"A lush, thoughtful, seductive reimagining of the Dracula mythos that had me under its thrall from page one, Dao's darkly dreamy book will leave you thirsting for more. Let Lucy sink her teeth into you and draw you into her new world." —Kiersten White,
#1 *New York Times*–bestselling author of *Hide, Mister Magic,* and *Lucy Undying*

"This novel will leave you breathless and make you question what you thought you knew about the original tale. Julie C. Dao is the master of nuanced, complex female leads who will not just demand but forcibly take exactly what they deserve." —Beth Revis,
New York Times–bestselling coauthor of *Night of the Witch*

"Dazzling, sensual, sparkling with danger. Lucy Westenra is a force of nature in Dao's capable hands, taking control of her own story with a vengeance long overdue. A vibrant, chilling reimagining that feels wholly its own."
—Natalie Mae, author of the Kinder Poison trilogy

"A sultry gothic that hooked me from the first sentence. Every page of this lush *Dracula* retelling is imbued with danger and darkness. It's a beguiling book and one I can't recommend enough." —Alexis Henderson,
author of *The Year of the Witching*

"Prepare to be swept away by this tale of romance, power, and immortality as Dao's enchanting Lucy Westenra fully embodies the dark feminine lurking within us all." —Jessica Rubinkowski, author of *The Bright & the Pale*

"Wild, wicked, sensuous fun. *Now Comes the Mist* is for all the dark romantics, the lovers of drama, and the ones who want to get bitten."
—Wendy Xu, bestselling author and illustrator of *The Infinity Particle*

NOW
COMES
the
MIST

— BOOK 1 —

JULIE C. DAO

Podium

To Tamar Rydzinski,
who helped bring this book from the mist into the daylight.

Copyright © 2024 by Julie C. Dao

Cover design by Damonza

ISBN: 978-1-0394-5747-8

Published in 2024 by Podium Publishing
www.podiumaudio.com

Podium

NOW COMES *the* MIST

"Then look for me by moonlight,
Watch for me by moonlight,
I'll come to thee by moonlight, though hell should bar the way."

—Alfred Noyes, "The Highwayman"

CHAPTER ONE

I wonder if any of these women have ever imagined their own deaths.
  This is the thought that creeps through my mind as I sit on the bench in the old churchyard. My skirts are tucked neatly around me. My ankles are crossed at the hem. My hands are folded in my lap. I appear to be every inch a lady, for anyone who cares to look at my silhouette against the billowing snow—and even in the midst of their deepest mourning, they look. But inside my head, where no one can see, I am sprawled six feet beneath the ground on which their feet tread, my limbs splayed and hair mussed, choking on the frozen dirt. The earth swallows me whole, savoring the taste of my last warm breath.

It is a far more romantic death than lying in a coffin in our family tomb, which will be the likelier fate for me. But there, my skirts would be tucked, my ankles would be crossed, and my hands would be folded—and what is the point of dying exactly as one lived? If I must pass into the arms of Death, I want to do it as no one of my acquaintance would think proper.

Two women approach me, arm in arm, swathed in black bombazine. Both wear heavy crape veils but have folded up the fabric to reveal their faces. I remember how Mamma used to complain about the scratchy material irritating her skin, but she had endured it in public as all widows must, so I am pleased by the boldness of these ladies. They nod in greeting as they pass, and I see that they are not much older than Mina or myself. In fact, they could be a glimpse of us five or six years from now. One is plump and dainty with yellow corn-silk hair, like Mina, and the other is small, slender, and dark, like me. They walk in perfect unison, step for step, and lean confidingly on each other like sisters. Or lovers, I suppose.

They stop at a grave nearby, and the fair-haired woman places a bouquet of white lilies by the headstone. The petals sink into the snow to begin their slow decay, and then the women retrace their steps with a parting nod for me. I imagine them strolling through the churchyard gates, stepping into a carriage, and driving back to a house of bright windows like eyes glad to see them. They would pull off their offending veils and sit down to a cup of fragrant tea, the memory of the grave in the snow and me on the bench already fading from their minds.

Death slips so easily from other women. But on me, it lingers like a perfume, seeping into my skin until every breath I take is a reminder that the grave awaits me. I cannot shake its iron grip, and as I rise trembling from the bench, I am not certain I want to.

In my black silk skirts, I weave through the sleeping-places of the dead. I wonder if they can hear the snow crunching beneath my slippers, and whether the sound makes them jealous. It would make *me* jealous. I would hate the girl creeping over my grave like a wraith at dusk, her skin winter white against her black, black hair, and her eyes burning with life in a place where life is not welcome. I soften my steps so as not to offend the bereaved unduly.

At the rear of the churchyard, against the iron gate, stand seven tombs of fractured granite. Interspersed by drooping yew trees, they loom over the headstones like lords regarding a sea of peasants. *Gladstone* is etched into the first, and *Taylor* on the next. I pass *King* and *Price* and *Browning*, and then, beside *Shaw*, I see the object of my visit: the seventh tomb, adorned with stone roses. Metal lanterns hang on either side of the door, unlit, but the name *Westenra* inscribed above seems to glow as though there were flames.

I push open the heavy door and step inside. It should not be bright in here, not in the gloom of a February evening, but somehow I can see everything as clearly as if I held a torch: the cobweb-strewn floor, the remnants of dead flowers, and the cold granite walls carved with the names of every Westenra who lies here in eternal sleep. Stone steps lead into the vault below, where multiple Johns and Henrys and Georges I have never known are interred beside their wives and children. But here, in the main chamber of the tomb, rest the people I *have* known. The thick, sweet smell of decay fills my nostrils as I move, dreamlike, toward a set of stone coffins. They are rather grand affairs, in keeping with the honor of their occupants.

The first inscription reads: *Lord Alexander, 6th Viscount Westenra, and his wife, Vanessa.* My great-grandfather had never wanted his title or estate. All he had ever wanted was my great-grandmother, and in order to keep her, his parents had forced him to return to England. No more youthful escapades across the world, no more learning war and bloodshed and domination from his volatile French uncle, a high-ranking minister in the court of the emperor of Vietnam. "Come home," his parents had commanded, according to family legend. "We will accept your bride as long as you come home and take responsibility." And he had.

He had died before I was born, but my great-grandmother had lived until I was three. She had been just a slip of a girl when her English husband had stolen her away from the Vietnamese court, and she had remained small and delicate all her life. I remember her feeding me ginger candy and laughing her lilting laugh as she tried to navigate our hard-edged consonants. The month she had taken to her bed forever, I had not understood. "Why do we have to say goodbye?" I had asked, as she lay pale and silent—and sleeping, I thought—on her pillow.

"Because she is going to the old churchyard," Mamma had explained.

"But she will come back. Won't she?"

"No, my darling. Never again."

Still, I had not understood. I had waited by the window day after day, hoping to see her carriage come clattering up to the door. I do not remember when I learned what death was—only that as the years passed, I began to dream endlessly of wandering through the mist, searching for Mamma, screaming for Papa, terrified that one by one, they would go and leave me all alone.

Now, I stoop beside the second coffin, which reads *The Honorable Phillip J. Westenra and his wife, Lucy*. I run my fingers over the name I share with my grandmother. She gave it to me, along with the smile with which she had captivated London society half a century ago. I had clung to her as a child, frightened that I would lose her, too.

"We all must go sometime," she had said, hugging me close. "Life cannot go on forever."

"But it should," I had told her fiercely. "I'll *make* it go on forever."

That she lies here beside my grandfather is proof of my failure. I press my cheek against the icy stone of their coffin and think of everything I had read in Papa's library after her death. Volumes about the afterlife and medical treatises, barely decipherable, with complex diagrams of the body after death. When I had exhausted those, I had turned to outright folklore: ghost stories, superstitions surrounding funeral rituals from around the world, and tales of people getting buried alive and walled up inside dark catacombs.

After that, all my dreams were of dying. I drowned in the sea. I clawed at the inside of a coffin until my nails tore off. I plummeted from a castle tower to the river waiting below.

"It's a defense mechanism," the doctor had told my concerned parents. "Lucy is learning how to cope with grief. She will grow out of it, I promise you."

But I never have.

Because here I am, alone in a tomb surrounded by the dead. With my face still resting inches above my grandparents' skeletons, I turn my eyes to my father's coffin. *Phillip Westenra, Jr.*, it reads, with room to add Mamma's name one day. My gaze moves above the inscription.

There is a hand there.

It hangs over the edge of the coffin, the fingers long and pale and limp. As I watch, the wrist slowly swivels until the palm is upward. The index finger crooks.

Come here.

I rise, and the dust rises with me. I walk toward Papa's coffin. The lid is gone, so I can see him clearly: jet-black hair, high cheekbones, and pale skin warmed with a touch of gold, all of which I have inherited. His eyes are open, and as I come closer, he turns to look at me.

"Lucy," he says, pleased. "I knew you would come."

My heart surges with longing. "Papa," I say, taking his hand. It is big and warm and steady, and mine disappears within it. "Oh, Papa, I've missed you so."

"And I've missed you, my child." He sits up in the coffin, his broad shoulders and heavy body shifting the dust around him. His wide, dark blue eyes crinkle at me. "Why have you not come sooner? I've been waiting for you."

I kneel beside his coffin. "Waiting?"

"This is where you belong. What wonderful talks we will have, you and I. We have so much to discuss and all the time in the world to do it." Papa studies me affectionately. "You get prettier every time I see you. You have my grandmother Vanessa's eyes, you know. The same color and shape. It feels like she's looking out at me."

The longing in his voice is palpable. My father had been close to his grandmother and had learned much at her knee: respect for elders, a passion for the spices of her home country, and even her language, though he spoke it only in the safe confines of his home and never in the smoking rooms or parlors of refined English society. All of this, he had taught to me in turn.

"My beloved Papa," I say, pressing a kiss to his fingers. The inside of the tomb feels bright and warm when he is with me, and I imagine us sitting here side by side. I am safe and happy and cherished, no longer plagued by dreams full of shadows. The worst has come and gone—Death has sought me, and I have answered, and the world will go on outside.

The world outside . . .

I see sunlight filtering in through high windows. I see Mamma weeping alone in our great house. I see Mina in her wedding dress, her face sorrowful beneath her veil. I see all the men I have ever known, all the men I have danced with, all the men who might have married me and shown me a side of life no woman can ever properly tell me about, but for which I long with every fiber of my aching, untouched body to know.

"What is it, Lucy? What's wrong?" Papa asks, concerned.

Behind me, I hear the scraping of a stone lid as my grandparents awaken. They sit up in their coffin, like Papa, but they look nothing like him. They are shreds of decomposed flesh clinging to bone, their gaping mouths stretched in fossilized smiles. A smell of rot sweeps the chamber. A fat pink worm slips from my grandmother's nostril.

"What's wrong, Lucy?"

"Stay with us, Lucy, forever."

I turn back, horrified, to see that my father is covered in great black beetles. They devour his skin with razor-sharp pincers, tearing the meat like paper, stripping off layers of bloodied sinew and pulsing muscle. His hand is a cage of cold chalk bone around my fingers.

"Your place is here, Lucy," he says lovingly as a beetle plunges its pincers into the soft wet jelly of his right eye.

And even as I scream, I feel myself clinging to his hand with all the strength I have left in me. Some force is separating us. Some voice speaks in my ear.

"Lucy. Lucy! Wake up!"

I am kneeling in the snow. Splatters of blood surround me like paint on a bone-white wall. My fingers are bleeding. I have been clawing at the door of our family tomb.

"Oh, Lucy, why? Why does this keep happening?" Mamma moans. She is the image of a woman who left her bed in a hurry. Her hair is coming loose from its plait, and the hem of her nightdress flutters beneath her heavy woolen robe. She has brought my own robe for me, as she always does, and hastily wraps it around my shoulders.

Only then do I realize how cold I am. I am wearing only my night-gown, the white lawn material so thin I can see my whole body through it in the light of the lantern carried by Harriet, my maid. She places a pair of slippers on the snow beside my bare feet, which are also bleeding—I must have cut them walking from our house to the churchyard—and so numb with the cold that she has to help me lift them into the slippers.

"What time is it?" I ask, my teeth chattering.

"Half past midnight," Mamma says wearily, steering me away from the tomb. Harriet leads us out of the churchyard, lighting the way. "If only you sleepwalked during decent hours. An afternoon nap, perhaps. Though I suppose I ought to be grateful that you don't." She glances at my bare legs, which are clearly visible through my thin nightgown. Had I wandered in my dreams in daylight, all of respectable London would have seen every inch of my body. "Let us go home. Harriet will draw a warm bath, and I'll have Agatha heat some broth for you."

I shiver uncontrollably as we pass through the gates. "I . . . I saw Papa."

Mamma gives me a sharp glance. "This must stop, Lucy."

"I can't help it. The doctor . . ."

She waves away my words impatiently. "I do not speak of your con-dition. Your father also sleepwalked, as did his father and grandmother before him. I am speaking of this"—she gestures to the graves in the snow—"this unnatural, unhealthy obsession with death and loss."

I grip my robe tightly around my shoulders.

"It has been five years since Papa died." In the light of Harriet's lantern, Mamma looks much older than she is. "You must let him go."

We stand for a moment in the snow, looking at each other, our breath emerging on the frigid air like ribbons of mist. Finally, my mother sighs and continues leading me down the street, and I obey without a word. What can I possibly say?

How can I tell her that I will never let go of Papa, or my grandparents, or anyone I have ever lost? How can I tell her that they . . . that *Death*, will not allow it?

And so I remain silent, and we walk home beneath the winter sky.

CHAPTER TWO

I am the moth, and Mina is the candle.

That has never been clearer to me than tonight in my room, dressing for her engagement party. She stands before the full-length mirror with her lips pursed in contemplation, examining every inch of her gown. The silk envelops her figure and trails behind her in a gleaming cascade of sky blue, a perfect match for her eyes. I knew it would be when I chose the material for her. She is studying the rippling sheen of the fabric, but I am distracted by the way the candlelight dances in her pale gold hair, gathered at her nape with one of my diamond pins.

"Lucy, I can't accept this dress," she says for the thousandth time.

"I told you, it's not *from* me, silly," I reply, also for the thousandth time. "I arranged the dressmaker, but the gown is an engagement gift from Mamma."

"Nevertheless . . ." Mina runs a hand down the bodice, from which her round shoulders and bare arms emerge like snowy marble. "You've done so much for me already, both of you. Throwing this party, ordering the flowers and champagne, sending out the invitations."

I laugh and stretch luxuriously across my bed, the bones of my corset pressing into my torso with the movement. "We thrive on spoiling you. You know that," I tell her and catch sight of my own reflection in the glass. I am the picture of ease and languor, lounging back on my elbows, my long, glossy midnight hair splattered across the pristine coverlet like spilled ink. My eyes, dark and tilting at the corners, sparkle in the light, and my pale olive throat glows above the expensive French lace that barely contains the plump, warm half-moons of my breasts. I shift my weight and the hem of my short chemise rides up a few inches.

If Mina is the angel in every man's hopes, then I am the devil in every man's dreams.

The sky-blue silk rustles as Mina turns to face me, her eyes darting to the expanse of naked thigh between my chemise and the lacy edges of my stockings. Her cheeks flush, and for a moment, I wonder if she, too, is remembering our kiss that sun-dappled day by the sea. "Lucy," she says in a playful, scolding tone, picking up my abandoned cream-colored drawers from the floor, "aren't you ever going to get dressed?"

I gesture at myself. "Whatever would be the point? I would catch a husband much more quickly as I am."

"You wouldn't have trouble with that even if you wore a potato sack," she says, laughing.

"Men are so easy to manipulate." I take the drawers and reluctantly step into them. "Wear a low neckline, flutter your lashes, stroke your finger over their hand, and they call you a *charming girl*. There's no trick to it. No beauty or wit required."

"Though it certainly helps that you have both."

"I never said it didn't."

We laugh as Mina helps me into my gown of pale blush pink silk. "How wonderful you look in this color. I'm the one getting married, but you will be the one they all look at tonight," she says without a trace of envy.

"Only because no one has entrapped me yet, as Jonathan has you." The moment his name leaves my lips, I regret it. Her gaze turns inward at once, to thoughts and hopes and memories that have nothing to do with me. She twists the simple gold band on her finger, and it gives me a childish degree of satisfaction that the tiny sapphire Jonathan chose is nowhere as near the color of her eyes as the silk I picked for her.

"I don't know what I'll do with myself when he goes away this spring. He expects to be gone almost a month, and we've never been apart that long," she says, her eyes downcast. In the soft light, she looks like a painting I would keep on my wall, if I could not keep any other part of her with me. "You must think I'm silly. I spent almost twenty years thinking of him as a friend and have loved him for only three. But he seems as irreplaceable to me now as my own heart."

I feel her love and pain like splinters in my skin. They embed themselves in me until I can no longer tell whether I am moved by Mina's passion or jealous that she will go into that blissful unknown before me, and with someone else. I imagine the soft, sibilant promise of the bedroom door closing, cotton and lace slipping down her body to pool at her feet, and her heavy sunlit hair tumbling down her smooth bare back. I see her walking to the bed where Jonathan sits, his eyes afire with want, and sliding a knee on either side of his lap.

Jonathan.

The first time I met Jonathan Harker, I had assessed him with one glance and found him wanting. Rather tall, but what man of our acquaintance wasn't? The slight, quick build of a fencer. The unmarked hands of a man who shuffles paper for a living, a lawyer's clerk with money of his own and rising in his employer's estimation every day. Dark gold hair, a sloping nose, and a smile that appeared suddenly, when least expected. Even his conversation was too clever, too interesting for my liking. And the way he gazed at Mina, his grey eyes warm and soft on her, as though afraid she would vanish if he looked away.

No, I have never liked Jonathan Harker.

Mina looks up from the ring. "You will understand very soon, my Lucy," she says lovingly, "what it is to care about someone in this way."

I smile at her, my lips closed so that the words I can never say will not escape. Carelessly, I gather up my long black hair and affix it to my head with snowy pearl-tipped pins. My maid would have done a neater, more thorough job, but I prefer it recklessly windswept, as though I've been walking through the London gale. Or someone has just run his rough hands through it, his lips burning on my neck. "Well," I say lightly, stepping back to look at my full reflection in the glass, "you'll still have me when Jonathan is called away to business."

"And I'm glad of it." Mina rests her chin on my shoulder. We are the same height, both of us small and dainty, and she presses her cheek against mine as I adjust the simple jewelry I always wear: a gold locket embedded with jet, which holds Papa's photograph, and a ring with a stone of green Vietnamese jade that had once belonged to my great-grandmother.

"Where on earth is he going again? The plains of Africa? The steppes of Asia?"

She laughs. "Not that far east, I'm afraid. His client lives in the wilds of Austria-Hungary, along the edge of the empire. He's an elderly nobleman with a castle somewhere in the Eastern Carpathians, in a region translated roughly as the Mountains of Deep Winter. Isn't that poetic?"

"You are the writer, not I. People speak of me as the useless one and of you as the talented one, with your daily diaries and gift for observation and knowledge of shorthand."

"Nonsense. I write more than you do, that's all. I keep it up so that I may be useful to Jonathan in his work. I hope he won't always have to travel so far." Mina sighs. "The mountains sound beautiful and full of history. I'm not certain why the client wants to move here to London when he lives, as Jonathan tells me, on a peak above a deep blue river."

Her words bring to mind my dreams of plummeting into raging water, the visions dark and disturbing and endlessly seductive. I close my eyes as Death whispers to me. I envision emerald peaks dotted with villages and forests blooming in the shadow of old stone towers, and I feel an envy that is almost hatred. "I'd give anything to trade places with Jonathan."

Mina wraps her arms around me, smiling. "Why? So you can leave me, too?"

"No. So I can marry you, of course," I say, with just enough gaiety to make it a jest. "And travel the world and see all those glorious sights. Can you imagine sitting on a steam train, watching foreign castles pass outside your window?"

"He won't be taking a train the whole way," she points out, ever the practical one. "The geography won't allow it. It will have to be hired carriages after a certain point. I've marked his journey with a red ribbon pinned to a map and read about all the places he'll go. I suppose I know more about the history of that region than any self-respecting governess ought to."

I give a dismissive wave. "Carriages, trains. It doesn't matter. Just to go somewhere, *anywhere*, and see new faces and hear new voices. To order tea in a foreign hotel or sit in a dark theater full of strangers or send telegrams home from far-off cities. That's freedom. That's *living*, my Mina. You could be anyone you wished to be, and no one would be any the wiser."

"That does sound nice," she admits.

"Can you imagine rambling around some strange country?" I lift my hand to her neck and trail my fingertips over her porcelain skin, feeling her shiver slightly against me. "Seeing the sights, exploring? Sleeping in a dark room, in a bed you don't know?"

Mina pulls away, leaving my shoulder cold. "Perhaps Jonathan will take me one day."

"I don't mean traveling with a *husband*," I say impatiently. "I mean traveling the way that men do. Alone . . . or with a friend."

She laughs. "Alone! Fancy going anywhere alone, without protection."

"And why not? What do we need protection from?"

"I don't know," she says helplessly. "Dangerous men. Thieves, rogues, murderers?"

"Maybe *they* need protection from *me*." I feel the sudden, furious urge to rip the pearl-tipped pins from my hair. "I could be dangerous, too, out there on my own. I just don't know it because I've never been given the chance, and never will. I haven't the faintest idea who I am."

"Oh, Lucy," Mina says, distressed.

I move to the window and yank aside the plum silk drapes. It is dark outside, but beyond the reflection of Mina and me, I can just barely see a deepening winter sky that weeps lacy flakes of snow. "There's a whole world out there we will never see," I say, and the familiar despair—urgent, immediate, overwhelming—almost chokes me. "Castles and mountains and forests, and so much more. Is this truly all there is? Silk dresses and engagement rings? It seems to me there is more freedom for us even in death. At least it would be a choice we make for ourselves."

"Dearest, you are in one of your moods again," she says gently. In the light of the streetlamps, we can see carriages pulling up in front of the house and people stepping out into the snow. A few curious, eager male faces turn up toward my bright window, and Mina reddens even though we are both fully dressed. She pulls the curtain shut and puts a hand on either side of my face. "This is only youth and high spirits talking. The excitement of the evening. Soon, you'll be downstairs with your usual parade of admiring beaux, and you'll forget all of this."

This is the foundation of our friendship: I produce a wild, unsanctioned idea, always and forever inappropriate for a young lady of my station, and Mina willingly stretches her hand out to meet it—but then always pulls back. Back into safety, into the smothering cloisters of traditional womanhood and all the expectations that bar the way out. And then, to keep from upsetting her, I retract the thought and hide it deep within me once more.

This was exactly how we kissed, that day I was bold enough to try.

I am so tired of hiding.

"My beautiful Lucy. My beloved, my sister, my friend," Mina says, still holding my face between her hands. "This is partly grief, too, I know. You still miss your father, who told you all about the world. This need to be free is only your longing for him, don't you see?"

I touch the locket at my neck and turn away, both because she sees far too much and because not even she is allowed to speak of Papa. I am saved from having to think of a response by a light knock at the door. "Who can that be?" I ask, too brightly, too gaily, and sail over to it.

Harriet, my maid, stands outside with her arms full of fragrant flowers. "Begging your pardon, Miss Lucy, but these bouquets just arrived for you and Miss Mina."

"Bouquets!" I repeat, still in that overly delighted tone. I drag Harriet into the room and run my fingers over an ostentatious bunch of scarlet roses, red as the devil. Mina is watching me warily, all too knowledgeable about my moods. "Exquisite. Who could they be from?"

"This one is from Mr. Jonathan Harker, for Miss Mina." Harriet hands my friend a small cluster of forget-me-nots. I note smugly that, like Mina's engagement ring, their shade of sky blue does not even remotely match her eyes, but she still brings them to her nose, beaming.

The maid gives me the huge bouquet of roses. "And this is from Dr. Jack Seward."

"Jack Seward!" Mina says, astonished. "Doesn't that man work every hour of every day? And yet he took the time to send you such lovely flowers, Lucy!"

"Don't excite yourself. It's likely he got his assistant at that dreadful asylum to send these," I say offhandedly, though I am certain he *did* make the effort himself. That brief interlude with him at the Stokers' autumn ball, the two of us alone in the conservatory while everyone else was in the drawing room, tells me so. Otherwise, I never should have expected the serious, dark-eyed young doctor to harbor such intense passion beneath all his mundane talk of psychology and human nature. His desire is evident, too, in the flowers he has gifted me tonight, each lurid, luscious rose so full blown as to be almost obscene, the petals readily yielding and opening to my touch. "They are stunning, though, aren't they?"

"Oh, Lucy, he *must* be in love with you. Red roses mean adoration, of course," Mina says, her eyes shining. "To think you might soon be a doctor's wife!"

"Now I think you're being silly," I tell her indulgently and look at the third and final bouquet in my maid's arms. "And who on earth are those from?"

Harriet hands me the picturesque bunch of old-fashioned camellias, each soft rounded flower a warm, rich red. "The Honorable Arthur Holmwood, miss."

"Arthur? Are you quite sure?" I ask, dropping Dr. Seward's roses on the dressing table.

"Yes, miss. He handed them to me himself as he came in just now."

"You may leave us, Harriet," I say, inhaling the scent of the camellias as she curtsies and closes the door behind her. "Arthur Holmwood, early to a party? This must be another man of the same name. The Arthur I know hardly dares to speak in my presence, let alone attend a large gathering of strangers."

"Don't be so hard on him," Mina chides me gently. "He's just bashful. And I happen to know he is admired by many girls, even if *you* think nothing of him, dear."

"I don't think nothing of him. I simply never remember him when he is not in front of me," I say to make her laugh at my incorrigible thoughtlessness. But it is a practiced thoughtlessness, one I have honed over the years to protect my innermost feelings.

Arthur Holmwood, indeed. His parents, Lord and Lady Godalming, are friends of Mamma's, and it had been inevitable that their only son and heir be a part of my childhood. But among the acquaintances with whom I had spent many a summer, he had always faded into the background: a quiet boy with skinny arms, mousy hair, and a perpetual sniffle. Papa used to tease me about my lack of interest in Arthur and call me "Your Ladyship," joking that one day, years hence, the awkward boy would grow up to be the handsomest man of our circle and sweep me off my feet.

Papa never lived to see his joke come true.

"I don't believe you truly mean that about Arthur," Mina says knowingly. "You told me he asked you to dance at the Stokers' ball last October."

That autumn ball, again, and another man who had changed my opinion of him there.

"He had been away at school for so long. And then his family went abroad for his father's health." I study the camellias. A soft gold radiates from the warm red center of each flower, like a secret tucked inside their hearts. "When I saw him at that ball, I almost didn't recognize him. He looked so different. Stronger. More self-assured."

Mina's eyes glow with excitement. "You never told me this, Lucy," she reproaches me. "You only said he looked like his mother had dragged him there kicking and screaming. Except he would have done it all silently because a peer of the realm never causes a scene, not even in his family's private carriage."

A startled laugh escapes me. "How on earth do you remember my insipid comments?"

"I remember everything you say. You were surprised when he asked you to dance because he could barely look you in the eye. He was always staring at your nose or chin."

"Or something lower still," I add with a dazzling smile.

Mina tries but fails to look stern. "You do know what camellias mean, don't you?"

"Of course not. As my former governess and the expert on all things pertaining to etiquette, I was hoping you could tell me."

"Camellias mean *my destiny is in your hands*. They are unutterably romantic. More so than roses, in my opinion. I've never liked roses. They always feel too bold."

I look between the camellias in my hands and Dr. Seward's bouquet on the table. "Are you trying to tell me something, my Mina?"

She leans over and kisses my cheek. "I wouldn't dare. Besides, your mind is already made up one way or another, even if you don't know it yet."

Mina knows me so well that I wonder if she has guessed what else I did not tell her about that ball and that dance with Arthur. How the shyness I had once mocked had seemed endearing and gentlemanly in this tall, elegant almost-stranger. The walnut hair, hazel eyes, and quiet demeanor had still been there, but all else was different: the broadness of his shoulders beneath his suit jacket, the newly confident fluidity of his movements, and the low, soft timbre of his voice. And such hands! Tender and firm and big enough to envelop mine, applying gentle pressure on my waist to move me exactly how and where he wanted me. I wonder if Mina has guessed how I dreamed of those hands for weeks afterward, and what they did to me in the most secret recesses of my subconscious.

Arthur, however, had seemed calm and collected. He had thanked me for the dance and returned to his mother's side without a backward glance. No passionate whispers, no straying touches, no notes slipped into my hand, like my other admirers. For the first time, I alone had been affected. A reversal of roles . . . or so I had believed.

I bring the camellias to my nose once more. *My destiny is in your hands.* "Lucy?"

I realize that Mina has been speaking to me and I haven't heard a word. "Yes?"

She tilts her head to one side thoughtfully. She has tucked a few of the forget-me-nots over one ear, and their soft azure is enchanting against the deeper blue of her eyes. "Which flowers will you wear down to the party?"

She looks from Arthur's flowers to Dr. Seward's, and there is a coyness in her voice that tells me she will read a great deal into my answer.

But I am not one to easily satisfy, not even when it is my most cherished friend.

"Neither," I say lazily and toss the flowers in an untidy heap on the table without bothering to get them any water. "Come, let us join the party. Mamma is expecting us."

CHAPTER THREE

A ll their eyes are on me.

I feel it the moment Mina and I enter the drawing room. I have followed every rule to perfection, after all. "You must be above reproach at all times," Papa had always advised me. "People with an unusual heritage like ours must prove to society that we belong."

And there is no place I belong more than a party. I have stabbed my gleaming upswept hair with pins so that my long neck will appear to best advantage. I have been tightly laced into my corset so that my breasts will look soft and full and my waist impossibly small. I have pinched my feet into costly slippers to make them look delicate and feminine.

I am a dazzling, glittering doll in pink silk, constantly in danger of tripping or having to faint into someone's strong arms. Helpless and fragile, just the way men want me.

And oh, how they want me, from that rosy-cheeked boy by the door who looks scarcely old enough to be drinking champagne to that aging marquess by the fireplace, talking calmly of business even as he ogles every inch of me.

Every move I make will be observed. When I run my fingers over my collarbone, twirl to greet a guest, or bend to speak to someone seated so that my décolletage is on full display, it will set their hearts racing and fingers clenching on the stems of their wine glasses. My younger naïve self had been uncomfortable with this avid attention once. There was an unease in knowing that I could never hide my being different, with my tilting dark eyes and gold-touched skin, and that this very difference made me desirable to men. An exotic trophy, a status symbol to be pursued and flaunted. But like my corset, I have learned to think of it as armor, this beauty passed down from my great-grandmother. And tonight, though I have not had a sip of champagne, I feel half-drunk with my own power over these men who rule London society.

"Lucy, your mamma and Jonathan are over here," Mina says. She has recognized the signs of intoxication in me and steers me away from a cluster of men who are watching me with hungry eyes. "And look, they're with Lord and Lady Godalming."

"That means Arthur must be close by," I say with incorrigible sparkle. I am not to be quenched, not even by my beloved friend. Not tonight.

"There you are, girls," Mamma says pleasantly. She and I look nothing alike, but she is almost as pinned and trussed and pinched as I am, though to a more forgiving degree. Men relax their expectations when a woman has passed a certain age. Still, her maids have taken great care with her appearance, swirling her ash-blond hair into a perfect knot above her ropes of pearls and eminently suitable gown of lavender silk moiré. She also wears a gold locket identical to my own, embedded with Yorkshire jet and carrying a photograph of Papa. "How pretty you both look tonight! Mina, I adore that dress on you."

Jonathan Harker is perhaps the only man in the room who does not spare me a glance. His attention is all for Mina, and his eyes on her are so full of wanting that I feel a familiar ache deep inside me. "I agree with Mrs. Westenra. You look like a mermaid, my love," he says, taking Mina's hand and rubbing his thumb over her fingers.

Lord Godalming, on the other hand, is gazing at me as intently as any other hot-blooded man in the room. "My goodness, Lucy, how you've grown," he says. "I don't believe I've seen you since you were just a little thing. And *now* look at you."

"It wasn't that long ago, dear," Lady Godalming tells her husband, laying a hand across the back of his wheelchair. "We saw Mrs. Westenra and Lucy only a few years ago, before we went to the Continent. Don't you remember? She was full grown then."

But not like this, he is clearly thinking, even as he replies, "Of course. You're right."

"How are you, my lord?" I ask demurely. "I heard you had gone abroad for your health."

His wife interjects before he can respond. "He is as well as can be expected. His heart still acts up from time to time, and so he avoids walking when possible."

"I suppose dancing is out of the question, then?" I press a hand over my heart in disappointment. "I regret losing the opportunity to have such a distinguished partner."

His Lordship's face reddens with surprise and delight.

"Out of the question, indeed," Lady Godalming says with a tight smile. "Though I am certain you will not want for partners tonight, so charming as you are, Lucy." *Save your flirting for the other men, you little tart,* her eyes tell me.

Meanwhile, Mina's eyes are begging me to leave the poor man alone, and I can scarcely ever refuse her anything. "Congratulations on your engagement, Jonathan," I say, turning to him. "And on your impending business trip to Austria-Hungary. Mina has told me all about it."

"Thank you," Jonathan says, still holding her hand. "I'm a fortunate man. The job seems straightforward enough. My client wishes to purchase property here in London, and Mr. Hawkins has given me authority over the matter, to increase my independence in the business."

"How wonderful," Mamma says. "I assume by that show of confidence that he expects you to take over the practice for him one day? I understand he is advanced in his years."

"He is approaching seventy, though you wouldn't know it to look at him," Jonathan says, laughing. It makes his grey eyes dance and his whole face light up, damn him. Mina gazes up at him like he is a pastry she could devour. "Yes, he has shown me every kindness as an adopted son and now potential heir. I am grateful that someday, if I prove myself worthy, I will have the means to take care of Mina in the way she deserves."

"And any children you may have," Lady Godalming adds, looking indulgently at them.

Mina tucks her head into Jonathan's chest, blushing.

"May they be many in number," Mamma chimes in. "God willing."

Someone moves to stand quietly by my side. I know he is coming before I see him because I smell a scent I recognize from the Stokers' ball: a combination of shaving cream, a whiff of pine, and cigar smoke. Immediately, I think of his hand on my waist and the distracting warmth of him as we danced. I remember how small I had felt against him, as though his body could swallow up the whole of mine. My pulse picks up, my breath seems to stop short in my lungs, and it takes every ounce of my self-control to appear serene and unaffected. I do not turn my head to look at him. *Good lord,* I think. *I must really be lost.*

"Mrs. Westenra, please forgive me for not coming over right away to greet you," Arthur's low, calm voice says. "I ran into an old friend I have not seen in some time. I hadn't realized you were acquainted with Dr. Jack Seward."

Mina and I exchange glances. Her lips fold inward, holding back a laugh that the two admirers who had sent me flowers tonight happen to be friendly.

"That's quite all right," Mamma says, her eyes darting between him and me, enjoying the sight of us together. "Dr. Seward was a friend of my late husband's. He's a fine young man."

"As is Mr. Harker, from what I hear," Arthur says politely, bowing to Jonathan. "I must congratulate you on your beautiful bride-to-be, sir. I understand you are the guests of honor."

Jonathan returns the bow. "Thank you, Mr. Holmwood. I am grateful to Mrs. Westenra and Lucy for giving us this party. We had intended to have a small, quiet engagement to go with our small, quiet wedding, but these kind ladies would not hear of it."

"Of course not," Mamma says, chuckling. "I can never do too much for such a lovely young couple, especially when the bride is like a sister to my Lucy."

I wait for Arthur to acknowledge me, but he says only, "I am sure your generosity is well deserved, Mrs. Westenra," before turning the conversation to Jonathan's upcoming travels, as though I had not been brought into the conversation at all.

So, I think. *He asks me to dance in October and sends me flowers tonight and has now decided to ignore me.* I am long accustomed to toying with the feelings of men, but having my own emotions manipulated is not a pleasant sensation. Or indeed, acceptable.

"Excuse me, Mamma. My lord and lady," I murmur to our elders as Arthur is asking about the route Jonathan will take through Germany. "I must see to our other guests."

Mamma nods with approval at my sudden conscientiousness. She has never known me quite as well as Mina, who raises an eyebrow as I curtsy and move away. Arthur is still speaking to Jonathan, but I hear his voice grow ever so slightly louder as he turns in the direction of my back. *Good*, I think, and while he is likely still watching, I walk right up to Dr. Jack Seward.

"Dr. Seward," I say, my voice high and lilting so it will carry back to the group. "Thank you so much for your exquisite roses tonight. They were most appreciated."

"Miss Westenra. Lucy." His dark eyes light up as he brings my hand to his lips. He does not leave it there any longer than is considered proper, but his mouth opens a fraction against my skin. The heat of it sears up my arm and down my spine before he releases me, and I wonder how I could ever have thought the doctor a boring, bloodless man.

We had first become acquainted six years ago, when he was a mere medical student and assistant to my father's physician. I had been a child, too self-absorbed and concerned for Papa's ailing health to harbor the silly infatuations that girls of my age often did for young men, and anyway, Jack Seward had seemed dull, forever prattling on about the connection between mind and body. Imagine my surprise when he had caught me alone at the Stokers' ball last year and lowered his lips to my ear. "I think you are the most beautiful woman I have ever seen," he had whispered, his close-shaven hint of a beard scratching most delightfully against my cheek.

"Dr. Seward," I had replied, smiling, "you astonish me."

"It is you I find astonishing." His eyes had glittered as he ran a finger over my wrist, feather light, and suddenly I had wanted nothing more than for him to take me by the waist as Arthur had moments before. I had seized his hand before he could pull away, both of us gasping at the sudden heat of our palms meeting, and tugged him close to me. He had stumbled forward a bit, off-balance, and for one glorious second I had felt all of him pressed against me.

He had released my hand and stepped away at once, looking discomfited and perhaps even displeased. In my excitement and frustration with Arthur's cool detachment, I had forgotten my place: as the woman, I was the quarry and not the hunter. I was to be alluring and desirable through my appearance only. *Never* my words or actions. I had broken Papa's stern rule of being above reproach at all times.

Luckily, I had known exactly what to do. "I am so sorry, Doctor," I had said, putting my hands over my cheeks in feigned maidenly embarrassment and lowering my eyes shyly to the floor. "I was overcome by your kind words. Please forgive me."

Dr. Seward's displeasure had slipped away at once. "There is nothing to forgive, Miss Westenra," he had said gently. "Lucy."

I have always known too well the part I must play in this ridiculous game of courtship between men and women, and I have played it brilliantly. For here he is in my mother's house, standing before me with the same spark of interest in his eyes, with his bouquet of roses, devil-red and wantonly full-blown, upstairs in my bedroom. From the slow smile parting his lips, I know he, too, must be remembering that night in the conservatory.

"I'm pleased you liked my gift," he says. "I thought of you when I saw them."

"And here I believed you too busy with your medical practice to care about something as frivolous as flowers," I say archly.

"Ah, but flowers are far from frivolous." He leans toward me as though to confide a secret, and a lock of black hair slips over his forehead. He smells like soap and clean linen. "They carry messages in code, you see. They are like innocent spies."

"Dr. Seward!" I say, pretending to be shocked. I know Mina would shake her head at the overly coquettish tone I am wielding, but the young doctor looks charmed. "Are you telling me you have sent a bouquet of spies to my bedchamber tonight?"

A slight startled look crosses his face. I have again been too forward. But this time, he recovers quickly and says, "Perhaps *spies* is the wrong word to use. I would not presume to send such intrusions to a lady so modest. We could say they are . . . mere couriers, perhaps."

I tilt my head back and laugh, knowing that the bell-like sound will carry to almost every corner of the room. "You are a very amusing man, Doctor."

He is all smiles again, looking pleased with himself.

"And what do we have here, Seward?" asks a deep, drawling voice, the vowels peculiar and stretched out flat. "Is it possible you've found the most dazzling lady in the room?"

"More than possible," Dr. Seward says, frowning a little at the interruption, though he claps the newcomer genially on the shoulder. "Miss Lucy Westenra, may I introduce my friend, Mr. Quincey Morris? We met last summer when I was completing my studies in America."

I can't help staring at the stranger, and I notice that many others are, too, though not quite with admiration like me. The man stands out like a beacon, and not just because his skin is a rich gleaming ebony where everyone else's, excepting mine, is lily-white. His merry, intelligent eyes dance in an otherwise stern face with thick brows, a strong wide nose, and full, beautifully shaped lips. He wears a most unconventional outfit of a long sporting coat of grey wool over a tan waistcoat, his dove-colored ascot contrasting with the dark masculine edge of his jaw. He and Dr. Seward are matched in height, build, and age, with both men around thirty or thereabouts.

But the manner in which the stranger stands is different from the languid ease of all the other gentlemen in the room: feet slightly apart, wide powerful shoulders drawn back, and hands braced on his hips, revealing a flash of silver metal tucked into a leather holster around his trim waist. He looks like a man accustomed to having to fight at a moment's notice, and as I take in some of the guests' barely veiled stares of hostility directed at him, I believe I can see why.

"M-Mr. Morris," I stammer, most uncharacteristically, dazzled by his appearance. I see from his grin—straight, flawless teeth, white against his dark skin—that he is pleased by my reaction. "Are you a sharpshooter of the American West? I seem to remember someone with such a stance as yours in a play Mamma and I once saw."

Quincey Morris laughs, a bright and cheerful sound that softens some of the grim faces watching him. "I am not a sharpshooter, ma'am, though I do know a thing or two about hitting targets. I've knocked plenty of bottles off a fence in my day," he says with a kindly wink, and his smooth, buttery accent is so attractive I can't help gasping up at him. "A more accurate term to use for me would be cowboy, like my father before me. There aren't many of us left these days, but I keep the profession to honor his memory. Jack here," he adds, putting a hand on Dr. Seward's shoulder, "met me when he was doctoring in Texas. Brave man that he is, he couldn't resist the excitement of the lawless Wild West. Could you, my friend?"

"I was there studying Indigenous medicine," Dr. Seward says, relaxing under the other man's gregarious cheer, though he darts nervous glances at me. My admiration of the handsome, strapping American is much too apparent for his taste. "*That* was what drew me, as well as the need for doctors. Quincey is the heroic one. He saved me from bandits."

Mr. Morris rolls his eyes good-naturedly at me. "And *he* saved *me* and ten others on my homestead from the wasting fever. We would have all gone to glory had it not been for him. I don't know anything about medicine myself. Give me a cow to rope or a horse to ride."

"And a fire to light under the open night sky, I suppose?" I ask, struggling to recover as best I can. I smile at Mr. Morris's delight. "I have read a few tales of the American West despite my mother's disapproval of them. I suppose sharpshooters and gold mines are not the most suitable reading material for a young lady, in her eyes."

"No reading material is out of reach when a lady is as intelligent as you clearly are, Miss Westenra," the cowboy says smoothly, bowing with his hand on his heart. For just a brief second, those molten brown eyes flicker to my mouth, so quickly I might have imagined it.

"Lucy's late father was my good friend and as educated a man as you could meet. He passed down his gifts, as you can see," Dr. Seward says quickly, trying to win my attention back.

But I cannot take my eyes off Mr. Morris when he is smiling at me. It's blinding, like gazing directly into the sun.

"You're a diamond in the rough, then, Miss Lucy," he says. "And all it took for us to meet was several thousand miles across land and sea. Do you believe in destiny?"

"Yes, I think so," I say breathlessly, and that beautiful smile widens even more. I do believe I would have said yes to anything he asked.

"Ah, Arthur! Come join us," Dr. Seward says loudly, not bothering to hide his relief.

Once again, Arthur Holmwood comes to stand beside me, and I struggle to suppress my delight. So, the sight of me with two other interested men was enough to send him over. The doctor introduces him to Mr. Morris and the two shake hands.

"How long will you be staying in England?" Arthur inquires.

"I originally planned to stay a month or two with my friend Jack here. But I wouldn't be averse to staying longer, if I felt inclined to do so for some reason," the cowboy answers, with a sly little glance at me that makes the doctor scowl. I feel a pleasant little flutter in my stomach, because Quincey Morris is apparently a man after my own flirtatious heart.

This would have been the perfect opportunity for Arthur to acknowledge me at last. Instead, he gestures to the flash of weaponry beneath Mr. Morris's coat. "I assume you're an excellent shot, sir? Jack will be joining me on my estate for a hunt next month, if the weather favors us, and I'd be glad to have you along if you're interested."

"Now that's a kind offer I'd be glad to take, Mr. Holmwood," the American drawls, and then he and Dr. Seward politely look at me, ready to turn the conversation so that it includes me.

But Arthur presses on. "What is your experience with rifles? I have a few that were given to me by my grandfather. Rather large, unwieldy affairs, but they are reliable and—"

The sound of violins interrupts his speech and my returning annoyance. Arthur seems bent on ignoring my existence, aside from following me around. He has yet to even look at me tonight.

"Ah, the dancing is about to begin," I say, watching as the guests begin filtering into the ballroom. Deliberately, I move forward and offer my hand to the cowboy. "May I be so bold as to claim you as my first partner, Mr. Morris? I hesitate to ask Dr. Seward, as it would no doubt shock him to be invited by a woman. But I believe you, with your New World sensibilities, might be somewhat more adventurous in this regard?"

A deep furrow forms between Jack Seward's brows, but Mr. Morris is grinning from ear to ear. "You can read me like a book, little lady," he says, and the endearment is captivating from him when it might sound condescending from any other man. He places my hand on his arm. "Who am I to say no to a dance with the most glorious woman in the room?"

I smile up at him as we glide away and spare a glance for Arthur, expecting him to look calm and politely bored as usual. Instead, his expression is one of hurt and surprise, and a strange ache tugs at my chest. *He could have claimed me if he had wished to,* I tell myself, *instead of going on about that silly hunt.* I place my other hand on Mr. Morris's arm as well and lean against him, determined to enjoy myself. What have I to be guilty for?

"Do you waltz, Mr. Morris?" I ask as the elegant sound of Strauss fills the air.

"For you, Miss Lucy, I reckon I would dance the mazurka if I had to," he says, his eyes twinkling down at me. "So I can most assuredly exert myself to the waltz."

"How absurd you are," I say, laughing. We turn heads as we enter the ballroom together, and I stare pointedly at the people who are glaring at the cowboy. They avert their eyes, unwilling to displease the hostess's daughter. "Are all Americans this prone to hyperbole?"

He leans down, and again, his eyes flicker to my mouth. "Let me answer your question with another question. Are all English women as utterly enchanting as you are?"

"Flattery will get you everywhere with me," I say lightly.

"I'm glad to hear it." He sweeps me into the throng of dancers and executes a perfect waltz, much more gracefully than I would have expected.

"Where did you learn to dance like this?" I ask, amazed. "I thought a man who spent his life herding cows on horseback wouldn't know much about a ballroom."

Mr. Morris's cheeky wink is as irresistible as his laugh. "They have ladies in America, too, you know. Some of the ones who weren't so bothered by the color of my skin taught me to dance, so I could cross the ocean and impress you."

"You have the most beautiful skin I've ever seen," I tell him honestly.

"Now, ma'am, you need to stop complimenting me or I'll completely lose track of the dance." He twirls me, my pink skirts sailing around us. "On second thought, I don't really mind. Go on and keep complimenting me."

We laugh, and I catch sight of a group of matrons whispering. No doubt my name and Mr. Morris's will be entangled in much of the night's gossip, but I am enjoying myself so much, I truly don't care what the old hens are clucking about.

"My great-grandmother came from Southeast Asia. Vietnam," I say before I can think too much about it. "My great-grandfather swept in and took her back to London with him. The other French and English officers cared about riches, but the only treasure he wanted was her."

I am not certain why I am revealing this, not when my family has taken pains to keep it quiet. Even Papa, who had looked like any other English gentleman with a full beard, had never spoken of his ancestry in society. There had been whispers once that my great-grandmother had not been a royal lady but rather a lowly brothel girl who had bewitched an innocent young English lord. Papa had wanted to avoid feeding the gossip, and Mamma—always conscious of status and propriety—had agreed never to speak of Vanessa. But somehow, I have an instinct that Quincey Morris will understand. Perhaps it is the way he had stood in that room of unfriendly eyes earlier, defiantly turning his uniqueness into armor the way I do my own.

And indeed, the American's gaze on me is kind, as though he can hear everything I am not saying out loud. "That explains why you have the loveliest tint to your skin," he says, charming to the last. "Like the sun is following your face, even at night."

"Aren't you the poet?" I squeeze the hand that envelops mine. It is big and rough, nothing like Dr. Seward's clever, elegant ones, but I am glad to hold it just the same. It feels friendly—though the look in his eyes is anything *but* merely friendly. A fire burns there, promising delicious warmth if I find the courage to approach. He pulls me slightly closer, and the nearness of him is daring. Another inch more and it would be scandalous.

"There are Asian folks who live around my homestead. They work on the ranch and the railroad, and I'm lucky to call some of them my friends." Mr. Morris's eyes shine down at me. "And I hope I win *your* esteem as well, Miss Lucy Westenra. You're a diamond in the rough, like I said, and I don't tell many women that, I promise you."

"I don't believe you," I say gaily. "A man like you must know many special ladies."

"None I'd want to ride across an open plain under the night sky with. A great moon up above. Stars shining down. Wolves howling." His voice is as soft as a bed I would happily sink into. "But you don't need to be afraid of them, ma'am. Not with me around."

I lower my voice. "Will you tell me something? Something I'm aching to know?"

His eyes spark. "Anything."

I press my lips together, feigning nervousness. "I've heard that American cowboys have very, very big . . ." I am delighted to see that he is holding his breath. "Hats. Is that true?"

Mr. Morris throws his head back and howls with laughter. "You're one of a kind."

I beam up at him. Dr. Seward would have been horrified by the joke, but Mr. Morris is obviously a different kind of man. A man I wouldn't have to worry about offending—a man who might actually value my speaking freely before him. "I'd like to see that open plain you mentioned someday," I say frankly, and there is such warmth in his gaze that it fills my soul.

The music ends and I notice a couple near us. The man is glaring at Mr. Morris. I don't know him, but I recognize his partner as Penelope Worthing, a lively, pretty red-haired girl with whom I grew up and have always liked. I glance from the emerald ring sparkling on her hand to her pale, horse-faced partner, whose front teeth jut out from his thin lips. Penelope notices my observation, flushes, and whispers to him, but he continues to stare.

She gives me an apologetic smile. "Good evening, Lucy. How lovely you look tonight! I'm afraid I haven't had the pleasure of being introduced to your partner."

"I would be happy to introduce you. *And* your companion, who is looking most avidly at him," I say, and the man blinks his bulging blue eyes at me, startled by my directness. But I have long since learned that in company such as this—where women are trained never to say what they mean and must instead embed a myriad of insinuations into every innocent comment—it is best to force the knife to the core of a situation. And I am a woman who keeps my knives sharp. "This is Mr. Quincey Morris, an American friend of Dr. Jack Seward's. Mr. Morris, this is my childhood friend, Penelope Worthing."

They murmur polite greetings. "This is my fiancé, Alastor Hurst," Penelope says, sounding abashed as she indicates her smirking companion.

I feel a twinge of distaste and sympathy, for I recognize the name. The Hursts are social-climbing merchants who had tried for years to befriend my parents—to no avail, as Mamma despised their airs and pretensions—but their wealth is undeniable. And it is no secret that Penelope's philandering older brother has put their parents into dire financial straits. Clearly, this will be a marriage of desperate circumstance—not the outcome I would have hoped for Penelope.

Alastor Hurst scans Mr. Morris from head to toe, his lip curled to clearly telegraph his disgust. "Miss Westenra," he says. "Mr. Morris. You seem to be having a most amusing conversation. I've never heard such noise during a waltz before."

"Alastor," Penelope says, closing her eyes briefly.

"It's called laughter, sir," I say with a dazzling smile, even as anger burns in me like acid. "It must be a foreign concept to you if it puzzles you so deeply."

"Laughter?" Mr. Hurst repeats. "It sounded more like the braying of a donkey. It is rather distracting, trying to dance amid such noise."

Above reproach, Papa's voice echoes in my head. *At all times.*

But I cannot look at this simpering, equine-visaged fool and remain silent. "Oh, dear," I say with mock sadness. "If merriment is so repulsive to you, I find your presence at our party rather curious, Mr. Hunt. Or was it Holmes?" I remember his name perfectly, but I can't resist. This buffoon is not worth even the dirt on Penelope's shoe.

Mr. Hurst turns white with fury, but he directs his venom at the cowboy. "I didn't realize you people were allowed in places like this. I'm astonished at Audrey Westenra for inviting you. Shouldn't you be shoveling coal somewhere or cleaning horse dung out of the stables?"

There is absolute silence in the room. Even the musicians have stopped playing.

Penelope closes her eyes again, looking as though she wishes a hole would open in Mamma's expensive French carpet and swallow her.

I draw myself up to my full height. "Sir, you have insulted my guest quite enough. I find no other recourse but to ask you to leave at once."

Gasps of shock and delight sound out around us.

"Miss Lucy, please," Quincey Morris says quietly. "I reckon there's no need to send him away on my account, not when he is escorting a young lady."

But Penelope speaks up at once. "I don't mind leaving. Come, Alastor," she says, seizing her fiancé's arm, her face red with mortification. "Take me home."

"Am I to be dismissed with so little courtesy?" Mr. Hurst sputters. "Do you know who I am, Miss Westenra? Who my parents are? So high and mighty as you are."

"I will not tolerate such appalling behavior at a party given in my home," I say calmly.

"We're leaving," Penelope says, pressing my hand in farewell. "I am so sorry, Lucy. And Mr. Morris, I hope you will enjoy your time in England."

"Do come back and have tea with Mamma and me soon," I say with an apology in my own voice. Mr. Hurst deserved to be attacked, but I regret having done so at Penelope's expense.

Mamma unsuccessfully attempts to intercept them at the door, then rushes over to me as the music starts up again and the spectators scatter. "Lucy," she whispers, with a big smile on her face to mask the horror in her eyes. "What on earth just happened?"

I gesture to the cowboy. "That man insulted my guest, Mr. Morris."

"Oh, I see," Mamma says helplessly. "Well, I am very sorry for his rudeness in that case."

Mr. Morris bows. "No need to apologize, ma'am. I have heard much worse before, and it is I who am sorry for the interruption of your party." When he turns to me, his gaze is not as warm as it was. "Miss Lucy, thank you for the dance and conversation. Will you excuse me?"

I stare after him as he walks away. "Well, I never!" I say, laughing and trying to make light of the situation. "You would think *I* had been the one to insult him."

Mamma's smile is still plastered on her face as she takes my arm and leads me across the ballroom. "How many times have I told you? Men are scared off by outspoken women."

"Why shouldn't anyone speak out against incivility, man or woman?"

"There is a time and a place to do so. And putting aside the fact that you are a woman and expected to be modest and demure," Mamma continues, "a party thrown in *your* home for *your* guests is not that time or place. You should be generous toward everyone here, Lucy. I thought you knew better. Think of what poor Papa would have said if he had seen you just now!" Even as she chides me, she gives a welcoming nod to guests strolling by.

"Papa hated the Hursts as much as you do."

"He believed in decorum above all, and you have shown an appalling lack of it in ordering that guest to leave with such little civility."

The fight goes out of me, and I feel the giddy energy of the night ebbing. What is it all for, really? This dancing and flirting in the name of finding a husband to fill the hole Papa left behind in my heart? This is what Mina knows: that my gaiety and charm are just an act to hide the gaping emptiness inside me. And for all their admiration, Dr. Seward and Mr. Morris and even Arthur Holmwood would see this eventually if I married any of them. Away from the façade of parties and in the light of reality, they would realize that I am another woman entirely—one who wears a mask of cheer to hide the smudges on her soul left by Death.

My mind reels away from this crowded room and back to the cool, misty churchyard with Papa and my grandparents. There, I might be alone and peaceful, surrounded by the silent memories of those who had once loved me and can never return.

"I know you were only trying to do the right thing, my love," Mamma says, squeezing my arm. And then her gaze sharpens. "Or is there more to the story? Who is Mr. Morris to you? I only invited him at Dr. Seward's request, thinking it harmless. I should have thought you would be dancing with Arthur instead of a perfect stranger. And an American, at that!"

"He's no one to me," I say dully, catching Mina's eye from across the room. Her brows knit with concern, recognizing my mood. "And Arthur has not even looked at me once tonight. He isn't in the least interested in me, Mamma, and the sooner we accept that, the better—"

"Excuse me, Miss Westenra." Arthur Holmwood is standing close enough to have heard every word I was saying. A muscle twitches anxiously at the corner of his jaw, but his eyes on me are calm. In this light, they are more of a true green than hazel.

"Mr. Holmwood," Mamma says, flustered. "I . . . I hope you are enjoying the party?"

"Very much. But I believe I would enjoy myself more if Miss Westenra would give me the honor of the next dance?" He holds out a hand that is neither slender and sly like Dr. Seward's nor rough and weather-beaten like Quincey Morris's. It is simply *Arthur*.

I stare at it, making no move to take it, then look up at him with no small degree of frustration. Arthur Holmwood has puzzled me to the brink of insanity these past few months, showing interest one minute and apathy the next. The camellias he sent tonight had been warm and open and honest, but the man himself is a fog of indecision. If not for the flowers, I would have assumed that he never thought of me from one moment to the next. I hate that it matters so much what Arthur thinks of me— what *any* man thinks of me, aside from Papa.

"Lucy," Mamma whispers, shocked by my silence.

Arthur's hand wavers and a flash of worry flickers in his eyes, and it is this that saves him. I place my fingers in his. "Yes, I will dance with you, Mr. Holmwood," I say. "But only if you are being truthful about it being an honor."

My mother's mouth is agape at my nerve. Over her shoulder, I see Mina, Dr. Seward, and Mr. Morris all watching us, despite being in conversation in their respective groups.

Arthur applies a bit of pressure to my hand. "I would not have said so if it were not true," he says, and as he leads me toward the other dancers, I wonder if he can feel my traitorous pulse thundering in my wrist.

CHAPTER FOUR

The waltz I danced with Quincey Morris had been lively, but the music for my dance with Arthur is lush, melancholy, and romantic. Arthur, of course, is a perfect dancer as is required of men of his class, and I know that he and I make a beautiful pair to watch as we move across the ballroom. His feet touch the hem of my skirts, light as feathers, and my waist seems formed to exactly fit his hand. If only we could be as serene on the inside as we appear on the outside.

From the muscle still twitching in his jaw and the involuntary tightening of his hand around mine, I can see that he is as discomfited as I am. At least he is looking at me now, so directly that it is almost shocking. To his credit, he does not miss a single step of the waltz.

The other couples laugh and talk in low voices as they dance around us, but Arthur and I remain silent. I know he is waiting for me to say something, but after that reproach from my mother about being too outspoken, I will not utter a word until he does so first.

"Miss Westenra, thank you for the pleasure of this dance," he says at last.

"You are welcome, Mr. Holmwood," I say with chilly formality.

"I couldn't help overhearing what you were saying a moment ago." His gaze falters, but his eyes do not stray from mine. "Do you believe what you said? That I . . . do not care for you?"

"I would not have said so if it were not true," I say, repeating his words with an ironic smile. My reply seems to distress him, but relenting is not in my nature. "I must be honest. I do not know what to make of you. This is the second time in our acquaintance that you have asked me to dance, and tonight, you sent me flowers. Yet you never look at me or speak to me. You do not acknowledge my existence. Why are you astonished, Mr. Holmwood, to hear my assumption that I never cross your mind?"

The dismay on his face would be comical were it not so genuine. "Miss Westenra, I am grieved to hear that my behavior has led you to this conclusion."

"It is not just your behavior," I say calmly as we sail past Mamma and her friends. My mother is putting on a decent show of appearing cheerful and gay, but I can tell she is wondering—and fearing—what I could be saying to Arthur. "But also the behavior of other gentlemen, to which I have been comparing yours. I can name at least seven other men in this room who seem more willing to converse with me than you are."

"Seven?" Arthur almost groans.

I look up at the ceiling, pretending to think. "Seven who are age-appropriate and unattached. If you expand that number to include the men who are either too old or too married to even think of speaking to me, then the list of names grows significantly longer."

He blinks down at me. "You are . . . teasing me."

"A bit," I admit.

For a moment, we stare at each other. And then the most unexpected thing happens.

Arthur Holmwood laughs.

He laughs, and it transforms him. And every memory of Dr. Seward's beautiful hands and Quincey Morris's charm disappears from my mind in the light of Arthur's face laughing. His eyes crinkle, his jaw softens, and on the right side of his mouth is a perfect, kissable dimple. And now that I have made him laugh, I am filled with the most urgent need to do it again and to hold on to his smile before it disappears.

"You are so full of life," he says, and that is unexpected as well. "You always have been, ever since we were children playing in your garden. Do you know . . . I believe I have never known anyone in our circle as long as I have known you? When I look back at my childhood, it seems that you have always been there."

I am stunned. This is the most that Arthur Holmwood has ever spoken in my presence, and I am afraid to reply for fear of scaring him off, so I let him surge on. He seems to be talking as quickly as he can, letting the words out before his courage fails him.

"But we were never friends," he says. "And I think that was my fault."

"How so?" I ask.

"Well, I was always afraid of you."

It is my turn to laugh, hoping he will laugh with me so I can see that dimple again.

But his face remains serious. "You were too brilliant, you see, with your frocks and your smile and the way you beat everyone at every game. I still remember how you destroyed Peter Redmond and Edward Hart at cricket in every sense of the word one summer. They were angry at being defeated by a girl, and you told them they should have been more upset about losing so spectacularly after boasting about their skills."

"How do you remember that?" I ask, astonished.

"I remember everything about you," Arthur says softly, and a warmth spreads out from the core of my body to every fingertip. "But I only watched from afar because I knew I didn't deserve you. A timid, coddled boy like me? With no gift for sport, no courage, no cleverness, and no conversation? I suspected I would always remain in the background of your life."

The waltz ends, but we continue dancing as another piece of music begins.

"I went off to school, and every holiday, I came back to find you even more brilliant. Even more beautiful." His cheeks redden, but his voice remains steady. "You grew up into the woman I expected you to become, and I knew someone like you could never notice me."

"Arthur," I say helplessly. It is the first time in our adult lives that I have said his name to him, as though we are more to each other than what he has described. As though that name is very dear to me. He hears it in my voice, and emotion washes over his face.

"With all your liveliness, I could see there was something different about you after you lost your father. Forgive me for touching on a painful subject," he adds quickly. "But I know you've been sad for a long time. I . . . I still watch you, you see. Even if it seems like I never do. You always touch your locket whenever someone mentions him, and your eyes . . . It's like you go somewhere. Somewhere you can be alone and not pretend anymore."

I look down at the gold and jet locket around my neck, stunned that solid, emotionless, seemingly unobservant and uncaring Arthur has seen so much of me. "There's a photograph of Papa inside," I say. "It was the last one taken of him before he died."

We are both silent, lost in thought, moving among the other couples without seeing them.

"I'm sorry, Lucy," he says quietly. It is the first time in our adult acquaintance that *he* has ever said *my* name. "Every time I saw you struggling, I wished I could help. But I didn't know how. Or whether my sympathy would be welcome to you."

I study every inch of his face, from his grave brow beneath his walnut-colored hair to his eyes, both tender and serious, and the slight cleft in his chin. And I realize that aside from Mina, this man might be the only one to have ever seen a bit of the true me. *Me*, the woman behind the flirtatious smile and the fluttering silk fan. The woman who is still the girl who had never gotten over so much loss and death, and who may never do so.

"I want you to know," I tell Arthur, "that you have not been in the background of my life for some time. You have been in the front, with your back turned to me."

His lips tremble. The hope in his eyes is almost terrifying and breathtaking to behold. "My back has never been turned to you," he says in a voice so low that I can barely hear it over the music of the orchestra, "and it never will be."

I am surprised to find my eyes are wet as I smile up at this shy, sweet, and timid man who has just confessed to being afraid of me for most of our lives.

Arthur smiles back, the dimple appearing again. "Jack Seward doesn't mean anything to you, then?" he asks, searching my face. "I heard you say that he sent you flowers tonight, too. Roses. And I feared that you . . . and he . . ."

I can't help it. I lower my eyelashes, enjoying his anxiety.

"And Quincey Morris. I saw you laughing as you danced with him, and I thought . . . I was worried that . . ." He groans at my silence. "Lucy, you're torturing me."

"Only because you've tortured *me*," I tell him.

It isn't even remotely an answer to his questions, but he reads the truth in my eyes. His hand is firm but gentle on my waist, and I am awash in memories of the first time he held me this way, on another night at another ball. This time, it is different. This time, we have come dangerously close to admitting that we are important to each other. That we have, each in turn, been watching the other from afar and wondering if we will ever share more than a childhood and a single dance.

I look at our joined hands and run my thumb slowly across the side of his palm. He swallows hard, a lump moving down the length of his throat. I lean closer to him, imagining the taste of his neck on my lips and tongue. I know that he, too, is envisioning my kiss from the hungry way he is watching my mouth, though he tightens his hold on my waist to keep us a decorous distance apart. There is a fierce possessiveness in his eyes that both inflames and repels me. I want to fling myself into his arms and feel him against me. But I know that to do so would be to become what society demands of me: the property of a man, even if that man is Arthur. Even if I have dreamed of belonging to him since October.

"Lucy," he says, very low, and then the music ends.

I pull away, letting go of his hand. I feel as though I cannot take in enough air.

"Lucy," he whispers, looking straight at me. It is far too easy to imagine us alone in a room together, and Arthur murmuring my name against my ear. I can imagine the weight of his ring on my finger and the warmth of his body on mine. He will know every freckle on my skin and every corner of my heart and my dark, dark mind. He will discover that I am not the bold, brilliant, laughing girl he thought I was. When I take his hand and his name for my own, I will no longer be able to hide myself from him.

And if I let myself fall for this man—if I allow myself to *truly* love him—he will become yet another person I must one day lose forever.

Arthur is not the one who is afraid. Not right now.

"Lucy?" His face is creased with worry. "I'm sorry. Have I said anything? I—"

I press a hand against my chest, struggling to breathe, and then I hurry away.

I almost run back to the safety of meaningless flirtations and long looks at men in whom I haven't the slightest interest. My slippers carry me to the very farthest corner of the drawing room, where I stay away from Arthur, and we do not speak for the remainder of the night.

CHAPTER FIVE

T he mist kisses my ankles as I move barefoot through the churchyard, searching for something. It is no physical entity I seek tonight,
but rather a feeling, nebulous and dim. I burn with the need for something
impossible to define, and underneath my thin lawn nightgown, my skin
feels raw and alive. My hands reach out and find nothing but empty air.

I am angry, I think. Or very, very sad.

There is no moon tonight and no sound but my own breathing and
dead leaves crumbling beneath my feet. I can barely see anything through
the thick mist aside from the vague shapes of headstones, but occasion-
ally, through the curtain of silver, I spy other wanderers, other hands outstretched, other faces in the night, and some of them are dead.

I am dreaming again, I think. *This is just a dream.*

But it feels real when the ground beneath me suddenly sinks into nothingness. I gasp and pull myself back, staring at the hole dug into the earth.
I have almost fallen into an empty grave. No . . . not empty. At the bottom
is a plush white bed, and a man and a woman lie upon it. They are not
corpses, as I would expect, but are very much alive and entwined, their
breath emerging fast on the cold air. She has long dark hair like mine,
which cascades over them both as she pulls herself on top of him. His
hands slide up her thighs to grip her bottom, hard enough to bruise.

I am on fire.

My feet stumble around the open grave only to find another, and
another, and another, all of them filled with beds shaking and tongues
meeting and hands pressing. Silk and lace slipping above tangled
haunches. My heart races in a rhythm of frustrated longing. Every nerve
in my body is alight with the desire to join one of these graves, to feel

hungry welcoming arms and starving wet mouths on my naked skin. But it is so very far to fall, and I know I would not be able to climb back out again.

Suddenly, a man is standing behind me. I lean into his broad chest and feel the line of his jaw on top of my head. His long, elegant hands span the width of my waist. And in the way of dreamers, I know that it is Jack Seward without having to turn around.

Why Jack? I think, dazed. I remember another man's hazel eyes in ballroom candlelight, another man's walnut hair, another man's hand holding mine. Red camellias and a melancholy waltz. I know instinctively that it is neither he nor Jack I seek in the mist, but I am electric with yearning, and I will settle for whichever one of them appears. I turn around in Jack's arms.

All at once, the churchyard vanishes and we are in the conservatory at the Stokers' ball, alone in a dome of glass that shows the night sky. Somewhere beyond us, I hear laughter and conversation, violins and tinkling glasses. Leafy green plants and trailing vines conceal us from view, but someone could still walk in from the ballroom at any moment and discover us.

Jack's brown eyes are liquid with desire, but when I tilt my face up to his, his arms slacken. "Kiss me," I command, trying to hold him close, but he shakes his head.

"Not up here," he says, pulling my hand. "Down there."

An open grave yawns behind him, somehow—in the shaky logic of dreams—cut right into the fine stone floor. The bed at the bottom lies empty, waiting for us.

I let Jack lead me to the edge, but this grave is deeper than all the others. It would be like falling into an abyss. Jack's grip is tight as I look around desperately, my bare feet slipping on the stone, fighting to remain above ground. The conservatory is neat and orderly, with perfect rows shaped by well-cut trees and precisely placed plants, but through the foliage, on the other side of a monstrous orchid, black as death, I see a path almost hidden from view.

I yank my hand free of Jack's and run to the secret path. It is lined with sharp, lethal brambles and thorns thirsty for the blood of anyone brave or foolish enough to wander off the neat brick aisles of the conservatory. Other women would not risk their skin and their gowns being torn to wander off into the darkness. But I have never been one to flinch from danger.

As soon as my foot touches the path, I am rewarded. The brambles draw back and bow as though for some lost queen. Sinuous strands of mist beckon me into a garden beneath the night sky. Marble statues, towering and elegant, reach for me. Here, a woman arching her back, cold breasts exposed. There, a man whose robe slips down the line of his hips, his gaze feral. I touch hands and limbs like ice, all the while aflame in my own skin.

And then, in the center of these silent marble people, I find a man.

He wears the mist like a cloak and stands so still that I take him to be another statue at first. I cannot make out his features in the moonless dark, but somehow I feel I know him, and that I would recognize his face. I sense him watching me, surprised that I am there. The mist outlines his form—that of a big, powerfully built man, slightly taller than Arthur, broader than Quincey Morris. He has a quiet, thoughtful presence, tipping his head to one side as he studies me with eyes I cannot see.

My longing thrums harder in my chest, for I have found that which I was seeking.

"Lucy." His velvet baritone is like the music of a cello, warm and rich and dark. Never has my name been spoken with such unfettered yearning, not by any man who has ever wanted me. I want to sink into the depths of that voice and all the promise it holds. "Lucy."

I want to go to him, but I hesitate, thinking of Jack recoiling from my embrace, Quincey's cold eyes when I had spoken for him, and Arthur's hand keeping us properly apart as we danced.

The stranger holds out his long white hand. On the smallest finger shines a brass ring set with a garnet of deep wine red. "Lucy," he says for the third time. His tender, melodic tone is veined with both kindness and aching desire, and it is an invitation I cannot refuse.

It is only a dream, I think, giving myself permission before I run into his open arms.

He is as cold and solid as a marble statue. He has no smell and no warmth, but somehow his embrace is as familiar to me as my own name. I press my face against his chest and close my eyes, feeling a greater peace than I have known for some time. He holds me securely, but not tightly. Here, I am free to go whenever I wish, and there are no open graves to swallow me.

The man presses his icy lips to my forehead. I feel small and protected in the cradle of his arms as his hands stroke my back, arctic through my thin nightdress. His fingers teeter on the precipice of my waist, a tantalizing inch from the curve of my bottom. I lift my face to his, which is still masked in shadow, and hold him closer to me.

It is only a dream, I think, *and no one need know what we do here.*

"No," the man agrees, and in his voice I hear a smile.

I put my hand against his cool cheek, expecting him to pull away. Everything about this would be shocking by the light of day: me alone with a stranger, caressing his face so intimately as his hands learn the topography of my body. But he does not move as I trace his sharp jaw, clean-shaven but rough with bristle. My fingers find a long straight nose and a wide mouth. His lips, still smiling, brush a knowing kiss on my thumb.

Another invitation.

A flame ignites in my chest. This man will not refuse me like the others. He will give me everything I desire. He cares nothing for propriety when I am in his arms. Quickly, before I lose my courage, I press my mouth to his. His lips slide over mine, soft and delicate as a feather, and grow warm as I kiss him. I wrap my arms around his neck, pressing my breasts tightly to his hard chest. His hands stroke my body from shoulder to hip, and I shiver at his cold fingers on my bare arms. I am aching, melting. I sigh into his mouth, but he stops me at last with a quiet laugh, touching my face in a mirroring caress of how I had explored his.

"Lucy," he says again, heartbreakingly tender.

I hear a farewell in his voice and tighten my arms around his neck. I have no shame in the dream, not for the possessive way with which I hold him to me or for the urgency in my voice when I whisper, "Please don't go." *Not when I have found you.*

He leans his forehead against mine. "I will find you again," he vows. His accent is one I cannot place, but it makes me think of sprawling ancient cities, ruined castles embraced by dark tangled trees, and wild peaks glinting in the light of a cold sun. His arms wrap around me, gentle and protective. "I will find you, Lucy."

And then I wake up.

I am shivering alone on a bench in the churchyard. The moon has emerged from a blanket of thick clouds, and the garden, conservatory, and statues have all vanished. But there, held upon the wintry breath of night, is the stranger's promise, lingering like the mist.

CHAPTER SIX

B y afternoon, my dream has vanished into the sunny reality of the sitting room, where Mamma and I sip tea and wait to be fitted for our new dresses. The dressmaker arrived today with a coterie of apprentices, each carrying an armful of colorful garments. They divide them neatly onto two racks, one for Mamma and one for me, busily smoothing fabrics of lilac, rose, and pearl—all the cheerful hues we plan to wear on our holiday in Whitby this summer.

I struggle to hide a yawn as the dressmaker orders her workers about. Fortunately, I had woken no one else with this latest bout of sleepwalking and had crept home to wash my cold, dirty feet just as the first light of dawn had appeared in the sky.

"You look exhausted, Lucy," Mamma remarks. "Did you have trouble sleeping after all that dancing? At least the party was a triumph."

"It was. Mina enjoyed herself a great deal, even if Jonathan did not." I pour myself another cup of fragrant jasmine tea. It had been Papa's favorite and had reminded him of his grandmother, and he had never cared about the cost of having it shipped from overseas.

Mamma laughs. "Poor Jonathan. He dislikes being the center of attention, and an engagement ball was not something he ever wanted."

"Well, Mina likes parties and dancing, and *someone* has to give her what she likes."

My mother raises an eyebrow at my tone. "You don't like Jonathan, then? I've never gotten a sense of what you think of your Mina's husband-to-be."

"It's not that I *don't* like him," I say slowly. "I just always imagined that when I ended up losing Mina, it would be to a far more superior man than he."

"You're not losing her. You may not see her as often, once she sets up house in Exeter, but I'm certain you will write many letters and visit." Mamma sips her own tea—chamomile, her tastes ever sensible in contrast to Papa's and my more adventurous preferences. "And I disagree. Jonathan may be of humble origin, but then so is Mina. He is hardworking, honest, and educated. He adores her. And they've known each other for years, like you and Arthur." She glances at me. "Everyone talked of how beautifully the two of you danced last night. My friends were jealous that you secured him for *two* waltzes when their daughters couldn't manage one."

I look down into my tea, remembering the jolt of fear I had felt before parting from him. "He is so shy," I say softly. "I thought he wasn't interested, but he was only shy all along."

"I never doubted that he had feelings for you. What man could resist you?" Mamma asks, with a proud sniff that makes me chuckle. "And Lucy, I hope you aren't angry with me."

"Angry? Whatever for?"

"For scolding you after that incident with the American. You have a great deal of spirit, and I hate reprimanding you about something you can't help."

"Oh, Mamma, it's all right. I shouldn't have sent Mr. Hurst away." I shake my head ruefully. "Mr. Morris clearly didn't appreciate my defending him. He seemed almost affronted. As much as I hate to admit it, you were right that men don't like an outspoken woman."

"I wish I could give you a different world, my love, one in which women are respected for speaking out. But I cannot change the rules of society." She laughs. "I was much like you when I was young. You would be surprised. I threw champagne in a suitor's face once."

I gasp, delighted. "Mamma!"

"I don't recall what he had said to deserve that. Only how ridiculous he looked with his hair and shirt soaked. And it did the trick, for he never proposed marriage again."

"My prim and ladylike mother! I wish I had known you then."

"So do I. You would have approved of that wayward girl who longed to run off with the circus. What a life of adventure I dreamed for myself once." Mamma laughs again, her eyes wistful. "So you see, we are not so different."

"How could we be? Any woman, in any time and place." I twist the jade ring on my right hand. Tiny letters are etched into the band: Van, the name my great-grandmother had forsaken when she had married Lord

Alexander Westenra and become a respectable English lady. "Do you think that Vanessa . . . *Van* will be the only woman in our family to ever have a real adventure?"

"That depends on how you define adventure. She had to endure a difficult voyage and many trials in an unfamiliar land. But you don't need that to have joy and love, as I did with your father." Mamma takes my hand. "I must apologize for something else, Lucy. I worry that I have never been there for you the way Papa was. I know you felt you could tell him anything and I'm glad you were close, especially because my own father cared nothing for my troubles. When we lost Papa, I vowed to be everything that he had been. But I feel as though I've failed you."

My free hand flies to the gold locket around my neck. If Arthur were standing across the room, he would know exactly what my mother and I were discussing. "Mamma, why are you saying this? You have only ever been kind and loving, and I have nothing to reproach you with."

"I suppose I saw you dancing with Arthur, and it made me realize how grown up you are." Her smile is heartbreaking in its regret. "You've become a woman almost overnight, and soon you will no longer confide in me. You will be a wife . . . and perhaps a mother as well."

I smile back to hide my consternation as I imagine a screaming bundle in my arms, wet and smelly and writhing, with dirty sticky doll hands reaching for my hair. Me, a mother? I push away the horrid thought. My mind returns to the memory of Arthur's gaze on me last night, as though I already belonged to him. "Why look so far into the future?" I ask. "We are here now, together. Let us enjoy the present and speak no more of this."

"Bear with me. I don't know if we will have many chances to talk like this."

"What do you mean?" I demand. "We have many more years together yet."

"I only meant that you may be living in your own household soon. Away from me. And I have not properly prepared you for the . . . requirements of being a wife," my mother says with the caution of someone stepping barefoot around broken glass.

I laugh. "Are we truly about to have this conversation with all of these people around?" I gesture to the dressmaker and her apprentices putting the finishing touches on our garments. "Mamma, I may be innocent, but I know. I *know*."

Relief flatters my mother's elegant features. "Mina told you?"

I nod, though that isn't completely truthful. It was I who had found the book in Papa's library and shared it with Mina, the two of us giggling like naughty schoolchildren as we read the more lurid passages. The diagrams had been informative, somewhat terrifying, and—if I am to be honest—titillating as well. Mina had been aghast at the content, but I had argued that we *needed* this information so as not to be overly shocked by our wedding nights.

"One last thing," Mamma says. "I told you how much I used to be like you. But I am glad I gave all of it up when I married your father. It is the honor of a woman's life to be chosen by a good man as his wife and the mother of his children. It is a duty, but it can also be a joy."

I stiffen. "Gave all of what up? Your cleverness? Your high spirits and liveliness?"

She looks at me with knowing sympathy. "I thought I was getting the worse end of the bargain, too. But Lucy, this is what is asked of us. I am not saying you must change who you are. Just . . . suppress it. You will understand when you are a wife, too."

Thankfully, the dressmaker comes over to us at that moment. I watch Mamma touch and exclaim over each dress, feeling suffocated by our conversation and the expectation that society will dictate what I choose and what I give up. I am no more than a farm animal with a yoke to its neck, propelled to do what I am bid instead of living like a free being.

My lungs tighten and spots dance before my eyes. I take a deep breath, recognizing the signs of an attack. I cannot let it overtake me as it almost did last night, with Arthur watching. I must keep my mind from flying back to the churchyard where Papa waits, the mausoleum inviting against the dark. Something drifts across my memory like snow in the wind: a cold marble hand in mine, a kiss of ice pressed to my burning lips, and a man murmuring my name. The strange, half-forgotten images vanish when I try too hard to remember them.

Lost in my reverie, I scarcely hear our housekeeper answer a knock at the door and am only roused by the sound of footsteps approaching the sitting room. A hearty voice says in a flat American accent, "Good afternoon, Mrs. Westenra. Miss Lucy."

Quincey Morris beams, his eyes as bright on me as when we first met last night. He is wearing his long coat again, but today it is buttoned against the chilly weather and there is no sign of the weaponry I know is hidden beneath it. A hat is pulled low and rakishly tilted over his forehead, making him look every inch the gallant cowboy.

With him is Arthur, who bows in greeting. "Mrs. Westenra, I beg your pardon. And yours, Miss Westenra," he adds, looking directly at me. I stifle my laughter. In just one evening, I have trained the bashful Arthur to ignore me at his own peril. "Quincey and I wished to call and thank you for a wonderful evening, but I see we have interrupted an appointment."

"Nonsense. You are both most welcome," Mamma says warmly. She signals for the men to take the sofa across from ours and for the house-keeper to bring them tea. "My daughter and I are only preparing for our holiday in Whitby. A seaside town in Yorkshire, Mr. Morris, where we go each summer," she adds politely, looking at the American.

"It sounds delightful, and no doubt it will be even more so when you are both there," Quincey Morris says with the coy charm I am beginning to recognize as his signature. His eyes shine at me. "I have half a mind to see it and prove myself correct."

The housekeeper appears with tea and cake, and as Mamma serves and chats with Arthur, I smile at the cowboy. "I'm glad to see you today, Mr. Morris. I did not expect to, for I was worried that you were more like Dr. Seward than I thought," I say in the teasing voice that is *my* signature. "Shocked by my bold ways. You did not like my dismissal of Miss Worth-ing's fiancé."

Mr. Morris blinks, seemingly at a loss for words.

"I thought perhaps I had disturbed you with my frank and forward manners," I continue, enjoying his consternation. "I have the habit of being overly direct, I'm afraid."

"It is an admirable habit," the American says quickly. He sits up straight, looking eager to show me that he is not as old-fashioned as the doctor. "Miss Lucy, thank you for your kindness in speaking up for me. Any displeasure I showed was for the rude gentleman and not you."

I laugh. "You speak so warmly that I *almost* believe you."

He gives me a good-natured grin. "Well, I hope I find a way back into your good graces, ma'am, and can show my gratitude properly."

As Mamma begins serving Mr. Morris, Arthur takes a sip of his tea and coughs. Embarrassed, he dabs at his mouth with a napkin and puts the cup down in a hurry.

"Too hot for you, dear?" Mamma asks, concerned.

"Forgive me," Arthur says. "I have never tasted such a variety of tea before."

Frowning, Mamma lifts the teapot to inspect it. "Oh, dear. Agatha has mistakenly prepared Lucy's tea for both of you instead of my chamomile."

Quincey sips his tea, pauses and then takes a second sip. "I think it's delicious. I've never tasted anything like it before, either. Fragrant, very floral."

"Yes, but also quite bitter?" Arthur suggests.

"No. Not to me," the cowboy says, shrugging. "Why do you call it Lucy's tea, ma'am? Do the young lady's considerable gifts extend to growing tea as well?"

I answer for my mother. "Not quite, Mr. Morris. You are drinking a jasmine tea that my father loved, though I find I am the only one left to enjoy it now." My last words come out so quietly that they are almost a whisper. Arthur picks up his cup, looking stricken as I run my fingers over my locket.

"I won't let you enjoy it alone anymore, Miss Lucy," Quincey says, and I give him a look of gratitude. "May I have another cup, please, Mrs. Westenra?"

Mamma obliges him. Her eyes dart between us, displeased that the dashing cowboy is gaining so quickly in my favor. "Lucy loves this tea so much that we will have to bring it with us to Whitby," she says gaily, turning the subject. "It is truly the loveliest place in the summertime. Lucy loves the cliffs and walks there often, don't you, my love?"

Perhaps it is the melancholy of remembering Papa, but all it takes is the word *cliffs* and I can feel the briny sea wind whipping my hair as I stare down, down, down to the water's edge, where the hungry white foam would rise to meet me if ever I fell. I have often imagined how it would feel to fling myself into the air, to suddenly lose the ground beneath my feet and feel my stomach drop as I plummet. Imagining the freedom of it, the *choice*, is almost ecstasy.

I look up, realizing they are all waiting for my answer. Quincey is smiling, eager to approve of whatever I say, but Arthur's face is solemn and watchful. He has seen again what he does not understand in me, and I push away the awful feeling that perhaps this is what attracts him—that if I married him and unveiled the mystery, he would no longer find me compelling.

"It is a beautiful place," I say.

"You look peaked, dear. We *have* been sitting here a long time," Mamma says, and I hear in her voice that a plot is afoot. Subtlety is an art that my beloved mother never quite learned. "On the subject of walks, I believe a stroll outdoors might revive you. Arthur, would you take her? I'm a bit busy here." She gestures to the women sewing across the room.

"And I was hoping that *you* in particular, Mr. Morris, would stay and give me your advice."

"Me, Mrs. Westenra?" Quincey's expression while regarding our colorful summer frocks is so nearly frightened that I laugh, and Arthur does as well. "I wonder if an American cowboy might not have the elegant and sophisticated taste you would wish for in dresses . . ."

"Nonsense!" Mamma guides me to my feet so that Quincey can take my place beside her. "You are exactly the person I need. You can tell me what colors the ladies in America prefer."

"Shall we, Miss Westenra?" Arthur asks quietly.

"We shall, Mr. Holmwood," I say, matching his formality.

I slip on a coat and gloves, and we step out into the chilly February day. Another man might have given me his arm or I would have taken it, offered or not. But Arthur is not like the others, nor would I have him be. He folds his hands behind his back, I keep mine at my sides, and we walk with a respectable distance between us. No one watching us would suspect that we were anything more than friendly acquaintances taking a polite stroll.

"Are you all right?" he asks.

"Yes, thank you. Now that my mother has prescribed this medicinal walk with you."

"You were sad just now, when she mentioned Whitby. But you weren't thinking of your father. You didn't touch your locket." As though embarrassed by his own observation, Arthur looks away, pretending to study the passing carriages. "Were you thinking of Miss Murray's wedding later this year, perhaps? And her having to move away to Exeter with Mr. Harker?"

I sigh. "No, but well guessed. Jonathan will leave in the spring and may not return until full summer. I am trying to persuade Mina to put the wedding off until autumn, so that she may join us at Whitby. It would be nice to have someone to walk with." *And to keep me away from the cliff's edge*, I think as a little thrill rises up in me, all the sweeter for having to be kept secret.

Arthur glances shyly at me. "I have not been to Whitby myself for years. The doctor thinks the sea air would do my father good, but Papa is so reluctant to leave the house these days." It is his turn to sigh. He has never been one to show much emotion in public, and I take this as a sign of very serious worry indeed.

"Is his health worsening?" I ask, touched that he would show me this private grief.

"I'm afraid so. I'm not sure what I would do if he—" He breaks off abruptly.

"I'm sorry, Arthur." I am surprised to find how unbearable his pain is to me. I touch his arm and he looks down at my gloved fingers. I half expect him to pull away and take me back to Mamma at once, as Dr. Seward might. But instead, he applies the gentlest pressure to my fingers.

"Thank you," he says, very low.

"Death is cruel and cold and steals loved ones away too soon. I worry what you will think of me, Arthur, when I tell you how often I dwell upon it. I . . . I think about death all the time." The words slip out before I can stop them. But perhaps it is my conscience revealing this small glimpse into my mind, in hopes that it will save him from me. *Run, Arthur, while you can.*

But Arthur does not run. He turns toward me, his face open and expectant. He hears in my voice that this is important to me, and so he will make it important to himself.

"There is so little choice for a woman in life. A man can go anywhere and be anything, but a woman has not that freedom. She can select which dress to wear and what meals to serve her guests, but these are decisions without meaning, because they are already expected of her. Do you see?" I ask as a furrow forms between Arthur's brows.

"I . . . I believe so."

"Even in the matter of marriage," I go on, pretending not to see the flush that creeps onto his cheeks. "A man can choose who he likes, but a woman can only decide whether or not to accept a proposal. She must receive one first, and she cannot select from whom it comes."

Arthur blinks down at his shoes. He is trying so hard to understand. "But she can choose who she encourages, and that is something, is it not?"

I look away to hide my frustration. I cannot seem to put into words what sours and festers inside of me: the knowledge that everything in life has already been decided for me by men, by society, by my family name and position, and that the only meaningful choice I might ever have is to relinquish that life. To give it up on my own terms, in a manner of my choosing. To leave the neat, precise path and plunge into the bram- bles, to fall into the sea and be with Papa and be understood again. But I have never been able to explain this even to Mina or Mamma, and I can- not expect Arthur to comprehend it. I am alone, hopelessly alone, and I always have been.

My hand finds my locket once more. "I think about death all the time," I say again.

"Lucy, you are grieving," Arthur says, his voice full of emotion. "That is all. You have lost your beloved father and miss him dearly. I know . . . I can imagine . . ."

I turn back to him and see the shine of tears in his eyes.

"I would not have you be otherwise. To be unable to forget the ones you have lost is the mark of a very warm heart, and no one could ever question the propriety of that."

My own eyes sting from the grief and the empty certainty of knowing that I will never be understood, not even by poor, sincere Arthur, who only wants to think the best of me. He offers me a handkerchief of pristine white linen, embroidered with his initials, ALH, and I dab at my eyes. "How well the letters of your name look," I say with a shaky laugh. "I've always thought that *A* and *L* were so pretty side by side. The second letter like an extension of the first."

"Perhaps they were meant to be together," Arthur says, and the light of hope in his eyes makes my stomach clench. "Not just on handkerchiefs."

"Yes, they would look well on napkins and tablecloths and—" I stop myself from adding the word that would likely appall Mamma even from this distance: *bedsheets*. But Arthur seems to hear it just the same, and as I return his handkerchief, his fingers find the inch of skin between my glove and my sleeve. The heat of his touch makes my stomach clench in a delightful way.

"Are you in earnest, Lucy?" he asks, low and urgent. People stroll past us—couples, servants bearing packages, governesses herding children—and I know we are feeding gossip with our intense gazes on each other. But I hardly care as I look into Arthur's face taut with longing, feeling the intoxication of knowing that as powerful as he is in this world, a man with a title, estate, and old family name, *I* have the upper hand here. And he is mine for the taking.

And then the moment has to be ruined by, of all things, a child.

A little boy has fallen near us and scraped his knees upon the ground, and he is screaming as though he has been run through with a hot fire poker. The sound sets my teeth on edge and my blood rising, and I move away from Arthur in a half-dazed rage. The child's nurse runs over from wherever she has been socializing and hovers over him, fussing.

"Master Graham, you have torn your breeches! How careless you are," she croons with that peculiar mix of scolding and praising I have never been able to understand in other women.

The boy continues squalling, no doubt enjoying the attention from sympathetic onlookers. Other passersby are smiling, pursing their lips, or gazing indulgently at him.

Even Arthur's attention has been monopolized by the diminutive monster. "Poor little chap," he murmurs, his eyes soft. "That was a bit of a fall."

"Hush, now," the nurse says, holding the child close. "Quiet."

The boy's wails soften into sniffles as he tucks his head against her shoulder. And what should happen next, but for his attention to turn to me. His eyes are round and dark and shining, ringed with lashes like writhing spider legs as they squeeze out fat tears. Slimy white matter crawls from his nose and directly into his open mouth as he stares at me, unblinking, his dirty and smudged doll-like hands gripping the nurse's arm.

She notices his interest in me and offers an apologetic smile to Arthur and me. "Master Graham, don't stare," she chides the boy. "It isn't polite."

The child mumbles something in reply, his words indecipherable as more mucus enters his mouth. I swallow hard, trying not to gag as I stare at his repulsive little face. I am reminded of an image I saw once in one of Papa's books, a lurid illustration accompanying one of the many tales of horror I loved to read. It was of a dead child with an uncanny resemblance to this boy, down to the slimy lash-ringed eyes and gaping mouth . . . a child that had crawled out of its grave to terrify and punish an uncaring mother. I have never been able to look at a child since without revulsion and distaste and, at best, utter apathy.

The nurse gives us another apologetic smile. "What did you say, my pet?" she asks him gently. "Did you say that something is blue?"

"Bloofer," he mumbles, pointing his dirty chubby finger right at me. "Bloofer lady."

Even though pointing is much ruder than staring, both Arthur and the nurse start laughing, as though the boy is the cheekiest, cleverest little thing.

"What on earth is he saying?" I ask, trying to speak in a light tone. But my words are tinged with the rage and disgust I am trying to hide, and Arthur and the nurse look at me quickly.

"He's paying you a compliment, Lucy," Arthur says. "He's saying you are beautiful."

"I beg your pardon, miss." The nurse scoops up the boy and rises, her friendly face now apprehensive as she looks at me. I wonder what she sees in my eyes. "Master Graham means no harm. He's always liked pretty faces and yours is lovely, that's all." She bobs a curtsy to us and hurries off with the little boy, who is still looking back at me.

"Lucy?" Arthur asks, studying me carefully.

Somehow, I feel that this has become a test for me. I rearrange my features and laugh up at him. "What an adorable child," I say brightly. "Where would we be without these little angels? His compliment has improved my entire day. Did you hear him? He called me a beautiful lady!"

Arthur's face relaxes and his gaze grows warm on me. "He is not wrong, you know."

But as we walk back home, all I can think is *Yes, he is. The very existence of that child, of any child, is wrong.*

CHAPTER SEVEN

Winter ebbs into spring, and as the days grow longer and our journey to Whitby looms, Mamma enters a state of frenzy. In March, she suddenly decides to replace all the draperies in our London house, and her days are spent visiting cloth merchants before finally settling upon a deep green brocade only a shade darker than our original fabric. In April, she leads an army of servants in polishing every surface, repairing errant clocks and wardrobe doors that hang askew, and uprooting the garden so that neat stone paths and useless statues may be installed.

"What has gotten into you, Mamma?" I ask more than once, to which she replies, "I want everything to be perfect for when you inherit all of this, my love." And when I tell her that there are many more years before that happens, she only pats my cheek before returning to her manic activity, causing me to wonder if my obsession with death is catching. Perhaps I breathe so much mingled longing and fear that Mamma has taken it from the air into her lungs and heart. I cannot see any other reason for this sudden and morbid desire to ready her affairs for me.

In early May, a week before our journey to Whitby, she knocks on my door before dinner—something she almost never does, for by unspoken agreement between two adult women living together, she and I do not disturb each other in our respective sanctuaries. I am on my window seat in the open spring air, dreaming in the light of the setting sun and contemplating the multiple bouquets that grace my dresser and send a cloying scent into the air.

"It looks like a florist's shop in here," Mamma says, plucking a few dying blooms out of a vase of snow-white roses. "I'm surprised your young men haven't exhausted their wallets yet, buying you every flower to be had in London."

"They aren't *my* young men, Mamma," I say, laughing, though I get a thrill from the words. *My* men, whom I own. *My* property.

"Well, I certainly hope that changes very shortly." She brings the dead flowers out to the hall, placing them on a table for the servants to discard, before returning. "One of them will have to tire of courtship soon and make the deal official by asking for your hand."

"Mamma, I am not a business contract," I protest. "You know very well that these matters of the heart take caution, tact, and time."

She sits at my vanity table, facing me. "Time? What time do they think *any* of us have?"

I study the lines around her mouth, her blue eyes, and the shine of her ash-blond hair. "Mamma, what dark thoughts you entertain lately," I say playfully to mask my anxiety. "Why, pray tell, are you suddenly so eager for me to marry and inherit all of your property?"

"These aren't dark thoughts," Mamma says, waving a hand. "You know how impatient I am when things are left unsettled. I like tasks to be done, affairs to be completed, agreements to be reached, and all that. The sooner you marry Arthur and have a dozen children, the sooner I may rest easy and enjoy my old age, knowing that my work as your mother is done."

"It's hard to believe that you will ever grow old." I look down at my hands, slender and pale, the nails like gleaming shells. "Mamma, are you so certain that I will marry Arthur?"

She laughs, looking pointedly at the bouquets around her.

"Those are not all from him. Only the camellias. The other red flowers are from Dr. Jack Seward, and the white roses are from Quincey Morris, as a sign of surrender in a battle of wits we have been waging." I look with satisfaction at the snowy blooms, thinking of the notes the handsome American and I have exchanged over the past few months. Everything we have written is perfectly innocent, but the meaning between the lines . . . those, I am relieved no florist shall understand, for they would be horrified by the thought of the virtuous Miss Lucy Westenra expressing herself so openly to any man.

"Lucy, you must choose one eventually. And I think we both know who it will be," Mamma says indulgently. "You are twenty in September, and it's time you settled down."

"Mina turned twenty-four, and *she* is not married yet."

"Because Mr. Harker has been working hard to build up his savings for her and prepare for their life together," Mamma says. "He is a lawyer's clerk. *Your* young men are in vastly better positions and need not wait to take care of *you*."

I lean my head against a plump satin pillow, lazily enjoying my reflection in the mirror behind Mamma. "Well, then," I say archly, "since you insist upon me marrying at once, I shall propose to one of these men before we leave for Whitby. Will you ask Harriet to lay pillows upon the parlor floor, so I will not hurt myself when I get down on one knee?"

She shakes her head, chuckling. "How absurd you are."

"No more than you, dear Mamma. You know perfectly well that I would prefer to propose, but society forbids it, so I must linger on until one of my suitors finds the courage to speak. And since you are determined to hope for Arthur, I'm afraid it will take years yet."

"Years!"

"It took our entire childhood and years of adulthood for him to even *look* at me. So I'm afraid I will be your age before he musters the willpower to ask for my hand."

"I am not one of your lovesick men, impertinent miss," Mamma says, waving her finger at me. "Do not tease me the way you do them. Years to ask for your hand, indeed! I wager with you that he will ask before we leave for our holiday. I saw him at the Marshalls' dinner party last week, watching you talk to Dr. Seward and Mr. Morris."

I place a hand against my heart in delight. "Was he green with envy?"

"Like the first peas of spring, which Cook will be serving us at dinner," Mamma confirms, and we both burst into peals of laughter.

"Dear silly Mamma," I say affectionately.

"Speaking of dinner, I have invited Dr. Seward to join us this evening. He's bringing a friend, a foreign gentleman who is also a physician."

"Why Dr. Seward, when you favor Arthur so?" I lift my head from the pillow, alarmed once more. "And *two* physicians for dinner? Are we returning to the subject of your dark thoughts and the reason for your preparing my nest for me without you?"

My mother frowns and busies herself with smoothing imaginary wrinkles from her skirt. "Papa liked Dr. Seward, as you know, and I think it is important to maintain these friendships. I happened to see the young man in town and thought it might be nice to invite him, since Arthur and Mr. Morris call on us often. When he told me he had a friend visiting, I saw fit to invite the friend as well. Control that wild imagination of yours and get dressed," she adds, getting up.

"But what if you singlehandedly destroy Arthur's chances with this invitation?" I tease. "Suppose Dr. Seward, or even this foreign physician, if he is unmarried, proposes tonight in such a way as I cannot refuse and must accept at once?"

"Then I will be pleased, for that is vastly better than waiting for Arthur to take years," Mamma teases back as she leaves and shuts the door behind her.

I smile and shake my head as I rise from my seat to dress. She is where I get my playful nature from, and I cannot imagine her ever growing old . . . or not being here.

Dr. Jack Seward is a man who is as precise in his social life as he is in his work, and so just as the clock strikes eight, Mamma and I hear the door open and two sets of heavy male footsteps come down the hall toward the parlor. Dr. Seward enters first, and his eyes find me unerringly even as he greets my mother first. "Miss Westenra," he says, turning to me with a slow, warm smile. "I would like to introduce you and your mother to a dear friend of mine who has almost become a father to me. May I present Dr. Abraham Van Helsing of Amsterdam?"

The name is of Dutch origin, but the man who bears it does not look even remotely Dutch. He is a head shorter than Dr. Seward but taller than Mamma and me, with a slender build. When he politely takes Mamma's and my hands in greeting, I feel the strength and quickness in his fingers. He has jet-black hair, a sharp jaw, and narrow dark eyes on either side of a flat nose. In the firelight, his skin is even more olive than my own. He looks to be in his late forties.

Mamma's face remains calm and polite, though I can see the surprise in her eyes. She had expected someone old, grey, and European, just as I had.

"Mrs. Westenra. Miss Westenra. Thank you for the pleasure of your invitation. I am honored to meet you both after how much Jack has praised you." Dr. Van Helsing hands my mother a lovely bouquet of yellow daisies. His voice is calm, deep, and impressive, and his English, which is perfect, has shades of both a German and Dutch accent.

Mamma's eyes shine at his fine manners. "You are most welcome. Any friend of Dr. Seward's is a friend of ours. Shall we go in? I'm sure you are tired and hungry from your journey."

Dr. Van Helsing gallantly offers her his arm and she takes it.

"I suppose that makes you *my* charge tonight, Miss Lucy," Dr. Seward says. His arm is warm and solid beneath my hand, and I let myself imagine for a moment that he is my husband and that we are in our own home. It is almost too easy to picture, and as I look up at him, I see in his darkening eyes that he is thinking along the same lines. My breath catches, and the realization comes at last that what Mamma said was true: as much as I love flirting with these men and enjoying our intrigues, jests, and playful dances, one day soon I *will* have to choose from among them. And I will not be able to make them all happy.

"I am glad to be in your care, Dr. Seward," I say, squeezing his arm lightly to hide my emotion. "How have you been enjoying this weather?"

"Very much indeed. I spent an exciting day last week shooting with friends."

"With Mr. Morris?"

He darts a quick glance at me. "Why, yes."

"On Mr. Holmwood's estate?"

"Yes," he says, with an uneasy laugh. I hide a smile at his obvious hope to keep my mind only on him. "Well guessed. And you?"

"An uneventful week for me, aside from preparing for our summer holiday."

In the dining room, a fire roars despite the mild spring night, giving the space warmth and cheer. Mamma takes the head of the table, gracefully directing Dr. Seward and Dr. Van Helsing to the chairs on either side of hers. She seats me—to my amusement and Dr. Seward's dismay—beside the older physician. To the men, it must seem like a hostess's courtesy, placing her newer guest between herself and her daughter to ensure that he feels welcome. But the twinkle in Mamma's eye tells me she is thinking of our earlier conversation in my room.

It's no mystery who Mamma wants for her son-in-law, I think, obediently taking my seat next to Dr. Van Helsing. I have an inkling that even if Arthur took a whole year to propose, my mother would consider it worthwhile, no matter how she jests when we are in private. I smile, imagining what his proposal would be like. Probably a dry, gruff question put to me in a formal manner, his hands behind his back and his chin lifted. I do not think Arthur would be the kind of lover to get down upon one knee. That would be much more in Dr. Seward's style.

I glance across the table as the servants bring in the soup and find him watching me, as though he knows I am thinking of him. I blush and look down, and he smiles broadly. I feel Dr. Van Helsing looking indulgently between us and wonder how much Jack has told him about me.

"How did the two of you meet, sir?" Mamma asks Dr. Van Helsing. "Dr. Seward did not specify. Did your friendship begin in England or elsewhere?" It is her tactful way of asking about his heritage. Someone else might have bungled the attempt into something offensive, but the grace with which she puts the question makes him smile in complete comprehension.

"We met over ten years ago, when I was a young and very green professor in Germany," Dr. Van Helsing explains, giving an appreciative sniff of the whitefish bisque the servant places before him. "Jack was my brightest student and challenged me with many an irritating question."

Dr. Seward laughs. "You are too modest. I don't believe you have ever been young or green. That is," he corrects himself hastily, "green. Of course you were young, and still are!"

Both Dr. Van Helsing and my mother have burst into laughter.

"I see how it is, Dr. Impertinence," the older man teases, and his smile transforms his serious face into a bright, happy one. I glance at his hand for a wedding ring and see a simple gold one. "You accuse me of being elderly when I have scarcely entered my prime."

Dr. Seward grins. "You will never be elderly, sir, not even when you *are* elderly."

"Before I taught in Germany, I was raised abroad," Dr. Van Helsing says, turning back to Mamma. "I was born in a village in China, where my mother worked as a laundress. By chance, she befriended a kind Dutch couple. The husband was a physician studying rare illnesses in that region of the world, and he and his wife offered my mother employment in their household and an education for me. They became our family, and we gladly took their name. We lived in Amsterdam until my adopted father sent me off to the best schools in England and Germany, having recognized my aptitude for medicine. And now I find myself back in Amsterdam, which feels more like home to me than anywhere else. I was offered a nice little position there."

"And by nice little position, you mean you are running the entire branch of physicians dealing with rare diseases all over the world," Dr. Seward adds, and I favor him with a glowing look, touched by his eagerness to boast about his friend. "He will never tell you ladies, but he is a respected leader in many fields, especially that one."

"How impressive," Mamma says. "You must know about all sorts of conditions, Dr. Van Helsing. For example, diseases of the heart?"

"Ah, for that, I concede to my boy Jack," the physician says modestly. "I myself focus primarily on the blood, in which many contagions can be found. But I beg your pardon. This is not a pleasant conversation for a dinner with two such lovely ladies."

I laugh. "My father was not a medical man, sir, but he was interested in the field, and strange and grotesque topics were a matter of course at our table while he lived. I am certain I know more about lung conditions or how to prevent biliary upset than any young lady should."

Dr. Van Helsing beams. "Miss Westenra, your intelligence and charm do not surprise me, as I had heard much about them before I met you," he says, with a knowing glance at Dr. Seward. The young man blushes and quickly engages Mamma in conversation.

"What a fascinating life you have led, full of travel and experience," I say wistfully.

"I have been most fortunate," the physician agrees. "If the Van Helsings had not adopted me, I would never have been afforded such opportunities."

"I am hungry to see the world as you have, though it is unlikely that I ever will."

"You may have a chance." Smiling, he looks again at Dr. Seward, who is still talking to Mamma, and then back at me. "My late wife, Eleanor, used to say I was her ticket to the world. We had no children, and I took her with me to every medical conference and lecture."

"Was she so well educated?" I ask, surprised and envious.

He laughs. "She was the most supportive of wives, but my line of work was not for her! During my lectures, she would explore or happily spend the whole day lost in a book." A touch of melancholy softens the lines of his face, making it rather handsome.

"We need not speak of her if it is too painful," I say gently.

"On the contrary. I am glad to speak of her, for I am not often able to do so," Dr. Van Helsing says as the servants place the main course before us: delicate slices of roast beef with root vegetables. "In fact, she is the reason I became interested in folklore and superstition, for everywhere we went, she would learn all she could about the local customs."

"I, too, am fascinated by folklore. I have read everything in my father's library on traditions surrounding death." As soon as the words slip out, I wish I could take them back.

But the doctor seems intrigued, not repulsed. "You, Miss Lucy, a student of death?"

"We have had much loss in our family, and seeking knowledge comforted me," I explain. He gives me a look of fatherly approval so like Papa's that I surge on. "I enjoy reading of how cultures across the world perceive death and immortality, whether as a gift or a curse."

"And what is your opinion?"

I hesitate. "To have my loved ones go on and the world continue as though I had never existed is a chill I cannot shake. I think, sir, *that* is the true curse. Mortality."

The doctor studies me, and as adept as I am at reading the thoughts of men, I cannot discern anything in his sharp, clever eyes. "I see your reasoning. But you have many long and happy years ahead of you, I think, and need not worry about such things."

I make myself give a light, careless laugh. "Of course. These are the mere musings of a sleepless mind. Or rather, a sleepwalking one. An inherited family affliction," I add, seeing his interest. "My father sleepwalked, as did *his* father and his grandmother, Van."

"That is an unusual name."

"She was an unusual woman. In English society, at least." His eyes follow my gaze to the jade ring on my finger. "She became Vanessa before her foot even touched English soil."

Dr. Van Helsing nods with perfect understanding. "When my adoptive parents took us in, my mother urged me to give up my native language at once. Some of us must sacrifice a great deal, must we not? Names, tongues, and roots. I have colleagues who are still perplexed by my existence, even though I turned my back on my heritage and worked harder than any of them."

"Above reproach at all times," I say softly, echoing Papa's words.

"Just so, Miss Lucy." His solemnity lifts when Mamma asks him a question, bringing him into her conversation with Dr. Seward, and soon they are all talking in animated voices.

But our conversation weighs upon me, as does his expectation that I will choose Jack for my husband. Once again, it occurs to me that I will have to decide soon. Even if Arthur cannot muster the courage to propose, I doubt Dr. Seward or even Quincey Morris would hesitate.

I feel Dr. Seward looking at me again, but I keep my gaze lowered, knowing that my long lashes are put to best effect that way. I know that I appear beautiful and demure to him, but inside, I am boiling with frustration at Arthur. It is my fate to be tied to a man, an inevitable evil. Even Dr. Van Helsing, who had listened to me with respect, had suggested that

I would never travel unless my husband took me, as he had generously done for his own wife.

If I must belong to someone, I would rather it be Arthur than any other man, but it is not my choice to make, and many months have passed without him even alluding to the topic again. *Perhaps*, I think bitterly, *I ought to accept someone else to show him that I will not wait forever.*

But as soon as the thought crosses my mind, I recoil at the sorrow I know I would cause him. And now that I have seen him laugh, I do not want him to do anything else. Of the two of us, I am stronger and bolder. Perhaps all he needs is a nudge.

I lift my hand and whisper my instructions to a servant, still watched by Dr. Seward.

Tonight, I will guide Arthur to the decision he must make.

CHAPTER EIGHT

This time, when I walk to the churchyard, I am wide awake. Though it is spring, there is still a touch of winter in the night breeze, and I wrap my shawl tightly around my shoulders as I pass through the gate. I am beginning to ponder the wisdom of sending Arthur an urgent message to meet me here. Instead of waiting for him to speak, I have shown my hand. I have crept out of the house to speak to him unchaperoned, and such audacity might lose him to me forever.

"But I *must* know," I whisper, following the moonlit path.

This meeting will determine both our fates. I will know, irrevocably, whether he loves me enough to claim me. And if he does not . . . I bite my lip, wondering what I will do if he rejects me and turns me away for my impropriety. Or worse, if he does not come at all.

"Lucy," a hoarse whisper sounds out in the still air.

I close my eyes and exhale. "Arthur, you came."

"Of course I did." He hurries toward me, panting as though he has run from his carriage. He looks as genteel as ever: elegant coat, beautifully knotted cravat, gold cufflinks gleaming at his wrists. The image of a future lord even on a secret midnight tryst. His eyes widen as they take me in. If he is the image of a gentleman, I am afraid to say I am not much the image of a lady.

Beneath my shawl, I am wearing a white satin wrapper over my nightgown, the lacy hem of which can clearly be seen. I could have worn my dinner dress and appeared as pure and virginal as anyone could wish . . . but where would be the fun in that?

And how fun it is, I can't help thinking with glee, watching him swallow hard.

"Your urgent message worried me so," he says. "I thought something was amiss. Are you unwell? Is your mother—"

I shake my head. "All is well. I am sorry to alarm you. I did not consider the prudence of sending you such a message. I only wished to see you so much." I look down, then back at him.

His expression softens. "Lucy," he says, very low, with such affection that I want to melt against him that instant. "I will come whenever you call me."

"Do you mean that?"

"I am here now, am I not?"

I am desperate to throw myself into his arms, but I remain where I am. Arthur is like the deer he and his friends hunt—easily spooked, requiring a light step or he will be lost. I turn away, facing the direction of my family's mausoleum, and catch sight of a statue beside an opulent grave. The marble glows in the moonlight, stirring the dying embers of a memory in my mind: a pair of long white hands, a garnet ring, and a voice caressing my name like dark music. It must have been a dream, strange and feverish. I shake my head to clear it.

"Is anything wrong?" Arthur asks.

"Mamma invited Dr. Seward to dinner tonight."

In my peripheral vision, I see him go absolutely still. "Dr. Seward?"

"He is a favorite of hers, after the close friendship he had with Papa. He brought a doctor friend with him. A kind and lovely man, still young and . . . I was sad to hear, a widower." I have no designs whatsoever on poor dear Dr. Van Helsing, but Arthur does not need to know that. He moves toward me, barely breathing, and my eyes find his in the gloom. "I talked and laughed. I enjoyed their smiles and compliments. But all I could think of was you."

Arthur's expression changes, reminding me of his unexpected laugh when we had danced at the party. But he is not smiling now. There is clarity in his eyes and determination in the set of his jaw. He stops an arm's length away, and I can feel the warmth of him through the air.

"You thought of me?" he asks.

"Yes." I face him, my heart surging with hope. He will speak at last, and I will accept my fate as happily as I can because it will be shared with him. I wait, but he says nothing. "Arthur, do you not have something to say to me?"

My frustration builds as he remains silent, though his eyes on me are full of longing. We are in an empty churchyard on a dark spring evening.

There is no one to watch, no one to listen, no one to say what is proper or not. I am in my night clothes, tendrils of hair soft against my face and dark eyes shining up at him. But still, he refuses to speak. Still, he will not propose.

"Arthur?" I ask.

He tenses and opens his mouth, but then closes it again.

My chest tightens like twisted wire as tears of shame and disappointment blur my vision. I know that he cares for me, but now I also know that it will not be enough for him to claim me. "I am sorry for taking up your time. Good night." I hurry past him, stumbling in my slippers.

His hand finds my elbow. "Please don't go," he whispers, anguished.

I turn my head to hide my tears, but he takes my waist and turns me to face him, his touch scalding hot through my robe. He is so much taller than I am that I must tip my head back to look at him. My breath comes in choked gasps, and I am shaking—not from cold, I realize, but from aching, uncontrollable desire. And I am not alone in this, for his hands tighten on my waist.

"You know all that I cannot find the words to say," Arthur says gruffly.

Hope knifes through my despair. "Then do not say it with words."

I do not think. I do not hesitate. In one step, I close the distance between us. I press all of me against all of him and pull his mouth down upon mine. His soft, warm lips taste of both sugar and salt, an intoxicating combination that stokes my hunger. I feel the delicious rough scrape of his chin and smell pine and brandy and cigars. His heart drums against my palm and I wonder if he can feel mine thundering, too. I lean into his long, solid frame and gasp him in like air. He wraps his arms around me, locking me tightly against him as we kiss with starving desperation.

I have never been kissed like this outside of my dreams, and as his silken lips move hungrily on mine, I regret all the time I have spent on this earth *not* kissing. I feel slick and wet and formless, a bank of snow melting in the heat of his mouth. I am grateful for his arms around me, for my legs seem unable to hold up my body. I *need* more. I clench the lapels of his coat, deepening the kiss, and slide my tongue into his mouth like he is a confection for the tasting. And my elegant and reserved Arthur utters a growl deep in his throat as his tongue meets mine. My hands move to the burning skin above his cravat. His blood is rushing, and his pulse is racing, all for me. For *me*. I wrap my fingers around his neck. In this moment, he is once again powerless. In this moment, he is mine.

And then he ends the kiss.

One second, we are exploring the lining of each other's lips, and then the next, he is a full ten feet away with his back turned to me, shoulders heaving and hands clenched into fists.

I hug myself, shivering from the chill of his absence. "Arthur? What is it?"

He lifts his trembling fists to either side of his head and breathes in and out.

"What happened?" I ask, moving toward him.

At the sound of my feet on the path, he darts even farther away. I glimpse his flushed face, eyes pinched shut as though in pain and distress. "No," he says shakily. "Don't come any closer, Lucy. I'm not myself. If we go on, I wouldn't be able to . . . we shouldn't . . ."

Hurt knifes through my gut. I offered myself to him freely. I gave him the honor of my first kiss when there were dozens of other men who would have promised me the moon for it.

"This doesn't feel right," Arthur says in a low voice, as though to himself. He shakes his head. "You and me. This is not the way it should be . . . not like this."

"You don't want me," I whisper.

His eyes pop open. "Lucy."

"You don't want me," I repeat, my eyes stinging with tears for the second time tonight.

"Lucy, you know this isn't right. We are not meant to—"

I back away, struggling to breathe. The pain in my chest is almost unbearable. "You don't feel for me as I do for . . . oh, Arthur!"

"Please wait," he begs, his hands clasped as though in prayer. "Just hear me—"

"I wanted to see how you truly felt about me tonight," I say, and under my desolation is a rising wave of shame. "And now I know for certain."

"Lucy, wait," he says despairingly.

But I am no longer willing to stay with a man who does not want me. "Goodbye, Arthur," I say, unable to see his face through the haze of tears.

And then I turn and run.

CHAPTER NINE

ours later, I am still tossing in bed in a frenzy of embarrassment and frustration, unable to calm myself. When sleep finds me at last, I am suddenly standing in a grove of trees with no notion of how I got there until I see the mist swirling around my ankles, a garden of white marble statues, and moonlight glinting on a great glass-domed conservatory. I am dreaming again. My chest is tight, and my breath comes fast. I am *furious* and I cannot remember why.

"Lucy!" Arthur calls.

The revelation comes with both pain and relief. It is *Arthur* with whom I am enraged. I stay motionless beneath the trees, petulant even in my dreams.

"Lucy, come here," he pleads. "I have something to say to you."

He sounds so desperate that I reluctantly follow his voice to the conservatory. The mist is cold upon my feet as I wend my way through the headstones in the grass. A chill light illuminates the building, which is humid and warm and choked with a jungle of twisting plants. Gaping wide in the center of the stone floor is an open grave, next to which Arthur is waiting for me.

He looks remorsefully at me. "I'm sorry, Lucy. I'm sorry I didn't drink the tea."

A table stands in the corner. The steaming teapot releases coils of rich, fragrant jasmine.

"Will you forgive me?" Arthur holds out his hand. He looks like a lost little boy and his eyes are strange tonight, black and ringed with thick spider leg lashes. "Jump with me."

I look into the open grave and see a great drawing room with a roaring fire, handsome furniture, and silk drapes at the windows, through which a light snow is falling. A dog dozes near the hearth, where another table is set for tea, though the pot smells only of bland chamomile. A servant enters the room. "All is ready, my lady," she says, looking up out of the grave at me.

"Jump with me," Arthur repeats. "I'll take care of you."

But I am suddenly, desperately afraid of falling. I look around in a panic, and once again I see between the neat paths of the conservatory that there is a hidden walkway covered with brambles. I try to pull away, preferring the thorns to the fall, but Arthur begins to cry. His sadness is unbearable, and so I let him tug me into the grave, expecting us to land before a warm and inviting hearth. But the drawing room is gone, and all that awaits us is a cold dirt floor.

I claw at the sides of the grave, terror-stricken. "I did not want this. I do not want to be here, not even with you. Let me out, Arthur!"

"Don't go," he pleads. "Stay with me."

I am as frightened as I was angry earlier. Every clod of dirt I dislodge flies back into place as though I had never moved it. It is impossible to climb out of this grave. *I will not see the brambles anymore*, I think, grief tearing at my lungs. *I will never drink Papa's tea again.*

"Stay with me," Arthur says, and this time, it sounds more like a command.

A shadow falls over the grave. Through a curtain of mist emerges a powerful hand with a red gem shining upon the smallest finger. "I am here," says a voice I know, a low baritone with shades of an accent I cannot place—French, perhaps, or German. Memories flood my mind: a broad frame, a face hidden by night, a kiss that promised me everything I have been denied. And a vow spoken on another evening, in another dream: *I will find you again.*

"It's you," I say with wonder. A familiar longing pierces my heart, like a hunger for that which I cannot name and have no words to describe. It has haunted me in every dream in which I wander through the mist, end-lessly searching. I sense that this stranger's long white hand holds all the answers. "Have you come for me?"

"Don't go," Arthur says at my elbow.

I turn and scream at what I see. Arthur is gone. In his place is some-thing shaped like him but made entirely of writhing green vines as thick as my arm. They slither and twist and undulate like hellish snakes, each one pocked with gaping, seeping black holes full of tiny little teeth.

"Stay here," the nightmarish mouths command me.

I seize the stranger's hand, and in one powerful movement, he lifts me from the grave and away from the monster. And suddenly, we are no longer in the conservatory but a sprawling ballroom full of mist, dark but for the starlight filtering through the windows. Vases of dead roses surround us, and a waltz plays, hypnotic and seductive, though the room is empty.

The stranger takes me in his arms. Again, I detect no warmth or smell, only a feeling of dangerous, all-encompassing cold. "Dance with me, Lucy," he murmurs, lips against my ear, and we waltz across the gleaming floor. I feel his hand on my waist and hear his breathing just above my head, yet when I look into the wall of mirrors behind us, I am dancing alone.

I gaze up at him, but his face is hidden in shadow. "You saved me."

"You took my hand," he replies.

"Where have you been?" I ask longingly. Time is often a twisted tangle in my dreams, but tonight I am certain that it has been months since our dreamed kiss in the statue garden, when I ran through the brambles to find him. I had forgotten until this very moment.

"I have been preoccupied," he says, amused, spinning me around so that my back is pressed against his front. He wraps his arms around me, and his lips find my ear again, sending tingles of pleasure down my neck. "I will not refuse you anything. Not like them."

I close my eyes and lean back, and I *believe* him. He would never recoil or turn me away as Jack has, as Quincey has. As Arthur has. Arthur, to whom I called with my heart in my hands. Arthur, whose rejection hurts me most of all.

"Lucy, look at me," the man says.

I turn my head over my shoulder and his lips are there, his head tilted down to kiss me. Our mouths dance and his hands study the geography of my body, exploring curves and valleys, but too slowly for my taste. Greedily, I seize one of them and try to place it where I want it.

He removes it with a soft laugh. "Patience. Everything you want, I will give you in time."

"When?" I plead.

He drops a cold kiss upon my neck. "Very soon. Wait for me."

And then I wake up.

The man is gone, and my maid stands before me, her face drawn with worry in the light of the candle she holds. "At last!" she cries, relieved. "Miss Lucy, I have been trying to rouse you."

"Harriet." I blink the sleep from my eyes. We are in the ballroom of my mother's house, but there are no dead roses, no hypnotic music from invisible violins. There is not even starlight, for the drapes are closed against the night. "How long have I been out of bed?"

"I don't know, miss. I woke up an hour ago, came down for a cup of tea, and found you in here by yourself." She shivers. "You were dancing all alone."

"An hour? I was dancing all that time?" I ask, stunned.

"Perhaps longer. I saw that the door was open, and there you were in your nightdress, waltzing in the dark. I thought you were a ghost at first." She gives an embarrassed laugh.

My mind feels scattered and fragmented. I clutch at the edges of the dream. There had been a man waltzing with me. Or at least, I *believe* we had been waltzing. My back had been pressed against him, and I had turned my head over my shoulder, and his lips . . .

"Miss Lucy?" Harriet asks, staring at me.

I press my hands to my hot cheeks. The dream had felt so real: the press of his mouth on mine, the feel of him behind me, his hands on my body. "Did you see anyone else here?"

Poor Harriet looks frightened now. "Of course not, miss. It's the middle of the night." She touches my elbow. "Please let me take you back to your room, or you'll catch cold. At least you sleepwalked around the house tonight instead of out to that dreadful churchyard."

Obediently, I follow her out of the room. Just before she shuts the door, I look back at the mirrors, almost expecting to see a shadowed figure gazing out at me. But the reflection is only that of my own small and slender form, draped in white and full of endless, futile yearning.

CHAPTER TEN

A few days later, Mamma holds another dinner party. Jack Seward is invited, this time without Dr. Van Helsing, who has returned to Amsterdam. The guest list holds other familiar names. One of them is Quincey Morris, to my satisfaction . . . and another is the Honorable Arthur Holmwood, to my chagrin. My mother has ignored my pleas to exclude him.

"It would be unconscionably rude to leave him out," she protests whenever I bring it up. "I am sorry he has displeased you, but at least give him a chance to redeem himself."

She believes that Arthur and I have had a lovers' quarrel, and I do not disabuse her of this notion, not when half a dozen bouquets from London's finest florists arrive every morning. From a bed of greenery spill red camellias, fragrant forget-me-nots, and last night, even a desperate two dozen roses. I tell the maids to throw them away, but I can still smell them in the hall; no doubt Mamma has hidden them away in her own room, unable to get rid of such lovely gifts.

That evening, as our guests begin to arrive, emotion rages inside me. It took three hours to decide what to wear as I tossed aside dress after dress for looking too desperate, too hopeful, or too aloof. But my goodness, what frock would properly assert "I am a beautiful, brilliant woman whose heart has been broken by the only suitor she ever truly loved, but must try to look unbothered to all the other men who desire her"?

And Mina is not even here to calm and advise me. She is in Exeter with her aunt and only knows of the latest developments through my tear-stained letters. Her responses are loving, sisterly, and full of encouragement that I will make the right choice and do the right thing.

But I do not deserve her confidence. I attempted to force Arthur's hand, and now I have lost him forever. When I think of how abruptly he had ended our embrace, I am filled with a shame so sour I can taste it. "This doesn't feel right," he had said, his back turned to me, and his fists clenched. I had been so conceited, so overconfident. I had never imagined such a rejection from anyone, least of all the one person I felt certain would accept me no matter what I did.

I do not know how I can face him tonight—how I can look at him and speak to him as though we were mere acquaintances mingling at a party.

And so I do neither.

When the sound of laughter and the clinking of glasses fills our home, I do not look at or speak to Arthur after a brief greeting, as is expected of the hostess's daughter. I devote myself to Jack and Quincey, who have singled me out, a pair of hungry wolves seeking out a willing lamb.

Tonight, I have chosen a demure gown of watered silk that covers my shoulders and décolletage, the blue-grey shade resembling mist over the sea. The front may be modest, but the neckline dips courageously in the back, revealing several surprising inches of skin above a row of gleaming pearl buttons. I have swept my hair into a knot with a pearl comb to display my back to best effect, and I feel many eyes on me as I chat to Jack and Quincey. Arthur's, in particular, are like a warm and lingering touch, but he does not make the slightest attempt to win me back.

He truly does not care, I think, throwing my head back to laugh too hard at something Dr. Seward has just said. The heartache is so powerful, it threatens to dissolve my façade. My breath catches in my tight throat and Dr. Seward notices at once.

"You look faint. Is it too warm for you?" he asks. There is professional concern on his face, but his brown eyes are full of yearning for any excuse to touch me. I hold out my hand to him, but to my never-ending amusement, Quincey Morris swoops in like a great thundercloud and takes it before the young doctor even has time to blink.

"Let me take you outside for some air, Miss Lucy," the cowboy says in his butter-smooth drawl. "It isn't dark yet, and dinner won't be for a while longer."

I look up at his strong and handsome face, his eyes crinkling as he smiles at me, and force Arthur from my mind with all the willpower I possess. Here is a kind, amusing, intelligent man who has made no secret of his affection for me. "I would like that very much, Mr. Morris," I say, and he leads me out of the room. I catch a glimpse of Dr. Seward's crestfallen expression and Mamma's sharp gaze before the American and I are alone in the garden under the darkening sky.

"I'm glad to have a moment alone with you," Quincey says. He glances over his shoulder at the curious faces watching us from the windows, one of them doubtlessly Mamma's. I try not to think about the others, and to whom they might belong. "I've been wanting to speak to you privately since our dance at Miss Murray's engagement party."

"Goodness. That long?" I ask, looking down at our joined hands. I like the sight of my delicate fingers in his big, weathered hand. "You could have written to me."

"There are some things you shouldn't rely on paper to say to a lady. Or . . . or to ask a lady," he adds, gazing at me with such significance that I begin to suspect what is coming.

A giggle threatens to burst from my chest, but I restrain it and look up at him demurely. "What is this all-important question, then, Mr. Morris?"

He takes my other hand, too, so that we are standing face-to-face, and shuts his eyes. His chest rises and falls with his deep slow breaths, and he rolls his head on his big shoulders as though stretching after a long ride. He swings my hands lightly like we are two children playing in the garden, and the desire to laugh overtakes me once more as I realize that this large, strong, effusive man who is full of courage and cheer, who carries deadly weapons everywhere he goes and looks ready to fight at a moment's notice . . . is *nervous*.

I press my lips together to suppress my merriment. "Mr. Morris?" I prompt him.

Quincey's eyes fly open. "America is a beautiful country," he blurts out. "And it's completely unlike anything you see here."

"I . . . I'm sure you're right," I say, surprised.

"I know you love London. But I think you would love Texas, too. It's a sight to behold, especially on horseback. Golden fields under a hot sun, a rolling green country with grass rippling like waves, the sky in summer endless and bluer even than the sea. I don't leave home often, but whenever I do, the sight of it coming back is like cool water to a thirsty man."

I ache with envy at the warmth in his voice and the way his gaze grows distant, picturing that far-off land he loves. He can come and go from home whenever he wishes, take ships and trains and carriages and explore the entire world until his feet grow weary and carry him back across oceans to the place where he is happiest.

"My family never had a true home, you see," he says quietly. "My ancestors were taken to America by force to work a land they couldn't even own. But by the grace of God, the laws changed when I was a boy. The man my parents worked for was fairer than most and gave them land in exchange for all their years of labor, free and clear. They built a homestead, hired hands, and expanded their livestock. Everything I am, I learned from them. How to stand on my own two feet, how to surge on in a world that tells me I don't belong . . ."

A lump forms in my throat as his gaze returns to me.

"And how to love. I was raised in the light, taught hope and faith. My mother told me to keep my heart open because there is always a chance for love even in this unkind world." He lets go of one of my hands to tuck a strand of hair behind my ear. "I can see us riding together across those plains, Miss Lucy. You laughing, with your hair flying out behind you. I'm happy to be going home soon . . . but I don't want to go alone."

Now that the moment has come, now that I have received my first proposal, I no longer feel the need to laugh nor the thrill I had imagined. Instead, I want to weep as dread rises in me, not from the terror of belonging to this good man, but from the guilt of knowing that I will refuse him. The realization that I have always known I would reject Quincey is sudden and sharp. As attracted as I am to him, as easily as I can imagine riding across the plains with him and waking up in his bed, I have never seriously considered saying "yes" when he asked me to be his.

I look up at his affectionate face and I know that I have been too free with him. I have encouraged him only to cruelly stamp out his hope, and that knowledge finally does bring tears to my eyes. I look away quickly to hide them, but it is too late.

"Miss Lucy, don't cry," Quincey says, shocked. "Have I upset you?"

I shake my head. "No. *No.* I am simply overwhelmed by your—" I pause, realizing he never actually asked the question. "You *were* going to propose marriage to me, weren't you?"

Quincey laughs his booming laugh. "You surprise me every time. Yes, little lady, I was."

"Well, then, I am overwhelmed by your proposal." I see his dawning realization that I will refuse him. "You are a kind and lovely man. Your smile, your laugh . . . Every time you're happy, it's like the sun is shining on me. I've enjoyed our talks and our letters—"

"But you don't wish to marry me," he finishes, his face solemn.

"I am so sorry to hurt you, Quincey, after I encouraged your attentions," I whisper, aching with guilt and grief. "I have done you wrong, and I understand if it makes you think less of me."

There is nothing but kindness in his eyes. "You could never do anything that would make me think less of you. I understand. Of course I do. I was feeling pretty guilty myself about taking you so far away from your home and your mother. I guess it was silly of me, thinking I could plant an English rose in Texas soil." He winks and squeezes my hands, and I have the overpowering urge to throw my arms around him—not out of desire, but true affection and feeling for him. But I hold myself back, knowing that we are being watched.

"Mr. Morris, I believe that *you* are the true diamond in the rough and I am glad to know you." Tears slip down my cheeks, for it is clear that as gracious and gentlemanly as he is being, my refusal has pained him. "Please forgive me. I want us to be lifelong friends, and I do want to see those plains someday . . . just not as your wife."

He lifts my hands to his lips and kisses them. "I *know* we will always be friends, Miss Lucy. And there is nothing to forgive." He clears his throat. "Now, I think I ought to go back inside. I reckon dinner should be ready soon. Will you join me?"

"In a minute," I say, and he nods, as understanding as ever, before leaving me.

I shiver despite the warmth of the evening, appalled by my own reckless manners and unguardedness over the past few months. In hoping to win Arthur's interest—and, if I must be honest, to satisfy my own pride and vanity—I tricked someone into proposing without any real intention of accepting him. I bite my lip, thinking of the bitter disappointment Quincey tried so gallantly to hide. I feel the urgent need to sob and sob, to give in to my hysteria and heartache.

"Miss Westenra, are you unwell?" Dr. Seward appears, his expression still an odd mix of professional scrutiny and desire. He glances from me to the house, where Quincey has retreated.

"I need to sit down," I say, and he places my hand on his arm and leads me to a bench by the garden wall. I sigh when I feel the coolness of the stone through my skirts. It reminds me of being in the still and quiet of the churchyard, and the memory calms me.

"Did Mr. Morris upset you?" Dr. Seward leans against a tree with his hands in his pockets. His posture is casual, but his tone is anything but. "Shall I reprimand him for you?"

"If you consider too much sweetness and lovely manners an offense, then by all means, please scold him thoroughly for me," I say shakily.

Jack goes rigid and his hands slip out of his pockets. "He has spoken, then? He has asked you to marry him?" When I do not answer, he sits close beside me, facing the other direction so that he can look directly into my face. His eyes flicker to my left hand, which is still bare. "Lucy, tell me how you answered him. Tell me what you said."

"Mr. Morris is a gentleman, and I will not betray his confidence."

"Lucy, I beg you. I need to know if he asked you what I . . . what I wish to ask myself." And before I even have time to process the knowledge that I will be getting a *second* proposal of marriage within minutes of the first, Dr. Seward pulls me close to him. "I will speak now because I am afraid I will not get another chance tonight. Lucy, I've loved you for years. I always hoped to have your father's permission, because he was such a kind friend to me, but there was no time." His gaze darts between my eyes as though hoping to find an answer in one of them.

I bow my head and see the glimmer of my locket against my dress.

"I'm sorry to bring up a painful subject. But I know your father would have approved of this." Dr. Seward's voice rings with such genuine affection for Papa that it makes my heart clench. But of course, it says less about the doctor than it does about my father, who was loved by everyone who knew him. "Your mamma likes me, too. She has hinted to me before that she would not be averse to our union. Both your parents approve of this, my darling."

The raw hunger in his voice catches me unawares. My mind reels as I try to imagine what Papa would advise me to do. But all I can think of is my father teasing me about Arthur.

Arthur, again.

I close my eyes, frustrated that I cannot stop thinking about a man who does not want me. Dr. Seward's arms tighten around me as he waits for my reply, and that, too, reminds me of Arthur and the night he had held me like this, as though afraid I would disappear if he let go.

But he let go, I think furiously. *He let go.*

"I have my own property," Dr. Seward goes on. "We wouldn't live in the asylum where I work. I have a lovely house with a garden and a piano for you and a parlor where you and I can sit in the evenings. Can't you see us there? Me reading aloud to you, and you laughing as we sip our tea?" I shiver as one of his clever hands toys with the pearl buttons on my dress. "And then I would carry you upstairs, my love, and I would make you a very, very happy woman."

It is not difficult in the least to imagine being swept up in his arms. Pressing my smile into his neck as he runs up the stairs with me held tight against his heart, and then falling into a feather bed in the shadows. His lips on my ear, my neck, and my shoulders, trailing kisses all down my skin as his skilled and capable hands drive my rising need for him.

Yes, I believe him. He would make me very happy indeed.

But I feel rising dread and the hot, panicked threat of tears once more. Because though I have enjoyed his attentions, his flirting, his flowers, and his eyes on me like melting caramel, and as many times as I have imagined him knowing me in all the ways a husband would, the truth is that I have never been serious about Jack Seward, either.

"Dr. Seward," I choke out.

"Jack," he whispers, his fingers still on the buttons of my dress. "Call me Jack."

His gaze is ravenous, and I know he wants to kiss me more than anything. Just as Arthur had been in my power that evening, Jack Seward is in a similar position here and now. He wants to claim me as his own, but he will not move until he is sure of me. He waits with bated breath, his eyes roaming my face, desperate for my agreement.

I consider that this is a good offer. Dr. Seward is a wealthy and respected man, barely thirty and yet already established enough to give me a comfortable position in society. He would be a passionate, adoring husband. Mamma would like him, and I think it is true that Papa would approve as well. If I said yes, it would be suitable and appropriate and smart. I would be safe and well cared for and ease Mamma's constant worry.

Jack Seward watches me with hope and terror, as though I hold his very life in my hands.

"Dr. Seward," I say again, my voice trembling.

Something in my face makes him stand up and stare down at me in silence. The shock and pain in his expression are indescribable. His hands shake at his sides.

I cannot bear it. I cannot withstand facing the consequences of my thoughtless behavior again and hurting yet another man. "I'm so sorry, Jack," I say, and then I burst into tears. It is a testament to my grief over the pain I have caused him and Quincey, for I know full well how blotchy and red crying will make my face. The thought of going into the house afterward to face everyone like this makes me sob even harder, and I bury my face in my skirts.

After a long moment, I feel Jack kneel in the grass before me. He places one gentle hand on my shoulder and, with the other, strokes my hair with the utmost tenderness.

"I'm sorry, Jack," I repeat as a handkerchief is pressed into my hands. I wipe my eyes, and it is then that I smell the scent of a deep pine forest with an underlying aroma of cigars.

I know that scent.

I look up, and it is not the doctor kneeling before me.

It is Arthur.

CHAPTER ELEVEN

W e are alone in the garden. Dr. Seward is gone, and all is quiet: I hear the muffled din of voices from the house, the rustling of the trees around the bench, and Arthur's soft breathing. He is on one knee before me in his fine evening clothes and his face is calm, though his eyes are not. He watches me apprehensively, as he had the night he overheard me telling Mamma that he did not care. I look back at him, remembering his laugh as we danced, and I wait to feel joy. After all, it was *his* face I pictured even as two other men proposed to me tonight.

But instead of relief, I feel an intensifying shame for my childish resentment toward Arthur. I was angry with him for toying with my affections . . . when I have only done the same to Quincey Morris and Jack Seward. Regret builds at my temples, a mounting pressure that feels like a pot coming to boil. I heartily despise myself but cannot find a way to express this to Arthur, not when his hazel eyes meet mine with such fear and hope and longing.

My torment is such that when I speak, my voice comes out cooler and more distant than I had intended. "Is there something you want, Mr. Holmwood?"

Arthur's hands drop to the bench on either side of my lap at my chilly formality. He takes a deep breath in through his nostrils, his shoulders moving with the inhalation. When he exhales, the breath comes out with words. "I want you to marry me," he says.

Inside the house, a man laughs, the bright brassy sound carrying toward us. The door has been left open, either by Arthur when he came out or by Dr. Seward when he went back inside. I wonder if the doctor and Quincey Morris are talking about me. Perhaps they are comparing their proposals and my refusals of each of them. I feel the inexplicable desire to laugh once more, and I know it must be the emotional turbulence of being tossed and turned between these men like a toy tugged between children. All wanting to play with it. All wanting it to belong to only them.

"I want you to marry me," Arthur says again. "Please, Lucy."

For the first time in my life, I am without words. I, who have always had the perfect jest or the wittiest, most sparkling retort, can think of nothing to say to this declaration.

"I know you're still angry with me about the other night, but it's only because you don't understand. You thought I didn't want to kiss you."

I put my hand up. "Arthur, it is I who owe you an apology. You don't have to explain—"

He continues speaking, his voice low and pleading. "You thought I didn't want you, but it was the opposite. I knew that if we kept kissing the way we did, I would not be able to control myself. You make me not want to remember what is proper, and most of all, you make me not want to *care*. I kept arguing with myself when you were in my arms, telling myself we didn't need a big society wedding, the kind that both of our mothers want. I kept thinking about my carriage waiting nearby and how quickly I could take you to Gretna Green by dawn."

My hands are claws around Arthur's handkerchief. I can feel the imprint of my own nails in my skin. "You wanted me? You wanted to marry me that night?"

There it is again: Arthur's smile, like a flash of light behind clouds, and I am sick, sick with the need to see it once more. "So badly, I would have gone against our parents' wishes and eloped with you, had our behavior led us to . . . to impropriety." He lays a large, warm hand on my clenched fists and it calms me instantly. "Lucy Westenra, I have wanted to marry you for almost twenty years. I have been desperately in love with you for almost twenty years."

I hold my breath, waiting to feel the prickle of guilty tears or the pain of knowing that I have to disappoint him. But I do not . . . nor do I sense overwhelming joy or relief. There is only numb unease and disquiet deep in my belly, heavy like a bag of stones in water. *This is it,* I think. *The moment in which I lose what small freedom I had.*

This is everything my short existence has led to from my very first breath on this earth. From the moment I was placed into my mother's arms, tiny and red and screaming, and been announced a girl, *this* has been expected of me. Nineteen years of learning how to curtsy, how to hold a fork, how to dance and sing and play music. Nineteen years of being educated and groomed and dressed like a doll so that I might first be a credit to my father, then to my husband. There is no other route my life could have taken, no hidden path of brambles leading me off the road that has faced every woman who came before me, even my great-grandmother with her royal and romantic past in a land far away.

There will be no journeys for me now, no voyages across the sea, no sprawling ruins or sun-touched mountains or deep shady forests. It had all been an unquenchable yearning and a useless hope only to be spoken in the dark. "Some of us must sacrifice a great deal, must we not? Names, tongues, and roots," Dr. Van Helsing had said, but he had not mentioned the sacrifice a woman must make of her own existence. Of course he had not. Only Mamma and Mina would understand, and they have spent years pressing me to accept my fate and be that ideal of womanly perfection and virtue. Someone modest and circumspect, someone who loves children, someone who does *not* desire her dearest female friend, someone who speaks and moves and lives with such elegance and grace as to be the perfect choice for a gentleman's wife.

Like Van, who became Vanessa so that she could be with my great-grandfather, I will be Lucy, who became what she was not so that she could belong to Arthur Holmwood.

There is only one correct answer to what he has asked of me.

My reeling, frantic mind searches for a way to stall. I reach for my favorite armor, my playful demeanor, and keep my eyes on my lap where his hand still covers both of mine. "Why have you not spoken before now? Perhaps," I add, with a touch of wickedness, "you only want me because you know that two other men wish to be my husband."

"Do you really believe that?" Arthur asks quietly.

"You never made clear your intentions before. You came when I called and kissed me in the churchyard, but you did not mention marriage until Jack and Quincey proposed. Neither of them ever made me wonder, you know." I sigh and turn away, watching the branches sway in the breeze. "Tonight, I considered securing my future at last with either the doctor or the cowboy."

"But you refused them." Arthur now lays both of his hands on mine. They are so much larger than my own that his fingers splay over my lap, and only my skirts separate his touch from my naked legs. He swallows hard, but he manages to hold on to his composure. "When Quincey came inside, I saw your answer in his face. And then Jack went out to you, and

I couldn't stand it anymore, so I followed after a while, and his eyes . . . I just knew. And it gave me hope."

"Refusing them doesn't mean I will accept you," I whisper, my playfulness dissolving as I try to take my hands away. But Arthur's grasp tightens, and I think again of how he held me in the churchyard, his arms locked around me like a drowning man's on a buoy. "That night, I told myself to forget you. And when the moment came, to choose another—"

"But you didn't choose another," Arthur says, calm and determined. He inches closer to me, his eyes level with mine. If he tipped his head forward, our mouths would meet again. He spreads his hands, expanding the heat of his touch on my legs and trapping my breath in my raw throat. His plea comes out in a hoarse whisper. "Please, Lucy, I am begging you. Marry me."

He has prostrated himself before me, helpless with longing. He will offer me his hand, his heart, and his home, and I have the ability to determine the course of his life with one word. I will choose whether this man is happy or heartbroken. But however immense this power seemed on the night we first kissed, it is pale and weak and silly to me now.

Already I am envisioning our life together. There will be a ring upon my hand, binding me to him. He will take away my name and give me his to let the world know that I belong to him as much as his horse or his carriage do. I will live in his home, entertain his guests, please his parents. I will sit by his side at every event, another hunting trophy won after a long and victorious chase. And—I swallow hard to clear the bile in my throat—any children I bear will be considered his, though I buy them with the pain and blood of my own body.

I will have nothing.

I will be nothing.

"Lucy, you're killing me." Arthur moves his hands to either side of my face, as though he might squeeze my answer from me like juice from a berry. "What are you thinking?"

"I am thinking of how much it hurt when you pushed me away," I say shakily. "And of how much more it will hurt when you push me away after we are married."

A fire ignites in his eyes. I have said *after* we are married, not *if*. "What do you mean by that?" he asks eagerly. "I already explained about the other night—"

"I mean that when I become your wife, Arthur, you will see all of me," I say. "And I am afraid you will turn away. I am a woman made of dark thoughts. Death is always with me, and I with it. There is a sadness I cannot shake, and you will grow tired and frustrated with me."

"I would *never* turn away from you." He moves even closer, until my knees are pressed into his abdomen. Whoever is watching us from the house will have quite an interesting view of his back, shielding whatever we are doing from their curious gazes. "I would love and accept all of you, Lucy. Please believe me. I know how you still mourn your father. Don't be angry, but your mother has told me that you often sleepwalk to the churchyard where he lies."

This startles me. "When did she tell you? *What* did she tell you?"

"Not much. Only that she and your maid have found you wandering in your sleep." The corners of his mouth lift shyly. "I think your kind mother hopes as much as I do that you will marry me. She told me she could never presume to know your heart, but she thought she sensed a regard in you that she had not seen for any other man. Was she right?"

I look straight into his eyes. "Yes," I whisper.

Arthur touches my face so tenderly that I almost cry again. "How can you think that I would consider your grief a failing? You are a woman who loves deeply and are marked forever by those you love. I . . . I only hope you think I am worthy of that love, too."

"I do think that." I place my hand over his with the feeling of someone standing on the edge of a crumbling cliff. Every second that passes is another rock, and another, and another, bringing my feet closer to the fall. "But why did you wait so long to ask me?"

He gives a short, rueful laugh. "You know how bashful and awkward I am. I'm not a dashing cowboy, painting beautiful pictures with my words, or a handsome doctor who always knows the right romantic gestures to give." He indicates himself. "This is all I can give you. And I know it is a poor offer compared to the ones you've received tonight."

As stunned as I had been to see him smile, I am even more shocked by the tears in his eyes. Arthur Holmwood is crying before me as he professes his feelings, and through my muddle of grief, confusion, and anxiety is the overpowering need to make him happy. I want him to know only joy, this gentle soul who might ease the pain of being forced down this road for me.

"I love you," I say quietly.

The change that comes over Arthur's face clears my mind of any other man walking on this earth. It is like he is a candle and I have lit the wick, and the flame is dancing before my eyes, bright and searing where moments before there had been nothing, only darkness. He puts his arms around me and whispers, "Say it again."

"I love you," I tell him. Only when I taste a drop of salt do I realize that I, too, am crying—though I am not certain whether it is because of that long-awaited happiness or the dreadful certainty that I have now embarked upon an irreversible course. Perhaps it is both. "I love you, Arthur. My answer is yes. I will be your wife."

And then he is kissing me, as passionately as he had that evening. I lean into him, feeling all the warm points of connection between us: our lips, moving with urgent intent; his arms gathering me close to him; my breasts against his jacket; the warmth of his torso against my legs; how soft his hair feels in my fingers as I stroke the back of his head.

He stops the kiss, panting, but does not move away. We look into each other's wet eyes, and he holds me even tighter against him until I am pulled to the edge of the bench. I wrap my arms around his neck and over his shoulder, I see Mamma and her friends beaming at us through the windows of the house. Behind them are the other guests, Jack and Quincey among them, now fully realizing why I did not accept them. They are gentlemen, and they will toast Arthur and me with genuine congratulations even through their disappointment.

I think of how Mina will squeal and hug me when she finds out about my engagement.

With my acceptance, I have made so many people happy.

But am I happy? I wonder as I stroke Arthur's hair.

I look up at the stars in the darkening sky with a sorrow and a longing for something I cannot name.

CHAPTER TWELVE

"A re you going out, dear?" Mamma asks, glancing up from the rose-wood desk in the parlor. "Could you send this letter for me if the post office is on your way?"

I take the envelope. "I am going in the opposite direction, to the cliffs, but I would be happy to take a detour through town."

Sunlight streams through the window beside the desk, making my mother's fair hair glow. Her eyes are clear in the light, and she looks so sweet and pretty in her lavender gown that I bend down and kiss her cheek impulsively. She laughs and takes my hand, gazing up at me as though trying to untangle the thoughts in my head. It is a skill at which she has never been adept in all the years of being my mother. "Are you happy, my Lucy?" she asks gently. "*Truly* happy?"

I squeeze her hand. "Of course I'm happy. It is June, and it is a beautiful day, and I am in Whitby with you. Why shouldn't I be happy?" My tone is light, but her question sends a thrill of recognition through me. Perhaps Mamma sees more than I think.

She looks down at the gold ring on my hand. The small perfect gems—a diamond with an emerald on either side—were a family heirloom given to Arthur's mother, Lady Godalming, for her engagement, and had been taken out of the vault for me. "I worry that in my hope to see you settled and cared for, I've pushed you out of the nest too soon."

I wrap my arms around her, and she leans her greying head against me. "I turn twenty in September, which is too old to be in a nest anyway. But I love you more than anything, and I want you to come and live with us. I can't stand the thought of you all alone, and our house will have ever so much space. The servants will prepare a suite of rooms for you."

Mamma looks up at me, amused. "Live with a pair of newlyweds? Your husband-to-be may not be happy with that arrangement. And shouldn't you ask for his permission first?"

"Arthur adores me. He will do whatever I want." I brush a tendril of hair off her forehead, thinking of the letters he and I have exchanged since I left for Whitby.

It has been two weeks to the day since our engagement. That night, he and I had returned to the house to great cheer, and Jack and Quincey had toasted us with all the generosity of spirit I knew they would have. Later, when the guests had departed, Mamma had knowingly left Arthur and me alone in the parlor to say goodbye. He had written me the first letter and had posted it before I had even left. He insists that he is awkward when it comes to romance, but I find his love letters winsome and appealing in their simplicity. Nothing would mar my happiness but for the guilt and dread that fill me whenever I read his words. He is so earnest, so devoted, so innocent of anything that could stain me or our marriage.

"Mamma, there *is* something I would speak to you about." I sit on a chair upholstered in sky-blue silk. We have taken the same lodgings every summer since I was born, and over time, the rooms have become as much a reflection of Mamma's delicate tastes as our London home. "I don't know if you will understand, but I am nervous about Arthur knowing everything about me once we marry. He will see it all, won't he? Not just the good."

Mamma chuckles and holds up the hand that still bears her wedding ring. "Let me remind you that I, too, have been married. It's natural to worry about your husband finding out your faults." Her eyes twinkle. "My mother called me *wild*. She believed no man could tame me and I would join the circus, riding horses for a cheering crowd and bringing shame upon our name. But then I met your dear papa, and he loved me . . . all of me, as Arthur will love all of *you*."

"I have no aspirations for the circus," I say, and she smiles. "But I find it difficult to have to give up so much. Dancing at parties, for instance. You know a ballroom is my favorite battleground. But now it will not be appropriate to dance or even speak with another man for long."

"But you wouldn't wish the ballroom to be a battleground forever, would you? Now that the war has been won, and Arthur is yours?"

"I suppose not." I sigh. "And I will not have time for books or walks or daydreaming anymore, as mistress of the Holmwood estate. Not with a household to maintain, servants to instruct, and guests to entertain. And

I will have to give up Papa's jasmine tea and incense entirely, as Arthur cannot abide strong smells."

"Neither can I, though I endured them when Papa was alive," Mamma admits. "I know you want to honor your father and ancestors, my love. But Arthur will be a lord with a proper English household. Surely it will not be such a sacrifice to please him, will it?"

I shake my head slowly and turn to gaze out of the window. Unlike our bedchambers, the parlor does not overlook the sea but the garden instead, where climbing honeysuckle vines perfume the air with their fragrance. Still, I can sense the presence of the ocean beyond: the tang of its salt, the waves crashing onto the shore, and the yearning emptiness beneath all that water. Arthur is the garden and I am the sea. They can exist together in harmony, but the sea will always have depths that the flowers cannot begin to fathom.

"Well, thank you for the advice, Mamma." I rise with all the gaiety I do not feel. "I will be back in time for tea. Tell Agatha to serve those cakes I love with the sugar rosebuds."

"I told her to buy them for you as soon as I woke this morning," Mamma says fondly.

I blow her a kiss and slip on my pale flowered hat as I walk into town, the image of a carefree young woman of leisure taking in the picturesque sights of Whitby, with its winding cobblestone streets and the North Sea glittering beyond. Carriages clatter up and down, and ladies in summer frocks walk arm in arm, looking in shop windows and blushing at passing gentlemen.

I post Mamma's letter, enjoying the admiring glances from passersby. Even outside of a London ballroom, and with the expectations of what it means to be a woman of my family ever so slightly relaxed, I will still welcome smiles and compliments and gallantries. I stroll out of town exactly as people see me: a happy-hearted, light-footed girl relishing summertime.

But all of it slips from me, bit by bit, as I climb the one hundred and ninety-nine steps to the cliffs and the old ruined abbey atop them. I am grateful for my light lawn dress, for the air is heavy with heat even at this early hour. On such a sunny June morning, there are fewer people up here—most of them preferring to walk by the water, where the breeze brings the strongest relief—and I feel free to dream and wander without scrutiny. The sea sparkles with such manic light that it is almost painful to look at, and the deep blue of the water blends into the paler azure of the sky, unmarred by clouds. The air smells of salt and beach grass, tinged with the fragrance of the roses that grow just out of reach of the sand. I fill my lungs with the breath of Whitby as I take the path fringed with thick yellowy grass and blue and white flowers.

I study the crumbling grey stone skeleton of the abbey, surrounded by willows bending their heavy heads over shady benches. In the shadow of the ruins is a graveyard overlooking the cliffs that plunge down to the ocean. My nursemaid often took me here as a child to run off my energy and give my parents a rest, and I have come back every summer since, sometimes with Mina when she was my governess. But today, I am deliciously alone, free to stare out to sea for hours, wander among the graves and read the names that have become familiar to me, or stroll around the towering hollows of the abbey without anyone to interrupt.

Here, I can be completely myself.

I settle myself in my favorite spot, a stone bench beneath an ancient willow, and forget the oppressive heat as I lose myself in the view: glittering water as far as the eye can see, dotted here and there with white sails or grey boulders, all hugged by a strip of gold sand. The grass beneath my feet ends a short distance away, where a low wooden fence has been installed to keep people from tumbling to their deaths. Just on the other side is a steep drop hundreds of feet high, where the cliffs pour their stone tears down to the water's edge. My bench is set at an uphill angle from this drop, and it is exhilarating to imagine it lifting and tipping me over the side.

A childhood memory stirs in my mind of running down a hill behind my grandfather's estate in the country. I remember the breathless anticipation of scurrying up the slope, ignoring my mother calling me to come back at once, and then that moment—like a pause between heartbeats—of standing atop the hill before spreading my arms wide and letting the earth propel me downward, my pulse pounding and my mouth agape in an exclamation of shrill delight.

I have often imagined that plunging over those cliffs and rushing down to meet those foamy waves would be much the same. The thought is gripping in its terror and ecstasy as I picture townspeople finding my body crumpled in the sand or floating on the waves, my delicate pale dress contrasting with the dark water. I imagine men pulling me from the sea, Mamma hurrying to the beach, and Arthur prostrate with grief when the telegram reaches him in London.

I sigh.

This is where the fantasy always ends, whether I am dreaming or awake. The loss of Papa, my grandparents, and Van have scarred me so deeply that I would rather lose them all over again than force Mamma or Mina or Arthur to feel even a fraction of what I have.

Last night, I had sleepwalked again, but only to the parlor in our lodgings. Very often, in the light of morning, I forget what I have dreamed—aside from a vague feeling of pleasure or fear or worry. But this latest episode insists upon lingering. In the dream, I was in the churchyard, watching grave robbers defile my family's mausoleum. I screamed and shouted, but they could not hear me as they dug pick-axes and shovels into the coffins where my loved ones lay, taking what jewelry they could find. I had expected Papa to sit up and protest, but all that had lain in his tomb—and in those of every other family member—had been nothing but bones and dust. And when the grave robbers had finished their grisly task, they had locked me in with the skeletons and silence and death, pounding my fists on the door with no one to hear.

This is what dying would truly be like, I imagine my mind telling me.

Not a joyous scene in which I would reunite with Papa and be free of a life I never chose, but the stark reality of dust and darkness and bones, while in the world outside Mamma grieved, Arthur mourned, and Mina wept as she married without me there to fix her veil.

My morbid pleasure dissolves, and I am brought back to reality as I look down at my feet, firmly and securely planted on the ground.

I will be Arthur's wife, and no matter what he claims, he will neither like nor understand these fantasies of death that seduce me. *This* is what I had tried to convey to loving Mamma, who believes that I am anxious about Arthur discovering the untidy way I discard my dresses in my room or my fits of temper whenever I am hungry. She thinks I fear what any other young lady would, when the truth is that I am not like any other young lady. I am not like anyone at all.

I think of how much it had hurt when Arthur had pulled away from our kiss in the churchyard. To imagine his *true* rejection after our marriage, when he learns about the peculiar workings of my mind, is even more excruciating, for he would not be able to put me aside. He would be trapped as my husband, and I cannot do that to him. Not to Arthur.

"I must truly love him," I whisper with a rueful laugh.

My only solution is to be completely truthful. If I had pen and paper with me, I would confess everything in a letter to him this very moment. "This is me," I would write. "This is all of me, and I want you to see it before it is too late."

The urge is so powerful that I walk back to our lodgings a full few hours sooner than I had intended, but when I walk through the door, I have no opportunity to run to my room and my pen. For on the hall table is a gentleman's hat, and drifting out of the parlor is a man's voice.

Arthur is here, I realize. Arthur is here, and I could tell him everything I meant to write.

I find him sitting with Mamma. He rises at once when he sees me, his face so open and bright that I am seized by a pang of indecision. If I tell him the truth and he turns away . . .

Do not be cowardly, Lucy, I think, trying to appear light and easy. "Why, Arthur," I say, holding my hands out to him. It is one of the advantages of being engaged, for I can touch him now in the presence of my mother, who beams upon seeing our joined hands. "What a wonderful surprise. You didn't say you were coming in your last letter."

"It was a spur-of-the-moment decision," Arthur says sheepishly. He releases one of my hands to turn toward my mother, politely including her, though he keeps a firm hold on my other one, my fingers warm and secure in his. "I'm afraid I didn't think much before I purchased a train ticket this morning. I just wondered how you were faring at Whitby."

"Well, you're just in time for tea," Mamma says with an affectionate smile, getting up from the sofa. "Let me see how Agatha is getting on with the preparations. Excuse me."

And then Arthur and I are alone. We look at each other shyly, as though we are fifteen and he is the first boy brave enough to declare himself my suitor.

"I couldn't stay away," he says softly. "I missed you too much."

"I'm glad you're here." I reach up to fix his cravat, even though it is already impeccably straight. I can't help thinking that it might be my last chance to do so, now that I will tell him the truth about me. We sit side by side on the sofa, still holding hands. He angles his long legs to the side so as not to bump into the glass table, and his knees press into mine comfortingly. "I was sitting up on the cliffs just now, near the abbey and the graveyard."

"A graveyard doesn't seem the right place for you, darling." He reaches out to smooth my hair right above my ear, the gesture tentative and sweet, sending tingles down my neck.

I take a deep breath. "Arthur, I want to tell you something that's been on my mind."

His gaze, which has been fondly roving over my hair and my ear and my chin, focuses on my eyes. "What is it? Is something troubling you?"

I nod and lower my eyes, for his trusting gaze is almost too much to bear. "You know how I am still in mourning for Papa. We have talked of it many times. But what you don't know is that death fascinates me. It always has and it always will, and if you are to be my husband, I want you to know everything before you are tied to me."

"Do you mean that it frightens you?" he asks.

"No. And yes at the same time," I say, struggling to explain. "Who among us is not afraid of dying? But there has always been a part of me that longs for it as well."

"Longs for it?" Arthur echoes, alarmed.

"When I was on the cliffs, I imagined tumbling over the fence. I thought about how it might feel to plunge into the waves and what would happen afterward, when I was found. I don't mean that I *want* this to happen, exactly," I add, seeing his concern growing with every word. "I only mean that I often envision my own death. There is something almost . . . pleasurable in it."

He looks at me in silence, trying to understand.

"I did this even as a child. A doctor explained that it was my way of coping with grief. It began after my great-grandmother and my grandparents died, and it continues on even after the loss of Papa." I take Arthur's hand in both of mine, holding it tightly. "Mamma told you that I often sleepwalk to the churchyard where they lie. Even in the depths of sleep am I drawn to death. It is something that attracts me, a moth to a flame."

"I see," Arthur says quietly.

"I can't stop," I say. "And I am not certain I want to. It is a part of me and how my mind works. I want you to know so that you have a chance to take back your proposal of marriage." My throat chokes on the words, but I look into his eyes with all the resolve I possess.

"You think that this makes me want to marry you less?" he asks, startled.

"Well, yes. What man wants a wife who thinks of death constantly?"

Arthur gives a low, gentle laugh and moves closer to me on the sofa. "I have no intention of taking back my proposal. I love you and I want you to be my wife."

I search his eyes. "None of this disturbs you, then?"

"You are a woman who loves very deeply, and so death leaves a stronger impression upon you. I have said this before. Of course it occupies your mind, after the losses you have suffered."

He is saying the right words. He is being kind and accepting . . . and yet I am unsatisfied. My wayward heart wanted him to know the truth and still love me. So why, then, this emptiness?

Arthur kisses my hand. "Have no fear. When you are busy with the wedding, running our household, and planning our first party in our home . . . and later, when you have your hands full with our children," he adds, blushing, "you will forget all of that, I know."

"I will forget all of that?" I repeat, dazed.

"Like a bad dream," he reassures me. "You won't ever think about death again with so much happiness ahead of us, Lucy. And I swear to you, I will make you happy."

He does not understand me. I have told him what death means to me—something I long for, something that means freedom. And yet he thinks I can easily let go of my longing and melancholy in favor of inviting dinner guests, ordering cuts of meat, and wiping the noses of our beastly children. He does not *see* me as I am, but then no one has, not even those who love me.

And he is looking at me with such devotion that I cannot find it in me to be angry with him. I have bared all. I have told him the truth and he still wishes to marry me, and I will delight Mamma and Mina when I become the wife of this gentle, trusting man. The thought does not bring much relief, the way a sip of water cannot satisfy a person dying of thirst.

But it is enough, I tell myself. *This is enough.*

Arthur kisses my hand again, the touch of his lips sending heat rippling down my arm. My frustration is already a kindling flame, desperate for escape, for some sort of release, and now it is a bonfire in my very bones. Without a second thought, I lean forward and kiss him.

"Lucy," he mumbles against my lips. "Your mother . . . the servants—"

"Let them see," I say fiercely, throwing my arms around his neck and drinking from his lips with greed. He tastes like both sugar and salt, heady and intoxicating. Vaguely, I realize that I have somehow maneuvered myself into his lap, draped across his legs like a woman of ill repute, but I hardly care. I am afire with want as I shift my weight on his lap, delighting in his low moan.

"Lucy, stop," he whispers, though his arms are fastened tight around me.

"Come to me tonight," I murmur, my lips still on his. A shiver of pleasure runs down my spine at the friction of our mouths and the contrast between his silken kiss and the rough scratch of his chin. I shift in his lap again and feel something rigid press into my thigh as he groans again. "Come to my room. I want you and I know you want me, too."

"I can't," he groans, sounding pained, even as he goes on kissing me.

"I do not just imagine death, you know," I say, moving my mouth to his ear and licking it like a greedy child sampling dessert. "I imagine what it will be like with you."

His hand trails down my back tentatively. Ever impatient, I seize it and place it on the curve of my bottom, and he gasps even though several layers of clothing separate his skin from mine. I am drenched between my legs. I think of the forbidden books I found in Papa's library, the ones I giggled and gasped over with Mina, and of a particular illustration of a woman in a man's lap, facing him, both of them naked. I am ravenous to know how it will feel with Arthur.

"Come to me tonight," I whisper again, moving myself against what has grown between us. It is granite hard, but it yields to me eagerly. I reach for it, needing to touch, but that is too much for Arthur. In one quick and powerful move, he lifts me off him and onto the sofa and flies clean across the room. But this time, I know that he wants me. I have *felt* it.

I press my legs together, panting as I watch his shoulders rise and fall with his ragged breaths. I can't help laughing at what we have begun . . . and what we will soon finish.

"Arthur?" I ask playfully. "When will you come to me, then?"

"I cannot," he says, his voice strangled. "I will not."

I rise to my feet. "Yes, you can. And you will."

At the sound of my skirts rustling, he startles like a skittish horse and almost runs for the door. "I will not. Not until we are married." He is still turned away from me, but from his profile, I see that his face is as red as that of a man who has been under intense labor.

I laugh in disbelief. "You cannot be serious. You want this as much as I do."

But Arthur shakes his head. "I am going back to London. There is a train leaving in half an hour. I will not stay tonight. Please make my apologies to your mother for missing tea."

My pleasure dissolves into shock and disappointment. "Arthur!" I exclaim. "What is wrong? What has happened? Are you angry?"

He looks at me quickly. "Not at all. But I must go to avoid temptation . . . for you and for me. When I come to you, Lucy, it will be as a husband to his wife."

"But we will be married no matter what," I say, fighting the urge to scream, so frustrated as I am. "I *will* be your wife and you *will* be my husband. What difference can it make if you spend a night with me before our wedding? You want this, too."

"Yes!" he cries, his eyes wild. He glances at the door and lowers his voice. "I want you more than I have ever wanted anything. I forget myself near you. But I will not . . . intrude upon your privacy until we are man and wife. It is important to me to keep my honor and your virtue."

"Damn them!" I proclaim, and he stares, appalled by my language. "What should we care of honor or virtue when we have each other? Arthur, I am dying for you."

"I am going," he says calmly. "I will write to you when I return to London."

I clench my skirts in my fists, too furious to speak.

Quickly, he closes the distance between us and kisses my forehead, as chaste as if we were in full company. "I love you," he says, tilting my chin to look deep into my eyes. "And I promise you that our wedding night will be everything you desire. I will make you happy then."

And then he strides away, leaving me hungry and full of desperate, unsatisfied desire.

CHAPTER THIRTEEN

N ight has fallen, and I am standing in the shadow of the ruined abbey atop the cliffs of Whitby. The moonlight is so bright that I can see every stone in the crumbling walls, every bench beneath the graceful trees, and every flower beside the path. I stoop to pluck a luminous white blossom, and the scent of it is like ephemeral sugar, melting and pure. All is still, and aside from the rumble of the ocean hundreds of feet below, there is not a sound to be heard. I hold the flower to my nose and continue up the steps, feeling utterly at peace.

The month of July settled upon Whitby like a thick smothering blanket, but tonight, the ocean air is cool and refreshing, and my bare feet are kissed by a delicate mist that seems to shimmer in the dark. I enjoy the wind riffling through my hair and the folds of my long silk nightdress as I make my way toward my favorite seat overlooking the water.

Someone is already sitting there.

A man gazes out to sea, his long arms propped behind him on the bench. From his serene posture and the way he tips his head back to look at the stars, he seems as appreciative of the air and the view as I am. He does not turn, and yet I sense the exact moment in which he becomes aware of me. There is a slight straightening of his torso, the merest tilt of his head to the side, and an intake of breath that I can feel more than I hear. The sensation of his focus shifting from the ocean directly to me is like sitting with closed eyes in a pool of moonlight.

He does not speak, but I sense his patient expectation.

I find my voice. "Good evening."

"Good evening," he says, and my heart clenches. I know that voice, deep and rich and full of music, with the slight trace of a foreign accent.

My head feels light and buoyant as I sift through the ashes of my dark dreams, searching for this man, but they elude me. Perhaps my mind is playing tricks on me; perhaps he is only a stranger after all.

"I am sorry to disturb you," I say politely.

"You do not disturb me in the least." The rhythmic cadence of his words is like a lullaby, filling me with calm and well-being. I am overwhelmed by a sudden powerful drowsiness and a longing to sink into the plush feathers of my bed. The scene around me grows hazy and dim, and the lines of the abbey dissolve against the night sky.

"Good night, then." I turn to go home, for I can barely keep my eyes open.

"Lucy."

My drowsiness subsides at once. In an instant, I feel more awake than I have ever been in the whole of my existence. That one word, my name, spoken in his soft voice, is enough to bring the cliffs and the sea and the sky back into sharp resolution. I can almost feel the cold heat of the stars from where I stand. All at once, I am certain that I have heard my name from his lips before, and he and I have stood together in the night.

"Yes?" I ask.

"Come and sit with me a moment."

His cordial tone implies that it is a request, but my feet obey as if it had been a command. I take a seat beside him, looking out at the great black expanse of ocean. I have never seen this view at night, and in the darkness, sea and sky seem to be one but for the keening of the waves below like some great sleepless beast in the depths. Strands of mist weave through the grass at our feet, and the air smells of fresh turned earth, peculiar but not unpleasant.

I long to study this man I suspect I have met in my dreams, but something holds me back. A languid heaviness hangs upon me like the stupor of coming out of sleep, when you cannot yet slip from its grasp. I am forced to keep my eyes on the sea and take in only what I can feel: the cool stone beneath me, the stem of the flower in my fingers, the warmth of my hair and the fluttering ruffles of my nightdress upon my shoulders. The bench is not wide, and though I am small and perched on the edge with my knees together, the stranger is very close to me.

From the corner of my eye, I see that his legs are much longer than mine and end in polished black shoes. He wears dark trousers and a well-cut jacket, from the sleeves of which his long pale hands emerge, one of them resting on the bench between us. I glean the sensation of a big, powerfully built man, but it does not occur to me to be afraid. I am in my favorite peaceful spot in Whitby, after all, and my companion has a quiet, thoughtful presence.

Something glints on the smallest finger of his hand, and my breath stops in my throat when I recognize it. I know that ring of brass, that garnet of deep wine red. I have felt it on my skin as he stroked my face, as he ran his hand down my bare shoulder. Images flash through the darkness of my mind like lightning: A pale hand reaching for mine. A ballroom of dying roses. A moonlit kiss in a garden of watchful statues. A path of brambles calling to me from the dark.

"Hello, Lucy. I told you I would find you again." He sounds amused. His attention on me feels like drifting into slumber on a languid morning, the muslin curtains diffusing sunlight into something soft and dreamy. I feel his gaze take me in, but it is a pleasant, rapturous scrutiny. I could happily sit here for all eternity with his eyes on me, warm and tranquil. "This is my first visit to these cliffs. I wanted my earliest glimpse of England to be a beautiful one."

A dozen questions form behind my lips. I want to ask who he is, where he comes from, why he is here, and whether we have met before. But try as I might, I cannot—nor can I look at him. It is as though my words and actions are barred by some invisible gate. I clear my throat to ask another question, which comes out easily. "And is it beautiful, your earliest glimpse?"

"Yes, it is beautiful," he says with a smile in his voice.

I have known much admiration in my nineteen years. I have received gifts and flowers, love letters and compliments, and three proposals of marriage. But from this man I still have not properly seen, the praise somehow means more than any silly flirtation. I am flooded by the knowledge that everything up to this point in my life has been meaningless. I have been waiting for this exact moment in time.

I have been waiting for him.

He runs his thumb over my cheek, and I close my eyes at his cool, soothing touch. The questions I long to ask fade like shadows. I am content not to know anything but what he chooses to tell me. "I come here every day," I say. "The cliffs bring me a peace I cannot find elsewhere. I sit on this bench and look out to sea, and it seems I am suspended between two worlds. The waking and the dreaming. The living and . . ."

The dreamy sunlight of his focus sharpens into a blinding ray of heat. "And?"

"And the dead."

He is surprised, I think, and the notion that I can astonish him with anything I say is heady and overpowering. I am oddly proud that I can affect this man.

"I often imagine what it would be like to slip over that fence," I say, my voice rising and falling with the music of a reverie. It is so easy to share my deepest self with him, as inevitable as rain pouring from the sky. "I picture climbing to the other side, my shoes sliding on the crumbling earth, and then nothing but air beneath me as I plummet toward the sea."

He smooths my hair behind my shoulder, as gentle as my own mother. "And what if you fall toward the rocks instead?" he asks as calmly as though we are conversing about the weather.

"Then I would accept that fate, too."

"Are you that tired of life that you would so readily embrace death?"

"It calls to me, though I have many people for whom I wish to stay. My mother . . . Mina, my dearest friend . . . and Arthur."

The man's attention is now so sharp I can almost feel its razor edge brushing against my throat. He places his large, cold hand on top of both of mine, resting in my lap, and I turn my palms upward to meet his. "Arthur is someone who loves you?"

"He has given me his heart and he will give me his name."

"But your heart? Where is that?"

"My heart is like the sea," I say sadly as the man's fingers close softly around my own. "It is deep and dark and belongs to no man, however many try to tame it."

"I disagree," he says in a quiet voice. "You are not the sea, but a sailor. A wanderer like me. You want to steer a ship to foreign lands, tread ground you have never walked, encounter wonders you have never seen." His thumb traces the lines of my palm as though he knows them by heart. "You want to taste all of life, but you are shackled here. And you're wrong, you know."

I am shaking as I listen, moved almost to tears. "Wrong about what?"

"About my not seeing your chains. I see them, Lucy." He runs his thumb down the inside of my wrist, so tenderly that my sorrow overflows. Tears scald my cheeks and splash onto our joined fingers. He lifts my wet hand but does not kiss it as I expect him to. Instead, he presses my tears against his own eyes, as though he would willingly take my pain and make it his own, to spare me. "I know why you are drawn to the places of the dead, to graveyards such as this one. There is freedom here. No one to watch or listen or try to change us into something we are not."

I choke back a sob. This man sees me. He *sees* me as no one in my life ever has or ever will. "Tell me this is not just a dream. Tell me I will not wake up and be so alone again."

"You will wake up," he says kindly. "But I promise you, Lucy: you will never be alone again. Not now that I have found you, here in a place only we two know. Suspended between the waking and the dreaming."

"Between the living and the dead," I whisper, and like an incantation, the words lift the dreamy, hypnotic stupor from me. I feel it all come back: the ability to ask any question I wish, to move my body as I like, and to look where I want to look. I sense that this return of my free will is a gift he has bestowed upon me and that I have proven myself to him in some way. And I am able, at last, to turn and see him for the first time.

The man beside me has the appearance of stone, as though every angle has been cut into unforgiving rock, hewn by no human hand but by the passing of years and the relentless wearing down by wind and water. He is like the cliffs, and it is every bit as tempting to imagine myself plunging against him to my doom. His skin is as white as the flower still clutched in my hand, contrasting with wavy dark hair slightly curling at his temples and neck. He has thick eyebrows over a long straight nose and a thin, pale-lipped mouth.

But it is his eyes that arrest me. If a painter could capture the ocean in a single gaze, it would be this one. I look into the deep blue-green of his eyes, and I can remember every summer I have spent on these cliffs, my lonely heart aching for the horizon. It is the color of solitude, of empty longing, of the pain of having to hide everything I am and everything I need. It is breathtaking, unsettling, like staring into a mirror and seeing my true self reflected for the first time. His eyes would be frightening, I think, if their expression was not so soft. I find that I am struggling for breath as I look at him. I seem to have forgotten how to take in air, an action I have done since the very first moment I came into this world.

"I have been waiting for you," I hear myself say as tears continue to spill down my face.

"And I have come," he says.

I am trembling as though I sit in the depths of winter, and I know it is from hunger and relief, from joy and sorrow all at once and not from being cold. But still, the man removes his jacket, which is of a beautiful dark wool too heavy for the weather, his movements slow and deliberate as though he does not wish to startle me. He wraps me within its folds and meets my eyes with that fathomless ocean gaze, a question on his starkly handsome, fine-boned features. Something in my face must answer it, for he gently lifts me—jacket and all—until I am in his lap, sitting sideways, and he hugs me tight to him. We do not speak for a long time, and I wonder with every beat of my yearning heart how he knew that I needed to be held like this: with infinite tenderness and no hesitation, no expectation of anything in return but for me to accept his care.

Not even Arthur would dare give me this intimacy outside of marriage, and to find it from an almost perfect stranger is dizzying, shocking, gratifying.

My face is pressed to the man's white linen shirt, which exposes a strong throat corded with veins. "Who are you?" I whisper in the shelter of his arms. "How did you find me?"

"For now, think of me as a friend from far away who will listen without judgment."

"Far away? Are you not with me right now?" I ask fearfully, burrowing deeper against him as though I am drowning in the sea and he is my only salvation. There is a stark reality to his existence, his voice, and his embrace that makes me forget that I am only dreaming.

His laugh is a low, pleasant sound. "You are extraordinary, Lucy Westenra. I did not think I would meet such a one as you when I have not even set foot upon this land." He presses a light kiss to my temple. "You see, England has held my interest for decades. How could a tiny country floating helplessly in the grip of oceans come to such godlike power? Always am I drawn to those who grasp for domination, and it is England that commands my imagination this century."

Century? I think. I long to ask about this curious, hyperbolic turn of phrase. But the soothing rise and fall of his voice is a stream of consciousness in which I am lost. I drift along its current as though he might dictate to me all the secrets of the universe if I listen intently enough.

"But it is not just her ships, commerce, and monarchy that interest me. It is also her society. Her people. The men . . . and the women." His hand strokes my back, as meandering as his thoughts. "Death links us all, no matter who we are. Man is born, man breathes, man lives, and man dies. Man is but an animal, and yet English society prefers to forget that. Is this true?"

"I am not certain." I lift my head to look at him, and his sea-glass gaze is the most intense scrutiny I have ever faced. I am a window he is looking through, and I sense that he can see absolutely everything inside my mind, my heart, and my soul.

"Babies emerge, screaming and bloody, from the pits of their mothers' wombs, yet this is not spoken of," he says, his hand moving yet lower on my back. "People rut in the privacy of their bedchambers, and sometimes carriages and darkened halls, yet this is not spoken of. All is prim and proper, buttoned to within an inch of its life, all to maintain a veneer of *politeness*."

My breath comes in short, shallow gasps. I have never heard such notions put into words, and I am faint with how easily I can imagine myself closed up in a carriage with him, with all the curtains drawn, or in a dark and empty hall, our limbs tangled in the moonlight.

He runs a hand softly through my hair, and I shiver as electricity dances through my veins. "I have learned that strict rules govern the manners of England's highest society, and the most rigid of these are laid upon the women."

Even in the haze of my rising desire, I pull away in surprise.

The man's mouth curves, sly and seductive, as his hand finds the curve of my bottom, exactly where I had placed Arthur's the day before. It squeezes deliciously and I gasp with stunned pleasure. "Women do not speak of unpleasant topics such as death," he murmurs. "They do not long to see the world or give in to their secret dreams, their private hopes, or their deepest longings. But *you* would if you could, wouldn't you, Lucy? And why not? Why shouldn't you be free for the first time in your existence?"

The coat slips from my shoulders as he pulls me to him, chest against chest, mouth against mouth. Slowly, tantalizingly, his tongue swipes across my bottom lip. "Because," I manage to say, "I would lose everyone dear to me, especially—" I stop myself from saying Arthur's name just in time, conscious of the sense of betraying him even in a dream.

But the man hears it anyway. "Ah, yes, the saintly Arthur," he says with wry amusement, "who would keep you safe in his lordly house like a trophy. But you would soon lose your shine. He does not know how to bring out the best of you." His mouth finds my neck, and the edges of his teeth graze my skin. "What if you gave him up and let yourself go? I wonder if you would be brave enough to make that choice. You who seem bolder than the women who follow your society's constraints. What if another path were laid before you?"

I think of the red-tipped brambles from my past dreams as his teeth slide over my throat, the promise of them as sharp as thorns.

"Are you yourself not worth choosing?" he murmurs against my skin.

"Women do not choose themselves." I have unconsciously crushed the flower in my hand, scattering fragile petals all over his coat. I close my eyes and tilt my head back, inviting his lips with abandon. "The perfect woman lives only for others."

"But you are not the perfect woman?" he asks, his mouth meeting mine again in a lingering kiss. His eyes are almost black with desire.

When he pulls back, I lean forward to kiss him again, but he holds me just an inch apart, smiling. "No. Not like Mamma or Mina, who snuff their own spirits like fingers choking a flame. They are like dolls, happy to be loved and touched and told what to do."

The man takes the remains of the destroyed flower from me and lifts its broken petals to his nose. "You will be the same if you marry Arthur, no? He, too, is bound by these rules and expects you to be as well." He chuckles at my consternation. "I can see every encounter you have ever had with him. I can taste your wanting like wine."

A small thread of fear comes loose in my chest. "How can you see all of this?"

He does not answer. He only runs the crushed flower over my lips, and my unease fades into that languid stupor once more. "I would not deny you anything, Lucy. Unlike Arthur, I will satisfy your thirst. Also unlike him, I understand your craving for death . . . your instinct that dying could be the one choice you will ever make of your own free will."

"Yes," I breathe as he tucks the flower in my hair, just above my ear.

"But have you ever considered that death might not be the escape you wish for?" he asks, studying my face in the pale light. "That it might merely be a different sort of chain?"

I think of my dreams of sinking beneath waves and lying in the mausoleum. Always, I see myself walking into the arms of death, but never what happens next, like a morbid fairy tale with no unveiling of what happens *after* the happy ending.

The man laughs gently, hearing my thoughts. "Tell me this," he says, wrapping one of my waves of hair around his fingers. "If someone were to push you over that fence and give you that dark dream you long for, would death not be yet another method of being controlled?"

I push through my hazy confusion and look fiercely into his eyes. "Not if I asked for it. Not if I embraced it willingly and stood on the edge of the cliff waiting for the push."

Something flickers on his face, half admiration, half recognition. "Do you know how else I am unlike Arthur?" he asks. One of his hands is still on my bottom, and the other finds my bare leg. It slides from my knee up to my thigh, dragging the hem of my nightgown with it, and my mouth goes dry with need. "This is what you wanted him to do to you on the sofa, with your mother and the servants only steps away. You wanted his hand where mine is, his lips where mine are." He presses his mouth to the pulse galloping in the hollow of my throat.

"Yes," I gasp, wrapping my arms around his neck. "Oh, yes."

"I will give you what he cannot," the man whispers as his hand drifts ever higher.

A shadow falls over our bench, blocking out the moonlight.

"Miss Lucy, wake up!"

I jerk awake, half falling off the bench. A pounding pain knifes through my temples as I look into the face of my maid. "Harriet? How long have you been here?" I ask, looking around in a panic. I cannot imagine what she must think of the scene she has just taken in: me sprawled in a stranger's lap with his hand on my thigh, my hair mussed and nightgown almost to my waist. But the space beside me is empty, and when I put my hand on the seat, it is chill.

It was only a dream. I have been sleepwalking again. The realization is both a relief . . . and a disappointment.

I press a hand to my heart, allowing myself to slowly regain full consciousness. My pulse is racing as though I have run all the way up the cliffs.

"A noise woke me," Harriet says. "I found the door open and saw you wandering up the cliffs. I was terrified you would fall into the sea! But you only came up here and sat down."

"You saw no one else?" I ask, though I know the answer. I gasp in air, still breathless from the dream and the feeling—so very *real*—of the stranger's hands and lips on my body.

"No one, miss," Harriet says, her face strained. She wraps a light shawl around me, unconsciously echoing the man's actions. "Let's go back. You shouldn't be out here alone."

But I wasn't alone, I think as she steers me home. I reach up and find the half-torn white flower in my hair, where I had dreamed that the man tucked it. *I wasn't alone at all.*

CHAPTER FOURTEEN

D o you have everything you need for the night, miss?" Harriet asks, standing in the doorway with a bundle of laundry in her arms. "Can I get you anything else?"

"No, thank you. I will be fine," I say impatiently, for she has been stalling her departure from my bedchamber for half an hour now. "Good night."

I have been in a flurry of distraction all day, thinking about the man and the dream I can remember in vivid detail. I burn with the need to see him again and to relive last night on the windy cliffs. Mamma wished me to pay calls with her all afternoon, and at each acquaintance's home, I dropped a glove, lost track of a conversation, or spilled my tea. My mother believes I am coming down with a summer cold, and I am in no hurry to convince her otherwise.

Harriet is still lingering by the door. "Miss Lucy, I don't think I should leave you alone."

"We've already discussed this," I tell her. "I am in no danger whatsoever."

"But how can you be so sure?" The poor maid looks as though she would like to wring her hands had they not been full of my clothing. "I don't think Madam would want—"

"You *promised*," I say sharply. "You gave me your word you would not tell Mamma."

"I know, miss, and I will keep it. But I don't like the idea of your wandering alone on the cliffs at night. I would blame myself if anything happened to you."

"You are not to be blamed for anything," I say in a gentler voice. "You brought me home last night and have taken good care of me since. You have done well."

"But perhaps if we put a chair against the door? Or if I slept on this sofa and—"

I throw my hands up. "Harriet!"

She leaves in a hurry, closing the door behind her.

Sighing, I nestle against my pillows. My room is darker tonight, as the clouds that covered the sun all day have remained to obscure the moon. In preparation for any stroll I might take this evening, I am in bed with my slippers on, a light robe tied over my nightdress, and my hair in a plait. If I am to meet the man in my dreams again, I will at least look more presentable.

I lie on my side, gazing up at the night sky and thinking about him. Even after waking up from our encounter, I had felt as though a part of me were still with him. The memory of his kisses and his hands on my body fill me with both frantic desire and the need to giggle like an enamored schoolgirl. I have never been alive until now. I have never been awake until he awakened me. Somehow, in the most remote recesses of my unconscious mind, my frustrated longing has created this man—this delicious escape from reality.

I twist Arthur's ring on my finger. All day, I have berated myself for betraying the man I love, and yet . . . I have done nothing wrong. My meeting with the stranger took place inside my head, the natural result of my loneliness and unsatisfied yearning for Arthur.

I glance at my dressing table, where the flower the man tucked over my ear has been steadily wilting all day. I know that I put it in my own hair as I dreamed of him. The encounter was not real. My mind knows this, and yet my heart, my soul, and my skin—which now knows the touch of his hands—wants desperately to believe that it *had* taken place, against all reason.

I can explain my deep connection to this man no more than the stars can express why they hang aloft in the heavens. It is as inevitable as the pull of the moon upon the tides. I think of his warm voice, his sympathetic gaze, and how he had held me as I had always longed to be held, and I am suddenly so cold and so sad at the certainty that a man who could so thoroughly understand me, who could see and accept everything that I am, cannot possibly exist. But it is better to have him only in dreams, I tell myself, than not at all.

It takes me a long time to fall asleep . . . or at least, I assume that I sleep.

One moment I am in bed, thinking these puzzling thoughts, and the next, I am climbing the cliffs and smelling the clean scent of the ocean once more. It is as though my mind has glided from one place to the next without any connecting memory in between, and that *should* disturb me. But instead, I am elated and hurry up the path beneath the spreading midnight sky.

The wind is stronger tonight. The heavy clouds have heralded the coming of a storm, and I smell rain in the air as I run with my heart in my throat. I do not linger by the old abbey tonight but make directly for the stone bench like an arrow loosed from a bow.

I see at once that my hopes have not been in vain.

He is standing, waiting for me beneath the willow tree with an eager welcome in his eyes. I feel no shame, no embarrassment, no concern for propriety as I run straight into his arms and he gathers me close to him. I know that one cannot love a stranger. What I feel for this man as he strokes my hair, the two of us sheltered by the whispering leaves of the tree, is sharper, more desperate and immediate. It is a need, a recognition so powerful that it steals the breath from me as he lifts me off the ground, my arms around his neck and my legs around his waist.

"Good evening, Lucy," he whispers in my ear, and I smile into his neck, my fingers tangled in his dark waves of hair. The rumble of his voice against me is already familiar, like a soft blanket I can wrap myself in. He has no scent, or perhaps he shares that of the ocean and the night. The mist rolls in off the sea, enveloping us in its tender embrace.

"I wish you were really here with me now," I say softly.

He pulls away to look at me, nose to nose. The blue-green of his gaze is deeper tonight, as though the sea of his eyes is mirroring the ocean ahead of the storm. "Am I not?"

"You are only a dream," I say, and he laughs. "Aren't you?"

His arms tighten around me, his hands respectfully on my back. But respect is not what I want from his hands. So when he asks, "Why don't you find out?" I mold my mouth to his, my lips and tongue starving for the taste of him, and he laughs again and rewards me by laying his fingers along my hip and thigh. He gently ends the kiss. "Enough now, or I will think you have come here only for this and not my sparkling conversation."

I lay my hand on top of his, touching the garnet that rests there like a drop of blood. One of his fingers has a rough callus that I recognize as belonging to someone who writes often; I have felt them on Papa's and Mina's hands as well. I squeeze lightly, and the hand squeezes back.

He sets me down on his side of the bench, where he had sat the night before, and takes a seat on my side. Already, I am thinking of *his* side and *my* side. "I don't want your feet to get wet. It has rained here," he says, carelessly putting his polished shoes into the puddle as though defying its disrespect toward me. We look out at the ocean, which is as agitated tonight as I feel.

I touch the cool surface of the bench, and my fingers find a crack in the stone. "This is the most vivid dream I have ever had," I say as my robe flutters around my legs in the wind and an errant leaf sinks to the grass, wet with rain. "It all feels real. *You* feel real. But it is not possible."

The man tilts his head. "Why not? Is it so impossible that you are a dreamer and that I am also a dreamer, and somehow, in our dreams, we have found each other?"

"You would have to sleepwalk as I do. And you said last night that you were not even on English soil." A sigh escapes me. Such a lack of logic is irrefutable proof that I am dreaming.

The man seems amused. "I think you will find that not even I can walk across the sea. But perhaps I am both here and *not* here. Perhaps my body is on a ship headed to these shores and I am dreaming from the safety of her hull. Perhaps I am with you in every way that matters." Last night he had seemed more guarded, but tonight, he turns to look at me with openness, his beautifully accented English smooth and free. In recent memory, the only acquaintance I have met who speaks with an accent is Dr. Van Helsing. Perhaps my subconscious mind recalled the softening of his English, and indeed, I hear shades of German in the stranger's speech.

"Where do you sail from, then?" I ask playfully. "Amsterdam, perhaps?"

"A port in Bulgaria. It has been a long and tiresome journey, with no good company on board, so I am grateful for our conversation." The man looks sideways at me with gallant charm.

"Are you Bulgarian?"

He laughs, displaying strong white teeth as he takes my hand, studying it as though reading something written upon it. "Bulgarian, French, German, Russian, and everything in between. I am connected to almost every noble house in Europe. I simply chose a Bulgarian port for convenience." He sighs. "The *Demeter* has a provincial crew and no passengers with whom I can hold educated congress. And so I dream to pass the time, especially at sunrise and sunset."

"Sunrise and sunset?"

"The times when I rest. When I am most vulnerable." He looks thoughtful but does not explain further, and I do not press him. Somehow, I sense I would not be able to, and it is both interesting and disturbing, this feeling that I can only ask what he will permit me to. As though he is steering me the way a captain is steering the ship he is on. "I dream to explore the land I will soon call home. I am moving to England for a time and have just purchased a property outside of London, in Purfleet."

I blink in surprise. "That is not far from my own home. I almost lived there myself."

He raises an eyebrow. "Almost?"

"I know a gentleman who is a doctor," I say, blushing. Clearly, Jack Seward still lingers in my mind, even after my engagement. "He works at an asylum there."

Again, the stranger seems to hear everything I am not saying. "Ah, I see! So this gentleman might have brought you to live with him in Purfleet, had it not been for the noble Arthur. Well, I am glad my property will not be far from you. We will be almost neighbors."

I laugh at the wonder and the absurdity of this dream. "Do you think we shall meet in person?" I ask, playing along. "Outside of dreams? It will be strange."

He turns my hand over, still examining it. "Strange? How so?"

"Well, we have already met, and it would be a lie to pretend otherwise. Though it *would* be highly inappropriate to admit the circumstances under which we became acquainted."

"A lie? Why not say a secret?" The man's eyes shine at me, the lashes long and thick, giving his stern face a hint of softness. "A delicious secret shared by two friends."

I smile, for being called his friend and sharing a secret with him feels oddly like an honor.

"Perhaps I will call upon you here in Whitby," he says, squeezing my hand. "Perhaps I will find you in town and you will invite me in for tea, since we are in England, after all. And we will converse as though we are newly acquainted, not as kindred souls who have met before."

My heart leaps. "Do you believe me to be a kindred soul? I feel that about you. I feel that I can talk to you about anything, the way I cannot with many people in my life."

He puts an arm around me, and I lean against him. His presence gives no warmth, and yet the gesture is comforting and natural. "I am glad for your confidence in me. It is good to have a friend one can speak to without fear, and I shall be that for you."

"Have you ever spoken to other dreamers?" I ask lazily. "Do others dream of you, too?"

"Sometimes. When I call to them."

"Have you called to me, then?"

"Perhaps unwittingly. You and I are like-minded souls, and our paths seem destined to cross." He rests his head on top of mine. "Are you glad we have met? Or does it frighten you?"

"I'm not frightened," I say at once. "I am glad I can be myself with you. In the waking world, there is no circumstance under which I could sit with a man after dark like this. But here in my dream, I have complete control over what I do. It feels like traveling, in a way."

He toys with my plaited hair, wrapping it around his wrist. "Do you?"

"I beg your pardon?"

"Do you have complete control over what you do here in the dream?" His voice is as gentle as ever, but there is a dark, sardonic amusement in it that reminds me of last night's spells of unnatural drowsiness and my inability to ask questions. He must sense my rising uneasiness, for he quickly adds, "You say that dreaming is like traveling. Is travel something you aspire to?"

"It doesn't matter. It is not possible for me." I look at the raging sea, the waves stirring as though some great invisible hand has reached down from the sky to disturb them. "Arthur prefers to remain at home. He will inherit his father's estate, and it will be a great deal of work for him, becoming Lord Godalming. A great deal of work for both of us."

"You are not much alike, then," the man says thoughtfully. "I prefer a couple to be like-minded. It is not comfortable to always be disagreeing and bickering." He seems to speak from experience, as though there is— or possibly *was*—a woman in his life.

"Arthur and I will not bicker," I say, a bit defensively.

"No," he agrees. "You would defend your opinion when needed, but he is too well bred to argue. He might concede your point and then go and do whatever he thinks best. His word would always be final. How interesting. Yes, I see how these well-bred English gentlemen manage their women." He chuckles. "But over time, Lucy, do you not think these little grievances will build up inside of you? Will they not gather in some dark recess of your mind, growing so large that they eventually topple out of the shadows?"

I stare at him, stunned.

"You think I am sowing discord between you and your lord-to-be," he says, placing a hand over his heart in apology. "But I am only telling you what I have observed. I have lived many years and have seen much of human nature. Forgive my frank manners."

I want to defend Arthur and insist that he would always agree with me, or if not, he would at least welcome my opinion. But I know that the stranger is speaking the truth; I can feel it.

His eyes on me are full of pity. "Tell me where you would travel, if you could."

"Anywhere," I say desperately. "Everywhere. I want to see mountains, walk through forests, ride trains through the countryside. There is so much world out there, and the thought that I can only ever experience it through books and hearsay feels like *pretending* to live. Soon I will have a husband and a herd of children, and it will be like losing a chance I never even had."

The man is silent for a long moment. "I have traveled much in my life. I have been to the greatest concert halls of Europe, the plains of Africa, and even the Far East. I have done everything I have ever dreamed of doing, and I cannot imagine being shackled as you are."

I listen longingly but without the envy I feel when I hear about Jonathan Harker's travels. It occurs to me that perhaps it is not Jonathan's freedom I envy, but the woman he will possess. Hastily, I push away the thought. My love for Mina is not something I wish to share with this all-knowing man, not yet—even if he is only just a dream. "What else have you done?" I ask.

"Everything." The man traces the lines of my hand, his gaze turned inward to memories he has had the privilege to collect. "I have been a soldier and a statesman, waging wars and punishing enemies. I have been a leader, caring for my people and protecting our land. I have been a scholar of every subject: astronomy, philosophy, alchemy, religion. I have heard music that would thaw the coldest heart, seen artwork that would shape civilizations, and witnessed the most splendid architecture the human mind can dream up."

"You cannot possibly have lived long enough to do all of that," I say, smiling as I scan his unlined face. "You cannot be more than forty. You are teasing me."

"I would not dare tease such a charming lady." His dark ocean gaze finds me once more, as intent as though he is studying a portrait and not a person. "You really are very beautiful, Lucy, though you do not need me to tell you that."

"I wish you were real," I say with a pang of sadness. "Though I should be grateful you are only in my mind. I feel as though I have known you for a very long time. As though I could sit here and talk to you forever. But even dreaming of you is wrong."

"Why?" he asks gently.

"I will be married soon. The wedding is in September, and sleepwalking away from my husband to have nice long chats with another man . . . that is something that the future Lady Godalming should absolutely not do." My short, low laugh is full of aching sorrow. "As Arthur's wife, I will need to be everything that is virtuous and admirable."

The stranger looks down at our joined hands. My palm is as fragile and ephemeral in his as the white flower I plucked last night. "He isn't what you really want. Becoming a fine lady will starve your soul. Trying to make him proud will take everything out of you that I so admire."

"What alternative is there?" I ask bitterly. "There is nothing else for me, unless you can somehow step out of my imagination and take me on those marvelous journeys of yours around the world. Waging wars and visiting concert halls." I meant for it to sound like a jest, but the earnest grief in my voice turns it into a serious plea.

"I could, you know." He looks straight into my eyes. "I could take you away with me and make you forget him. I could make you mine." He places a kiss upon my wrist, searing cold. His lips move down my arm to the crook of my elbow, where he drops another kiss.

I close my eyes as he leans his forehead against mine. I wish I could live for eternity in this dream, sheltered beneath the trees on a stormy moonless evening with this man.

"This is my advice to you, Lucy, from someone who has lived so much to someone who has not yet fully lived at all," he says. "Be careful what you wish for, for you may just get it."

CHAPTER FIFTEEN

H e calls for me every night, and soon all of July bleeds into heady, dazed half memories, languorous and incoherent. I begin to feel that the daytime is the dream, that walks into town and dinner parties with Mamma are the confused visions of a sleeper, while my evenings, sharp and clear and bright, are the true reality. My conversations with the stranger are all-encompassing, and at times the breadth and intricacy are enough to render me to tears.

Starved for knowledge, I beg him to discuss history and law and philosophy, all the subjects that have been kept from me until now, and he obliges, taking pleasure, I suppose, in the shaping of my sheltered mind. I am certain he is teasing, yet when his musical baritone lingers on a particular note—whether a rapturous description of Florence during the Renaissance or the burning seventeenth-century shores of a Dutch-occupied South Africa—I can *almost* believe that this man had been there, that he had actually lived and breathed and loved in those lost centuries.

My rational mind understands that everything he knows is what *I* know. Perhaps I have gleaned more from the books I have read and the years I have spent under Mina's tutelage than I thought. But I wonder how I could have possibly forgotten so much, only to recall it vividly in my sleep. Perhaps it is another disquieting quality of my dreams, this suspension of logic.

"Let us say, for the sake of argument, that you *did* see the forests of the Amazon in 1502," I say one night after he mentions the beauty of the South American continent.

A smile plays at the corners of his mouth. "1582."

"I still don't believe you," I say in the playful tone I would use with a suitor. "But if I did, and you *have* lived for five hundred years, I imagine such a long life would be a burden."

"Burden?"

"Yes. It would grow tedious. The world is only so big, is it not?"

He laughs. "In some ways, you are right. Humans are tiresome. The same mistakes and the same wars, only with different people. Civilizations rise and fall and rise again. But there is always some novelty, some new path to trace . . . such as this one that takes me to England and to you." As always, one of my hands is cradled in his. His skin is so cold that it feels more like clay than flesh and blood, but I find it more soothing than unpleasant.

"If a person could live five hundred years, and assuming no one else can," I venture, "I think it would be lonely, observing the world in solitude."

The man looks at me, and the light that was briefly in his eyes when he laughed is gone. "Do I seem lonely to you?" he asks quietly.

"You have spent night after night talking to a strange girl," I point out.

"Then by that definition, *you* also are lonely."

"I am. I have no one I can talk to the way I talk to you."

The stranger sighs. "Tell me. If you had five hundred years, what would you do first?"

My answer comes at once, without hesitation. "I would go to Vietnam to learn more about my great-grandmother. I should like to see the place where she first met my great-grandfather. His uncle was a French minister in the emperor's court."

The man touches the green jade stone upon my finger. "As was I and many men in my family. I know the court well. I am familiar with a lady of that country." I sense a dark and bitter melancholy settle over him and surmise that the lady meant—*means?*—something to him. But he does not elaborate, and I tactfully change the subject.

"And with the remainder of my five hundred years, I would spend half a century living on each continent," I say. "I would learn every language, read every book, study every culture."

"You would be a scholar like me. A kindred soul, as I have said." He strokes my palm with an icy fingertip. My hand looks like a leaf in his, easily crumbled between his powerful wrists. I close my eyes as he touches the pulse fluttering in my wrist. "You were right. I *am* lonely. And I am glad to have met you and to see, on your lovely hand, a long life . . . if you wished it. I wonder if this hand would take mine if I offered it."

My eyes fly open. I know by now what a proposal of marriage sounds like. But then the stranger brings my palm to his mouth and traces its lines with his tongue, dissolving any rational thought. Electricity ripples through me, making my bones feel formless and liquid as his lips close around my thumb. He licks circles around the tip, and then a long, slow stroke down the base, as though drinking honey from it. All the while, his eyes are on me, blazing and intent.

I am burning where I sit. Somehow, I can also feel his freezing tongue on my lips, breasts, and between my legs and gasp at the delicious impropriety of my own mind. I tense as his mouth moves rapturously down to my wrist. Never before have I dreamed of kisses like these. My desperate longing to be touched has grown feverish indeed.

"Would Arthur kiss you like this?" the man murmurs.

"No," I gasp, only half recognizing the name.

He presses his knowing smile against the tender inside of my arm, but then stops. When he lowers my hand, I actually whimper in desperation. It is not a sound I have ever made in the whole of my life, but I am not ashamed. I want more. I want him.

"In time," he says with a quiet laugh. "I have much to teach you, my beautiful and willing Lucy. The waves are carrying me to you now on the ship called *Demeter.*"

I choke in air, trying to calm my racing heart.

"A strange name for a ship. Demeter," he says matter-of-factly, as though I am a dinner guest and not a woman who had practically just begged him to ravish her. "The Greek goddess of the harvest and all things that grow. It is not quite fitting for *me* . . . but then Demeter was the mother of Persephone. You know the story, of course?"

I nod, still taking air into my straining lungs.

He tightens his hold on my hand possessively. "In a way, because she gave birth to her, you could say that Demeter brought Persephone to Hades. But in our case . . . in yours and mine, the *Demeter* will bring Hades instead." He chuckles and strokes my cheek. "I will see you soon, my Persephone. Very soon."

I wake up on the bench, cold and alone and aching with unfulfilled desire.

"Lucy, how tired and slow you are this morning," my mother scolds me, coming over with a frown. Her dress of light grey mousseline de soie rustles as she bends to examine me.

I look up languidly from the sofa. "I'm all right, Mamma."

"You look pale, and you've seemed distracted for weeks. Perhaps we ought to call the doctor. And my goodness, these dark shadows beneath your eyes."

"I'm fine." She lays her cool hand upon my forehead, and my cheeks flood with heat, remembering other icy fingers touching me. I grab my mother's hand and press it harder against my face, giggling. "I feel wonderful. And so, so happy."

Her worried expression deepens at my wild laughter. "Arthur has written again, then?"

It takes a minute for me to place the name. "Oh, Arthur. There is a letter from him almost every day," I say listlessly. "He should not write so often if he wants me to miss him more."

"Lucy, he isn't just another lovelorn admirer. Are you writing him back?"

A sharp prickle of conscience bursts through my haze of languor. I sit up and smooth my hair. "Of course. I have already begun a very long letter to him, which I will finish tonight for the morning post. So do stop ruffling those dear feathers of yours."

"You won't have time tonight. Have you forgotten? Mina's train will be here soon."

I blink slowly. "Mina. Of course. Can it really be the eighth of August already? How easy it is to lose track of time in all this heat."

Mamma's face softens. "It has been uncomfortably hot, hasn't it? But there is a lovely breeze off the ocean today. Wouldn't you like to walk into town and wait for Mina's train?"

I recognize a command masquerading as a suggestion when I hear one. Sighing, I stand and straighten my skirts. My head feels light, like a dandelion ready to blow away with one puff of wind. I collect my hat and gloves as Mamma looks on, her lips pursed with concern. But the minute I step outside and the salt-laced breath of the sea touches my face, I feel more awake. I will never again see, hear, or smell the ocean without thinking of my evenings on the cliff with the stranger. He occupies every corner of my thoughts as I wander distractedly into town.

At the station, I sit down to wait for Mina's train. I have not decided if I will tell her of the nameless man in my dreams. She would be shocked if I confessed the things he has done to me in these secret, burning reveries. But she knows me too well, and even if I stay silent, surely she will still be able to see that I am different—that these encounters of lust and connection and conversing about history and philosophy have irrevocably changed me.

When she steps off the train, however, she only hugs and kisses me as if I were the same Lucy she has always known. I breathe in the familiar floral scent of her hair and skin and hold her tightly against me. The comforting warmth of her arms clears my dazed mind at once. "How splendidly Whitby has treated you," she says, pulling away to look at me. "That color in your cheeks! Though you do look a bit tired."

"Only because I was sleepless with excitement for your arrival," I say, trying to sound as cheerful as always. "I've been desolate without you."

Mina's eyes sparkle. "Now *that* is a lie. I can tell you're happy. Arthur writes daily?"

"Like a great big grandfather clock, punctual to the minute. He even paid us a surprise visit in June and rode the train in just to stay an hour." I feel a sudden pang of yearning for Arthur and his smile and his simple, uncomplicated self. Perhaps seeing Mina and remembering my life at home in London has made me realize how much I miss him. Since he left, his letters have been even more loving and tender, reassuring me that he eagerly awaits our wedding day.

"Oh, Lucy, what a lucky and loved girl you are." A shadow passes over Mina's face, one that might go unnoticed by someone who loved her less. But before I can ask her what is wrong, a porter approaches to take her bag. "Thank you. Would you point us to a carriage, please? I know the walk isn't long, but I don't feel quite up to it today," she adds, glancing apologetically at me. For the first time, I notice the circles under her eyes and the peeling of her lips, as though she has been chewing nervously on them.

I slip an arm through hers. "You look even more tired than I feel. Whatever's the matter?"

In the carriage, Mina confesses, "I have not heard from Jonathan in two months. He left in May and last wrote to me at the beginning of June, and his letter was so cold and curt. I've been torturing myself, imagining him hurt or lost or . . . or worse."

I frown. "That doesn't sound like him, not when it comes to you."

"He warned that this trip might take longer than expected," she says, and my heart aches at the pain in her eyes. "The route is difficult, and one can't simply take a train and be there, the way I've come to you. He promised he would write often, so why hasn't he kept his word? And why was his letter so short and formal? Oh, Lucy!"

"Hush," I soothe her. "I'm sure there is a good reason."

"Sometimes I think I love him so much, I can feel everything he feels." Mina presses her white knuckles to her mouth. "I know something is wrong. I *know* it. Somehow, I feel that he is worried and afraid. But why doesn't he tell me, when he has always told me everything?"

She begins to weep despite the presence of the carriage driver. For my ladylike Mina to cry before a stranger, she must be distraught indeed. I rock her gently and stroke her hair, wondering if Arthur and I are connected the way she believes she is to Jonathan.

I give her my handkerchief. "This is the first journey his employer has entrusted to him, is it not?" I ask, and she nods, blowing her nose. "Perhaps the client keeps him so busy that he had time to send only a quick note. I am certain he wrote you a longer letter afterward, perhaps several, and they were delayed by a bad storm of some sort. That would explain his unease. What was the region called in English again?"

"The Mountains of Deep Winter," she says, looking a bit relieved. Where crying makes me red and blotchy, tears brighten the vivid blue of her eyes and the delicate softness of her face. "He did tell me they tend to have snowstorms there. I had not thought of that."

"And you notified the post office that you would be on holiday in Whitby," I remind her. "You gave them my address here, so that is yet another layer through which a letter must pass. I wager that soon you will be overwhelmed by a packet of fifteen letters, all come at once!"

She squeezes my hand. "I hope you're right. I'm so glad you're here. When I'm alone, I think all sorts of horrible things." She glances at the carriage driver and lowers her voice to a whisper. "I have even imagined that he has forsaken me for someone else."

I can't help laughing at that absurdity. "Have you lost your mind, Mina?"

"Such things happen. Devoted husbands go astray. Men are not like us. I often think they are weaker-willed and less steadfast." She hesitates. "Sometimes I worry Jonathan is only marrying me out of habit and only wants me because I am comfortable and familiar to him."

I stare at her in disbelief. I have never seen her in such doubt, not when it comes to her beloved Jonathan. "How can you say that? Surely you can hear how wrong that sounds."

Mina gazes out the window. "We've known each other almost twenty years," she says softly. "I was six when I came to live with Aunt Rosamund and met her neighbor Mr. Hawkins and his adopted son. To me, Jonathan was never just the boy next door." A smile touches her lips. "We were like-minded from the start. He knew he would be a lawyer one day, and he never scoffed at my intention to find a living as a governess, the way other men might have done."

I roll my eyes. "Yes, indeed. How dare you hope to earn money and secure independence for yourself, Mina? I should hope Jonathan never scoffed at something so logical!"

"You know how traditional some people are," she says, smiling again at my irreverence. "They do not hold such modern ideals for women as you and I do. I have my aunt to thank for that. She never married and taught me to be self-sufficient whether or not I found a husband."

"And you listened and came to me, and I would still be a mannerless hoyden if not for you. But now you *have* found a husband, one who loves you not because you are familiar, but because of all you are: kind and good and true. I think you know I've never liked Jonathan as much as you would wish. I am jealous that he will take you from me, but even I know that he would never forsake you. Why allow a few delayed letters to bring you such pain and doubt?"

"I can't tell you why," Mina says quietly. "I can't explain this dread. This fear that I may never see him again and that our kiss goodbye was our last."

"Wait and see," I reassure her. "In a month or two, when we are dancing at your wedding, I will remind you of this and we will laugh."

She brightens a bit. "Perhaps it will be at *your* wedding." Her eyes hold such hunger for Jonathan, and for the safety and comfort of marriage and children. I think of how everything she desires is what repels me most, and my heart feels a tug toward the cliffs and the bench in the shadows, but I pull myself back. I must be here, in this moment, for her sake.

I take my handkerchief back and gently dab at her face. "Jonathan will do everything in his power to come home to you. I know it as surely as I know my own name. He would fight any danger with his bare hands, despite being the soft, coddled lawyer's clerk he is!"

But instead of smiling, Mina takes my comment seriously. "He did not go without protection. He brought a weapon with him—a kukri knife that his explorer father had carried back to England and left him when he died. Mr. Hawkins and I laughed when Jonathan packed it, but perhaps he had a presentiment . . . perhaps he sensed that the journey would be difficult."

"I would have laughed, too," I say as brightly as I can. "Were you and I to travel, we would think of packing warm scarves or hardy boots, but here your Jonathan brings a knife that was likely stolen from some poor man in South Asia who needed it."

This time, she does smile, but I know it is only to humor me.

"Cheer up, darling," I say as the carriage pulls up in front of our lodgings. Mamma is already at the door, waiting for us. "I promise that his silence is not for lack of loving you."

Mina only has time to give my cheek a grateful kiss before stepping into my mother's embrace. I follow her, heavy with the weight of all we have said . . . and left unsaid.

CHAPTER SIXTEEN

W̲e are merry that night, sipping wine and gossiping like a trio of naughty, dissipated sisters. Mamma fusses over Mina like a mother hen, and Mina is all sunshine in her presence, even responding to her inquiries about Jonathan with a calm "I haven't had a letter recently, but I hope I shall soon." I am cheered by their chatter and determined to enjoy our time together, knowing that soon, such evenings will only be things of the past. But I cannot help my growing impatience as the moon rises ever higher.

Mina lays a concerned hand on mine. "Are you tired? You seem out of sorts."

"Lucy hasn't been sleeping well," Mamma explains as the servants clear away the dishes. "At least she hasn't been sleepwalking as often lately, have you, my pet?"

My eyes meet those of Harriet, but my maid's face remains expressionless as I say, "Of course not. But I *am* rather tired, and I think I will go rest."

"You should too, Mina," Mamma says. "Agatha has prepared the room next to Lucy's."

Upstairs, I slip on my nightgown, plait my hair, and blow out the candles, heart pounding with anticipation. But as soon as I get into bed, the door opens and Mina climbs in with me. And for the first time in all my years of confused love and longing for her, I feel a twinge of irritation. "What are you doing? I thought you would be exhausted and slumbering away by now."

"It's tradition. Have you forgotten?" Mina asks, hurt.

My annoyance fades at once. We always share a bed on our first night in

Whitby and have done so ever since she first became my governess five years ago. It was a way to keep me from sleepwalking, since she would wake me up if I did . . . or so my fourteen-year-old self had explained to my approving mother. And every summer since then, on numerous occasions, I have watched Mina sleep, her pale lashes fluttering against her cheeks, thinking of how I wanted nothing more in life than the privilege of seeing her dream.

But now, with the stranger waiting for me on the cliffs, Mina's face seems vague and intangible and imaginary, a palette of blues and greys in the shadows. She looks more like a painting from my dreams, meant to fade with the coming of day, than a woman.

"We can't break tradition when this is our last summer holiday together." She hands me a silver bracelet. It is simple and cheap, the kind of trinket I would never buy, and indeed, it would not even be sold at the shops Mamma and I patronize. But to a former governess of modest means, it must have been an extravagance indeed. The locket opens to reveal a photograph of Mina, her heart-shaped face solemn within waves of golden hair. "I hope you like it. You, Jonathan, and Aunt Rosamund are the only people to have my photograph."

"Oh, Mina, thank you," I say, touched.

She shows me an identical bracelet on her own wrist. Inside is a photograph of me, a rather bad one taken on my eighteenth birthday. I am looking off to the side, with a slight smile playing on my lips. "Now we will always have each other, even when we're not together."

She means when we are both married, of course, but I cannot help thinking of death, the ultimate door that will part us forever. I want to say something, anything, but I have no words.

"Lucy, what's wrong?" Mina asks quietly.

What's wrong is that something has changed in me, something I cannot easily confess in the light of day. If this were morning, I would give her my usual response: a flippant remark, a sparkling laugh, and then a change of subject. But night has fallen, and I have no desire to pretend in the shadows of the bed we share. I feel braver by moonlight. And I am so tired of pretending.

Mina rolls onto her side to face me. "You cannot hide anything from me, you know. I told you this afternoon that I feel connected to Jonathan, and I am to you, too."

My heart gives a little leap. "You love me that much?"

"I always have." Mina by daylight would have spoken the same words, but in a different manner: fond, sisterly, careful. But Mina by moonlight allows a tremor to enter her voice, and I remember again that day at the beach and the first tentative press of our lips. "You said earlier that you were jealous of Jonathan. Well, I am jealous of Arthur. I can feel how happy you are, happier than when you left London. But there is something else. Something like . . . a kind of thirst, as though you have tasted a wine you wish to drink forever."

I can't help shivering. But the thirst she senses in this moment is not for Arthur, and how can I tell her I desire another man, even if he is only in my dreams? Even with the courage the shadows give me? She might never look at me the same way again, my tender-hearted Mina who is devastated by the mere idea of Jonathan straying. "There's nothing wrong, exactly," I say. "I think I am nervous about giving up my freedom for marriage."

"As am I. It will be wonderful, but it will be an immense change."

"Arthur cut his visit short because of me, and I am still embarrassed about it," I confess. "I'm afraid I threw myself at him as soon as Mamma left the room."

Mina chuckles. "Kissing your husband-to-be is nothing to be ashamed of."

"We didn't . . . we didn't just kiss."

She lifts her head from the pillow. "Lucy!" she says loudly.

"No, no, not *that*," I say hastily. "We were alone in the parlor, on the sofa, and I climbed into his lap. He got a bit . . . excited, threw me to one side, and fairly ran back to London when I asked him to come to my room that night."

Mina's hands are pressed over her mouth, though whether from delight as well as horror, I cannot say. "Oh, poor Arthur. Is that why he stayed only an hour after coming all that way?"

"Yes," I say miserably. "And I'm still angry with him."

She laughs and puts an arm over me. "I don't blame you in the least," she says. "There have been times with Jonathan where I've felt a bit . . . impatient myself. Like something had taken hold of me. A kind of hunger and longing and curiosity."

"It feels like electricity to me. Or free falling." I think of the delicious scratch of Arthur's chin against mine as we kissed in the parlor, my body pressed to his even though we could hear the servants' voices a room or two away. And I shiver when I remember the stranger's soft, cold lips closing around my fingers. "Have you and Jonathan ever . . . How far have you . . ."

Even in the darkness, I can sense her blushing. "Certainly not as far as you and Arthur, by the sound of it," she says, giggling. "Though we, too, have been alone in the parlor. No, we've only kissed and held hands, and he touches my face sometimes. I think if I were brave enough to try with him what you did with Arthur, he would have reacted the same way."

"How, by fleeing like a panicked rabbit?" I ask, and she laughs and gives me a squeeze. "Would you? I mean, would you ever be brave enough to climb into Jonathan's lap?"

Mina by moonlight gives me a playful smile that sends a flutter through my stomach. "I don't see why not," she says, and I grin at her, delighted by the bravery the darkness lends us both. "They pursued *us* for marriage, did they not? Why shouldn't we pursue them back?"

I hug the arm she keeps draped over me, almost clinging to it, because I know what comes next. This side of Mina, full of fun and mischief and daring, never lasts long, however much I want it to. And indeed, she sighs a moment later and removes her arm, rolling away onto her back. When she speaks again, it is in the prudent, cautious voice of governess Mina.

"Ah, but this is silly talk," she says gently. The sober expression that has replaced her smile is like a cloud obscuring the moon. "We are fortunate girls to be marrying two kind and honorable men, who only wish to do what is proper and right."

I feel it again, that knife of disappointment that cuts me each time she and I dance along the edge of such a conversation, only for her to pull away at the last moment. For some reason, it hurts more than ever tonight. "But what is more proper and right than pleasing one's wife?" I argue. "Arthur and I will marry on September twenty-eighth, my birthday. I will be Mrs. Holmwood."

"But you are speaking of the future. It has not happened yet, and so Arthur feels that he cannot come to you. Not in that way, not yet, for the sake of your virtue."

"But what difference does a wedding make?" I ask, irritated. "It is only a party. I wear a white dress and we receive gifts. It is no one's business what happens between us or when."

"I see your point," Mina says, trying to soothe me. "I do. But upholding tradition—"

"Is required only of women. Men have needs they satisfy elsewhere. Did you not allude to that earlier?" I ask, deftly aiming my sharp words, and she flinches. "Arthur and Jonathan, I am sure, will not come inexperienced to the marriage bed. These misgivings of theirs are only to preserve *our* virtue. Why should we not satisfy our needs as well?"

"Because this world was neither made by us nor for us. Believe me, I see the unfairness of it, too," Mina pleads. "I only meant that doing everything you can to start your marriage off properly can only be a good thing. Arthur believes this, too, don't you see?"

I sit up in frustration. "You always do this," I say. "Deep down, you agree with me, but then you pretend not to. You are never truly on my side."

She sits up, too, flustered. "But, Lucy, I *am* on your side! You know that I see your point, and that I love you too much to blame or judge you."

I press my face to my knees. I am not certain why I expected anything different. Even with her determination, her intellect, and her belief in the importance of female independence, Mina will always sit quietly in the boat life gives her, trying not to disturb the water, while I swim frantically against the current. She and Arthur love me, but they will never understand me.

She moves to sit close to me, leaning her cheek on my back. "Do you remember what your father used to tell you? That you must be above reproach at all times?" she asks, stroking my hair when she feels me go still at the mention of Papa. "I think about that advice often because it is how *I* live my life, too. I know you think I am a coward—"

"I think nothing of the sort," I say, shocked.

"Overly careful, then. For hiding in the safety of rules." Mina presses a kiss to my back, her lips warm through my nightdress. "My family never had money or status. I was never going to make a grand match like yours. I would never have even seen high society if not for you."

I close my eyes. My heart is still beating a rhythm of displeasure, but I am listening.

"I want to be a credit to Jonathan. I want us to be respected and admired, to *belong*. To be above reproach . . . even if my true thoughts, deep inside and known only to you, are not." I feel her smile against my back. "Things are changing. A new century is almost upon us, my Lucy, and we will see the world alter, bit by bit, until the next generation of women is freer than we are, and the next, and the next. But change doesn't happen overnight. It takes time, just as you and Arthur must. And won't it be sweeter to wait for something so special?"

"Let's just go to sleep," I say shortly, lying back down. "I'm exhausted."

Mina wraps her arms around me, cuddling close. When her breathing is as steady as the tide, I slip away to her room and into her cold, abandoned bed. In my agitated state, it takes much longer to fall asleep, and I begin to fear that I will toss and turn uselessly until dawn.

But between one breath and the next, I am on the cliffs beneath the night sky once more. A massive bank of clouds shrouds the moon, revealing jagged pale veins of light that bleed over the ocean. The wind is restless, turbulent, and cold, and I hug myself as I hurry up the path.

The stranger is on the bench as usual, but he does not greet me with a smile or open arms tonight. His rigid posture cuts through the curtain of mist, and he keeps his eyes fixed on the raging waters below as I take a seat beside him. "It is very late. I was beginning to think you would not answer my call tonight," he says, his voice clipped and as chilly as the wind.

I shiver in my thin nightdress. "I was delayed."

"Were you?"

I glance at him, never having heard him speak so coldly to me. The wind blows a fold of my nightdress over his knee, and he gets up abruptly, as though he cannot bear to be touched by any part of me. He goes to stand near the fence with his back to me.

"Delayed by what or whom?" he asks. It is clear he expects some sort of apology or justification from me for being tardy to my own dream.

"What can it possibly matter? I am here with you now," I say, irritated, to which he remains silent. The air hangs heavy with his expectation.

My annoyance rises as I watch the waves churn, beaten by the powerful wind. The roiling clouds move to reveal a corner of the moon. In the dim light, I see a sea bird struggling against the gale, and I feel angrier than ever that a mindless wild creature might understand me better than the people who profess to love me. I am in no mood tonight to be treated like a willful child.

The man turns and starts walking away from me, his broad shoulders stiff with anger.

"Where are you going?" I demand, rising from the bench. He ignores me. "If you refuse to give me even your name, then I can't be expected to tell you every detail of my day."

As soon as the words leave my mouth, I know that I have made a terrible mistake.

The wind stops gusting, the waves freeze their frenetic stirring, and the clouds halt their uneasy movement across the sky. A strange, thick, heavy silence settles over us, and I am suddenly seized by the absolute certainty that I will be struck dead by lightning where I stand.

The man stops walking but keeps his back to me. "I see that my company has become distasteful to you," he says, his soft deep voice carrying an undercurrent of wrath. "Perhaps it is time we stopped meeting if you feel you do not wish to continue the friendship."

"Why are you saying this?" I ask, my anger shifting at once into the panic of never seeing him again. "I have come to you gladly, willingly, every night you have called to me. Whenever I am not with you, I long to be. Of course I wish to continue the friendship."

He turns around, his face impassive and his eyes fixed on a point above my head, as though I am invisible. "I want this to be clear, Lucy. You cannot hide anything from me."

I stare at him. Mina had said those exact words to me as we lay in bed together earlier—though how different her meaning had been from his. As her face appears in my mind, I feel an odd sensation akin to needles prickling at my consciousness. Somehow, I can sense my thoughts being violently sifted through, and every thread of everything I have ever thought being ripped from the seams of my brain. I gasp at the sudden pain, my hands flying to my head.

Colors flash before my eyes, buried memories and scenes that have long passed. Mina's golden hair flying as she runs on the beach, laughing; her cheek pressed against mine as we stand before the mirror, dressed for a party; her sky-blue eyes sparkling at me from across a crowded ballroom; our hands clasped, our lips meeting, as wild and reckless as the summer wind.

Every word, every look, and every touch I have ever shared with Mina has been laid bare, plucked from my mind like a bleeding tendril of a vein from my skin.

"You could have saved us all of this trouble had you only told me why you were late," the man says quietly. "All I wanted was an answer."

The pain in my head subsides as though it had never been there, but I keep my trembling hands on my temples, afraid it will return. Tears leak from my eyes as I take in gasps of air. "I thought you were my friend," I whisper. "I trusted you. Why would you hurt me like this?"

"Because you hurt me first," he says, and his voice is as gentle as it has always been. He looks at me for the first time tonight, his gaze full of sorrow and regret, and pulls me against him, stroking my hair just the way Mina had. "You made me feel that I am not important to you."

I am crying in earnest now from the pain, confusion, and relief of being once more what I had been to him. "I thought of you all day," I murmur into his chest. "I missed you all day."

He hugs me tighter to him, bending his head protectively over mine. "I thought of you, too. I was waiting for nightfall just so I could see you again, my little Lucy, my kindred soul," he says longingly, and with his words, the wind gusts, the sea crashes against the rocks, the clouds resume their swirling, and I feel that I can breathe deeply again.

"I am not myself tonight," I whisper.

"No, you are not. Or you would not have so rudely demanded my name." He leads me back to the bench, where we sit with our arms still around each other.

"Everyone disapproves of me this evening. First Mina, then you."

"Dear me, how self-pitying we are," he says, not unkindly, resting his chin on top of my head. "You did shock her with your confession regarding Arthur's visit, but I don't believe she thinks less of you for it. She loves you too well, that much is clear."

A trickle of disquiet poisons my relief at having won him back to me. How easily he had combed my mind for secrets, scraping my thoughts from the inside of my brain like butter from a sharp knife. He himself is a creation of my mind, I know . . . but still, for the first time since I have known him, I feel the urge to pull away. I do not know why my dreams, so pleasurable until now, have soured to this degree—perhaps it is a result of the agitation I felt tonight. All I know is that I want to break free of the man's arms, wake up, run down these cliffs, and curl up in bed next to Mina, safe and warm behind a locked door.

But I stay where I am, wrapped in his embrace with my head tucked into his chest. I am so inexplicably afraid of what will happen if I dare move. *Think of something else*, I tell myself, my heart in my throat. *For God's sake, think of anything else, for he can hear you.*

A lazy, drowsy calm suddenly settles over me. I feel my heartbeat slow and my breathing grow even, and my desire to run dissipates as the mist rises around us, cooling my heated face. I snuggle closer to him. There is nowhere I can be safer than here, with him.

"You are not angry with me, but with everyone you love. They don't accept you as I do." He smooths my hair off my neck and bends to kiss the burning skin there. I close my eyes as the soothing touch cascades down my spine. He parts his lips and I feel his teeth, icy and sharp, graze over my fluttering pulse. "I will teach you what you long to know and give you all that you have imagined in your darkest reveries. I will not push you away as they do."

I am so sleepy, so calm, so happy to be with him. I clutch him tightly, wanting to be even closer to him, wanting his teeth to stop their teasing and push deep inside me. With a whimper of impatience, I pull myself onto his lap and tilt my head back, offering him everything. The contrast of his soft mouth and tongue with his rough chin and sharp teeth sends my pulse racing and my need rising. I put my hands on either side of his head, holding him to me.

And then I am saved, in that moment, by three things.

The first is the memory of how minutes before, I had put my hands on my own head in just such a way, not in passion, but in excruciating pain.

The second is the cold flutter of Mina's silver bracelet against my wrist.

The third is his whisper against my throat: "You will give me what belongs to me?"

Belongs.

My trance breaks like the crack of fingers snapping. I pull back and put my hand over my neck, panting as the deep blue-green of his eyes washes over me. Once more, I feel the prickling pain in my head, and this time it is Arthur's face in my mind and Arthur's arms around me just like this, when I had sat on his lap in the parlor. *No,* I think fiercely. *No, not again.* I squeeze my eyes shut and imagine something, anything, shielding my vulnerable mind. Mina's silver bracelet gives me an idea. *Let it be silver,* I think, drops of perspiration sliding down my back. *A plate of silver protecting my mind that is so strong, so solid that the needles can't get through.*

I open my eyes to see a furrow between his brows. If I did not know better, I would have thought he was straining, fighting the barrier I have put into place against his invasion of my thoughts. "I do not belong to you," I hear myself say, weak but distinct. "I am not yours to take."

His eyes glitter, sharp as diamonds. "You think that is *your* decision to make?"

My heart pummels my rib cage, but the prickling pain lessens to a dull throb in my temples. "I do not belong to you," I repeat, my voice stronger this time.

"You would rather," the man says slowly, as the corners of his sly mouth turn upward, "that when I come to you, it will be as a husband to his wife?"

They are Arthur's words. From the man's widening smile, I see that in the quick moment before I had fought him off, he had glimpsed enough of what had happened between Arthur and me. Everything we had said, everything we had done, everything I had been thinking. Arthur kissing me with frantic passion, flying across the room, and leaving in haste to avoid temptation. Arthur, who loves me so much that he will not stain my virtue until I am his—so unlike this man, who would greedily take everything I had without another thought.

"You will not be my husband," I say. I am frightened, but I am angry, too, as I slide off his lap and back onto the bench. "You do not exist. It is for Arthur to come to me, and not you."

I half expect him to threaten or punish me again, but instead, his gaze holds amusement and renewed interest. *He is intrigued*, I think, *by my refusal, my belonging to someone else. He likes a challenge.* "There, now. You may very well be a perfect woman of the age after all."

I blink in disbelief. "What does that mean?"

"In every age, every country, and every culture, there is a class of woman admired above all others," he says, returning to the pleasant, conversational tone of our weeks together. "She is the model, the ideal, and represents every aspiration of her society in that period of history. As a scholar of the world, with all the time I could wish, I have made it a game to seek out such women and make their acquaintance. I find myself easily bored, you see."

I hug myself, shivering on the cold bench in the icy wind. The air hangs heavy with the smell of rain, and an ominous light touches the storm-racked sky.

"Most people bore me quickly, which is why you, with your hidden depths," he says, gesturing to me with gallant charm, "entertain me so. But always, I find myself turning back to perfection . . . or what is considered perfection in a certain place and time. Do you remember when I told you of how England's tightly buttoned, polite society fascinates me?"

"I remember."

"We know that *proper* women do not speak of death, nor are they entranced by it, and so you would be considered odd by those standards. But tonight, you refused me to keep yourself pure for your husband. Purity is prized in women of your society, I think?" He looks at me with a smile that I cannot be sure is not mocking. "Hence, a perfect woman of the age."

I touch my bracelet, thinking of how Mina had said that this world was neither made by us nor for us. She may accept that fact, but I do not. "You're wrong. I have never wanted to be perfect. I refused you because I belong to another, but it isn't Arthur. It is me. I belong only to myself, no matter what the world has to say about it."

He follows my eyes to the silver bracelet. "I have seen that photograph you carry before. A woman with sunlit hair and an angelic face, her eyes shining out at the viewer."

I go still. "I have not yet shown it to you."

"And yet I tell you, I have seen it before," he says calmly. "Perhaps your Mina is the perfect woman of this age, and it is *she* I have been seeking and not you at all."

Fear knifes through me at the thought of Mina helpless on this bench, drowsy and unable to ask questions, crying from the prickling pain in her head. It is impossible, utterly impossible for a man I have only imagined to hurt her, and yet my chest is tight with dread. I stand up. "Leave her be," I say. "I don't want you involved with her or Arthur or anyone else in my life."

The man is smiling. "You don't wish to share me." And then he is standing, too, with his arms locked around me. It happens between heartbeats, similar to the way I move from my bed to being on these night-smothered cliffs with him. Where his previous embraces had been tender, I now feel as though I have been swallowed up by some cold dark star or a column of granite, for there is no affection in the way he holds me. Only possession. I am a butterfly caught in an iron net, and with one movement, he could extinguish the whole of my existence. "Do you truly think you can turn me away, Lucy? After all that we have been to each other? After I told you my secrets and shared with you what scraps of my soul remain?"

I cannot respond. My answer is trapped in my throat by his strange, intangible power, and I can only look up into his face, as brutal and wild and beautiful as the arctic.

"You say you belong to yourself." He pushes my head back with one hand, exposing the length of my neck to him. His teeth graze me, harder this time. "But I can make you mine if I want to. I can make it so that no one on this earth could fight my claim upon you."

This is no longer a dream. It is a nightmare.

Wake up, Lucy, I tell myself fiercely as the points of his teeth threaten to penetrate me.

But then drowsy, aching, uncontrollable desire returns, so suddenly that it is almost like a spell. I tilt my head back even more, my blood galloping, even as some rational part of me presses my hands hard against his chest, trying to push him away. He looks down at them and gives a low, pleased laugh. He likes when I fight him. When I fit his definition of a virtuous and *perfect* woman, it makes him want me even more. I am a helpless creature in his thrall, but lord help me, this dangling thread of power that I hold, weak as it may be, is utterly intoxicating.

"I do not belong to you," I say again. "You are a stranger. And you are not really here."

He presses his smile to my ear and whispers, "My name is Vlad. And I am here at last."

I wake up.

An enormous clap of thunder has shattered the air and torn me violently from my dream.

A heavy, relentless rain that must have begun some time ago pummels me. I am soaked to the skin and freezing cold, my thin nightgown plastered against my body, and I shiver uncontrollably in the maelstrom that came upon me unawares. The wind howls through the willow tree, ripping leaves down with wild abandon, and several hard branches slap at my back and shoulders like desperate hands pushing me to go, go, go.

But before I can run back down the path toward home, a ship's horn screams in the night, drawing my attention to the vicious, roaring sea below. In between brutal, disorienting flashes of lightning, I see a gargantuan vessel approach Whitby harbor with inexorable speed, careening madly in the white-capped waves: a battered foreign ship with black sails, jagged as bats' wings.

CHAPTER SEVENTEEN

A soft knock sounds on my bedroom door. "Is she still asleep?" my mother whispers.

"Yes," Mina whispers back. "She hasn't moved an inch."

Slippered feet pad over to me, and a soft hand touches my forehead. "She doesn't feel feverish, but it was wise of you to cover her well," my mother murmurs to Mina. "Who knows what sort of chill she might have caught last night, wandering around in that storm?"

I breathe as evenly as I can, pretending to be asleep. To awaken to their fussing would mean fully returning to reality and leaving the frightening, puzzling, enthralling dream of the lightning-ripped seas, the rain, and the man's lips on my neck. *Vlad's* lips.

"She was soaked to the bone," Mina says in a low voice. "It was my fault, Mrs. Westenra. I should have heard her leave, but I was so tired. To think I could have prevented this—"

"Nonsense. It isn't your fault," my mother reassures her. "No one else heard her go, either. At least she got back safely without any injuries."

"Not a scratch. Though Harriet and I did see a little bruise last night when we put dry clothing on her. Just there, on the side of her neck."

A bruise, where he had kissed me. I almost stir in my surprise but manage to remain still as Mamma lifts my hair away from my jaw. "Yes, I see it. Nothing serious, thank goodness," she says, and the bed shifts as she sits down beside me. "Lucy? Wake up, dear."

I open my eyes and yawn. "Good morning. Are you already dressed to pay calls?"

"Good *afternoon*, you mean," Mamma says, touching my forehead again. "You slept the whole morning away. How do you feel? Any aches or shivers?"

I sit up against my lace-edged pillows. "I feel wonderful. I slept like a stone. I'm sorry to have worried you so last night, Mina," I add, holding my hand out to her.

"Harriet and I feared you had fallen into the sea," Mina says. "You were dripping water all over the rug and shivering dreadfully. When on earth did you slip out of bed?"

"I'm afraid that's rather the nature of sleepwalking, darling. I can't remember a thing."

"Well, we will put an end to that," Mamma says as my maid enters the room. "Harriet went into town just now and says there are wild dogs running about. Isn't that so?"

The maid sets down a tray of tea and my favorite strawberry pastries. "Yes, madam. A ship came into harbor late last night, and people are saying that an enormous dog, or perhaps a wolf, jumped off and ran through town. Everyone is still quite nervous about it."

"A ship? In this weather?" I ask as innocently as if I hadn't witnessed its arrival myself.

"Yes, miss. I expect it will be all over the papers today," Harriet says, her face drawn and frightened. "Such terrible things as I heard in town. I'm sure I shall have nightmares from what the men were saying. They found none alive on board. Just thirty boxes full of earth."

"Boxes full of earth?" Mina repeats, exchanging glances with me. "Strange cargo."

My mother shakes her head. "What a needless tragedy! I wonder at the captain's decision to sail in such a storm. He might have waited safely elsewhere for a day or two."

"There was no one on board?" I ask, frowning.

"Only two people, miss, both of them dead. The captain and one sailor. People were saying that such a large vessel must have left port with a sizable crew, and yet only these two men were found. What became of all the others, no one can guess," Harriet says miserably, and my mother covers her mouth in horror and Mina crosses herself, whispering a prayer. "But I heard someone say that something had drained these two bodies of all their blood. That beastly dog that got away, perhaps."

I hold my breath as I listen, every nerve in my body tingling with apprehension.

Mina sinks into a chair, her eyes wet. "Those poor men. They must have wives waiting for their return," she says, her face white as a sheet. She brings her engagement ring to her lips.

"The captain was dead?" I demand. "How did he steer the vessel into harbor?"

"No one knows, miss," Harriet says. "They found his body lashed to the ship's wheel with rope, as though trying not to go overboard in the storm. Oh, it's too awful!"

"That's enough," Mamma says, glancing at me. "I don't want Miss Lucy upset any more than she already is. Return to your duties and try not to think about all this."

"I'll try, madam," Harriet says, though the doubt is plain on her face. At the door, she turns and looks back at me with pleading eyes. "Miss Lucy, please let me lock your bedroom door tonight. I couldn't bear it if anything happened to you!"

"I'm to be shut up like a prisoner, then?" I ask, though I am touched by her concern.

"It is a sensible suggestion," Mina says gently. "You should not be walking around at night, unconscious, when there is a dog or . . . or worse, lying in wait."

My mother nods. "I agree. But," she adds, seeing the look on my face, "perhaps we need not resort to such measures yet, if you would stay with Lucy for a few more nights, Mina."

"Of course." Mina closes her eyes, shuddering. "A dark ship coming into harbor at night, carrying the dead. It is such an evil, *evil* omen, and I fear for us all."

"Wait, Harriet," I call. "Did you hear anything else about the ship? Perhaps its name?"

The maid nods. "It was a Russian vessel out of Bulgaria, they said. The *Demeter*."

A shocking cold spreads over me. If I had any belief left that my nightly visits with my strange friend were merely the visions of a troubled sleeper, then this has destroyed it for good. It is impossible that I could have dreamed such a ship ever existed, let alone predicted where it would sail from or that it would disembark here in Whitby. Everything that passed between Vlad and me this summer—every word, every look, and every kiss—really and truly happened.

Mina is studying me. "Are you all right, Lucy?"

"She needs food," my mother says. She stands up and glances out the window at the brightening sky. "And perhaps some fresh air. Now that the storm has passed, won't you both come to town with me to post a few letters? It would do you good."

Mina looks reluctant, but I am desperate for news of the *Demeter* . . . or of Vlad. "We'll meet you downstairs," I say, and my mother nods and leaves the room.

"Are you quite well?" Mina asks again when we are alone. "When Harriet told you the name of the ship, you looked as though you might faint."

"A good thing I'm still in bed, then," I say, taking a large bite of pastry to keep from having to say more. But Mina gives me her best stern governess look, and I brush the crumbs off my coverlet, wondering how I could possibly explain to her. She would not believe me, my Mina of the methodical brain. She would not accept that I had met a man in my dreams and had learned of his ship's arrival before it had even happened. "I can't tell you. Not yet."

"This ship means something to you," she persists. "This *Demeter*."

The name is disturbing coming from her lips, as though she has spoken aloud my private dream. "Please, Mina, not now," I say, and I must look so distressed that she sighs and gives up.

Within the hour, we are walking into town with Mamma. The grey sky is clearing, the ocean is calmer, and the air smells clean and new. There are people everywhere, flitting into shops or gathering in the streets to gossip about the *Demeter*'s macabre arrival.

"Come along," Mamma says, hurrying us away from them. "Here is the post office."

"Might Mina and I wait outside? There's such a crowd in there, and I prefer the fresh air," I say, and my mother agrees. Mina and I stand like obedient children by the door, surveying the cobblestone street. It is tidy and picturesque, with pots of flowers and little iron tables and chairs full of people on holiday, some of them chattering in foreign languages. Through the sound of steady conversation and laughter is the tinkle of bells as customers go in and out of the shops. Suddenly, I hear children shouting as a tiny white dog, no bigger than my two hands placed side by side, scampers mischievously through the crowd, tongue lolling and tail wagging.

Mina laughs. "Oh, no, I think he's making his escape."

"And here come his jailers," I observe.

A boy and two girls, all under the age of ten, are chasing after the dog. They have short plump legs, well-made clothes, and almost identical faces, with round brown eyes and dimpled cheeks. There is something eerie and uncomfortable about watching them, as though my vision has been distorted and I am somehow seeing three versions of only one child.

To my consternation, the impossibly small dog runs over to us and begins pawing and sniffing at my skirts. I step back in disgust, pressing against the outside wall of the post office, but Mina laughs again and actually scoops the wriggling animal into her arms.

"What a delightful little thing you are," she coos, rubbing its floppy ears. She smiles at the children, who have stopped in front of us. "Hello there. Is this adorable runaway yours?"

"He is, indeed, miss," says the older girl solemnly. "His name is Biscuit."

"What a nice name," Mina says kindly. "Which one of you thought of it?"

"I did," the boy says at once.

"You did not, Edward!" the girl argues. "It was Emily's idea. Wasn't it, Em?"

But the younger girl is not listening. She is staring at me. I blink back at her, choking down my disgust at the slimy white matter dotting the corners of her enormous eyes.

Edward seems to sense my displeasure. "Sorry, miss," he says, taking hold of his younger sister's arm. "Emily looks too long at people sometimes, even though we tell her it isn't polite."

"She just thinks you're pretty," the older girl adds, and suddenly all three children are gazing at me. My skin is positively crawling. They are so round and pink and tiny, with dripping noses, and it is impossible to imagine myself ever having been like them.

"She's bloofer," Emily whispers shyly, and gooseflesh forms up and down my arms. I think of the afternoon Arthur and I had taken a walk outside my home and a little boy called me that, mispronouncing the word in exactly the same way.

"Yes, she's beautiful," the other girl agrees, and they all watch me expectantly.

"Isn't that nice, Lucy?" Mina prompts me. "These lovely children complimented you."

I force a smile that feels more like a grimace, and my eyes dart away from the identical round faces for some relief. I realize that the tiny dog's escape has attracted spectators, and everyone at the tables nearby is watching us. "I am so glad," I say faintly. "So very glad."

"Here, let me return Biscuit to you." Mina hands the quivering pile of white fur to the older girl. "Keep a tighter grip on him so he doesn't escape again."

But no sooner has she finished speaking than the dog lifts its head, sniffing excitedly, before jumping out of the child's arms and tearing over to the cluster of iron tables nearby.

"Not again!" Edward groans.

Biscuit heads straight toward a man sitting alone and begins smelling his polished shoes and the cuffs of his dark trousers. The dog's tail wags frantically as the man reaches down to pat his head. Everyone is smiling at the pair of them, including Mina, but my heart seems to have stopped beating in my body. The man has a long, pale hand that wears a brass ring with a red garnet. It is Vlad's hand, and Vlad's ring, and when the man looks around at the crowd with a sheepish chuckle, it is Vlad's face—even whiter and handsomer by day—with its long straight nose, sharp jaw, and deep ocean eyes.

"No, I am not your owner, little one," he says gravely, his rich voice carrying easily. He seems to be exaggerating his accent. "I cannot take you home, for I have no food or bed for you. And I would likely think you were a cushion and sit upon you by accident."

Mina is laughing as hard as everyone else. The children hurry over, and the older girl apologizes to Vlad as she seizes the dog. Biscuit strains against her arms, trying desperately to get back to Vlad. Clearly, the animal is as charmed by him as everyone else.

"You have won him over, sir," says a young woman in pink muslin, her eyes roving over Vlad's well-dressed form with interest. "Perhaps you are an animal trainer?"

He shakes his head, a gesture so familiar that it almost takes my breath away. It is surreal beyond anything I could imagine, seeing in daylight a man I only know in dreams. "No, that is one calling in life I have not yet pursued," he says in a light, easy tone as his eyes move directly to me. The swiftness with which he finds me in the crowd proves he has been watching me this whole time. I feel mingled fear and excitement at the thought of him studying my face and form and listening to my every word without anyone else knowing our relation to each other. My breath comes a bit too quickly as his gaze holds mine.

"Lucy?" Mina takes my elbow, alarmed. "Are you unwell?"

Quick as a flash, Vlad leaves his seat and approaches us with an elegant bow. The power of his broad shoulders and the handsome head atop them draws every eye in the vicinity as he addresses Mina and me. "Forgive me, ladies, for we have not been introduced. But I could not help noticing that you may be in need of a chair," he says. "May I give you mine?"

"Please, sir," Mina says gratefully. "I'm afraid my friend might have caught a chill."

"From the storm last night? I would not blame her at all. A cold wet wind will trouble even the strongest constitution," Vlad says, holding out his arm to me.

Slowly, I take it as though in a trance. Through the sleeve of his thick coat, I feel the strength of his arm as he guides me to his chair. He and Mina look at me, both expecting me to say something, but my throat feels too dry and raw for words.

"This is very kind of you, sir," Mina says to him, ever proper. "Lucy, how are you feeling? Won't you thank the gentleman for his assistance?"

"Thank you," I say, still breathless. "I am much obliged to you."

"It is my pleasure." Vlad turns to Mina. "Shall I fetch you a chair, miss? So that you may join your charming friend . . . *Lucy*, was it?" Quicker than she can see, he gives me the most fleeting and private of smiles, meant only for me. I close my eyes, trying to slow my heart.

"I don't wish to trouble you—" Mina begins.

"It's no trouble at all, as long as I may join the two of you?" he asks politely. "Weary traveler that I am, I would appreciate sitting a bit longer."

"Of course," she says at once.

Vlad takes two iron chairs from a nearby table, where the flirtatious girl in pink is still watching him hopefully. But he does not spare her a glance as he sets down a chair for Mina, gallantly wiping off the rain with his handkerchief, before taking the other himself. "I hope you do not think this improper, miss," he says, looking straight at Mina, his self-conscious humility clearly a show for her. "I am new to England's shores, you see, and where I am from . . . well, our ways are not your ways. Will you allow me to introduce myself?"

"Certainly," Mina says, looking charmed.

He proceeds to speak, very smoothly and fluently, a series of names and titles rivaling those of the Queen herself. I recognize a number of different languages, from French to Spanish to German to Russian. "I am of a very large family, with roots all over Europe, as you can see," he says, sounding apologetic as Mina stares at him, overwhelmed. "The equivalent of my title, in your elegant English, would likely be count."

"It's a pleasure to make your acquaintance, Count," Mina says courteously. "From where do you hail, with such wide-spreading roots?"

"My primary home is in Austria-Hungary, in a remote place in the mountains."

"The Carpathians?" Mina asks eagerly, and he nods, his eyebrows raised. "My fiancé is there now on business. I shall not try to pronounce the name of the region, as I would not do it justice, but he told me that it translates into English as the Mountains of Deep Winter."

"Ah! I know the area well," Vlad says, smiling.

"I read everything I could about it before he left," Mina says. "I wanted to know more about where he was traveling, you see. It was my way of going with him. He is a lawyer's clerk. And I am so sorry, I have not yet introduced myself," she adds, blushing at her oversight. "I am Mina Murray, and this is my friend Lucy Westenra."

"A pleasure." Vlad bows from the waist, ever graceful. "The mountains of which you speak are rather far from here, Miss Murray. You must miss your fiancé very much."

Mina's face falls. "Oh, yes, but I am certain he will return soon."

He nods, all kindness and sympathy, but I detect his wolfish amusement. He is like a river, concealing dark undercurrents beneath the surface, and the evident pleasure he takes in Mina's pain is troubling, considering he has never seen her before. *But he has*, I recall with a sharp intake of breath. *He mentioned that he has seen her photograph.* Jonathan and I are two of the only people to possess a picture of her, so perhaps Vlad has met him. He lives in the country where Jonathan has gone on business, after all. But why would he not tell Mina so?

His eyes cut to me, dagger sharp, detecting my disquiet.

I find my voice at last. "What a coincidence that you hail from the same country. Perhaps you crossed paths with Mina's fiancé on the journey."

"Perhaps," he says, answering me but looking at Mina. "I did leave home quite a while ago, however. Boat travel takes considerable time, as you know."

"I do not know," Mina admits. "I've never been on a boat or, indeed, left England."

"Truly? Even though you have a scholarly interest and the heart of a traveler?"

He is still addressing Mina alone, which nettles me, considering that he had spoken similar sentiments to me first. "Mina and I are happy to remain on land at the moment," I say, bringing myself back into the conversation, "considering what happened last night."

He does not take his eyes from Mina. "Something happened?" he asks, all innocence.

"A ship came into Whitby. The *Demeter*," I say, and his eyes dart to me at last with a flicker of humor. My brazenness amuses him. "She sailed into port with not a crew member still alive. Perhaps you have heard the news in town or seen her for yourself?"

Vlad spreads his pale hands. "Alas, I fear my English is not good enough yet," he says to Mina, humble and abashed. "I have not been listening to the talk, as I am still learning."

"I think your English is very good," she says politely.

But I am not willing to let go so easily. "I hear the *Demeter* sailed from Bulgaria. Is that not where *your* ship originated? That is," I add hastily, seeing Mina's surprise, "you did not tell us that, but I assume it is one of the most convenient ports to you."

The corners of his mouth twitch at my error. "Yes, you are correct. I sailed from Varna," he says, turning to me at last with friendly attentiveness. The glint in his ocean eyes is challenging me to say more in front of Mina and risk exposing our secret.

But I refuse to be intimidated and meet his gaze full on. "How many ships sail from Bulgaria to England within the span of a few weeks?" I ask. "I can't imagine that many, as the route seems quite circuitous. And are they all called *Demeter*?"

Mina looks between us, puzzled and ill at ease.

Vlad sits back, regarding me with approval and profound interest. I am more daring than he expected me to be. But before he can reply, the people around us utter pleased murmurs as the sun begins filtering through the clouds, casting a soft golden light over Whitby. The sky lightens, and in a minute, the sun will free itself and burst upon the town.

"What a beautiful day it has turned out to be," Mina says, relieved to change the subject. "Are you staying here in town, sir?"

Vlad stands up abruptly, towering over us, and Mina startles. "I beg your pardon, Miss Murray, but I have just recalled an engagement I cannot miss. It was a pleasure to meet you."

"Oh," she says, surprised. "It was lovely to meet you as well, Count."

I wait for him to acknowledge me, but he holds his hand out only to Mina, smiling with chivalrous charm. Hesitantly, she places her fingers in his and flinches, no doubt at the coldness of his touch. "It will be easy to love England if everyone I meet follows your shining example," he says.

"You seem a remarkable lady, Miss Murray. And quite a beloved one, I think. I hope we will meet again. Good day." He strides away without a second glance at me.

"What a strange man," Mina says thoughtfully, rubbing the hand he had held.

"You did not like him? Even after all the pretty compliments he gave you?" I frown, annoyed by how he had almost ignored my existence.

"I don't know him well enough to like or dislike him. But I find it interesting that he spoke with a heavy accent when we first met him, and by the end of our chat, his English was almost perfect. Did you notice? And how quickly he left when the sun came out. Perhaps his skin burns easily, as mine does. He is paler than anyone I've seen."

"He does seem the sort to be vain and use a parasol," I quip.

But Mina isn't listening. "He seems well spoken and amiable enough, but I got the strange sense that he was laughing at us. There was something in his voice, perhaps, or the flash of his eyes. As though he were an adult speaking to two amusing, precocious children."

I look at her, surprised. "How observant you are, my Mina."

"The diaries I keep have taught me to use my eyes and ears," she says, smiling. "He was very cool toward you, darling. Perhaps you offended him by questioning him so thoroughly about his travels. You seemed to think he was lying to us about his journey."

"Oh, what does it matter?" I ask, sick of the subject of Vlad. "He's no one and nothing to me. And here is Mamma at last. Let's go home. I've a frightful headache."

My mother comes out of the post office with Mrs. Edgerton, a widow with whom we had become vaguely acquainted last summer. "Girls, how on earth did you manage to meet the count so quickly?" Mamma asks, glowing with excitement. "All the ladies in the post office are in a flutter over him. And Mrs. Edgerton here knows all about him."

"You do?" I ask the widow, astonished.

Quiet, reserved Diana Edgerton is in her midthirties and pretty in a faded way, with light brown hair and soft dark eyes. She is often overlooked and forgotten at parties but is tolerated by Whitby's high society because of the lofty fortune and beautiful summer home her elderly husband had left her. She keeps herself apart and spurns any and all advances of true friendship, including my own, but I do not take offense as the other ladies do, being so fond of solitude myself. And I have always liked the romance of her mysterious past: according to the gossips, she had been a harpist of some fame, disowned by her family for pursuing a musical career, and had met her husband in one of the great houses where she had performed.

"I made the count's acquaintance this morning," Mrs. Edgerton says in her soft voice. "He got lost on the beach in front of my house, and as it was cold and rainy, he begged to come in for a cup of tea. We spoke for an hour or two before I directed him into town."

"An hour or two?" I say playfully to hide my growing annoyance with Vlad. Clearly, I am not as special as he had made me feel on all our evenings together, and he is still searching for that *perfect* woman. "Then you truly *do* know all about him."

Mamma laughs. "Mrs. Edgerton was forbidden to leave the post office without giving the ladies a full account of the meeting. They even kept me from going out to you girls, for fear of interrupting your tête-à-tête! I think they were hoping he might make one of you his countess."

"But that is impossible," Mina says, upset. "Lucy and I are both engaged to be married."

"I know," my mother says, touching her shoulder. "It was all in fun, of course. If anyone is to be a candidate for countess, it would be *you*." She raises an arched eyebrow at Mrs. Edgerton, who blushes and stares with her wide doe eyes. "And why not? You are quite pretty and of a good age for him, and the gentleman is so very dashing."

"I beg you would not say such things, Mrs. Westenra, even in kindness and jest," Mrs. Edgerton murmurs, though she cannot hide her pleasure at the suggestion.

I stand up, faintly nauseated by the sight of the widow blushing over Vlad. "Mamma, do stop mortifying the poor lady and let us go home. I would like to rest. I was feeling faint earlier."

"Oh, yes, that was how we met the count," Mina says. "He gallantly gave her his chair."

"Poor Lucy. We will go at once." Mamma smiles at the widow. "Mrs. Edgerton, I hope you will visit us soon. You are welcome at any time. One must not be alone so much."

"Yes, perhaps, thank you," Mrs. Edgerton says quietly.

Mamma, Mina, and I head toward home just as one last cloud obscures the sun on its way out to sea. The sudden gloom jars the brilliance like an incorrectly played note in a piece of music and only intensifies my ill humor. I remain silent as my mother and Mina discuss the widow.

"How reserved Mrs. Edgerton is," Mina says. "She seems lonely. I feel for her."

My mother nods. "She's a bit of a shrinking violet. Lucy and I try to befriend her, but she always has some flimsy excuse for not accepting our invitations. It would be good for her to marry again and choose someone who seems as sociable as the count."

"He is still a stranger," Mina protests gently. "We know next to nothing about him."

"Well, then, we should throw them together a few more times," my mother says with a dazzling smile. "Perhaps if I had a tall, dark, and handsome count on hand, we could finally induce her to come over for tea. What do you think, Lucy?"

"Oh, Mamma, do leave the poor woman alone," I say, exasperated. "I have always liked her despite her aloofness. She clearly enjoys her solitude, and I think she is brave for remaining unmarried. In fact, I envy her the freedom of widowhood."

"Lucy!" Mina says, shocked.

I shrug. "It is plain to see that Mrs. Edgerton has had a difficult life, *and* she was married to an old man. We ought to leave her in peace and let her be unattached if she likes."

"Perhaps she only remained so because the right man never appeared . . . until now," says my mother with mischievous sparkle, unbothered by my protests. She glances down at my arm, which is linked in hers. "Why, Lucy, have you left your reticule behind?"

I sigh. "It must still be on that table. I will go back."

"Let me. You ought to go home," Mina offers, but I shake my head and hurry off, eager to be alone. I have had more than enough of other women fussing and blushing over Vlad for today, after more than a month of having him to myself. I fume as I stalk back toward the post office, thinking he might have spared me a kind word today after all the time we have spent together and after I had almost caught my death of cold last night on his account.

My reticule is not on the table. I bend to look beneath it, frustrated, and when I straighten, Vlad is standing next to me. My little blue silk handbag is dangling from his long fingers.

"Did you steal my reticule?" I ask, annoyed.

He holds it just out of reach, his eyes bright. "How else could I speak to you alone?" he asks, keeping his distance with all the curious eyes on us. I am sure we make a striking pair: me in cornflower blue with my hair swept up beneath my hat, and him tall and imposing in all black.

"You didn't seem very keen to speak to me when Mina was here," I say coldly.

"Lucy, please don't be angry with me," he coaxes, handing me my reticule as though it is a peace offering. His voice is soft with regret. "I was trying to protect you. We wouldn't want Mina to realize that you are more to me than just a stranger, would we?"

I loop the chain over my arm. "You have no shortage of willing company now, so I am no longer necessary. Perhaps you will find someone more worthy of knowing about your journey."

"Come to me tonight and I will tell you everything. I promise." His hand reaches out to touch my arm, just stopping short. "You know how much you mean to me. You weren't jealous, were you?" He speaks in a kind, pleasant, and cajoling way, so reminiscent of our earliest evenings together, but on his face is a smirk that strengthens my resolve.

"I will not be coming tonight. Good day, *Count*," I say, turning on my heel.

Vlad walks beside me, matching me step for step. "I *did* want to tell you what happened on the *Demeter*, but I couldn't until we were alone. You understand that, don't you?"

My curiosity is unbearable, but he knows it and he is smug, and he thinks he can beckon to or ignore me as though I am a dog. I stop in my tracks and look up at him. "I cannot see you anymore, Vlad. You are here in town. You have met people I love. I do not know how any of this is possible, but I *do* know that it is no longer a dream atop the cliffs. It is a reality now, and it is dangerous. *You* are dangerous."

He takes a step closer to me, his eyes moving all over my face like a caress. "When did danger ever frighten you, my Lucy?" he asks softly.

"You hurt me last night," I say, unable to keep my lips from trembling. I turn away from him. "The pain in my head, the invasion of my thoughts. I don't know how you did those things, but it was not the act of a friend. And you hurt me today by ignoring me."

"I am truly sorry," he says quietly. "I only wanted to know what you were thinking. I want to be important to you, the way you are to me. Let me make amends." He bends to look beneath my hat, his face earnest. "Come tonight and you will know all. I give you my word."

I look up at him, torn between fear and frustration, curiosity and longing. As I hesitate, the clouds shift in the sky and sunlight bursts out upon Whitby in all its blinding radiance. I shield my eyes with my hand, but when I lower it again, Vlad is gone and I am standing alone.

CHAPTER EIGHTEEN

T hat night, in my dreams, I find myself on an empty stretch of beach in front of a stately house, white with blue shutters, standing snug against the rocks and facing the sea. It looks like a fairy tale, all drooping vines and beach roses blooming against the sand. Light winks from one of the windows. Through the fog, I climb onto the veranda, find the door open, and enter an elegant and sumptuously decorated hall. Gold framed art hangs on the walls, curtains spill puddles of dark brocade upon the rich carpet, and fresh flowers burst from marble vases on every surface.

I hear harp music as clear, golden, and sparkling as champagne, the melody rising and falling as naturally as breathing. I follow the sound into a parlor lit by dozens of slim white candles and find Diana Edgerton on a velvet stool beside a great, shining brass harp, her dainty fingers plucking its strings with practiced ease and confidence.

"Mrs. Edgerton?" I ask, surprised.

She neither responds nor looks at me. In fact, she seems to be asleep. Her gleaming light brown hair hangs about her shoulders in waves, her eyes are half-closed, and her lips are parted as though in ecstasy. Her lace nightdress is slipping, revealing a round white shoulder as she plays the harp. A dark ribbon woven into her hair cascades down one side of her neck. I cannot help staring, never having seen the shy and retiring widow so full of life and passion.

"She bloomed like a rose for me," Vlad says, and I turn to see him on a sofa nearby. "Her soul has been sleeping for years and unfurls only with her music. What depths she conceals, what secret desires no man can satisfy, least of all that doddering old husband of hers. She is not like you, Lucy, with your anger and ferocity and fathomless longing right at the surface."

"Why are we here?" I ask uneasily.

"I thought I would expand your social circle."

"Why have you called to me when you already have company?" I ask, affronted. "You said you would tell me everything when we were alone, and we are not."

Vlad regards me for a moment. "You are quite right. Allow me to rectify that."

He gets up and moves to Mrs. Edgerton's side. As gently as a lover, he moves her curtain of hair behind her, exposing her neck. And I realize that what I thought was a ribbon is actually a stream of dark liquid, trailing from a wound and soiling the pristine white lace of her nightgown. It glistens bright red as she continues playing her music in a joyous trance, unbothered.

My hands fly up to my own throat as a terrible shiver takes hold of me. I feel deathly cold as I take in the two gaping holes on Mrs. Edgerton's slender neck. Blood weeps onto her gown and yet her face registers neither pain nor horror, only a chilling and perfect bliss so at odds with her condition. But there is something else beneath my fear—something I recognize, shocked, as envy. I am *jealous* of how happy and content she looks, such as I have never been in all my life.

Vlad is watching me with silent intensity.

"What is happening to her?" I croak.

"She is dying," he says, kneeling behind her. He wraps his arms around her and rests his chin on her shoulder. She leans her head back adoringly on him with no interruption in the music, no pause of her fingers on the strings. "Have you ever seen the life leave a person, Lucy?"

"Yes," I say, thinking of Papa and of my grandmother, motionless in her bed.

"But have you ever seen it leave like this?" He kisses Mrs. Edgerton's naked shoulder, and I see that his eyes have changed. Instead of their usual deep blue-green, they have become entirely black with a ring of poisonous red encircling each pupil. He offers me a wide smile, and the candlelight glints on his perfect white teeth, two of which have elongated like daggers of bone. The space between them is exactly the same distance as that which separates the holes on the woman's neck, and my breath snags in my chest as I realize . . . I *realize* . . .

Vlad lowers his mouth in one smooth, merciless maneuver, puncturing her with his long, sharp teeth. I hear his lips moving like the softest of kisses, and she moans as her body seizes—with pain or pleasure? Her music never ceases as she thrashes in his embrace with unadulterated elation. I tremble at the sight, but this time the envy, the *want*, is stronger than the horror. I have never seen such unbridled passion outside of my dreams. Vlad's hand slides to Mrs. Edgerton's breast as he deepens his kiss, adjusting the angle of his lips, and I let out a ragged breath.

After what seems like an eternity, her hands fall from the harp. The air hangs heavy with her unfinished music as she sinks against Vlad, bone white and drained of life. He detaches his mouth and faces me, teeth gleaming scarlet in the light. Slowly, deliberately, he licks them clean, then wipes his mouth with her nightdress and pushes her away as he stands, his eyes returning to their normal color. Mrs. Edgerton slumps to the floor at the base of her harp, head tilted back, her wounds no longer seeping. And I remember what Harriet had said about the *Demeter*'s luckless crew, of which only the captain and a single sailor had remained, dead and empty of blood: "Such a large vessel must have left port with a sizable crew," she had told us. "What became of all the others, no one can guess."

"It was you," I breathe. "You came in on the *Demeter*, as you said you would. You sailed from Varna, and you *drank* the crew members. Did you . . . dispose of all the other men?" In my mind's eye, I see pale drained bodies slipping into the sea one by one.

"Yes. Unfortunately there was no time to hide the two left on board. The storm pushed us into harbor too quickly and people were running to help, and I had to get myself away as soon as possible."

For a moment, there is no sound but my labored breathing. "How did you disembark? People only saw a dog—"

"In town this morning," he says calmly, straightening the collar of his shirt, "did you not notice how interested that tiny creature was in me? What was its name . . . Crumpet?"

"Biscuit," I say faintly.

Vlad shrugs his powerful shoulders. "Animals always know. They have stronger senses than humans, and our friend Biscuit recognized me. He can see better, smell better, and move faster than you, and he might even outrun me . . . or at least try. But you, Lucy, would not be able to. You could not hide from me anywhere in the world if I wished to find you."

It is clear from the curious and intent way in which he studies me that I am being tested. He is weighing my words and my reaction. He knows I am unlike others of my society; he knows that death attracts and compels me, but how will I respond when it stares me in the face with scarlet-stained teeth? I feel, then, the urge to show him that I am more equal to him than any other woman who blushed for him today.

"You say that Biscuit recognized what you . . . what you are today." My eyes flicker to Diana Edgerton's crumpled body. "And here I thought you were just good with dogs."

Genuine surprise flickers across Vlad's face. He laughs, the sound warm and inviting, and the candles seem to burn more brightly around us. He looks at me, his strong and handsome face alight, and I know that I have passed his test. "What a marvel you are, my little Lucy, my kindred soul," he says affectionately. "Are you not afraid of me in the least?"

"Of course I am. I would be a fool otherwise."

"Quite."

I cannot stop looking at the corpse. "But I am as curious as I am afraid. I ought to be more disturbed by the manner in which you took her life. But it makes me want to *know*," I say, and with the admission comes the smallest bit of shame. Any other person would be running and screaming, disturbed by the scene, and here I am wishing to learn. It would be easier to shrug away my morbid desire in a dream . . . but now I know that this is reality.

Vlad seems to take it as a matter of course, however. He is as focused on me now as he was distant this morning. "Ask your questions, then," he says indulgently, sitting back down on the sofa and gesturing for me to take Mrs. Edgerton's abandoned stool. I obey, angling my feet to avoid the woman's still-warm body. "I will answer whatever you want to know."

"Who are you?" I ask at once. "What are you? And why do you drink blood?"

He laughs again. "I am who I say I am. The names and titles I gave you and Miss Murray this afternoon do belong to me, but only *you* know my private, given name. That is how special you are to me." His eyes are soft on mine, and in that moment—try as I might to fight it—I feel myself forgive him. "I told you that in life, I was a scholar, a statesman, a philosopher, a warrior. Since then, I have inhabited many existences in many ages."

"You are no longer alive?"

"Not in the way you are." Vlad places a hand on his broad chest. "You see me before you, yet my heart does not beat. I breathe, yet my lungs do not need air. I am a being of fearsome physical and intellectual faculties . . . and I ought to be. I gave up my very soul for it long ago."

I grip the edge of the stool. "Then death cannot touch you?"

"Not in the way that it does humans, but make no mistake, I *can* die." His smile is a thing of ferocious beauty. "I was born into a powerful family, but with power comes the fight to keep it. My father's lands were torn between dueling empires and allegiances. Like you, I saw much loss in my youth. And when I in my turn became the lord of my people and inherited my father's enemies, I heard the footsteps of death behind me wherever I went." He pauses. "And that would simply not do."

I feel as though I have forgotten how to breathe. "And so you cheated death?"

"In a way. But death is forever the last, the greatest, and the ultimate enemy, and it holds sway even over the bargain I made." Vlad gazes out the window to where the sea roars, invisible in the shadows. "I was accepted into a . . . what is the English word? An academy, deep in the dark heart of the Carpathians. A school to which all of the sons of my family had been invited for centuries but had always refused out of fear. This place is a secret I must keep even from you, Lucy. Its whereabouts, what I learned . . . and who taught there. But this I can tell you: I was the first of my family to go, the only one brave enough." His eyes meet mine once more. "Seven students are accepted every seven years, and the greatest of these, the Master takes for his own."

"You."

"Me. At his feet, I learned about immortality and traded in my soul to become what I am now: vampyr. A vampire. But in return for my gifts of power, strength, and long life, I must drink the blood of mankind." He looks down at the corpse with detachment. "That is how I sustain myself and how I repay death for escaping its gaze: by taking other lives in the place of my own. Just as there must be a balance in the natural world, there must be a balance in the *unnatural*."

I exhale at last, my body shuddering with relief. "You are the only one of your kind?"

"No," he says, soft and contemplative. "There are two others like me, created by me, but far inferior. Over the centuries, I have taken a small number of men and women as lovers and confidantes, but I always end them when the time comes, and I am careful when I drink now. I will not be like the Greeks' Cronus, forever waiting for one of my children to overthrow me."

"*Created* by you? You turn them into vampires by drinking their blood?" I ask, looking down at Mrs. Edgerton's corpse in mingled anxiety and fascination. "Will she revive?"

"No. Nor will any of the crew of the *Demeter*, I'm afraid." Vlad gets up and walks over to the window to gaze up at the moon. "Draining a human of every drop will simply kill them. Creating another of my kind takes a bit more forethought than that."

I wait eagerly, but he does not explain further, and something about his pensive silence warns me not to press him now. "Why are you telling me all this?" I ask instead. "You were evasive when I asked you about the *Demeter* earlier."

"You expected me to speak of this in front of Mina, that fragile flower you love so much? No, I cannot be open with her. Only with you." He turns and looks at me with wonder and affection. "I never expected the mist to bring you. I never called to you those times before you came to Whitby, you know. And yet some sense or awareness helped you find me somehow."

"The mist?" In my mind, I see open graves, marble statues, a moonlit ballroom. A path of thorns tipped with red and all around us, the silvery blanket of the mist rising, hiding our kisses and my bare arms around his neck and his head tucked against mine.

He lifts his hand, and outside the window a thread of mist appears. "I use it to call to other dreamers. It is how I came to see the land I would call home whilst still on board a ship. It was a tedious necessity, that long route by sea. It took more than a month, but had I gone over land, there would have been curious eyes, train delays, and prying tax collectors. A ship is a world of its own, one that humans cannot easily leave any time they wish."

"How frightened the crew must have been of you," I say softly. I imagine being trapped on a vessel tossing in the turbulent sea, unable to escape as something with red-ringed pupils and teeth like knives stalked me in the shadows. Bodies being drained, one by one, with ruthless efficiency. I resist the urge to shudder, for Vlad is watching me closely. "My maid heard that the *Demeter* carried a curious cargo: thirty boxes full of earth."

"It is the soil of my homeland. The earth on which my many castles, my sanctuaries sit. I plan to distribute the boxes throughout England, so that I may have a resting place wherever I go, away from human eyes and from the sun, which I cannot abide, as you saw this afternoon."

"The sun hurts you? Powerful and immortal as you are?"

He chuckles, pleased, though I had been stating a fact and not attempting flattery. "Yes. I, too, have my limitations, insignificant as they are." He approaches a mirror on the wall, and I expect to see his reflection looking at me, but the glass only shows the room around us. "Mirrors no longer see me. They are backed by silver, which is said to repel evil. Nor can I be painted, for any attempt to capture my likeness becomes warped. Twisted. But these are mere trifles in exchange for everlasting life, do you not agree?"

"I don't know," I whisper, staring at the empty place where his reflection ought to be.

"I cannot enter a home without invitation. But that would be rude, so I am glad for that limitation." He turns to me with a touch of humor. "The very sight or smell of garlic offends me. Something to do with its ability to cleanse the blood, which is anathema to the venom I carry. But I have never liked pungent flavors and smells anyway, and all human food is repellent to me now."

For some perverse reason, I am reminded of Mamma and Arthur and their aversion to Papa's tea and incense, and I marvel at the ridiculousness of having such a thought at such a moment. "But the drinking of blood must be a heavy limitation indeed," I say, looking down at Mrs. Egerton's crumpled body, my heart aching at how fragile and pale she looks in death. At how easily her flame was snuffed out. "To take a life as though you are a god."

Vlad shakes his head dismissively. "That cannot stop me. I can subsist on animals if need be. And as for the sun burning my skin, that matters little when I have always preferred the night. So many more interesting things can happen in the dark, don't you think?" There is a hunger now in the way he looks at me, not that of a beast for his prey, but an empty, fathomless longing.

And God help me, I feel my heart and soul respond to him, this being of unnatural gifts and untold power who, even in his invincibility, might just understand my loneliness. Perhaps that is why I do not feel as afraid as I should be . . . because I know that beneath his monstrous nature, he is vulnerable, and he has chosen to show that to me. This man who trusts no one.

"I almost died from boredom on that ship," he says, mouth quirking at his own choice of words, "as we sailed slowly west through Gibraltar and then north through the Celtic Sea. But I had you, Lucy. You who are young and innocent and yet seem to understand that I did not so much as take this woman's life as I gave her a moment of the perfect happiness that had always eluded her. The grand passion of which she dreamed . . . and of which you dream, too," he adds, so knowingly that I blush. "And now that I have told you everything, I would like you to do something for *me*. I am in need of music. Will you play?"

I glance at the harp in surprise. "I am much better at the piano."

"Indulge me."

I tentatively touch the strings, half fearing that they might still be warm from the widow's touch, but they are not. "You request that I play? You do not compel me as you did her?"

His eyes gleam. "I like you with free will. Now, no more talking. Play something."

Mamma had always insisted that I learn and excel at music. I had hated the piano as a child, but as I grew older, I saw that it was a useful excuse to be the center of attention at parties and allowed men to watch me openly. I had only ever played the harp with Mina, who had taught me some duets, sitting side by side, our four hands making a beautiful harmony. It is the opening chord of one of those duets that I play now, though I will perform alone . . . or so I think.

As my fingers play the notes with an ease that does justice to Mina's teaching, I sense Vlad moving behind me. I hold my breath at the nearness of him, and my heart races as his white hands reach out on either side of me. But instead of touching me, his fingers find the harp and he begins to play, with perfect precision, the other half of the duet. His breath stirs my hair as he moves even closer to me, the buttons of his waistcoat pressing into the back of my nightgown.

In a daze, I shift forward to the very edge of the velvet stool, my knees touching the sides of the harp. There is no break in the music as Vlad sits behind me, his arms and legs framing mine. He buries his face in my hair as he plays, and I shiver uncontrollably, never having felt so close to him before, even after so many embraces in the night. I am helpless, lost in his body like a shell in the arms of the sea. I lean into him and feel his icy lips on my bare shoulder.

The tempo of the music increases with the intensity of his kisses. His mouth explores me with light scrapes of his teeth, and I gasp. This passage of the duet requires him to play the strings at the very center of the harp, and his arms tighten around me as he takes the melody and I the harmony, my fingers somehow steady even though every nerve is blazing with need for him. His lips push my nightdress off my shoulder, exposing the vulnerable, pristine skin of my neck.

Half of me is terribly afraid, remembering the holes in Mrs. Edgerton's neck and imagining my fragile flesh tearing beneath his teeth. But the other half burns with unquenchable lust and desire, needing him to enter me as badly as I need air. "Please," I moan, though I am not even certain what I am begging for. "Please, Vlad."

With one hand still playing, he takes the other and pulls the nightdress farther down to expose my left breast. His cold fingers cup me tenderly as his thumb finds my nipple, sending waves of unbearable excitement through me. Never have I been touched this way, and I wonder how on earth I have lived without it before now. I lean fully against him, not caring if I send us both over the back of the stool, but he is like solid granite resisting me. His thumb strokes, his mouth tastes, and I no longer have any idea what melody I am playing.

I am as wet where I sit as if I had lowered myself into the ocean. As the music escalates into a rising crescendo, I feel as though I am running up, up, up a hill with my arms flung wide open, anticipating the blissful moment when I will plummet down the other side.

Vlad's hand leaves my breast to find my throat. I feel a sharp, hot sting as his fingernails scratch the skin below my ear, and then his mouth is there, sucking greedily at my blood, though he is careful to keep his teeth away. I close my eyes and let out a long moan as the downhill comes and colors explode behind my lids. It is as exhilarating a freefall as jumping off the cliffs toward certain death. My hands drop away from the harp at last and I shake like a leaf in his arms, gripped by overwhelming sensations, as he finishes drinking me with a soft kiss.

His low laugh tickles my ear. "Sleep now, Lucy. I will see you again soon."

I blink my eyes, and the candlelit parlor is gone. I am lying in bed next to Mina, who is fast asleep with her cheek pillowed on her hand. Outside the window, the sky is still dark, and my room is wreathed in shadows as though I have been here all night, like I am supposed to be.

Like a good girl should be.

But when I sit up and meet the eyes of my own reflection in the mirror above my dressing table, I see that my disheveled hair is coming out of its plait and my nightdress is pooling around my waist. I am damp between my legs, and when I touch the left side of my neck, I gasp when my fingers come away with the faintest trace of blood.

I cannot help smiling at my reflection because I know that I am not a good girl.

I am not a good girl at all.

CHAPTER NINETEEN

A ll my life, I have believed one truth: that I am born to marry, to give birth, and then die.

Never in the farthest reaches of my trapped and anguished soul had I ever imagined an alternative. Never in my duality—half of me resigned to the expectations of society and the other half yearning for the grave—had I considered that there might be a way out.

Now, I know that it is possible to cheat death and to live on without bending to the rules of humanity. My soul has heard the music of immortality, of boundless time to do everything I have ever dreamed of doing, and now that it has awakened, it will never sleep again.

Vampyr. Vampire. The words run through my mind like a melody.

Vlad does not summon me for a week after our duet, and outwardly, I am as obedient to Mamma and Mina as they could wish: I sleep all night without leaving my bed, pay calls whenever they ask me to, and pretend to choose flowers and linens for my wedding. But inside, I am reliving that evening over and over again and rejoicing that I will never have to leave the ones I love. Death would have freed me, but also torn me from Mamma, Mina, and Arthur. I would have inflicted upon them the same pain that has tortured me since Papa's passing.

Now, they will have me forever and I will love them for as long as they live. I can marry Arthur and make him happy, knowing it will not be the end for me. After him, there will be infinite centuries in which I can walk the earth and savor my freedom.

Vlad had spoken carelessly of the limitations of his power, and they would mean just as little to me. I could feed on animal blood and not harm a soul. I could sleep during the day to avoid the sun. And I would never be alone. I would have Vlad to teach me, guide me, and protect me for eternity, and in return, I would be his lover and confidante and stave off his loneliness.

I am not so silly as to imagine perfection, nor would I want anything like an eternal marriage. I desire him, admire him, and yes, I care for him . . . but he has tendencies that disturb me, not least of all the invasion of my mind at will. If the need arose, we could occupy separate countries or even continents for as many years as we wished, and then find each other again.

I have thought it all over. And I am finally happy, so happy I could dance and sing.

That is what I tell Arthur, even if he does not believe me. He came back to Whitby from London two nights ago and keeps watching me in a thoughtful way. Not once have I made any inappropriate advances toward him, and my new reticence worries him.

"Lucy, are you angry with me?" he asks wistfully.

It is a bright, sunny morning in mid-August, so warm that Mamma proposed breakfast in the garden. And then, so smoothly that it could only have been planned, she and Mina vanished into the house with excuses, leaving me alone with Arthur. I am seated by the rosebush, watching butterflies float by as blithely as if they could never die. But they *will* die. Everything dies. It is only Vlad who lives on, and I wish to live on beside him.

I smile across the table at Arthur. "Why would I be angry with you after you came all this way, and I missed you so much, and you brought us such lovely gifts?" Thoughtful, generous Arthur had come bearing flowers and trinkets for everyone, even Mina, and had presented me with a sapphire necklace, another heirloom piece from his family's vault.

"I don't know," he says. "You have been quieter than usual. Pensive, I think."

I laugh. "What should I be pensive for? I am with the people I love best in all the world, it is a beautiful day, and I feel as though I could live forever and ever and ever." I lean back in my chair and stretch my arms lazily toward the brilliant blue sky.

Arthur relaxes, hearing me laugh. "And you haven't kissed me once yet," he says shyly.

"How neglectful of me," I say playfully. "Come over here and I will make amends."

He gets up at once and moves around the table, bending down to meet my lips. I breathe in his familiar pine scent, enjoying the feel of his mouth moving gently on mine. He kisses with such consideration, never asking more of me than I give, a sharp contrast to Vlad's possessiveness. Thinking of Vlad as I kiss Arthur is so jarring that I pull away before I mean to. The concern comes back into Arthur's expression, and I reach up to touch his face, soothing him.

"I love you," he says, with such artless truth in his honest hazel eyes that I impulsively wrap my arms around his neck, moved almost to tears. He kneels in the grass beside my chair and gathers me close to him, as he had done the night he had proposed.

I kiss his cheek. "And I love you. I'm sorry for worrying you. I didn't mean to."

"I'm sure your mind is occupied by wedding plans. Your mamma tells me you have been busy sending invitations." Arthur pulls back to look at me fondly, and his gaze falls upon the left side of my neck. "What is this? Did you hurt yourself?"

I press a hand over the skin where Vlad's scratches have healed but are still visible as red lines. And now I am thinking of Vlad again, damn him, while Arthur is looking at me in that innocent way. "I was petting a neighbor's cat and it did not like my attentions," I say, and because the lie sounds thin even to me, I add, to distract him, "Well, darling, how about a stroll into town? I would love to show you around Whitby."

"Could we go to the cliffs?" he asks eagerly. "The breeze might be cooler there."

I hesitate. I have not been there with anyone but Vlad all summer, and it almost feels like betraying him to bring Arthur there. But then again, I owe him nothing. And he need not know, for he would likely not be out in all this sunshine. "Let me get my hat," I say.

Within minutes, Arthur and I are walking arm in arm toward the sea. He prattles on about everything under the sun—our acquaintances in London, his mother's desire to go abroad again, and rearranging the gardens on his estate. I try to listen and show interest in these everyday subjects that he considers so absorbing, even as I find myself searching the faces of men passing by.

All week, I have only encountered Vlad in the conversation of others.

"The count was at Mrs. Whitaker's card party last night! What a fine figure of a man."

"That foreign chap, Count what's-his-name? From Russia, or some such place. He's really rather a decent fellow—insisted on paying far too much for my old curricle."

"At the Parkers' supper, I asked if he was married, and he spoke most pleasingly for half an hour and quite turned my head around. Never did answer, though."

"The count seemed upset about poor Diana Edgerton's disappearance and the fact that she simply up and left without telling anyone or even shutting up her house. The two of them had been friendly, you know. She was the first person in Whitby to whom he spoke."

When Mamma's friend had said that, I had pressed my lips tightly together. No one knows *I* was Vlad's first friend, long before any other swooning girl. It has been frightfully irritating, wondering if he has not called to me this week because he is with some other woman who caught his eye, perhaps calling her his *kindred soul* . . . or considering giving her his gift.

"Lucy, did you hear what I said?" Arthur asks, a bit impatiently.

I bring myself back with a powerful effort. "No. Could you say it again, my love?"

"I only wondered if you would dance with me tonight. That's all."

I laugh and kiss the shoulder of his jacket as we walk. "I would dance with you anywhere and at any time you wished," I say cheerfully. "I would dance with you right now on this path, if you asked me to. But why tonight especially?"

"You really *haven't* heard a word of what I said," he tells me, his brow furrowing. "It's the Wilcoxes' ball tonight, of course. I've been talking about it for the last five minutes."

I had forgotten about the damn ball. "I am delighted that you're escorting me. The Wilcoxes are quite wild to meet you after how much I've talked about you! I was only distracted because I was pondering which dress you would think me prettiest in." I have been flirting for far too long not to know what men like to hear, and I feel Arthur's unease fade at once.

He looks around to see if anyone is watching, then ducks his head under my hat to kiss me. "You look pretty in everything," he says softly, and I feel the old quiet tug of longing for him. I hug his arm tight, wishing I could be the simple, uncomplicated girl he deserves. "And I am certain you will look like an angel at our wedding. Only one more month until you are all mine, Lucy, and I am going to make you so happy."

"You already do," I say, kissing his shoulder again.

We ascend a steep section of the path and Arthur holds on to my waist to steady me, unaware that I know this climb like the back of my own hand. "Speaking of the ball, I heard there might be some distinguished people attending tonight," he says. "Did you know you have foreign nobility visiting? Someone mentioned a count from Bulgaria. Or was it Germany?"

My heart seizes. "Yes, Mina and I met him briefly in town one day," I say offhandedly to hide my confusion. For some reason, I had never imagined Arthur and Vlad crossing paths. And why shouldn't they? No one would blink an eye at the man I am engaged to marry making the acquaintance of the man I have recently met, and only Vlad and I would know the truth. I wonder if I will be able to hide, on my own face, the memory of his hips framing mine and his eager mouth on my neck. Mamma and Mina can never know. *Arthur* can never know.

"Would you like to sit down for a while?" Arthur asks.

To my horror, he is pointing directly to the stone bench where Vlad and I meet. "Let's sit elsewhere," I say, my cheeks hot with guilt and embarrassment at the prospect of sitting with him where I had kissed and embraced another, thinking it was only a dream. "I don't like that one."

"Why not?" he asks, surprised. "It has a wonderful view."

"Many of the other benches do, too," I point out.

"And it looks so romantic with the willow branches hanging down, doesn't it?"

I tug at his arm, nearing desperation now. "Come, let's go farther down the path."

"But it looks so nice and cool in the shade of that tree—"

"Arthur, please," I say, more sharply than I had intended. "I don't want to sit there. I'm afraid of falling. It makes me nervous to be that close to the cliff's edge."

His face is a mixture of hurt and bewilderment. "Would you rather not sit at all?"

"I would prefer to show you around town. The heat is beastly up here, and I want you to see the streets of Whitby at their best." I take his hand in both of mine and lead him away. He is silent as we walk, still looking wounded and confused, so I whisper, "I'm glad you're here."

"Are you?" he asks and does not speak all the way back down.

That night, Mamma, Mina, and I enter the Wilcoxes' beautiful home, escorted by Arthur. The heat of the day has vanished, and a cool wind is blowing in off the sea, prompting us to bring wraps. We are greeted at the door by Amelia Wilcox, a cheerful, energetic girl about my age who just married this spring. Her husband, Edgar, is a loud, boisterous, and jovial man who is thirty years older than she and whose normal speech is almost always a shout.

"Glad to see you, Audrey!" he bellows at Mamma. "Don't stand on ceremony! Give your wraps to Desmond. Desmond, don't make these ladies carry their own things! Miss Murray, a pleasure! And little Lucy, of course! Though not so little anymore." He scans me appreciatively in my white dress with silver embroidery, the neckline just low enough to tempt the imagination.

Meanwhile, his wife is gazing admiringly at Arthur. "You must be Mr. Holmwood. How coy Lucy is! She didn't say you were *this* tall and handsome. Have you chosen a wedding day?"

"The twenty-eighth of September," Arthur says, blushing.

The ballroom spans the width of the house and boasts ocean-blue walls and mother-of-pearl floors. The musicians play a merry waltz, though not many are dancing yet, preferring instead to mingle or partake in the refreshments. Everyone is dressed in their finest, and my vain heart—not to be quenched even in my almost-married state—rejoices to see that most women have chosen jewel-toned gowns, making my white one stand out to anyone looking for me.

My ever-popular mamma is swept away into a group of gossiping ladies, and Arthur finds chairs for Mina and me before going off in search of champagne for us.

"What a dreadful crowd," Mina says, smoothing the skirt of her forest-green gown. "I would have much rather stayed home and waited for the mail. Sometimes letters come late."

I have been scanning the faces without finding the one I seek, but at her words, I turn to her and take her hand. "I am certain Jonathan will write soon," I say with a twinge of guilt for having been so absorbed in my own affairs that I had all but forgotten hers. "But I know he loves you very much and would want you to laugh and dance, not stay at home all alone."

Mina laughs. "Who would ask me to dance?"

"I would," says a deep voice.

Vlad is standing in front of us. All the other men are wearing black tonight, but he is dressed in crimson velvet, drawing admiring glances from everyone in the room. He gives an elegant bow and extends a hand to Mina. Even though he is ignoring me once again, I can feel how aware of me he is, especially after our evening of playing music in the dark.

"Miss Murray, may I have the honor of your first dance?" he asks.

Mina turns red. "You are very kind, Count, but—"

"Forgive me. I understand you are engaged to a fortunate man, and if he were here, I would ask his permission," Vlad says gently. "This would be a dance between friends only."

She smiles at his charming, old-fashioned courtesy. "You are very thoughtful, but—"

Arthur returns at that moment with champagne, and he and Vlad look at each other. I cannot help fidgeting in my chair at how amusing and embarrassing it is to see them together. They are almost of an equal height, but Arthur resembles a young and gangly calf beside a powerful bull, standing next to the imposing older man.

The men bow and introduce themselves, Vlad delivering the names and titles he had given Mina and me that day in town. "I met Miss Murray and your lovely bride-to-be the other day, and as I hope to continue the conversation, I am asking Miss Murray to dance."

"Ah, Miss Murray! I see," Arthur says, looking relieved.

But Mina shakes her head. "I'm very sorry, but I do not wish to dance with anyone but my fiancé. Tonight or any other night."

"Of course. I understand completely." Vlad looks at Arthur. "Well, here is a fiancé whose permission I may ask, though I daresay your Lucy will have the same misgivings."

Arthur looks taken aback, and I know it is not lost on him that Mina is *Miss Murray* while I am *Lucy*. "It's her decision to make," he says uneasily, and they both look at me, him with apprehension and Vlad with an ironic smile. They have put me in the position of openly choosing between them and having to be disloyal either to one or the other.

But I have never liked the games men make us play.

"My first dance," I say archly, "will be given to he who amuses me the most. So I suggest you each think of something clever to say or do. A joke, perhaps, or a little jig?"

Mina utters a shocked laugh. "Lucy, they are gentlemen. Not dancing monkeys!"

Arthur looks bewildered, but Vlad says at once, his lips twitching, "I know a secret about two people in this room. One has lived for far too long and the other has not lived nearly enough, yet they are as alike as petals on the same porcelain rose."

"Is this a riddle, Count?" Mina asks, intrigued. "Why a *porcelain* rose and not fresh?"

"Because a porcelain rose lasts much, much longer," I say, and Vlad's eyes flash at me with humor and approval. "Arthur, my dear, the count has presented a riddle as his way of amusing me. What do you have to offer this evening?"

But Arthur is not in the mood. He looks down at his shoes, frustrated by a conversation he does not understand. "I have nothing clever enough. She is yours, Count."

"Mine? What a generous man you are, Mr. Holmwood," Vlad says with a wolfish smile.

I get up and take Arthur's hand. "I will save every other dance for you, my love," I say, and he gives a gruff nod and sits down next to Mina. And then I am free to take Vlad's hand in front of my friend and my fiancé. "Shall we?"

Vlad leads me to the center of the ballroom, where five other couples are dancing. Even so, I know instinctively that everyone is watching the two of us, and that in Vlad's arms, I must look as fragile and dainty as a flower plucked by his brutal hand. The silver threads in my gown catch the light as we move. He is as divine at the waltz as he is at everything else, which is unsurprising now that I know he has had multiple lifetimes to perfect every skill.

"Your fiancé is a very earnest, forthright young man," he says. "Full of feeling and nobility and, I believe, very deep love for you."

"Arthur is the best of men." My tone is almost defensive, perhaps because of the dry sarcasm I hear in Vlad's words. "He is honest and true, and I am proud to be his."

He chuckles. "How loyal of you. Perhaps you are more like Miss Murray than I thought."

"Even though I am only your second choice?"

Vlad looks down at me, his eyes as affectionate as they are pleased. He likes the touch of jealousy in my voice. "I asked Mina first because I knew she would refuse me. I cannot seek you out too obviously, or else I would make an enemy of your dashing Arthur." His hand on my waist pulls me a bit closer. "But you are my first choice, Lucy. Always my first."

"Then why have you not called me to you?" I ask, hating myself for the yearning in my question. I am not often ashamed to want to be with Vlad, but it feels different when Arthur is in the room with us. "I waited all week. I wondered if you had found another beautiful widow."

He laughs. "I have had business to attend to. Purchasing a property in England comes with a great deal of paperwork. Believe me, I would have much rather spent my nights with you." He strokes his thumb over my hand. "I have missed you. It surprises even me how much."

"Then call to me tonight. I need to see you."

"And what of your Arthur?"

I feel once more the clench of shame in my gut. "We will only talk, you and I," I say decisively. "It is no betrayal of him to have a simple conversation with you, is it?"

"Only talk?" Vlad repeats, his smile widening. "We *do* talk well together, don't we, Lucy? But we do other things well together, too." His thumb slowly strokes my hand again, and the aching, delicious memory of it on my breast makes me swallow hard.

"You are here in the flesh now," I say, looking straight at him. "It was different when you were on a ship far away and it felt like some sort of fever dream. But now, when I kiss you, I am kissing *you* . . . not whatever form of you I was kissing on the cliffs."

"Oh, you were kissing me," he says with knowing, vicious delight. "I can separate my physical self, one half in a state of rest elsewhere, one half wandering through the mist to you. I have always been with you. Every kiss, every touch has been real, and you know that deep down, no matter how you tried to tell yourself that it was just a dream. It is part of my attraction."

It is only a dream, and no one need know what we do here.

My cheeks burn at the truth in what he says, and the memory of all the excuses I have made to be with him. "I have promised to marry Arthur, and I will be his wife no matter what."

Vlad shrugs. "What does that matter? I care not for human vows. They hold no sanctity for me. What you want from me transcends something as ineffectual as a promise."

"And what do you imagine I want from you?" I ask.

"The world," he says, laughing as he twirls me in the dance.

"And you can give that to me, can you?" I meant to sound tart and flirtatious, retreating into the realm of what I know for comfort. But the question comes out with so much longing that even Vlad's face grows serious. "I am consumed by what you told me that night. About being a vampire." I whisper the word, but still, there is something as thrilling and dangerous about speaking it in company as publicly kissing Vlad fully on the lips would be.

"You truly aren't afraid of me, then?" he asks, shaking his head as though marveling at my naïveté. "I am an undead being who could crack your skull between my fingers like a nut. A monster who drained every last drop of blood from a helpless woman right before your eyes."

I look at the powerful hand cradling mine and the other curved around my waist, soft and protective. "I *am* afraid. But I also sense that you care for me, Vlad."

There is something in his eyes I cannot quite read, perhaps pity or regret. "Do not make the mistake," he says softly, "of ever thinking you are safe with me. For those who amuse and interest me the most, and those I regard most highly, are the ones in the greatest peril."

A sharp stab of jealousy pierces me. "Like Diana Edgerton?"

"She?" He raises a thick black eyebrow. "She was food."

I press my lips to restrain a shocked laugh as we dance past Mamma and her friends, all avidly watching us. "You told me you have created others like yourself before. How do you decide who is food and who is a companion, and how is it done?"

"Food is lonely widows and unfortunate crew members, easily gone and never missed."

A new dance begins. Around us, the couples change partners, but Vlad and I do not let go of each other, which would have been proper. I know that Mamma and Mina will reprimand me and that Arthur will be forlorn, but at this moment I need information like I need air. I look back to where Arthur is sitting and try to tell him, with only my eyes and my smile, how much I love him, how sorry I am to break my promise to save the rest of my dances for him, and how I will make amends. He does not look like he believes me, and I cannot blame him.

"Mrs. Edgerton died," I say, turning back to Vlad. "You drained her. But if you had wanted her to be a companion . . . perhaps you would have left some blood behind? Drank only a little, but not all of it? It's as easy as that?"

Vlad's laugh is full of shadows, though his pleasure is unmistakable. He likes me to be curious and awed by him, and he likes to shape my innocent mind. "*Easy* is not the word I would use," he says. "I bite my victim multiple times, taking care never to drain them. And when they are sufficiently infected with my venom, they must drink *my* blood and make their first kill before the next sunrise. That, my subversive little Lucy, is how it is done."

I shudder, and his eyes glitter with approval, thinking I am terrified and disturbed. But if he were to probe my thoughts and inflict my mind with that sharp, tingling pain, he would know the truth—that I am imagining the multiple times in which his mouth would find my neck and kiss me, bite me, drink me. I am picturing his hands all over my body and his teeth setting me free.

Endless time in which to be with my family, who would never lose me. Endless time to savor the world's delights, to wander, to learn, to *live* as I never imagined I could.

I tighten my grip on his shoulder. "Being a vampire is being more alive than ever, for you are *more* than a man. You have powers unchecked and you are beholden to no rules, least of all those imposed by life and death."

He raises an eyebrow, pleased by the awe in my voice.

"Don't you see? Vlad, it is everything, *everything* I want. What you have is what I desire for myself." I see his smile vanish so suddenly that I miss a step in the dance. "What is it?"

The satisfaction and approval on his face have been replaced by an icy cold so treacherous that it reaches deep into my bones. "What did you say?" he asks, very low.

I do not understand the hatred in his gaze, not when he had looked so tender and amused a moment ago, but I cannot take my words back. So I summon every last drop of courage before his glacial, ferocious eyes and say, "Vlad, make me like you. Make me your companion."

He drops his hands and we stand still, staring at each other, surrounded by swirling dancers. Fury radiates from him like a wildfire, but when he speaks, it is in his softest voice yet. "You dare to command me? You dare to demand this of me?"

I take a step back, frightened and confused. "Of course not. I only meant . . . I . . ."

He is looking at me the way I should have looked at him when he murdered the widow, as though nothing on earth could be more wrong or monstrous or disgusting. "I," he says coldly, "do not take orders from you."

"Vlad, please—"

Without another word, he walks away, leaving me alone on the ballroom floor.

CHAPTER TWENTY

Ignoring the stares and whispers, I follow Vlad onto the terrace. When I shut the doors behind us, muting the voices and music from the ballroom, it is like being in one of my dreams with him again. But this time, he is not looking at me with amusement or affection. He is looking at me as though he would like to tear my head from my neck.

I hug myself, shivering in the chill of the ocean breeze and of his gaze. "Why are you so angry? I never thought to command you. It is a request."

His sharp, gunshot laugh makes me flinch. "As if that is any better!"

"How can you be surprised? Every night we have been together, I have talked of how trapped and helpless I feel, and you have shown me a way out. Don't you see? You showed your true self to me, and this could be my escape to *my* own true self."

"You would so easily give up everything in your life? Your mother, your friends, Arthur?"

I shake my head in confusion. "Why would I give them up? They will have me as long as they live. They need never mourn me the way I do my father." I go to him and clutch the lapels of his jacket. "I have never belonged to the living, neither do I truly wish to be locked away with the dead. You inhabit the world between, and I want to as well."

Vlad plucks my hands off his jacket. He leans in, menacing and deadly, until our noses are almost touching. "What makes you think you have the right to ask this of me? A young woman like you should be modest and pure. Repulsed by the very idea of what I am, no matter how awed and curious you might have been at first. You should be running from me, not *to* me. Have you no dignity or virtue that you would dare choose this?" He turns his back on me and faces the sea, bracing his hands on the railing.

"*You* chose. You chose to bargain away your soul for this existence."

"It is not the same."

"How is it different?" I demand. "I don't understand. We both wish to evade death. You wanted more from life than forever grappling for power, and I want more from life than just becoming a vessel for children and old age. You said it yourself: I am your kindred soul."

He whirls, looking at me with utter disdain. "I talk nonsense when I am infatuated with a woman. And it *was* an infatuation, Lucy. I hope you are not stupid enough to think that I could ever *love* you. You are but a plaything, a diversion in my long and often tedious life, enjoyed briefly and then forgotten. Did you imagine yourself as some sort of dark queen by my side?"

"Of course not, for I do not love you either," I say as steadily as I can to hide my hurt. "It is not love I want from you, but something greater. Something no one has ever given me fully: sympathy and acceptance. You may be a master of deceit, but you cannot hide the truth."

"Enlighten me. What is this truth?" he asks sarcastically.

I meet his eyes without flinching. "That I might be very near your equal in feeling and intellect, even without the advantage of a similar education. What you call an infatuation could become . . . if not love, then genuine regard and friendship, yet you will not give in to it."

Vlad shakes his head and turns away, as though he cannot bear the sight of me.

"What disgusts you is that I am a woman," I say, frustrated. "You and I are the same at our core, but because I am not a man, I ought to be virginal, helpless, and afraid instead of being courageous enough to make the same choice you did. You can't stand that, despite all your years and intelligence, you were wrong about me."

He is not looking at me, but I can feel in my very bones the violent animosity radiating from him. "It is not for a woman to want the unnatural," he says. "This choice is not for her to pursue immodestly, only accept meekly if bestowed upon her."

As afraid as I am, I am angrier. "How could you imagine sharing with me everything that you are and expecting me not to want it, too? You, with your talk of seeing the world, of centuries of learning, of castles and pleasures and delights. You, to whom nothing is limited. No prey can outrun you, no object of desire can deny you, and the few rules that bind you are nothing!"

"Nothing?" Vlad gives me a cruel smile. "I thought you were intelligent, Lucy. You think I gave up my soul for a kind of paradise? A blissful existence of immortality?"

"That was what you told me," I cry. "You said you could not bear the sun or see yourself in a mirror or a painting. These, I can and will give up. You said you could subsist on animal blood, and I could, too, to avoid hurting anyone and—"

Vlad laughs mockingly. "You think not being able to preen in a mirror is the worst part of being a vampire? You simpleton. You utter child. You stand there and tell me to my face that you are my intellectual equal. You puff up with vanity over your romantic conquests and the suitors who would die for you, and yet you have no idea when a man is lying to you."

"Lying? But you had no reflection in the mirror—"

"Lying by omission, my dear." He faces me, and when he speaks again, it is with the pleasant, conversational tone he has always used with me. The ease with which he can switch between kindness and hatred is utterly chilling. "I told you that those who interest me most are in the greatest peril. I used that word, *peril*, and you did not question it. You did not ask why I equate vampirism with being in peril." His gaze is piercing and direct. "There is a reason that it costs such a high price as one's soul. Make no mistake: what I am is a curse."

My temples are pounding with the pain of anger and confusion. "What do you mean? You told me of your limits, of mirrors and sunlight, of sleeping in boxes of earth and not entering homes without invitation, but you made them sound like nothing at all—"

"Haven't you been listening?" Vlad taps my forehead with a cold, mocking finger and I jerk away from his touch. "I was infatuated with your innocence and beauty, and I wanted to awe and shock you. But there is much more to being a vampire than what I chose to tell you. Haven't you wondered why I have so many different homes? Why I am forever moving from this land to that? Why I had to take the longest, loneliest route by sea to England? Because most humans fear me, despise me, and want me dead. I am always running away, Lucy, as powerful as I am, because wherever I go, I will be outnumbered."

I look at him, shivering and silent.

"Most people do not like having a monster among them who might drain them of their blood," he says sardonically. "I am forever in hiding and in disguise. Could you live like that?"

"I already do." I close my eyes and turn away. "I thought you were a god, an immortal being who could hold the entire world in the palm of your hand. How disappointing to find that you are like any other man. You want me to be intelligent, but not more so than you. You want me to be beautiful and tempting, but unaware of it. You were happy to satisfy my curiosity, but now that you have whetted my appetite, you punish me for being hungry." I hate myself for the tremor of tears in my voice, but perhaps this is what saves me, for his ire melts away at once.

"You were right before," he says gently. "You are not my first choice. Mina is all that you ought to be: modest, innocent, and unstained by any thought of shadows or darkness. She is quick and curious like you, but her womanly qualities make her more ideal. The perfect woman of the age." He moves behind me and strokes my hair, and only my rage and hurt keep me from leaning into his touch. "Women like Mina or Diana run from me because they cling to purity and goodness. I am the antithesis of everything they believe in, and to infect such a chaste and virtuous woman is profoundly satisfying. By transforming her, I would make her the *opposite* of herself, whereas if I do the same to you, I fear you might become *more* yourself than ever."

I take in a deep, shaking, enraged breath.

"I am a predator, and I need prey. I need the thrill of the chase." Vlad leans his head against the back of mine almost lovingly. "I should not have become angry with you. You are very young, Lucy, and I cannot expect you to understand any of this."

I fly about in a rage. "Don't speak to me like I am a little girl. I understand you perfectly. Why, if you find Mina so appealing, did you call to *me*? I don't believe a perfect woman is what you really want. What drew you to me as I was drawn to you?" I meet his hard gaze straight on, seeing his shock. No doubt he has never been spoken to like this in five hundred years, and certainly not by a lowly woman. "*I* am what you want. Someone who is as hungry as you are. That is why we found each other, and yet you are afraid of me."

"I? Afraid of you?"

"Yes," I say, not taking my eyes from his. "You are a paradox, Vlad. You are so very lonely, but you are careful not to create other vampires, and if you do, you destroy them before they can grow too dear to you. You are outnumbered among humans because to be powerful, you must be without equal. But without someone to share your endless life, what is the point of existing? You will go on forever, yearning for companionship and then pushing it away when it is offered to you. For all your supposed intellect, you can't even see this simple truth."

More quickly than I can blink, his hand wraps around my neck. His thumb presses hard against my throat and I gasp for air. "You have insulted me quite enough, madam," Vlad snarls. A glowing bloodred ring, burning with wrath, forms around each of the dark pupils of his eyes. When he bares his teeth, I see two long daggerlike fangs piercing through his pale gums, bringing drops of blood with them. "This is what you want, then? You want me to bite you as I bit that widow? Answer me, damn you!"

He thinks I am too afraid. He thinks his hand on my throat and the sight of his fangs will shock sense into me. Even in his violence, his expression holds mocking amusement at being able to manipulate me so easily. And so, coughing, I touch his face. He pauses, surprised by the tender gesture, and his hand on my throat loosens slightly. We gaze at each other, and a moment later, I feel the prickling pain beneath my scalp once more, prying at the edges of my mind. He is trying to read my thoughts, to unearth what I am feeling in this moment that I am not telling him.

No, I think fiercely. I picture, once more, a shield of pure silver protecting my mind from the onslaught. Silver like Mina's bracelet, which she gave to me with love; silver like the ring belonging to Van, which she brought with her to a strange new land. I strain with the effort to protect myself, and I feel the prickling stop immediately.

"What is this?" Vlad spits. "How are you doing that?"

"You don't need to invade my thoughts. I will tell you exactly what I am thinking." I grit my teeth, staring into the unnatural red-ringed eyes. "I am thinking that I want you to bite me, if only to show that you do not fear me. You would have to bite several times to turn me into a vampire, so where is the harm, Vlad? What is holding you back if not cowardice?"

The impact of his fangs ripping into my skin comes with a burst of frenetic emotions. I can feel everything roiling inside of him: rage, astonishment, and overwhelming desire, all underlined by an unstoppable, insatiable hunger. He crushes me against him in an arctic embrace, his body as cold and brutal as winter. The only points of heat are where his fangs have embedded themselves into my throat. It is the most terrible, undeniable pain I have ever felt. My tender skin and the veins underneath bellow in agony at the invasion, and my lungs struggle to let out a sob, a shout, *anything* at all. But I only take in ragged gasps of air as my hands scrabble uselessly on his massive shoulders. In response, Vlad bites me even deeper and harder. Only when my feet kick desperately in the air do I realize he has fully lifted me off the ground.

I lose my vision. I can hear the sea and the wind and the awful gushing of my blood into his mouth, but I can see nothing except darkness. For the first time in my life, I genuinely wish to die. It is no longer a pleasant flirtation but a fervent need to no longer exist. I want to fade into oblivion so that this merciless pain that racks my body will disappear.

Someone is sobbing as though her heart will break.

A moment later, I realize that I am the one crying, lying crumpled on the ground. My vision returns in time for me to see a hot stream of blood pouring from my throat, splattering across my dress and the stones of the terrace. The world spins as I weep, tears scalding my face. The incredible pain is still there, but muted around the edges now that Vlad has stepped away to watch me sob, his bloodstained mouth set in a grim line. I curl up into a ball as a wall of heavy, freezing mist rolls in from the ocean. Vlad kneels beside me, and I press frantically against the railing, covering my wounded throat with my trembling hands.

"Please, Vlad," I beg. "No more. It hurts so much. Please, please."

But I am too weak to resist as he moves my hands away from my throat. When I look at him, however, his eyes have returned to their normal state and his face only holds a strange sort of weary pity. "I am only going to clean you," he says quietly. "May I?" I do not have the strength to nod, but he sees the consent in my eyes and slowly lowers his mouth to my neck once more. I sob, expecting the excruciating impact of his fangs again, but I feel only his lips and his tongue, gently removing the blood from my shoulder and neck. When he has finished, he takes one of my hands and places it over the two raised wounds. When he holds my fingers before my eyes, I see that they are clean of any blood.

My body feels as limp as a rag wrung out too forcefully. The mist surrounds us, blocking the house from view, and I shiver in the unrelenting cold. I feel as though I may never get warm again. "Am I dying?" I whisper. "Was all of this for nothing?"

"You are not dying."

A weak sob escapes me. "It hurt so much. I thought . . . I thought I would enjoy it as Mrs. Edgerton did. She looked happy. But I—" I break off as a wave of dizziness overtakes me. I feel as though I might float away with the mist if Vlad lets go of my hand. But he does not.

"I was rougher with you," Vlad says, smoothing hair off my clammy forehead. "Much rougher. I had to teach you a lesson. I didn't want to, but you forced my hand. You made me be the monster everyone expects me to be." He presses his freezing fingers against my wounds, which feels so soothing that I lean against his hand, crying weakly. Gently, he pulls me into his arms and lifts me like a child, and as he stands up, the mist rises with him.

My head droops over his chest where his dead heart lies still. I am so cold and tired that I only vaguely register us moving through the thick fog. We are floating away from the bright windows of the Wilcox home, which slowly fades into the distance.

"I took more blood than I planned," Vlad says ruefully. I feel no heartbeat in his chest, but I do hear the vibration of his voice. Alive, yet not alive. A man, yet not a man. "I'm afraid you will be very ill for some time. I wish you had listened to me and not forced me to bite you."

I close my eyes against another wave of dizziness, and when I open them again, I see my family's lodgings at the Crescent. Vlad carries me to the door and stops on the steps. "You brought me home?" I ask. "But Mamma and Mina and Arthur . . . the people at the ball—"

"I will take care of it." He lowers me to the ground. My knees quiver as though I am walking on mist instead of solid ground. "I must leave you here. I cannot carry you inside."

I press my hand against my neck, feeling the heat of the protruding wounds, and groan. "I am near death, and all you care about is my reputation and servants gossiping?"

"I cannot enter without invitation," Vlad reminds me. "I told you, but you wouldn't listen. What I am is a curse. And I am afraid," he adds, a trifle smugly, "that now you have been infected with my venom, you will feel something of these limitations yourself."

I blink at him, lightheaded and unsteady. "What do you mean? I cannot go into the sun?"

"Of course you can. You haven't transformed. But you may find that it hurts your eyes or stings your skin. That is the price of what you brazenly demanded from me." He strokes a long, icy finger down my tear-stained cheek, his face full of regret. "I think you will be extremely ill tomorrow, and the next day, and the next. You will need a doctor."

"Oh, what do you care?" I ask tiredly, pushing his hand away and dropping onto the doorstep. "I am only a woman. A plaything and a diversion, as you said, and even after all I have shared with you, you still prefer someone else. Go and leave me here to die."

"How dramatic you are," Vlad says brightly. "Are you jealous?"

I lean my head against the door and close my eyes. "No, I am not jealous," I say, exhausted. "I am only cold and tired and very, very sad. Please just go."

But he does not leave. Instead, he sits down beside me, as though we are on the bench on the cliffs again, and he pulls my head to rest against his shoulder.

"Why are you still here?" I ask.

"Because what you said is true. I believe I do care more for you than even I know," he says. "But what I told you before is also true: I do not love. It is simpler not to, and you must never hope for that from me, Lucy. No woman should . . . though many of them have."

There are ghosts in his voice, past lovers who had fallen for him and fallen to their deaths. The perfect women of every age, succumbing before he took everything, emptied them like wine from a glass. I think of his admiration for Mina and go cold with fear at the idea that she could ever suffer what I just have. And then I remember what I should not have forgotten all along, had I been a better friend to her and not so absorbed in my own affairs: that Vlad seemed to have known of Mina before the cliffs, as indeed he had known of me.

I sense that this is my moment to ask him, that I will get more answers in his unusual state of gentleness, the closest I will ever get to an apology for what he has done. Mustering what strength I have left, I say thinly, "You told me you have seen Mina's picture before. Tell me the truth, Vlad. Have you crossed paths with Jonathan Harker?"

"I have."

I swallow, my throat dry and painful. "Then you are the client he was working for? The nobleman whose castle sits in the Mountains of Deep Winter?"

"I am."

I am seized with an even more profound cold than what I already feel. Oh, Mina, my poor Mina. "But he left months ago," I say, my voice trembling. "And you are here, and he is missing and has not written in a long time. Is he . . . is he dead?"

"No. Nor is he like me, if that's what you're wondering."

With a monumental effort, I lift my head from his shoulder and look into his eyes. My voice is barely above a whisper. "But you did bite him as you bit me?"

His smile is a red slash in his face. Some of his teeth are still stained with my blood. "Several times, in fact, and quite enjoyed him."

"Where is he?" I ask, my heart clenching for Mina.

"Still there," Vlad says matter-of-factly. "He was extremely useful from the moment he set foot in my castle. He gave me such insight into his society and helped me with the language, in addition to assisting with the purchase of my home. I told him how his country fascinated me. Such a tiny land with such immense reach. Under the rule of a woman, no less!

Power calls to power, and England called to me. I needed an agent who would introduce me to her ways."

"And Jonathan served you well," I say bitterly.

Vlad leans his shoulder against mine in a confiding way. "I told you Mina is the finest example of womanhood of your society, and she and Mr. Harker are well matched. He is a paragon among Englishmen, I think, and a beautiful young man." He smiles, his eyes soft and faraway. "Such vivacity and intelligence, such boldness! I marvel at the strength in his character. No one can blame me for desiring him or being intrigued by his description of the perfect girl he was to marry. He showed me her photograph, kept in a pocket over his beating heart."

My anger is rising again with every word, and I somehow find the fortitude to pull myself to a standing position. My head spins as the infernal mist swirls around me. "You are keeping Jonathan from Mina," I say, my teeth clenched. "You are the reason her heart is breaking. She actually thought he had left her for another woman, but I will tell her the truth about you."

Vlad looks up at me with raised eyebrows. "Mina Murray seems to me like a woman of logic and reason, and will therefore worry a great deal about your sanity." He waves a dismissive hand. "Time will pass, and she will forget him. Humans are fickle creatures. Lovely as she is, she will marry another in no time. Mr. Harker is better off where he is."

"You were right," I say furiously, as my knees shake beneath me. "You know nothing of love if you think Mina could marry another. She only wants Jonathan, and to him alone will she give her whole heart. Your selfishness in keeping him like a disgusting *pet* will kill her." I am forced to pause, leaning heavily against the door, as the blood rushes to my head in my anger. "Mina only dreams of a life with him, and I will not let you take that away from her."

Vlad looks at me, so still that I wonder if I have enraged him again. I do not care.

"Bring him back," I gasp, for my lungs feel full of cotton and not air. "Send a letter, send people . . . I do not care how it is done. But bring him back or I will somehow find a way to do it myself, even if I have to sail the wreck of the *Demeter* in this state."

"You love Mina so much?" he asks quietly.

"More than I love myself. There is no one alive who is as kind and deserving as she is. I would do anything to bring . . . Jonathan . . . back for her . . ." I collapse, and Vlad is on his feet at once, holding me up as the earth spins wildly beneath me. I look up at him, dizzy and sick but still determined. "Please, Vlad, I am begging you. She loves him."

"Then back to her he will go."

"Do not toy with me," I say feebly. "Not about this."

"I am in earnest. I will release Jonathan. I have my ways." He leans me against the wall and knocks sharply on the door. "And now I must leave you, Lucy, for I am afraid you really will die if you stay out here much longer. Have your servant carry you straight to bed."

My body is heavy with the longing for sleep, but the rage shooting through me keeps me upright. "I thought you were my friend," I say, my voice shaking, "but now I am not certain I want you to be anything to me anymore. Not after the cruel things you have said and done to me tonight, and not after you imprisoned Jonathan and kept him from Mina."

He looks at me in silence as quick footsteps approach on the other side of the door.

"I don't want to see you again," I whisper. "In dreams or out of them."

"You don't mean that," he says gently.

"Goodbye, Vlad."

The door opens, and Harriet screams at the sight of me fainting and covered with blood. I fall into my maid's arms as more servants come running, and I vaguely register that Vlad is gone. Only the mist remains as I am lifted over the threshold he cannot cross.

"Oh, Miss Lucy!" Harriet wails over and over as another servant locks the door.

"I'm all right," I choke out, a dead weight in her arms. As they carry me upstairs, I turn to look out of the window beside the door one last time. Through the heavy mist, I see the glowing eyes of an enormous dog watching from the deserted street. "But I want you, please, to lock me in my bedroom tonight. And every night from here onward."

And then I sink into nothingness.

CHAPTER TWENTY-ONE

F or days, I am sicker than I have ever been in my life. I slip in and out of consciousness, raving, feverish, and weak as a newborn. An impossible thirst takes hold of my being, but no matter how much water I drink, it cannot be satisfied. The wounds on my throat throb with constant pain, and colorful lights dance in my vision whenever I open my eyes to see another face hovering over me. I recognize the elderly town doctor, looking utterly clueless; Mina with dark shadows under her eyes; and Mamma, weeping inconsolably over my frail body. But most of the time, it is Arthur who is there, kneeling beside my bed with his weary head against me.

"Lucy, don't leave me," he says brokenly. "Don't go away when I love you so."

Their grief is unbearable to me, worse than the pain of Vlad's bite, and in my moments of clarity, I curse his name with everything I have left. It is all his fault. I asked for kindness, for friendship, for a taste of immortality, and instead he gave me what I fear more than death itself: the devastation of having to watch my loved ones mourn me. I cannot, *will* not forgive him.

But then, one morning, I wake to find my head is a bit clearer, though light from lack of food and fresh air. My thirst has abated, and my stomach is loudly proclaiming its hunger.

Mina, who has been sitting on a chair nearby, hurries over to feel my forehead. Her face is drawn, exhausted, and white as paper. "Thank God! Your fever has broken. We thought you were going to . . . The doctor warned that you might . . ." She collapses into sobs that shake her body, and I wrap my arms around her, holding on as tightly as if she were a buoy in the sea. We stay that way for a long time before she pulls away to look at me. "How do you feel?"

"Never better," I say feebly.

She laughs and kisses my cheek. "I would run and call Arthur and your mamma this minute, but I hate to disturb their rest, especially Arthur's. How that man does love you. I thought he and I would come to blows when I insisted that he go get some sleep."

I smile at the thought of demure Mina and mild Arthur coming to blows. "I am glad to have you to myself for a little while. How long have I been ill?"

"Three days and nights. It was terrifying to see you so pale and still when we got home from the party. But the count graciously explained everything—"

"He was here? You invited him in?" I try to sit up in my alarm, but it brings on a wave of dizziness so nauseating that I am forced to lie back down at once.

"No, he spoke to us at the party." She smooths her cool hand over my brow. "Do you remember going out to the terrace with him? After some time, we went to look for you, but you were both gone. We were frantic until he returned and told us an animal attacked you." She looks thoughtful. "I may have been wrong about him. There was always something in his eyes and manner of speaking that seemed mocking . . . but that night, he was so gentlemanly."

I struggle to keep my face neutral. "Yes, I'm sure he was."

"He made a lovely apology to Arthur for keeping you for two dances," Mina says. "He said he was enjoying your conversation so much, and you only stayed with him to be polite, and it served him right that the second dance was interrupted when he saw a large dog outside."

"A dog?"

Mina nods. "Do you recall that unfortunate ship? The *Demeter*? People saw a black dog jump off, so the count assumed it was the same one and went out to investigate, as he has a way with animals. You bravely followed to see if you could help despite his protests. We were relieved to hear this, Arthur most of all. Forgive me, Lucy, but it *did* rather look as though you and the count had had a lovers' quarrel. However, I knew that could not be."

I offer a weak smile at Vlad's deft spinning of the truth. "What happened then?"

"On the terrace, the dog attacked you. It bit you just there." Mina indicates the left side of my throat. "Your gown was so bloody that the count did not want to call for help and terrify everyone, so he took you straight home in his carriage. He knocked and left at once, to protect you from gossip, and then came back to assure us that you were safe."

"How noble of him."

"It *was* noble," she says uncertainly, hearing my sarcasm. "He seemed very upset indeed that you had been hurt. I think you may have caught his fancy, darling, so I felt the need to remind him that you were engaged. He seemed amused, but grateful."

Yes, I can believe that. How his eyes must have shone as my righteous friend protected my honor. The perfect woman of the age. My hunger fades into exhaustion as emotions overtake me. I have lied to my loved ones, begged Vlad to bite me, and lain so close to death that I can still feel the grip of its fingers. In my fervent hope to save my family pain, I only ended up inflicting it. "I am tired, Mina," I whisper, closing my eyes. "I would like to sleep again."

Later that night, I am roused from my troubled slumber by a noise. Harriet dozes in the chair nearby with her mending in her lap, but she is not snoring or making a sound. My room is dark and peaceful, and the door is securely locked, as I had requested. I close my eyes, ready to drift off again, when I hear a tapping at the window. I turn my head, feeling light and buoyant and dizzy, and see shadows moving against the night sky. Are they birds or branches shifting in the wind? Or are they the wings of a great black bat, cutting through the heavy mist?

My mind feels unmoored, unsteady. I am caught between waking and the land of dreams as the shadow lingers a moment, then flits away. I fall back into a sleep full of disturbing visions: of bleeding profusely on a dark terrace, of running through the mist, of searching for Vlad and feeling his presence like trailing notes of dark perfume. When I am awake, I may hate him and curse him and think of him chaining Jonathan up in a castle far away—but in my dreams, I long ceaselessly for him. I miss the kind and gentle Vlad who listened to my troubles, who held me and understood me and seemed to be the very last person on earth who would ever hurt me.

But he *did* hurt me. And I told him I never wanted to see him again.

When I wake in the morning, dazed and delirious, I am sobbing as though my heart will break. Arthur hurries over and gathers me close as I babble over and over, "I am soiled. I am dirty. I do not deserve you." I cling to him, shaking with sobs as he comforts me, his face almost grey with worry and distress. I feel Mina's cool hand on my forehead and hear her say, "I don't understand it. She was better yesterday," before I sink back into oblivion.

On the fourth evening of my illness, I open my eyes to see a familiar man talking to Arthur as he slips out of a traveling coat. His smooth, unlined face crinkles in a smile when he sees that I am awake and there is something so like dear Papa in his handsome, olive-skinned countenance that I smile back and weakly reach my hand out to him.

He takes it and gives it a kind squeeze. "You remember me, then, Miss Westenra?"

"Dr. Van Helsing," I whisper. "And it's Lucy, please."

"It has been some time since that dinner with our friend Jack Seward, hasn't it? Where you and I spoke, most cheerfully, of death. But death is not welcome here," he adds hastily, seeing Arthur's alarm. "Not with me ready to fight it off with everything in my power. I came as soon as Jack told me of Mr. Holmwood's telegram for help. He could not be spared from the asylum at present, so here I am." His calm, fatherly manner puts me at ease, and even the pain in my throat subsides as he takes the chair beside my bed.

I hold on tight to his hand. "You traveled all the way from Amsterdam just for me?"

"Thank you, sir," Arthur says fervently. "We know it was a long journey."

"Pah! Thirteen hours on a train and a boat is nothing. I would have come a much greater distance, after the kindness Miss Lucy and her mamma showed me." Dr. Van Helsing speaks in a light, comfortable tone, but I can see his physician's sensibilities turning on. His keen eyes look between each of mine as his hands feel my forehead and jaw, pressing here and there. He leans in to examine the left side of my throat. "I hear you were attacked by a dog. Mr. Holmwood tells me it has been terrorizing people in town. It killed another dog this week, and also some cattle. Ripped them open from throat to belly, drained them of blood, and left them where they lay."

"Truly? They were drained?" I ask, surprised by the revelation that Vlad is feeding on animals. Perhaps he only wishes to lie low and evade suspicion after my attack. I do not believe him to be penitent for what he has done to me . . . but I cannot be certain.

Arthur throws the doctor a disapproving glance. "Sir, she has been in and out of consciousness for days. Perhaps we ought not to upset her with these violent details."

Dr. Van Helsing hums a noncommittal response. His fingers apply light, steady pressure around my wounds. "Does this hurt at all, Lucy? When I press . . . so?"

"A little," I say, wincing.

"Two large, long, and very sharp fangs," he says in a low voice, as though to himself. "The skin is warm around the injury and quite red. I see stark-white circles around these deep holes of red. I'm afraid you may have an infection, my poor young friend."

I almost laugh at his use of the word. If only he knew. But I can only draw in a few shallow, ragged breaths, which attracts his attention at once.

"Do you have trouble breathing?"

"My lungs feel like . . ." Unable to find the words, I place a hand over my chest and press down to mimic a heavy weight. "I feel it most when I am awake."

Dr. Van Helsing sits back, his face thoughtful. "Your mamma tells me you have eaten nothing for days. And I learned from Miss Murray that you were extremely thirsty until your fever broke. Your body is not overly warm, aside from the area of injury. Can you sit up?"

"Every time I try, I feel so faint." I look at Arthur standing beside him, his face drawn and sorrowful, and feel a pang of fear. "Do you think I am dying, Doctor?"

"You? A young lady of nineteen in the peak of health?" Dr. Van Helsing waves away my question, but I see in his eyes that there is a great deal of thought happening. "Your heart is strong. I felt that at once in your pulse. The dizziness, the light-headedness, the pallor . . . these are signs of significant blood loss. But you are staying awake longer, which I find encouraging. Your appetite will return soon, but until then, eat something even if you are not hungry. Your body needs fuel. A small bowl of broth, perhaps, which Mr. Holmwood can fetch for you?"

"Right away." Arthur leaves immediately, glad for something to do.

The doctor's eyes find mine, grave and focused. "Now that we are alone, Miss Lucy, allow me to be frank. I have treated many ailments in my career and have seen patients with animal bites before. But this, I'm afraid, is no animal bite. At least, not that of a dog. I don't wish to distress you with too much information, but—"

"Please, Doctor, you may speak plainly," I say, my curiosity rising at what he might guess.

Dr. Van Helsing nods. "Very well. An agitated dog will bite with both jaws. But let us play . . . what is the English phrase? Devil's advocate. Even if the dog bit with only the top jaw, there would be punctures from the other teeth due to the shape of the mouth. And here I see the marks of two teeth. Two teeth only." He cocks his head. "What did the dog look like? Can you describe it for me?"

I think again of that evening. As the servants brought me inside, I had glanced at the dark street outside the window to find Vlad gone and a dog in his place, huge and hulking, watching me from the mist. Both Vlad and the dog had been on the *Demeter*, yet I had not remembered to ask him about it. Was it a denizen of his, perhaps? A scrap of his soul torn from his body?

"It was like a wolf in shape and size," I say, and Dr. Van Helsing leans forward and closes his eyes to listen more carefully. "I do not remember the color. It was too dark to see, perhaps. The dog had pointed ears, I think. It was large and shaggy, and . . . and very thin."

I have stopped speaking, but the doctor remains in the same position, eyes shut and brow furrowed with thought. The existence of vampires would strain any physician's credulity, and yet I wonder what would happen if he discovered the truth—if he found Vlad. How could this slender, soft-spoken man hope to stop an all-powerful being untouched by death, with eyes like voids ringed with blood? I shudder at the memory of Vlad tearing into my flesh, a creature of wrath and vengeance, and Dr. Van Helsing opens his eyes in time to see it.

"I'm tiring you with so much talk," he says apologetically. "I beg pardon. But I hear Mr. Holmwood's foot on the stair, and before he returns, I wish to say one more thing. Know that you can tell me anything, Lucy, and I will treat it with the utmost discretion. I will not share a word of it with anyone, not even your mamma, if you charge me with secrecy."

"Why do you think I need secrecy?" I ask, touched by his consideration.

"I don't know," he says slowly. "But I have a hunch that there is more you could tell me. And if you'll forgive my arrogance, my hunches are always correct. Then there is the fact that I have no daughters and little experience with young ladies like yourself, but I believe secret-keeping is a common characteristic, no?" He pulls a funny face.

I smile. "You speak as though young ladies are creatures to be studied."

"Perhaps you are." He grows serious again when his eyes find the wounds on my throat.

The door opens and Arthur enters bearing a tray with a steaming bowl, an empty glass, and a pitcher of cold water. Dr. Van Helsing gets up and begins riffling through his medical bag, and Arthur takes his vacated chair to feed me hot, salty broth.

"Now, Lucy, I ask you to please finish that entire bowl," the doctor says as he scatters tubes, vials, and bandages on my dressing table. "You will need strength for this operation."

Arthur and I exchange looks of alarm. "Operation?" we repeat.

"Not to fear. I will not be chopping anyone up today," Dr. Van Helsing says cheerfully, and Arthur gives a good-natured groan at the man's levity. "But the truth of the matter is that Lucy has lost a great deal of blood to whatever bit her."

"You mean the dog," Arthur says, feeding me. "It was a dog."

"The symptoms I mentioned of faintness, dizziness, and so on," the doctor continues as though Arthur has not spoken, "are characteristic of anemia, but they can also occur when someone loses a significant amount of blood volume. Thus, that blood will need to be replaced. I specialize in a technique called transfusion, which I have done with great success."

"Replace the blood with what?" I ask, confused.

"With the blood from another person," Dr. Van Helsing explains. "As I said, you are young and healthy, and your body will make more of its own blood. But in the meantime, you need help, so I will give you some of mine. The transfusion involves a very small needle in your arm—you will feel only a pinch—connected to a tube, connected to a needle in *my* arm."

Arthur looks horrified. "Is this necessary, sir? With Lucy already so weak?"

"This will strengthen and revitalize her," the older man reassures him. "It is I who will be weak afterward, but none the worse for wear after food and rest myself, which the excellent Mrs. Westenra has already promised me." His manner is charming and jovial, and I feel a little more at ease, despite the disturbing mention of tubes and needles.

"But why does it need to be you?" Arthur persists. "I will gladly give Lucy my blood. Forgive me, but I am younger and stronger than you, and you are also fatigued from travel."

The doctor's dark brown eyes are twinkling. "There is no forgiveness necessary when what you say is true. Very well, Mr. Holmwood, we will do what you propose. Lucy, as brave as you are, I will give you something to sleep so that the operation does not distress you."

I lift my head from the pillow, ignoring the dizziness and frantic with sudden worry. "But, Doctor, won't this infection pass from me to him?" I ask, clutching Arthur's hand. "I have been stained by it. I have been dirtied. It is in my very blood, and I could not imagine—"

"There is no danger of that," the doctor says, so confidently that I nod my consent to be put to sleep. As Arthur feeds me the last spoonful of soup, Dr. Van Helsing pours me a glass of water and stirs a powder into it. I drink ravenously, but the water only seems to increase my thirst. "Do not worry. When you awaken, I promise you will feel well."

I smile up at the doctor, grateful for his genuine kindness and no-nonsense manner. My fear of death has all but disappeared after a short time in his company. "Thank you, sir."

Arthur and Dr. Van Helsing sit and chat about lighter topics, and I listen until I feel my consciousness slipping. But some powerful tug of resistance prevents me from fully giving way, despite my need to rest. Vaguely, I register a sharp pain in the crook of my arm, and my eyes fly open to see Dr. Van Helsing gazing at me in surprise. Arthur is on the chair with his sleeve rolled up and a cloth bound tightly about his upper arm. A long rubber tube swings between us, stained deep dark red. It is on this tube that I fixate in my dreamy, semiconscious state, for at the sight of it, my already unbearable thirst increases tenfold. The smell, oh, the smell! I am overwhelmed by the richness, the texture, and the exquisite shades of red in the blood flowing from Arthur to me.

In my daze, I feel as though I have left my body to float above. I see myself lying prone in bed with Dr. Van Helsing's hand on my shoulder, pressing me down hard into my pillow. He is much stronger than he looks, and I watch with detached astonishment as I try to fight him in my frail state, struggling to reach for the beautiful, fragrant scarlet tube. The second I pause for breath, he holds another glass to my lips. I drink and drink, my gaze never leaving the tube.

"You're giving her another dose?" I hear Arthur ask.

"She needs more than I thought. This is very interesting," I hear Dr. Van Helsing reply before I float back into my body and sink at last into a deep and dreamless slumber.

CHAPTER TWENTY-TWO

I awaken to sunlight pouring through the windows. I lie still, enjoying the warmth and comfort of it before noticing Arthur across the room, fast asleep with one arm over his eyes and his long legs cascading off the sofa. I sit up gingerly in bed, glad not to feel dizzy. In fact, I feel wonderful aside from a slight stiffness from sleeping in one position all night. I take in several deep breaths, delighting in how easily my lungs fill and expand. The raised bumps on my throat are cool to the touch. That blessed Dr. Van Helsing has worked his magic, and so has Arthur, who gladly opened his veins for me. Perhaps that was why Mamma had allowed him to sleep in here last night—though I note that the sofa has been pushed as far away from me as possible.

As if he hears me thinking about him, Arthur stirs and glances over. "Lucy," he says hoarsely, and the anguish and relief in his voice makes my eyes sting. I hold out my arms, smiling, and in two strides he has lifted me clean off the bed to hug me against him, so tightly I cannot tell where I end and he begins. I stroke his hair, murmuring to him as his shoulders shake. Finally, when he is calmer, he pulls away just enough to look at me. "I'm sorry. Did I hurt you? I was just so glad to see you looking well . . . Let me put you down—"

"Don't let go," I whisper. "Please."

Arthur does not even hesitate or glance at the door, where my mother or maid could enter at any moment. He gathers me up, one arm around my waist and the other under my knees, and climbs into the bed with me clasped against him. We lie there holding each other, our hearts beating in tandem, his lips in my hair and my face pressed to his shirt, drinking in the smell of him. He pulls the blanket up over my shoulders and gently moves my hair to keep it from getting caught under his arm. Even this small movement creates the tiniest gap between us, and I immediately make a sound of protest and tighten my hold on him. I hear him laugh, his warm breath stirring my hair, and I wonder how I could have ever wanted anyone but this deeply kind, gentle, and honest man who needs only to be with me. No games, no lies, no artifice. Just my heart in exchange for his own.

"I love you, Arthur," I say, my voice muffled against his shirt. "So very, very much."

He presses a hard kiss on top of my head. "And I love you." He smiles when I look up at him, his hazel eyes full of light. "You had me so worried. I doubted Van Helsing, but now I would trust him with my life. He was right about everything. You look so well."

"I *feel* so well," I say, and he laughs again and leans forward to kiss me. I feel safe and protected, lying there with him in the sunlight, our mouths softly moving together, neither of us asking for anything more than that moment. We end the kiss and stay nose to nose, just looking at each other, and I know that being married to him will be like this: waking up on the same pillow, caring and being cared for, and knowing that whatever calamity befell me, he would be there to offer me even the blood from his body. I run my fingers over his jaw, his cheek, and the soft fringe of his lashes, and I know that I want to make this man happy. I want to be with him every morning and every night for the rest of his life. "Mamma let you sleep in here?"

"Under pain of death if I dared leave my sofa." His dimple appears. "So I suppose my life is forfeit . . . now that I'm in bed with you. And soon, I'll be in bed with you every night."

"Why, sir," I say, grinning as his cheeks turn pink. "How bold of you to say so."

Still blushing, he touches his nose to mine. "I wanted to be here all evening. Right next to you. But Dr. Van Helsing was always looking in on us like some anxious father."

"I remember him holding me down during the operation. What happened?"

"You were trying to sit up," he explains. "Poor girl, you were frightened by the blood going through the tube. The doctor had to keep you from hurting yourself."

I frown. Frightened, I had not been. No . . . I had been *thirsty*. Unbearably thirsty, enough to pour the contents of the tube straight into my mouth. I glance at my bandaged arm and recall Dr. Van Helsing's use of the term *infection*. Yes, indeed, I am infected with something unspeakable. If Arthur or Mina knew, would they ever look at me the same way? Would they love me enough to understand why I had asked for it? Would they forgive me?

"Lucy? What's wrong?" Arthur asks, studying me.

"I don't deserve you," I whisper. "Not after what has happened."

"What do you mean? You had an accident, that's all. You are blameless." He hugs me tightly. "There is nothing but happiness ahead of us, my love, and you will forget all of this."

I bury my face in his chest and shut my eyes against the pain of knowing that I will *never* forget. I will remember that his heart, thudding a soft rhythm against my ear, will stop forever one day. Death will haunt us, lurking in the shadows, and I will lose Arthur or he will lose me. And I have seen for myself the depth of his suffering if he ever lost me, and God help me . . . I would do anything to protect him from sorrow, even if it meant walking into the mouth of hell.

A soft knock sounds on my door, interrupting my thoughts. Arthur jumps off the bed like a shot, his face bright red. But it is only Mina, not my mother. She looks at him and then back to me, her eyes dancing with amusement. "Oh, Lucy, those roses in your cheeks!" she cries, hurrying over to kiss me. "Arthur, you ought to go and eat something. I can stay with her now."

"I'll send her mamma up in a minute." He leaves, closing the door behind him.

Left alone with Mina, I breathe her in hungrily. She smells of sand and sea salt. "You are covered in the ocean breeze," I say. "How I long for a walk. I have been in bed forever!"

Mina laughs. "That was exactly what Dr. Van Helsing advised before he left. He told me to get you outside in the sun and fresh air. He knows such a great deal, doesn't he?"

"With your brain, you could have just as much knowledge if you went to school as he did," I tell her affectionately. "But you say he left? I was hoping to thank him again."

"He's on the early train to London." Mina chuckles. "I was a bit miffed that he didn't ask me to help with your transfusion last night, but he explained everything to me this morning and seemed amused when I took notes. He's gone to stay with Dr. Seward and do a bit of research."

"Research? On what?"

"Your condition, I think." She hesitates. "Do you know, I don't think he believes it was a dog that bit you. He was reluctant to speculate when I asked his opinion. All he said was that he needed to do some reading and consult with his friend Jack. Now! Enough chatter." She beams, holding up a small fragrant parcel. "I went into town at first light to get you straw-berry cakes. The baker thought I'd lost my mind when he saw me there so early, but when I told him . . ."

She continues chatting as she bustles around the room, but I am sud-denly having the greatest difficulty focusing on what she is saying. There is a sharp buzzing in my ears, like that of a fly, and when it subsides, I realize, shocked, that I am able to hear Arthur and Mamma conversing downstairs as distinctly as if they were in the room with me.

"Is that the telegram that just came, dear?" Mamma asks. "Is it bad news?"

"My father is worse. The doctors say he may not have much longer to live."

She gasps. "Oh, Arthur, I'm so sorry."

My body goes rigid at the revelation that I can hear *everything* from behind a closed door and an entire floor away: Arthur's feet pacing in the hall, the flutter of the telegram he is holding, and even Mamma's hands wringing her skirt in sympathy.

"I confess, I have been thinking about returning to London soon myself," Mamma says.

"And cut short your holiday in Whitby?" Arthur asks, distressed. "Not on my account?"

"No, dear. But on mine," she says sadly.

I hold my breath, waiting for her to explain, when I notice Mina wav-ing her hands for my attention. She calls my name in a loud voice, as though she has been doing it for some time. "Are you feeling ill again?" she asks, her blue eyes round with anxiety.

"No, no," I say, flustered. "But Arthur has just received bad news about his father."

"What? When? He looked so happy just now—"

The door opens and Arthur comes in, followed by my mother. I have not looked properly at Mamma since the night of the party, when she had been rosy and dressed in her best, and I am struck at once by the drastic change in her appearance. Purple shadows bloom beneath her faded eyes and her skin carries a sickly grey pallor, as though *she* has been the one lying ill and not I.

"Mamma," I say, unable to keep the horror from my voice. "Are you well?"

She kisses me and hugs my head against her side, perhaps to hide her face from me. "I will be fine after some food and rest. I have been anxious over you, that's all."

At the foot of the bed, Arthur holds up the telegram with tears in his eyes. "I have just received an urgent summons from London," he says. "Papa's health has taken a turn for the worse, and my mother and the doctors want me to come home at once."

Mina stares at me, flabbergasted that I had predicted what he was going to say.

But I am focused on Arthur, my heart aching for the pain I can understand all too well. "I am so sorry, my love," I say quietly, reaching out for his hand. "Of course you must go at once. Go be with your father and have no fear on my account."

He kisses me, presses Mamma's and Mina's hands, and leaves without another word. I shut my eyes, praying desperately that the doctors are wrong and that Arthur will not find his beloved father taking his final breaths, the way I had found Papa once. My eyes fly open, and I look up at my mother in alarm. Her waxy, unhealthy pallor is like a knife to my heart.

"Why are you thinking of leaving Whitby so soon, Mamma?" I ask.

"How did you know that?" she asks, shocked. "I mentioned it to Arthur downstairs."

"Lucy has been making some very astute guesses this morning," Mina says slowly.

"Why are you cutting our holiday short?" I persist. "We always stay for another week. Do *you* feel poorly?" I do not miss the meaningful glance that passes between my mother and Mina.

But Mamma only says, "Hush, Lucy. You are getting much too excited. I told you, I have been so anxious over you that I haven't been sleeping soundly, that is all. Dr. Van Helsing gave me pills to help and agreed that you and I might be more comfortable at home."

"This is all my fault," I whisper, taking in her hollowed cheeks and shadowed eyes. Hers is the face of a woman who has been mourning over the sickbed of her only child, perhaps wondering if she will soon have no one left in the world. "I have made you ill."

"Nonsense," my mother says firmly. "You haven't done anything wrong."

I want to shout "I *have* done wrong!" But I can see that my rising distress is upsetting her, so I try to calm myself. "Yes, I agree. We should go home. We will both rest and recover, and we can be near Arthur if . . ." I swallow hard. "If he needs us."

"Good." My mother gives me an approving kiss and moves toward the door, slow and deliberate, as though the motion pains her. "We will take the afternoon train tomorrow."

"Let me make the arrangements, Mrs. Westenra, and you lie down," Mina says anxiously, hurrying after her. She glances back at me. "I will return in a moment, Lucy."

Alone at last, I give in to my guilt and grief. My mother, always so full of merry gossip and energy, has become a ghost of herself in only four days. She seems to have aged years from care and worry. I have brought her closer to the grave. I press my hands over my eyes, weeping silently at my own folly. No. Not my folly. I had not wished for *this*.

Vlad could have granted my request without such brutality, but he had not. He had almost killed me to teach me a lesson, all because I dared to ask for what he himself had chosen.

I clench my teeth, cursing him and hating that I still long for him even after his cruelty. But he has made my last summer of freedom a dream of languorous moonlit nights, such as I will never have again. And now I will leave Whitby without seeing him or saying goodbye.

The sun streams in through my window, its warmth calming me a bit. I remove my trembling hands from my eyes and let the light soothe me. And then I sit up so fast that it almost brings back my dizziness. Vlad told me his bite might make me feel his limitations, but the sun is not hurting me. Fearfully, I look into the mirror across the room and exhale when I see my reflection, hair mussed, nightgown rumpled, and gaze a bit wild. Perhaps he did not infect me enough to feel any changes. Yet how can I explain my newly, unnaturally acute hearing?

Mina comes back into the room. "All is arranged," she tells me. "The servants will buy the tickets and pack, and I will come and stay with you in London awhile. Mail always gets there more quickly than it does to my aunt's house." Her voice drops to almost a whisper as she moves to the window, pressing her knuckles to her mouth.

I look at her drooping shoulders and her hair, soft and bright in the sunlight, and I know that I must tell her about Jonathan . . . but I have no idea how to say it. I open my mouth, hoping that the right words will somehow tumble out, when she speaks again.

"Oh, I forgot to tell you. The count has been calling every evening to ask how you are."

The air seems to stop in my lungs. "*Here*? At this house?"

She looks at me, puzzled by my tone. "Yes. He came last night when you were sleeping."

"Mina, come here to me." I hold out my hands and she obeys at once, alarmed. "Listen closely. You must never, *ever* invite the count inside. Have you done so?"

"No. He hands in flowers from the doorstep, and we leave them in the parlor to keep from disturbing you. I never ask him in because he comes so late, and also because I want to spare poor Arthur's feelings. I think the count cares for you more than he should."

I throw my arms around her. "Oh, you clever girl. Thank goodness!"

"What is this all about? I thought you liked him. As a friend."

My heart is beating so fast that I feel lightheaded again. I lie back down, trying to dispel the horrifying prospect of Vlad inhabiting the same space as Arthur or Mamma or Mina. "Never invite him in. He is not welcome over the threshold of our door. And please discard his flowers."

Mina studies me. "You're . . . afraid of him. Why?"

I look up at her beloved face, with her soft rose cheeks, summer-sky eyes, and her hair glowing gold in the light. "Mina, I have something to tell you and I cannot explain how I know it. It is similar to how I knew about Arthur's father and Mamma's decision to leave this morning before they had even come into the room. Will you promise not to ask how I know?"

She chews on her lip. "I . . . I promise."

After a long pause, I say, "Jonathan Harker is safe. He is not dead."

She goes absolutely still. The silence stretches on for so long that I begin to think she will not speak at all. And then she presses her hands over her heart and whispers, "He is not dead?"

"He is not dead. I know it for a fact. But that is all I can tell you."

"But how can you be sure?" Mina's eyes dart between each of mine, quick and keen. "Lucy, what does Jonathan have to do with the count?"

"Please, you promised not to question me." My eyes flutter shut. My heart has slowed a bit, but I feel an overpowering weariness take hold of me. "I must rest now. I'm still weak. Perhaps we will not get our last walk in Whitby after all."

Mina wipes her eyes with the back of her hand. "Oh, Lucy, I hope you are right. I *feel* that you are right. But why did—" She breaks off. "Rest, dear. I will be right here."

The last thing I see before sleep takes me is her standing by the window, a fist pressed to her mouth to keep from crying. And when I dream, I see the cliffs above the crashing sea, green countryside rolling by outside the train windows, and Vlad watching me from the shadows, his eyes at once pleading for my forgiveness and threatening that I will never be free of him.

CHAPTER TWENTY-THREE

There is something different about home.

The floorboards creak beneath my steps as always, the fires crackle as usual against the September chill, and the bones of the house—all sturdy dark-papered walls and gleaming wood bannisters—feel the same to my fingertips. I walk through the parlor where Mamma hosts her teas, the dining room with its fine pictures and my grandfather's prized brass elephant, and Papa's library, which still smells of his pipe and incense even after all these years. My room is just how I left it, hung with deep plum silks and strewn with old love letters and dead roses.

But I sense an otherness, a surreality that has never touched the house before. And after the first few days of our return to London, I begin to realize it is not our home that is different.

It is me.

I feel better than ever. I eat well, walk with Mina twice a day, and sleep soundly behind a locked door. But from time to time, I have a fit of unquenchable thirst that no amount of water can satisfy, followed by rage and the urge to rip a chair apart with my bare hands. I wake at night with my heart racing, thinking I have heard the beating of dark wings upon my window. I get a terrible headache daily from the buzzing in my ears, and I hear conversations that should not be humanly possible for me to hear: the servants gossiping in the attic, two full floors above us; carriage drivers chatting outside; or an old woman scolding a child on the next street.

Since our last day in Whitby, I have taken care to conceal this odd new ability from Mina, though she is too distracted to notice. Ever since I told her about Jonathan, it is as though she has gone into a room inside her mind and shut the door. True to her word, she has not asked me any more questions about it, though sometimes I catch her studying me thoughtfully.

After tea one day, I excuse myself with another splitting headache, and I hear from behind the closed door of my room—a full floor above the main level—our housekeeper, Agatha, saying, "Why, good day to you, Count."

I sit bolt upright in bed. In the mirror across the room, I see that my face has drained of all color. Vlad is here. He has found me, and in a moment, the housekeeper will invite him in.

My head throbbing, I leap off the bed and hurry across the room. My hand is on the doorknob when I hear Mina's light footsteps downstairs, followed by her clear sweet voice. "What a pleasant surprise to see you in London, Count. I'm afraid Mrs. Westenra and Lucy are both resting at the moment. Perhaps you might call another time, if that is convenient?" Her tone is as proper and polite as ever, but I detect the degree of strain within it.

"Ah! I am sorry to be a bother, Miss Murray." Vlad's voice is so warm, so familiar, that for a moment I have to brace myself against the door to keep from falling to my knees. I know every cadence, every vowel, and even the rhythm of his breath. "I only wished to say hello now that I am settling into my new home outside London. Forgive me. I will leave you to your quiet."

Moonlight on water. The ocean breeze in my hair. My hand in his, and his lips on mine.

I close my eyes against the powerful longing for him, despising myself for it.

"Please wait a moment," I hear Mina call. "I know it is not me you have come to see, but I would like to hear more about your new home. Shall we sit in the garden? May I offer you tea?"

I hear Vlad's coat rustle as he looks up at the sky. "I believe it will rain."

"Perhaps, but it has looked that way all morning. And it isn't as chilly today, I think." There is a note of steely determination in Mina's courteous voice. "All I ask is a few minutes of your time. I know you came to see Lucy, but I would like to speak to you, sir."

"With pleasure," he says with an unmistakable smile in his voice. "No tea, thank you."

I hear clattering as Mina collects an umbrella from the stand by the door. And instead of taking him through the house to the garden, she leads him around the side. I sink onto the chair in front of my dressing table, deeply grateful that she has taken my warning seriously. My heart is drumming so loudly that I am afraid I will miss even a second of their conversation.

But Mina's voice comes as clear as a bell. "How do you like your new house, Count? You say it is outside of London. Where, exactly?"

The iron chairs scrape gently against the terrace as they sit down.

"I have purchased a lovely property in Purfleet. Not far from you here in Hillingham. The house has a small library, a parlor, and a garden. Even a conservatory." Vlad says the last word with such playful meaning that I am absolutely sure he knows I am up here listening. A little joke, a secret between friends. An involuntary thrill of pleasure runs through me.

"Purfleet?" Mina asks. "The Westenras have a friend who lives and works there. His name is Dr. Jack Seward, and he runs a very respected hospital."

"Ah! What a coincidence, for the young doctor happens to be my neighbor. His mental institution is adjacent to my land. In fact, I can see it from my windows."

I tense in my chair. First, Jonathan Harker helped Vlad purchase his home, and now, the property is next door to none other than Jack Seward. These are far too many *coincidences* for my comfort. Something tickles the back of my neck, like the sensation of eyes watching.

"You say Dr. Seward is a family friend?" Vlad asks. "Of the late Mr. Westenra, perhaps?"

It does not take supernatural ability for me to know that Mina's cheeks are coloring. "Dr. Seward was a student of Mr. Westenra's personal physician," she says carefully. "And he and Mr. Westenra were friendly, but the doctor is more closely acquainted with Lucy, I believe."

"Ah, with *Lucy*. I see."

I, too, cannot help blushing at Vlad's tone of knowing amusement.

Mina clears her throat. "What is the name of your new property?"

"Oh, I have already forgotten," he says carelessly. "Something neither sentimental nor poetic, and my heart did not thrill to it. I have given it a new name, which has a bit more significance to me. I am calling it Carfax. It means—"

"Crossroads."

There is a moment of surprised silence. "Yes, Miss Murray, that is correct."

"From the Latin *quadrifurcus*. The place where four roads meet. I have developed a taste for folklore, as Lucy has always enjoyed reading it."

"Excellent," Vlad says, pleased. "As you know, legend has it that they bury murderers at a crossroads to keep evil ghosts from finding their way home. Other stories say the dead who lie there come back not as ghosts, but as something else entirely. So it is good to confuse them, no?"

Something else entirely. I know what he means, for I have read the tales and seen the illustrations in Papa's books: pale, creeping, blood-drinking monsters. Vampires.

Down in the garden, Vlad laughs, as though he has heard me thinking the word.

"Indeed." Mina sounds unsettled and quickly changes the subject. "How did you learn the property was for sale? All the way from your home in the Mountains of Deep Winter?"

My heart seizes within me. Vlad never confirmed living in that specific region of Austria-Hungary to Mina, and I know at once that she has put two and two together. Her logical brain has been ruminating on my words since we left Whitby. She has deduced that Jonathan is connected to Vlad because he helped him purchase Carfax, and now she wants to hear it from Vlad himself.

"And why England, of all places?" Mina adds, when he takes a beat too long to respond.

I cannot help smiling, despite my worry about her being alone with him. There is no one more dogged or persistent than Mina when she wants an answer, that much I know.

"I have always longed to see its shores and experience the excitement of London," Vlad says patiently. "I even hoped to catch a glimpse of Her Majesty the Queen! This must seem silly to you. I am but a sentimental foreigner." I know very well how his voice can take on that charming gallantry with a touch of self-deprecation. It has worked on me many times.

But for some reason, it does not work on Mina. "How did you proceed with purchasing your home?" she persists. "Did you write letters to a lawyer, perhaps?"

The buzzing returns to my left ear, and I hear the front door open as the post is delivered. Impatiently, I turn my focus back to the conversation in the garden.

"I wrote to a number of offices located around London, asking for their opinions on such a purchase and requesting the names of properties for sale," Vlad is explaining.

"And several of these lawyers must have mentioned Carfax?"

"Only one did."

I hear Mina's dress rustle as she leans forward. "Which one?" she asks, her voice low and intense. "Which lawyer mentioned that it was for sale?"

Even though Vlad is silent, I can sense his admiration of her. He approved of her modesty before, and now her quick mind and forthright manner have impressed him further.

But before he can answer, I hear footsteps hurry out onto the terrace. "I beg your pardon," Harriet says excitedly. "But an urgent telegram has just arrived for you, miss, from Mr. Harker."

I wince, my ears pained by the sudden sharp screech of Mina's chair as she stands.

"Mr. Harker? Are you certain?" she asks, already sounding near tears. "Count, I am sorry, but I must read this. It is the first communication I've had since—"

"Say no more, Miss Murray. I will leave you. Thank you for a pleasant conversation, and please let Lucy know I called. And Mrs. Westenra, of course," Vlad adds, his voice full of his slow smile. I hear his coat rustle as he bows and then his shoes walking back out to the street.

I go to the window to watch him leave and find him standing at our gate, looking right up at the window of my room. He lifts his hat to me when our gazes meet, his expression quietly wistful. It is the first time I have seen him look sad, and in his eyes, I see the ocean and the cliffs and our bench beneath the willow. But now I also see blood splattered on my ball dress, Mina crying, Mamma bent over me with grief, and Arthur kneeling heartbroken by my bed.

I turn away when my bedroom door flies open and Mina throws herself into my arms, shaking and weeping violently without making a sound. "What is it? What's wrong?" I ask, panicked that the telegram has brought her evil news.

But when she pulls away, she is smiling through her tears. She hands me the message. "Jonathan is alive! He wants me to go to him as soon as may be."

I close my eyes and sag with relief. Vlad kept his word. Quickly, I read the telegram aloud. "Ill, but out of danger. Hospital of St. Joseph and Ste. Mary, Budapest. Come at once. All my love. Jonathan." I hug Mina again, overjoyed. "Thank God, my darling. I am so happy for you. Go to him at once. Take the train out tonight."

"I hate to leave you at a time like this—"

"A time like what? I am perfectly well, and he needs you." I look into her beloved face, unable to keep my lips from trembling. "I have loved you well, my Mina, more than you can ever know or I can ever say. But it's time for me to let you go."

She touches my face. "Why are you saying this?" she asks desperately. "Why are you talking as though we will never see each other again?"

I laugh to take the edge off my pain. *Our* pain, for I see in her eyes what she will never admit even to herself. I wipe away her tears gently. "Of course we will see each other again. But the Mina I put on the train and the Mina who comes back will be different women. You will marry Jonathan in Budapest, I know. You could not travel back to London, alone together, otherwise. And I will have to give you up to him entirely."

"Not entirely," she whispers. "Never entirely. You claim a piece of my heart forever."

"But you were never mine, and you never will be." I lean my forehead against hers. "Oh, Mina, how much we have to lose as women. It seems only the other day we were girls, and now we must take our separate paths. It is like dying in a way, the impossibility of going back."

Mina takes my face in her hands. "Don't say that, Lucy," she tells me fiercely. "We will live, you and I. We will *live*."

She kisses me full on the lips, as she did that day on the beach, years ago. Her mouth is soft and tentative and delicious, but I feel a farewell in it, the closing of a chapter in our lives that will never come again. And as always, she is the first to pull away. She moves to the window and gazes out, and Vlad must be gone, for she looks down at the street with no expression.

"I am all aflutter," she breathes. "I hardly know what to do with myself. Jonathan is alive, and that is all I can think about. Not such unromantic details as train tickets and sensible shoes."

Her mind and heart are once again all Jonathan's. Our moment is gone, and I will have to make my peace with that. I press my hand over my lips, imprinting her kiss there, and stride over to the bell to ring for my maid. "Then let me take care of those details," I say as cheerfully as I can. "I will help you pack while Harriet runs to the station to secure you a ticket, and—"

"Wait," Mina interrupts. "Before you ring for her, I want to talk about the count."

My hand freezes in midair.

"He came again just now. He is living in Purfleet, near Dr. Seward's property. Aside from being much too interested in you, he seems charming and gentlemanly. And yet—"

I find that I am holding my breath. "And yet?"

Mina hesitates. "You seemed afraid of him before we left Whitby, and I think you were right to be wary. There is indeed something odd about him. A sense of wrongness in the way he looks at one and speaks to one. I believe he has an improper interest in me as well. I think some men must enjoy the ... *challenge* of a woman who is engaged to another." She studies me. "The day you warned me about him, you told me Jonathan was still alive in almost the same breath. I know I promised not to question you. But there is no way you could have known, unless ..."

My palm stings from the pressure of my fingernails digging into it.

"Unless it was that bond between us. That link I believe we share with our loved ones," she says, and I let out a slow and quiet breath. "Perhaps your love for me and, in turn, my love for Jonathan, led you to sense that he was safe. But I have been turning it over and over in my mind, the way you seemed to imply a connection between him and the count."

My throat is dry as bone, and I find that I cannot say a word.

"And I have been asking myself questions. Such as whether the count could be the client Jonathan was helping in the Mountains of Deep Winter. Or whether he could possibly have had anything to do with Jonathan's delay." Mina puts her hands on my shoulders and searches my eyes. "You had a feeling about Jonathan being alive. Did you somehow sense this, too?"

For one wild and reckless moment, as I look into the vivid blue of her eyes, I consider telling her everything. I consider baring *all*. The mist, the dreams, the secret encounters with Vlad. But then I would also have to confess to her what I have done—what I have asked for. And I am too much of a coward. We stare at each other for a long, charged moment before I hang my head. "No," I mutter. "I was so ill, Mina. I must have been feverish. Confused."

"You did not seem confused to me," she says quietly.

I keep my eyes averted. "As you say, there is no way I could know these things. It is only intuition, perhaps. A feeling, to use your word."

There is another silence, and then she squeezes my shoulders and forces a smile. "Yes, of course. This is all conjecture, and it may be unfair, casting suspicion on a man whose only fault may be liking women who are already spoken for," she adds in a lighter tone, and I make myself smile back, even as my pulse quivers like a cornered animal. "Perhaps I am overthinking it, as I tend to do about everything. But you know that about me, Lucy. My Lucy who I love more than life itself." She kisses me again, this time, a sisterly peck on the cheek. "I promise to be back in time for your wedding. Ring for Harriet, dear. Tonight, I shall be on the train to Jonathan."

I lie in bed alone that evening, feeling desolate with Mina gone, tucked into a train compartment somewhere with her trunk above her dreaming head. Part of my heart went with her, and I wish all of it had, for the piece that remains insists upon aching. I stare into the shadows of my room, wondering what else she may have pieced together from what I did not voice about Vlad. I would ask her if she were here in bed with me, but she never will be again. When she returns, she will be the wife of Jonathan Harker. And my beloved friend, my confidante and my teacher, my sister and my love, will almost be dead to me.

I curl into a trembling ball and hug myself. I cannot go on losing people, for every time I do, a part of my own self is destroyed. And someday, there will be nothing left of me at all—nothing left of any of us but ashes and shadow. How short, how full of loss life is. How unerringly bookended by death. I bite down on my pillow, hard, to quiet my sobs.

But my mother must hear me all the same, for there is a quiet knock followed by her soft voice asking, "Lucy?" The key turns in the lock and my door opens, revealing her thin face. The moon falls full upon her features, sharpening her skeletal cheeks, hollow eyes, and skin as fragile as crumbling paper. The truth of her illness is even clearer in the darkness, and it hits my aching heart like a powerful blow. "I had a feeling you needed me."

"Oh, Mamma," I sob as she comes over and puts her arms around me, rocking me and murmuring soothing words into my hair. "Whatever would I do without you?"

"You would live on, my precious one. You would have a happy life with Arthur, loved and protected. I have no fears on that score, so I can go whenever I am called."

I hug her so hard I can feel every one of her bones jutting out from her frame. "I won't let you go," I say fiercely. "You won't be called. I cannot allow it."

She laughs gently. "We talked about this when you were a little girl, remember? We cannot control death. It beckons and we can only obey, some of us earlier than others. I am glad, glad to the heart that I have had so many years with you."

"How can you say that when we haven't had nearly enough? Mamma, this is my fault. I should not have worried you so with my illness. I should not have—"

"Hush. I have been unwell for years now and I kept it from you." My mother smiles, her face softening into the one I know and love so very much. "I was not certain for a long time. I only suspected, and I did not wish to think of it, not with my daughter not yet married and under a husband's protection. But earlier this year, I began to accept it and to put my affairs in order. And recently, that marvel of a doctor Van Helsing put me at ease."

"What did he say?" I whisper.

"I told him everything in Whitby," she says. "He confirmed my illness, a malady of the heart, and assured me that I had prepared better than most. He praised me for seeing my lawyers early, organizing my papers, and ensuring that you would be cared for. And he gave me his word that you would always have his friendship. He holds such fatherly affection for you, my child."

I cling to her, my throat raw with tears. "But *you* are my true parent, my last parent."

"You are a woman now. In two weeks, you will be twenty and married. You passed out of my care some time ago without realizing it. It was why I pushed so for you to marry Arthur." She tenderly wipes my face. "You will have Arthur to adore you, Mina to be a sister to you, and Dr. Van Helsing and many others to help and advise. We only fear death when we have not done what we should have or lived life to the fullest, and I have done both. My story is ending, but yours is just beginning. My one regret is not being able to see your children."

I shudder. "I have no need of them when I still feel like one myself."

"You will change your mind," she predicts. "When Mina and Jonathan have their first baby, you will know that hunger for a child."

"I? Hunger for a child? What nonsense." I look pleadingly up at her. "Perhaps you and Dr. Van Helsing both will be wrong, and you will live to see a ripe old age."

"Perhaps. But it's better not to hope for something we have no power over."

"Will you stay with me tonight, Mamma?" I ask. "I feel so lonely without Mina."

We snuggle together in my bed, my mother's arms around me as though I am her little girl again. She believes I will come to accept our situation. But as I listen to her breathing grow steady with the rhythm of deep sleep, I think of how I have never been the sort of woman to accept hard truths. And I will not be now, not in the face of losing so much.

Something we have no power over.

Mamma does not know that I *do* have power over death. I *do* have a choice, and if I am brave enough to make it, I can be with her and Arthur and Mina for as long as they live, watch over them for as long as they live. I could spend all the years of Mamma's life nursing her back to full health as her devoted daughter, all the years of Mina's life proudly watching her build a home and a family, and all the years of Arthur's life being his wife and his true love. None of them would ever know the pain of losing me.

Two thoughts intrude upon my joyous fantasy.

The first: *Would Mina, with her perception and her cleverness, sense a wrongness in* me?

The second: *How would I ever convince Vlad to finish the job?*

I clench my jaw. If only he had met my request with compassion, rather than hatred.

To him, women are disposable. We are toys to be discarded when we have lost our shine. We are *belongings.* That is what this little game of finding the "perfect woman" is all about. That is what he is ultimately after: to possess, to dominate, to own. He wants me to be his. He wants me to give everything, all that I have and all that I am, to him alone.

I think of that night at Diana Edgerton's. The candlelit room, the urgent music of the harp, the feeling of plummeting down a hill as his hands learned the map of my body.

I have one card left to play. One part of myself I have not given to anyone.

I picture Arthur's face, and guilt blooms in my chest at the thought of surrendering to another what I should save for him. But I *did* offer it to him, and he refused. *And it is mine, and mine alone to decide whom to give it to*, I think. *Mine, and mine alone to decide what I want.*

And what I want is an eternity of cheating death, of delaying the inevitable for good.

Many hundreds of years ago, Vlad made such a choice. And though he denies me the same right, I know that it is within my reach.

It is then that I notice my bedroom door standing slightly ajar. Mamma came in without locking it again, and indeed, the key is still dangling from a ribbon around her wrist.

I gaze from the open door to the key.

But I do not take it from Mamma.

I do not lock my bedroom door.

CHAPTER TWENTY-FOUR

The mist leads me to the churchyard like a wanderer returning home. The cool night air cleanses my lungs with the scent of late roses and fresh-turned earth as I pass the silent graves to my family's mausoleum. Vlad sits on the bench across from it, gazing at the carved granite name of Westenra. When he turns, the rigid line of his mouth softens. The dark ocean of his eyes washes over me. "Lucy," he says, very low, and I hear in his voice that I have not been the only one longing for this. "I wondered if you would come back to me."

"I wondered as well."

He holds out his hand, strong and white and cold, and I let him pull me close. He presses his face into me and breathes me in. "I'm glad you're here," he says, lifting his head. His blue-green gaze is tender and mesmerizing, but I know now how cold and empty it can also be, and how easily his gentleness can vanish into the fanged beast lurking underneath. Which is the truth? The man who cares for me, or the monster who sees me as prey? "Why are you so sad? Tell me your troubles, and I will destroy everything that hurts you."

"Will you?" I whisper, smoothing a lock of soft dark hair from his forehead.

Vlad pulls me down beside him and wraps his arms around me. I shiver as the cold stone bench meets my thighs through my nightdress. But for the view of the mausoleum in place of the North Sea, we might have been on the Whitby cliffs again, late on a windswept August evening.

I look at the great death-house where generations of my family sleep. So many nights have I come here, seeking comfort. But there is no comfort for me tonight—only a road diverging, and a choice I must make.

"Everything seems to be slipping away from me," I say. "My mother. Mina. To live is to lose. That is what I could not make you understand, Vlad."

"What do I not understand?" he asks gently.

"Why I wished to make the choice I did. I thought you had killed me. I thought I would die from your bite, and I despised myself for bringing such pain to my family. In my haste to avoid death, I had almost welcomed it early instead. But here I sit."

"Here you sit."

"To me, what you are is protection from death. If I became like you, I would be with my family forever and also *free*. It is an escape." I look at him. "But I don't think you will ever understand. You only see it as some vulgar, disgusting perversion of womanhood."

"But I *do* understand. I should not have berated you," he admits. "You see my existence as a way out of what you fear. I have been doing a great deal of thinking during our time apart, and my reaction to your request— for I see now that it *was* a request—was regrettable."

"But you haven't changed your opinion of me," I say quietly. "I heard you talking to Mina today. I know you still value her high above me . . . and you are right to do so."

"I am impressed with Miss Murray, and I can see why you love her. But much of her appeal, I confess, is that she reminds me of my friend Lucy. She certainly interrogated me boldly enough to have learned it from that friend Lucy." He chuckles. "She has surmised that her Jonathan helped me to purchase Carfax. He heard of its availability from a man who lives and works near it. A man he knows socially, who had at one time hoped to marry his Mina's dearest friend."

"Jack Seward," I say, and Vlad's eyes twinkle at me. Something eases in my chest like a ribbon untangling. "I will not thank you for releasing Jonathan from captivity, as it was only the right thing to do. But I am glad you did for Mina's sake."

"I didn't do it for her. I did it for you, because you asked me to." His eyes find the marks on my throat. "You did not deserve such pain, not when I can choose to make it pleasurable, as you saw with the widow. Jonathan, too, though he is much more ill than you have been, for he was bitten many times and also had to survive the treacherous lands around my castle. That he did is proof of his strength. He will recover and marry that wonderful Miss Murray."

"Bitten many times." My words come out as both a groan and a gasp.

"He enjoyed it. We made certain of that." When Vlad looks at me, an image appears in my mind of the ever proper and self-possessed Jonathan Harker, looking neither proper nor self-possessed as he lies stark naked on a bed, his arms and legs sprawled apart while Vlad and two dark-haired women bend their heads over him, their wicked red mouths tasting more than just his blood. Vlad laughs, watching me shiver. "Oh, yes, he enjoyed it indeed."

I know full well that this is part of his strategy to possess me. He can choose unnecessary pain and violence when it pleases him to hurt and frighten me, and he can choose to be tender and playful when it serves him best, because he knows that kindness will win me back to him. Always, the choice is his. Not mine.

But I *will* choose. I have played the game of love for many years, with many men, and I can manipulate as well as he can, though I have not his powers.

Gently, I pull my hand out of his. "It felt wrong, the way you and I parted that evening, and so I came tonight to say a better goodbye. Thank you for being my friend, and for giving me a measure of freedom and happiness that I will never know again."

"Goodbye?" he echoes.

"I am marrying Arthur soon and must put all of this behind me." I feel no invasion of my mind at present, but as I speak, I imagine another shield around my skull, strong and silver, keeping my thoughts secret. I let it snap into place as I look up at the stars, taking care to show nothing upon my face. "I, too, have done much thinking this week, after you showed me the pain and brutality of being bitten. You say it can be pleasurable, but I have only known terror and suffering. So perhaps it is wise that I give it up. Give *you* up."

Vlad looks at me, his eyes piercing, and I wonder for a moment if I have overplayed my hand. And then he asks, "But why, if you have known freedom and happiness with me, must you give me up?" And I know that I have him. I have him, and we shall see who controls whom.

"It frightens me how right this feels, being with you. Even the marks you left on my throat feel right." I touch the scars lightly with a fingertip. "I can't stop thinking about how close I came to what I wanted. I don't regret asking you for it. But I think it is time we said farewell."

"Why do you think," he asks slowly, "it is yours to decide if we say farewell, or when?"

I ignore the flicker of anger that rises in me. "We must, for I would come closer to being the woman I ought to be. I must be perfect, the sort of wife Arthur deserves, for soon I will belong to him and only to him. You are the moon and the mist, beautiful and terrible . . . but now I must turn my eyes to the sun. To Arthur."

There is a long silence, and I know that I was right to protect my thoughts. Around my skull I feel a tingle, the sensation of Vlad probing for the truth inside me. I close my eyes and bow my head, as if in sadness, and focus on strengthening that shield and keeping him out.

"Marrying him will be the end of everything you are," he says. "You told me that you and I are equals. Is *he* your equal? What happened to your desire for *more*?"

"I have no right to desire more," I say calmly. "I will have a beautiful home, a good name, and a loving husband. Arthur is my kindred soul after all, and not you."

Vlad's eyes have darkened to a poisonous green. "But you and I found each other for a reason. Did you not imply that we were always destined to meet, perhaps for eternity?"

I stand up. Even on my feet before him, he is so tall that we are almost at eye level. "You exhaust me, Vlad," I say with honest fury. "I am tired of you pulling me like a kite in whatever direction you please. I begged you to let me be with you, and you rejected me. And now, when I want to leave you to regain my virtue and dignity, you lure me back? I cannot stand this!"

He takes my hands in his iron grip. "Lucy, calm yourself. You will not leave me," he says, his voice low and determined, spurred on by my refusal of him.

"Why should I stay with you?" I demand. "You don't want me. You like a challenge, not a woman who runs to you with her arms open. That is what *you* told me. And so I must belong to Arthur, when what I truly wish is to give myself to—" I cut myself off and turn my head away as though I can't bear to look at what I cannot have.

"Give yourself to whom?"

I close my eyes and do not answer.

He keeps my hand tight in one of his, and with the other, turns my face back toward him. His eyes are so dark now that they look almost black, and for a moment I see a flash of the great grey wolf in his features. "Give yourself to whom?" he asks, the words slow and deliberate.

"To you," I whisper. "I want to be yours, Vlad."

He stares at me, deep into my eyes, and I feel my resistance wavering as he begins to reach into my mind. But I steel myself, hard. I think of the silver of Mina's bracelet and of my great-grandmother's ring, and of all the people who love me, and I push away his intrusion.

"I want to be yours," I repeat as I bring his hand to my lips, feeling the sharp edges of his garnet ring. And then I grip his fingers, bring the gem to my neck, and scratch my throat as hard as I can beneath the two wounds. A bright, wet, hot line of pain bursts across my skin, and at the smell of my blood, Vlad's eyes shift at once into great dark pupils ringed with scarlet.

Roughly, he seizes me by the waist and pulls me to him, but I put my hands on his chest to keep us apart. He is a being that does not need breath, yet his broad shoulders are heaving as though from exertion. Slowly, I bring my face an inch from his. "This time," I say, very low, "I want to feel pleasure. I want you to give me what you gave to Jonathan."

Vlad's fangs snap down, and fear slips through my desire. I am in the arms of a monster that could tear my head off with a flick of his wrist, yet I dare toy with him as he does me. His hands slide to my bottom, crushing me against him as his mouth laps up the blood on my throat. I tense, remembering the awful pain of his bite, but his fangs do not touch me. Instead, I feel the long, slow stroke of his freezing tongue tasting my throat and my collarbone. He tears my nightdress off my shoulders, exposing my breasts to his cunning, clever mouth. The edges of his fangs just brush my nipples, featherlight. I cry out and lean my head back, closing my eyes at the unbearable sweetness of it.

He raises his head and fixes his wicked, blood-ringed eyes upon me. "If it's pleasure you want, Lucy, then I will give it to you," he whispers. "We both know you will not get it from Arthur, not like this. He doesn't know what you want. But I do."

With one swift and powerful movement, he lifts me onto his lap, facing him. He is like granite against me, and so, so cold. I lock my legs around him and shiver against the bulk of his massive body as his embrace devours me whole. His mouth sucks at the cut on my throat as his hands slide up my bare legs, bringing the hem of my nightdress with them. His thumb skims my upper thigh, and I shift impatiently on his lap, trying to bring it where I want it.

Vlad laughs against my skin. "I asked you before why you think it is yours to decide?"

He presses his brutal face against mine and kisses me. I gasp for air. It is like breathing in winter or feeling the first shock of cold as I dive into the sea. Somehow, he keeps his fangs from cutting me and maneuvers his mouth so that I only feel his lips forcing mine open and his greedy tongue tasting me. It is nothing like my kisses with Arthur. There is an underlying malice, almost hatred, as though he has realized that he has played right into my hands. I can taste the rusty wine of my own blood in his mouth, heady and thick and metallic.

I cling to him for dear life, my arms around his neck, and let his mouth have its way with me. He pulls his face away for a moment, his eyes glinting as I struggle to take in air. And then, without warning, his hand on my thigh slides across the drenched seam between my legs in one hard stroke, rough and slow. Electricity shoots through me and I throw my head back once more, almost weeping for more. He laughs again, pleased, and moves his fingers again in a sweet, savage glide from the back of me to the front. I am shaking uncontrollably, and my arms and legs are wrapped so tightly around him that I do not think even his prodigious strength could dislodge me.

"Do you think Arthur would know how to do this?" he murmurs against my mouth as his long fingers stroke me over and over. "Answer me."

"No," I gasp because I know it is what he wants to hear. Somehow, my untrained body knows what to do. I arch my back, my hips moving against his hand. I have lost all my senses. I can no longer see the church-yard around us, smell the soil, or hear the crickets singing. My entire universe has been reduced to this single point of contact between his hand and my body.

But I have never been one to relinquish the upper hand, so I lean forward and claim his mouth with mine, careless of the fangs. One of them pricks the tender underside of my lip and he sucks in the bead of blood that forms. "Give me what you gave to Jonathan," I breathe again as my hand slides down his chest to the rigid swell I know I will find in his lap.

Vlad shifts beneath me, removing the fabric that remains between us. "Another request?"

"No," I say. "That was a command this time. Can't you tell?"

His face tightens. "You have no power over me," he says through gritted teeth, but his actions disagree. His strong hands move to my bottom and lift me into the air, holding me helplessly crushed against him with my face just an inch above his. "Arthur is nothing. You will not belong to him. I am all you will ever know. Do you understand me?"

My body aches for him. I try, desperately, to lower myself, but he tightens his grip on me.

"Do you understand me, Lucy?" he asks, his voice like steel.

"Yes, I understand," I whimper.

He smiles, pleased to be torturing me into a frenzy. "To whom do you belong?" he asks. "Tell me or you will not have your reward."

Even in the heat of my desire, even in the agony of pleasure, I think, *I belong to myself.* But he is watching me, his blood-ringed eyes relentless and cruel, and I am dying for what he can give me. "I belong to you, Vlad," I say, panting. "I am yours for the taking."

In one quick, deliberate movement, he lowers me, and I cry out in relief and surprise as he plunges to the core of me, burstingly hard. There is no great pain, certainly nothing compared to his bite, but the sensation is sharp, foreign, and freezing cold. There is no other word for it but invasion. He holds still, giving me time to adjust to the frigidity of him inside my own burning heat. I shift my hips tentatively, leaning back and then rocking toward him, and feel the satisfaction of hearing him utter a low, pained groan. So much for not having power over him.

He presses his lips to my ear. "I'm going to hold you to those words."

And then he lifts me off him and brings me back down again, hard and rough. I cry out as my body envelops him, my muscles tense with pleasure. He repeats the movement again and again, controlling the slow and steady rhythm, and as on the night of our harp duet, I feel as though I am climbing a hill with mad eagerness, starving for the thrill of plummeting down the other side. I am there, upon the threshold, about to fall . . . when he suddenly stops. He has lifted me just high enough to still feel the icy edge of him between my legs. I moan and struggle against his broad chest, raving and wild for completion, but he only looks straight into my eyes.

"I will ask you what I asked you that night on the terrace," Vlad says, breathing hard, his arms like a vise around me. His cold black eyes rake down my face to my throat and back. "This is what you truly want? You want me to bite you?"

I have no dignity left. No pretension. I have given him what a good girl would save for her husband, offered myself up like a flower to be plucked. I have made my decision and he knows it, too, from the flash of disdain I see in his gaze, still repulsed that I insist upon my right to choose. But he wants to hear my consent to seal our bond like a spell spoken in the night air.

Somewhere in my haze of desire, my rational mind must still be functioning, for I hear myself say, "I want immortality. And I want to feel pleasure, and not to be so ill again as to worry my family. Will you promise me these things?"

He does not promise. He looks at me, waiting.

And I am so far gone, so greedy for everything he has given and can give me, that I hear myself say, "Yes. Yes, Vlad, I want you to bite me."

He lowers me in one sharp, deliberate movement, joining us together once more. I slide down the length of him to the root, gasping at the intense, delicious cold as he positions his fangs over the wounds in my neck and bites down hard. There is pain—of course there is, searing and red-hot, but not nearly as unbearable as before. I am too focused on where my naked skin meets his and how the jarring shock has risen to a crescendo as I plummet, crying out. His mouth remains on my throat, drinking lazily before he pulls his fangs away. We hold each other, his arms as tightly around me as mine are around him, and stay motionless for a long time.

Slowly, the churchyard comes back into focus around me. I rest my head on Vlad's shoulder and look, heavy-lidded, at the rows of graves behind him, the silent witnesses to what we have done. What *I* have done, gladly and greedily. The Westenra mausoleum, too, was watching the destruction of my virtue and my life as I have known it. I stroke the back of Vlad's head, my fingers tangled in his soft hair. My limbs feel heavy and drowsy and weak.

"Do you hate me for what I've chosen?" I whisper.

"Would it matter if I did?"

"No." I pull away to look at him, dazed. His mouth is stained with my blood.

"You are the only one who has ever demanded this of me," Vlad says, his face impassive. "Everyone else screams and fights and begs. Everyone else tries to run away. But you, who dare to desire this, expect my approval for that?"

"No. I expect only your understanding."

He runs his icy fingertips over my cheek. "Lucy," he says.

And then a shrill scream shatters the night.

I blink my eyes, and suddenly Vlad is gone. I am lying flat on my back on the cold bench. I turn my head to see Harriet running down the path, parting the mist over the graves. She sobs as she holds a lantern over me. "Oh, miss, are you all right?" she cries. "There was a wolf, a great ugly beast. It ran and jumped right over me! It was . . . You were . . . I saw . . ."

She trails off, her eyes widening in horror as she takes me in.

When Dr. Van Helsing performed my transfusion, I had felt like I was floating above my own body, watching the scene from somewhere above. That sensation returns to me now, as though the mist has lifted me into the night air, and I can see myself clearly through Harriet's eyes: my long hair is a dark tangle, my knees are spread wide apart, and my toes are touching the grass on either side of the bench. My nightdress is ripped down to my waist, baring my breasts, and the hem is rucked over my legs, hiding absolutely nothing, including the splatter of blood staining the inside of my thighs.

A hundred emotions flash over my maid's face in seconds.

I feel as empty as a shell or a husk. My throat throbs with pain and I am sore and bruised between my legs. "Harriet," I say faintly, "I think you ought to take me home now."

And then, in the darkness and the mist, I laugh and I laugh and I laugh.

CHAPTER TWENTY-FIVE

This time, I feel sure I am dying.

I lie in bed for days on end, struggling to breathe as my heart flutters in my chest instead of beating. I eat nothing, for I can keep no food in my stomach. I am too weak to stay awake for long, and thoughts flit in and out of my mind like bats in the shadows. One reigns above all others: the suspicion that this bargain between Vlad and me—my virtue in return for his dark gift—was only ever a bargain in *my* mind, and that he has simply taken what I offered him without any intention of granting me immortality. He tricked me.

And I, in my arrogance and stupidity, have allowed him to kill me. No vampire am I, not when I have been reduced to this weak, mewling husk of my former self.

I toss and turn, feverish and raving, and in the haze of my dreams I am dancing with Vlad again. I see his slow, knowing smile and hear his words, low and dark and private. "I bite my victim multiple times," he whispers. But what had he said afterward? I cry out in frustration as threads of memory slip through my fingers. There had been something about killing before sunrise, and another piece I have lost in the trauma of his first bite and the lust of his second . . .

Faces drift in and out of my consciousness. I see Mamma, her face white as she clings with trembling hands to my bedpost, and Arthur with shadows under his eyes, running from his ailing father's side to mine. "I will fight," I want to reassure them. "I will find Vlad and demand that he fix this. I will be with you forever." But none of it leaves my lips.

Jack Seward hovers over me, his brow furrowed and gaze shrewd, studying me as a physician now and no longer as a lover. Dr. Van Helsing's calm voice breaks through the gloom with quiet resolve. "She needs blood, Jack. A great deal of it."

"But what could have taken so much from her?"

"I am not certain." Dr. Van Helsing's solemn face floats into view. "But this is no dog. See how it bit her in exactly the same spot? Fitting its teeth into the old wounds . . ."

I slip in and out of sleep, only awakening fully when I feel a pinch in the crook of my arm and a rich, silky, metallic fragrance wafts into my nostrils like the finest perfume. Even if I had never seen blood, even if I had no idea what it looked like, I would still be able to smell its color: the deepest, most vivid scarlet red, swirling with vitality.

"Hold her down!" Dr. Van Helsing sounds frantic. "Hold her down, I say!"

Rough hands on my shoulders. A restraining grip on my grasping arms. I scream and cry and hiss to no avail. I could break every one of their fingers for denying me what I crave. Something is wrong with my vision. Everything near me is blurred as though I am looking at it through foggy glass: halos of yellow lamp light; the doctors' weary faces; and a long, swinging rubber tube stained brilliant crimson.

But when my bleary gaze finds the bedroom window, I can see a droplet of water upon a branch, a withered leaf on the ivy trellis, a beetle crawling along the trunk of a tree. I can smell rain on cobblestone, horse droppings on a passerby's shoe, a package of rotting food, and the musky scent from between a woman's legs on a man scurrying down the street after a tryst. It reminds me of my encounter with Vlad, of my arms and legs locked around him and the feeling of him inside me like a stake made of ice, his hands moving me on him with exquisite precision.

"Stop her, Jack," Dr. Van Helsing says sharply.

A strong hand takes my wrist, pulling my yearning fingers away from the seam of my legs, and I shriek in frustration. This, they dare to deny me also.

The buzzing in my ears is overpowering. I can hear a dozen conversations at once.

The cook, muttering in the kitchen. "I slave over these dishes all day only to have them come back untouched. And for what?"

Mamma, in her room. "What will I do? I cannot die before Lucy wakes. I must hold on for her sake. I must be here to care for her—"

My mother's maid. "What you must do is stop fretting, madam, for it will do you harm. Now, be a lamb and go to sleep."

Dr. Van Helsing, down the hall with Jack. "I have read of such things, of night creatures that feed upon the blood of the living." Jack makes a sound of disbelief, and the doctor adds, "But how? How did it know to follow her here from Whitby?"

Harriet, talking to the other servants downstairs. "The mail is to be kept here, so as not to disturb Miss Lucy. But she will be upset not to hear of Miss Murray's marriage."

And then, suddenly and violently, my illness grows even worse. I heave up water, though my mouth is as dry as a desert, and I am so hot that I feel as though I have somehow floated through the mist and up to the sun. I writhe in pain, chafed by every thread in my sheets and blankets. It feels that the very air is killing me and tearing through the tissues of my lungs.

"Her pulse is almost gone. What's happening to her?" Jack asks, hoarse with fear.

"The transfusion did not work," Dr. Van Helsing says grimly. "Something about your blood does not agree with hers, and I must give her mine. Quick, bind my arm."

"But, sir, it will weaken you—"

"I will not let this child die!" Dr. Van Helsing roars.

Once more, the prick of a needle in my arm. Once more, the blood-stained tube swinging and beckoning to me with its red iron beauty. Once more, strong hands pinning my body to my pillows, keeping me away from the sustenance I hunger for.

"She has the blood of *two* men in her body," the doctor says, his voice faint. "Two strong and healthy men. Can you comprehend how much blood the creature has robbed from this poor girl? And still she clings on, gripping the very edge of life."

"Please rest," Jack begs him. "You need your strength. I will sit up with her tonight."

"Very well. But do not, under any circumstances, leave her alone or fall asleep yourself. Do you hear me, my boy? She must never, *never* be left on her own."

"I swear to you, Quincey and I will watch over her all night. He is below. He wanted to see her before returning to America."

I do not know how much time has passed, but when I open my heavy eyes, the room is dark. My movements feel dull and drugged, and I am still weak and feverish, but the sheets do not seem to hurt my skin as much anymore. "Jack?" I croak, turning my head.

Jack comes to me at once. He takes my hand, but it is not the romantic gesture it might have once been. His fingers search for the weak pulse in my wrist. "Still not as strong as I would want, but better," he says, sighing. "Dr. Van Helsing finally went to bed, or I would call him this instant. It would set his mind at ease to see you conscious."

"Could I have something to drink, please?" I ask, my mouth like cotton.

He gives me a glass of water, looking relieved when I drink it all. "Thank God you are thirsty for water again. I thought perhaps—" He breaks off and pours me another glass.

"What? That I wanted to drink something else?"

"Of course not," he says, too quickly. "How do you feel? Do you have a headache?"

"No. Just sit with me a moment, please. I have something to say to you."

He takes the chair beside my bed. His black hair, usually immaculate, hangs in untidy locks and his eyes are rimmed with red, but he looks like the Jack I have always known, the ambitious and confident young doctor who had charmed Papa so. I look at him with affection, remembering how he used to make Papa smile even on the hardest days, toward the end.

"Jack, you have been a true friend to my family, and you will make some lucky girl very happy someday. I still regret what happened between us. . . . No, let me speak," I add when he opens his mouth to reply. "I am sorry for toying with your emotions when I preferred another man. Though there was a time when I truly was unsure if I preferred him."

He smiles, looking a little embarrassed. "Water under the bridge, my dear Lucy."

"You are wonderful," I say, tears filling my eyes. "And I am proud to have known you, and to have had the honor of having your heart once."

"Why are you saying this?" Jack asks, distressed. "You will be well, and in a week's time, I am going to dance with a light heart at your wedding. Your children will call me Uncle Jack, and you will scold us for running wild through the house."

"No. No, I can never go back to that. I can never again be the Lucy you knew."

"What do you mean?"

I close my eyes, feeling the sting of hot tears, my throat tight with guilt. "I have done a foolish thing, Jack," I whisper. "I have been so painfully, unbelievably stupid, and I have been tricked. All the books I have read and all the stories I have devoured, and still I did not comprehend that he who makes a deal with the devil will always lose."

"What are you talking about?" Jack demands. "A deal with the devil? Lucy, I think you must still be delirious." He reaches out to feel my forehead, but I push his hand away weakly.

"Listen to me, please," I say, my voice cracking and feeble. "I have made a choice that will hurt everyone I care about, including you. But most especially Arthur."

"You would never harm a fly," he insists. "And no matter what you think, you were only ever sweet and charming to me. Arthur loves you—"

"I have betrayed that love, and his heart will break." My tears flow faster at the thought of what I have done in the churchyard. What I gave up, from which there can be no coming back. "I did what I thought was right. I gave up what I had to protect him, to protect all of you, and it has only done the opposite of what I hoped. It wasn't a bargain after all. It was a lie."

Jack looks straight into my eyes. "Lucy, I don't know what you are saying," he tells me quietly. "You were viciously attacked by an animal, and you have been in bed for almost a week. You've done nothing bad in all that time." He regards me thoughtfully. "Can you remember the incident? Or describe the wolf? Harriet told us her account, but I would like to hear yours."

"What did she tell you?" I whisper.

"She woke in the night and came to your room to see if all was well. She found your door unlocked and your mother asleep in your bed, but you were gone. Sleepwalking, she supposed, so she went to the churchyard to find you." Jack hesitates. "She told Van Helsing and me that you were on a bench, struggling with a beast. A grey wolf, she believed, though she can't be certain. She thought it would kill her, but it only jumped over her and escaped, and she hurried over and found you . . . bleeding a great deal." He avoids my eyes, and I know he saw the blood between my thighs. He and Dr. Van Helsing must have examined me thoroughly, but what they thought of their findings, it would be improper and unthinkable for me to ask.

"Yes, I remember," I say softly. "I remember the wolf. But I was dreaming."

He pats my hand. "You had no idea what was happening, poor girl. It wasn't your fault."

But it was. All of it was.

I let out a long, slow breath. "I heard you say Quincey was here. May I see him, please?"

The room seems smaller when Quincey Morris fills it with his warm, cheerful presence. He and Jack exchange a quiet word before Jack leaves us alone, and then the cowboy is sitting beside me with his bright smile and kind brown eyes shining at me.

"I reckon it was about time you called for me." His broad, friendly accent with its long drawling vowels is soothing, and he is big and solid and sturdy. Everything about him seems reliable and poised for action, and when he bends to kiss my hand, I see the glint of his ever-present pistols at his sides. "I was ready to ride to the ends of the earth to get you whatever medicine you needed. How are you?"

"Better, now that you're here," I say softly.

Quincey furrows his brow as he takes me in. I must look very different from the lively, flirtatious girl he had danced with in February, but ever the gentleman, he says nothing of this. "I've missed your conversation and your pretty face. You left me bereft when you packed up for the seaside, you know. Though I have been keeping myself busy, staying with our friend Jack."

"What's this I hear about you returning to America?"

He gives a light, playful stomp of his boots. "Well, little lady, these feet of mine are getting restless," he says. "I hunger for those open skies I was telling you about not so long ago. And there's always work to be done on the ranch. Not to mention I've been in England for quite enough time, I think, imposing on good doctor Jack's hospitality."

"I don't think that's true. You imposing, that is. I think Jack would be happy to have you stay with him the whole year. Anyone would."

His eyes crinkle at me. "Now that there's a nice compliment."

I hold out my hand and he wraps his warm fingers around it. "I will miss you, Quincey Morris," I say, my heart aching. "You have been a light. You've cheered me and made me laugh, and I wish with all my heart that we could dance together again."

"But don't you remember?" he asks, puzzled. "You invited me to your wedding next week. I'm sure Mr. Holmwood wouldn't be so stingy as to refuse me a jig with his bride."

I swallow against the threat of tears. "I'm not sure it will happen. The wedding, I mean. I feel that it will never come to pass now."

Quincey's face crumples with concern. "Lucy, what are you saying? A woman like you has far too much life in her to let a little accident get the better of her. I knew it the first time I saw you. I said to myself, *That girl has got some grit.* You can fight anything you put your mind to, least of all this."

I can't help smiling. "You think I have grit? You, with your bravery and your pistols?"

"You've got heaps and heaps of grit," he says seriously. "Grit isn't just for cowboys."

"I wish I could tell you everything. I have a feeling you wouldn't hate me and you might understand better than anyone. Dr. Van Helsing or Mamma or Jack, or even my darling Arthur."

"You can tell me anything you want to, and I won't ever hate you. I promise."

But I cannot stand the thought of seeing his open, honest face warp into disgust. I could not bear it if he turned away, revolted by the sight of me and what I have chosen. "I can't. I'm not brave enough, and I don't want you to remember me that way," I say. "I want you to ride your horse on those grassy plains, in that clean open air, and think of me as a girl you once danced with who had a little grit. Perhaps I'll be watching you from that big, blue Texas sky."

"Lucy," he says, understanding dawning on his face. "Are you saying goodbye?"

My heart is breaking inside of me. "I'm saying goodbye," I agree. "Because they can fill me with as much blood as they like, and they can give me all the medicine in the world, but they cannot erase this stain from my soul. I am dying, Quincey—"

"You're talking nonsense," he says sternly, even as I see his eyes taking in my pallor and weakness. I must be a sight, having lain ill and exhausted and unwashed for a week. "None of what you're saying is true. And to show you I don't believe it, I'm entrusting something to your care that I want you to return to me when we dance at your wedding. All right?" He reaches into his breast pocket and pulls out three small objects, which he places into my palm.

I blink my tear-blurred eyes, and when my vision clears, I see a round, smooth grey stone veined with red and gold; a charred lump of silvery metal; and a piece of flat dark flint carved into the shape of a triangle, a sharp point at the tip.

Quincey points at the stone. "That is a piece of my land. Land my family has settled, free and clear, years and years after our forebears were taken by force to a country that didn't want them, only their labor. *That*"—he touches the flint—"is an Indian arrowhead, given to me by a great man. And *this* is a bullet I dug right out of my leg after a run-in with bandits. The dangers of the American West are as great as her beauty," he adds with a wry smile at my shock.

I run my thumb gently over the items, feeling the weight of their meaning in my palm.

"I carry many talismans of protection when I travel, but these, I keep against my heart. Right here." He pats his expansive chest. "The stone reminds me of what home means and what it has cost my family. The arrowhead tells me to never forget that the land I stand on was stolen from someone else. And the bullet is a way to remember that life can end in the blink of an eye." His voice is gruff with emotion. "They are objects of faith, respect, and strength. Choose one."

"Quincey, I cannot take these from you—"

"You're not taking them from me," he says solemnly. "You're just holding on to one of them for a week. I know you're a woman of your word, so you better keep this promise, you hear me? These talismans and what they mean to me—home, family, God's love and blessing—they've saved my hide many a time. Now let one of them be a talisman for *you*."

My thumb finds the charred bullet again, and Quincey nods and takes back the stone and the arrowhead. *Life can end in the blink of an eye.*

"Lucy? Are you all right?" he asks as sobs shake my frail body at his kindness and his trust in me. I start crying brokenly as I clutch the bullet, aching for the life I never wanted and pushed away with both hands, and through my tears I see Quincey going to the door to call Jack. Right behind them is Arthur, still in his coat as though he had just arrived. He hurries over and hugs me tightly to him, ignoring Jack's warning to be careful.

"Hush, love, don't cry like that," Arthur murmurs. "I'm here now. I'm here."

"She was trying to say goodbye to me," Quincey says in a low voice. His hands flutter helplessly at his sides. "She was talking nonsense and I got frightened."

Jack leans over Arthur's shoulder, lifting each of my eyelids gently and checking my pulse. "This is the longest she's been conscious, but her heart is a little stronger than before."

"When did she wake?" Arthur asks. "Have I missed anything?"

"Half an hour ago. She drank water but hasn't eaten anything," Jack says thoughtfully. "Maybe it's the lack of food that's gone to her head. She has been saying strange things."

"Should I go get some broth? Do you think she'd like that?" Quincey asks.

"Why are you talking about me as though I'm not here?" I ask, looking at Arthur with pleading eyes. "Why won't any of you believe me?"

"Hush, darling," Arthur says gently, lowering me onto my pillows.

They all look at me. Had I not been so weak, sad, and certain I would die, I might laugh at the sight of the three men who want to marry me standing there together. Instead, I shut my eyes and think of a fourth man, one who does *not* want to marry me, but who dangled a great gift before me without any intention of bestowing it. And now I will do what I feared most: leave my loved ones behind in grief, mourning, and utter disgrace. *Curse you, Vlad*, I think. *And curse the mist for bringing me to you.* "I want to be alone with Arthur, please," I whisper. My fingers are still curled around Quincey's bullet, and I tuck it carefully into my nightgown pocket.

Jack and Quincey move to the door at once. "We'll be just across the hall," Jack says.

Alone with Arthur, I see how exhausted he truly is. His face is grey with weariness, and his chin is rough from lack of shaving. "Now what's all this about saying goodbye?" Arthur asks, stroking my hair. "I know you have been very ill, my beloved, but this confounded dog hasn't harmed you as much this time. Thank God."

"What do you mean?" I ask, confused. "I feel immensely worse."

"Well, the first time it attacked you, Dr. Van Helsing had to give you some of my blood. Remember? And this time, you haven't needed any blood."

Slowly, it dawns on me that Jack and Dr. Van Helsing have not told Arthur about the other transfusions. Perhaps they wished to spare his feelings, thinking he might not like the idea of other men's blood flowing in his fiancée's veins. "How is your father?" I ask.

Arthur bows his head. "He will leave us soon. Any day now, I imagine. The doctors told me very quietly that he will not live to see us marry next week." He struggles not to cry for a moment, his face twisting, and I pull him close to me.

"Go on, Arthur. You may cry before me."

And he does, with his wet face pressed to my neck and his shoulders heaving in that silent, gasping way in which some men grieve. I rub his back, feeling that even with all the pain already housed within me, I would gladly take his too, to spare him.

"I was half-asleep, so I can't be sure," I say, still hugging him close. "But I think I heard a servant say that Mina wrote to tell me of her marriage in Budapest. She and Jonathan will be home soon, man and wife. They never wanted a big society wedding like ours. It must have been a simple ceremony, with him in a hospital bed. Just a chaplain, a prayer book, and their hands joined like this." I lace my fingers with Arthur's. "I would marry you like that, gladly."

He gives a soft laugh. "What about your gown and veil and flowers?"

"Mamma cares about those things, not me," I say, stroking his hair. The thought of further hurting him with my own death makes it difficult to breathe. *Curse you, Vlad.* But if I am to die, perhaps marrying Arthur on my deathbed would ease the pain. I would leave him a widower, unblemished by me. "You will be Lord Godalming and take over the estate. You must be strong."

"For you, I will try."

I put my hands on either side of his face and lift it to mine. "My heart is yours," I tell him. "And I will love you until the end of time. It will not fade even in death."

"I can't bear it, Lucy," he says, anguished. "Don't say goodbye to me, too."

He is waiting for a reassurance I can no longer give. What can I say to him? How can I explain what I have done? He would not understand. He has never been able to see into my dark and tortured soul, and he did not witness what I gave Vlad—and what I asked of Vlad in return—in the shadows of that churchyard, with my family's mausoleum hovering above us in the mist.

And so all I do is bring Arthur's face to mine and kiss him, hoping that my lips will tell him everything I cannot say. He kisses me back, hard, pressing my head into the pillow.

"Stop!" Dr. Van Helsing shouts. He grabs Arthur's shoulders and pulls him away from me. Behind him, in the doorway, I see Jack staring at the opposite side of the room. His eyes, so red-rimmed and tired before, are wide awake now. His face is white as a sheet.

Arthur twists furiously out of the older man's grip. "What are you doing?"

"You must stay apart," Dr. Van Helsing says sternly. "You must not kiss. Come over here and I will show you why. You see it, too, Jack?"

"See what?" I ask, frightened.

Dr. Van Helsing drags Arthur over to where Jack is standing, and Arthur goes quiet and still at once. They are all looking in the direction of my dressing table. "Forgive me," Dr. Van Helsing says. "I wished to give you and Lucy privacy, but I also had to keep myself nearby. This proves that I was right to worry." He sighs and runs a trembling hand over his tired face. It is the first time I have ever seen him afraid. "I stood in the hall outside, and when I saw that, I knew."

My weak heart picks up as I begin to wonder . . . I *wonder* . . . I struggle to sit up against my pillows, pleading, "Saw what? What is it? Tell me."

None of them seem to hear me.

"But . . . but *how*? This is not scientifically possible. A trick of the light?" Jack strides across the room, not to my dressing table, but to the full-length mirror I have looked into before every ball and every party for the past several years of my life. One of the last times had been with Mina as we prepared to celebrate her engagement, surrounded by flowers from the men who love us. It was not that long ago, but it feels as though a lifetime has passed.

"I will explain more later," Dr. Van Helsing says. "God help me, I will have to."

"But how can a mirror do that?" Arthur asks, his voice thinner and more ragged than I have ever heard it. "I am not as educated a man as either of you, but I know that a mirror cannot—"

"It is not the mirror's fault," Jack says slowly, exchanging glances with Dr. Van Helsing.

Arthur's already pale face goes even whiter. "What do you mean? You blame Lucy?"

"No one blames Lucy for anything," Dr. Van Helsing says evenly.

I cry out in frustration as I try and fail to sit up in bed. My limbs are shaking too hard, but not just from illness. I am also trembling because I think I know what they have seen in the mirror—or rather, what they have *not* seen. And if I am correct, then perhaps there is a sliver of hope that I have not given up everything in exchange for nothing. Perhaps there is still time, still a chance for me to find Vlad, to fix all of this. "Please," I call. "Dr. Van Helsing, show me!"

"Don't, Van Helsing," Jack says urgently, glancing at me. "It will weaken her heart—"

"It is too distressing," Arthur whispers as though to himself.

But Dr. Van Helsing studies my weak, tortured face, and then turns to look in the doorway. Quincey and two maids are standing there, grouped together like startled birds. In Quincey's hand is a large silver cross, attached to a chain around his neck. He is whispering a prayer, and I see

Dr. Van Helsing look thoughtfully from me to the cross and back. I stare back at him in confusion, and something must pass through his mind, some assurance, for he nods.

"One of you," he says to the maids. "Please bring Miss Lucy's hand mirror to her."

"Van Helsing, *no*," Jack says. "How will this help her? It will only frighten her."

"This is not a good idea," Quincey agrees.

But Dr. Van Helsing ignores them and nods again at the maids. Harriet collects my little silver hand mirror from the dressing table and brings it to the bedside. For the first time in the many years in which she has served as my lady's maid, she looks as though she is afraid of me. "Miss Lucy," she says hesitantly, clutching the mirror to her chest. "I don't want to do this."

"It's all right. Show me, Harriet," I say, my breath coming in short, ragged bursts.

A tear slips down her cheek as she holds the glass out, her hands shaking badly. I take it, half-hopeful, half-terrified that I will see nothing at all where my reflection should be, the way I had seen nothing when Vlad had stood before a mirror.

But what I see is infinitely worse than nothing.

My reflection is ghastly, a nightmare captured by light and silver and glass, and at first I cannot believe I am looking at myself. My eyes, dark and tilting at the corners, have whites that are dotted with blood. Those are my nose and my cheekbones and my clear pale skin tinted with gold, but they are all speckled with blood. That is my neck, long and smooth but for the wounds Vlad's fangs left behind—bright white weals with wet red centers, purple bruises surrounding them like halos—splattered in blood.

Blood, blood, blood. Every inch of me is covered in blood, droplets big and small, as though someone has opened a vein in front of me and covered me in the violent spray. All the drops are moving slowly, creeping over my body like living organisms, suspended in the unholy canvas of my skin. I scream and almost drop the mirror in my haste to run my hand over my face and my neck. But when I look down at my palm, it is clean.

There is no real blood splashed all over my skin. No evidence of what I have done or what I have asked for . . . except in my reflection in the mirror.

I stare into my own eyes, horrible flecks of scarlet dancing through the whites like gore on clean linen. I am breathing much too fast, and my weak heart is pumping at a rate it cannot sustain. I feel as though my head has been detached from my body and is hovering and spinning over the bed and the distraught girl gazing at the reflection not of her face, but of her soul.

Out, out, damned spot, I think. I feel the sudden urge to laugh as I had done that night in the churchyard when Harriet had found me, drained of blood and virtue. *Hell is murky.*

Vaguely, in my swoon, I register Jack pushing my maid aside. He seizes the mirror from my loosening grip. Van Helsing is there, calling out orders, and Arthur takes hold of one of my hands despite the doctor's warnings. "Lucy, Lucy," he weeps over and over again.

His voice is the last thing I hear before I give myself to the darkness.

CHAPTER TWENTY-SIX

The next morning, I wake to find Dr. Van Helsing at my desk, surrounded by books and papers and ink. His jet-black hair stands on end as though he has been raking his hands through it, and he looks exhausted, but there is a strange, intense, almost excited energy about him. He has angled the desk chair to face my bed, and so the second my eyes are open, he is coming over.

"How are you feeling, Lucy?" he asks kindly, though I notice he keeps his distance.

I have to think for a moment. "Better," I say at last, surprised. "My head isn't floating anymore. And I am not as weak or feverish." My stomach suddenly gives an immense rumble.

The doctor laughs. "Good! I will send for some food at once. What will you have?"

"I think I could eat every strawberry pastry in London," I say, sitting up without difficulty. I lean back against my pillows, cheered by my return to health and the blue sky and sunshine outside my window. But when Dr. Van Helsing goes to the door to send a servant for my breakfast, I see white sheets draped over my full-length mirror and the looking glass at my dressing table. The revelation of last night comes back to me all at once, and my heart sinks.

Dr. Van Helsing comes back and sees my changed expression. "That is just a precaution, my dear. I did not want you to be distressed upon waking up."

I touch my face, and my hands come away clean. "Please, may I see?" I ask quietly.

When he lifts the sheet off the full-length mirror, I am confronted once more by the nightmarish woman who looks like me: long black hair, dark eyes, pale olive skin with a tint of rose. But there are red droplets swirling across her skin and in the whites of her eyes, as though some unseen wind is blowing the blood around her face. I stare at the proof of Vlad's venom swimming in my veins, manifesting only—for some ungodly reason—in a reflective surface.

Dr. Van Helsing replaces the sheet, hiding my shadow self from view. "Do not worry," he says gently, taking the chair next to my bed. "Jack and I are working hard to find a solution. I have done much reading since last night, and we have a few promising leads."

My fingers involuntarily clench on my blanket. "Such as?"

"I will tell you when Jack returns. In the meantime, I want you to remain calm and to eat, so that those rosy cheeks remain when your mother comes to see you later."

My heart gives a tug of longing for Mamma. I did not see her face more than once or twice during this latest illness, likely on the doctor's orders, for which I am grateful. "How is she? Is she sleeping and eating better than she had in Whitby?"

"She is well taken care of," Dr. Van Helsing reassures me. It is not an answer, but I am beginning to see that he is a man who does not respond unless he can do so with the utmost truth.

I close my eyes, my chest tight with the guilt of what I have done to my beloved mother. "I have worried her into her grave, haven't I?" I whisper. "I will lose her as I lost Papa."

"Do not say that. Your mother's heart malady began long ago."

"But I have worsened it, and death will come."

"Death comes for us all," Dr. Van Helsing says calmly. "We have not the power to decide when, where, or how, nor does it serve us to predict or anticipate it."

"All those books I read in Papa's library," I say, swallowing past a lump in my aching throat. "And still I find no comfort. How can we live so haunted by death?"

The doctor folds his hands over one knee, looking thoughtful. "In some cultures, death is celebrated as an occasion to remember the life of the bereaved. In my mother's culture, no one is left to grieve or struggle alone. The entire community rallies when a person dies."

"Papa said his grandmother wore white at her husband's funeral. To her, it was the color of mourning and she would not be persuaded otherwise, though it caused a scandal. He said she was heartbroken and so alone, and I am afraid that Mamma . . . that I will . . ."

Dr. Van Helsing's eyes on me are kind. "It is hard not to have community. Just as your great-grandmother was cut away from her roots, so, too, were you and I, when I lost my mother and you lost your father. Being transplanted is not easy. It makes sense that death weighs upon you." He holds up a stern finger. "But we will not let it enter here. We will not invite it in."

I look at him sharply, but Harriet comes in at that moment and he gets up to take the tray from her. She gives me a nervous smile before vanishing, and the doctor himself places my bacon, eggs, bread, and tea before me, all of which tastes divine. I devour it in minutes.

Dr. Van Helsing claps his hands, delighted by my appetite, just as Jack Seward strides into the room with two large boxes in his arms, looking disgruntled.

"The shopkeeper thought I had lost my mind," he grumbles, setting them on my dressing table. "He must have assumed I was one of the patients at my own mental institution and not the physician responsible for them. What is this all about, sir?"

Dr. Van Helsing leaps out of his chair, looking energetic and cheerful despite his lack of sleep. He pulls some pale purple flowers out of the boxes. "These are for you, Lucy."

"That's very kind of you, Doctor," I say, bewildered.

His thick black brows form a stern line. "They are not for looking pretty. They are an experiment. You see, I have been reading an interesting book that may hold answers for us, particularly after what happened last night with the mirrors. Will you trust me in this?"

"Yes," I say with foreboding in my heart, wondering how close to the truth he has come. He approaches my bed slowly, his eyes on my face as he holds the flowers about two inches from my nose. I stare at them, puzzled. The stems are long, thin, and green and the blossoms are tiny purple spheres. But the most notable quality of the odd bouquet is its thick, strong, cloying smell. I look up at Dr. Van Helsing, who seems pleased by my confusion.

"We are not too late," he says, satisfied. "Hold these, Lucy."

Obediently, I take the flowers. I sniff them and immediately sneeze.

"Sir, you are going to frighten her if you don't explain," Jack says wearily as Dr. Van Helsing dives into the open boxes again. He brings out at least two dozen similar bouquets and looks around my room with an appraising eye, like a newly married woman decorating her new home. He puts flowers on my dressing table, hangs some from a string over my bed, and places more on the stack of books beside my bed. All the while, he hums a merry tune, and Jack and I exchange glances of mutual certainty that he has gone completely mad.

"These, my young friends, are garlic flowers," Dr. Van Helsing says at last, laying at least seven bunches along the two closed windows of my room. He bends to scatter two or three more bouquets under and around my bed. "And in that second box over there, which you so kindly brought at my request, Jack, must be the garlic bulbs themselves."

"I cleaned out the shopkeeper's entire stock," Jack says, shaking his head ruefully at me. "He must have thought I was planning some sort of pungent feast."

But I am not listening. I am thinking, as my blood runs cold, that one of Vlad's limitations is garlic. He told me that the sight and smell of it offended him. "Something to do with its ability to cleanse the blood, which is anathema to the venom I carry," he had said.

Van Helsing knows. He *knows*.

Neither he nor Jack seem to notice my discomfiture. "As I was saying," the doctor goes on, still happily absorbed in distributing the garlic flowers around the room, "I was reading an interesting book I found in Amsterdam shortly after your first attack, Lucy. It spoke of creatures that feed upon the blood of humans. For I strongly believe that is what happened to you."

Jack shakes his head and mumbles something.

Dr. Van Helsing ignores him. "I suspected from the very beginning that you had endured no dog bite. Dogs bite out of fear, protectiveness, anger . . . a host of reasons that do not include the drinking of blood. But you had lost so much from your person, and not even half of it was found on your clothing or the terrace. It must have gone *somewhere*. So the logical question would be: *where* did it go? And the answer is: into the creature that hell spat out."

I shiver and pull the bedclothes to my neck. If the doctor knew what had truly happened, would he think that *I* was a creature that hell spat out? Would Arthur and Mina and Mamma?

"I have also read essays and articles from leading men in science across multiple continents," the doctor continues. "Not just Europe, but my native Asia also, where they have seen attacks of this kind before. They are rare, but there *is* documentation. Creatures such as bats, for instance, sometimes live upon the blood of large farm animals. And there are other beasts and beings, though where science touches folklore, I cannot tell. Their threads are blended together."

"What do you mean by folklore?" I ask, my voice thin and strained.

Jack glances at me. "Sir, are you sure Lucy should be hearing this?"

"It will not frighten her. The most frightening event has already happened, no? Twice, in fact." Dr. Van Helsing lifts heavy white stalks of garlic from the second box and begins stringing them over the windows and door of my bedroom like strange, bulbous wreaths. "By folklore, I mean accounts of supernatural beings throughout history that subsist on the blood of the living. Some stories are mere fairy tales, told by firelight to thrill the soul. Others are more poisonous, propaganda originating from prejudice and hatred of certain peoples and religions."

I have to remind myself to breathe as he drapes the garlic over my full-length mirror.

"Some of the tales, however, are so plausible as to seem like first-hand accounts of true events. Fortunately, I have not one of those minds that rejects theories for being passed around by mouth and not gained by research." Dr. Van Helsing frowns at Jack, who has just scoffed. "I take all precautions. I look at nothing as impossible. And I read of how country people—farmers, peasants, the nomadic groups who migrate from land to land—deal with blood-drinking beings."

I clutch the purple blooms in my hand. "By using garlic?"

"It is one of the most common methods of repelling them, yes." Dr. Van Helsing surveys my room, which now feels stuffy and pungent with the heavy scent of garlic. "The wild rose has also been used. Some turn their clothes inside out and sleep with their heads at the foot of the bed, so as to confuse any bloodthirsty creatures who visit in the night."

"Forgive me, but this is errant nonsense and superstition," Jack interjects.

Dr. Van Helsing paces with his hands behind his back, as though lecturing in a classroom. "Perhaps. But perhaps not. Are you willing to take that chance?" he asks soberly, and Jack falls silent. "I have also read of these creatures being repulsed by sacred objects and images. It does not matter what religion. It seems that any item pertaining to faith may be harmful, from prayer books and scrolls to beads, candles, and statues of deities."

"And crosses, I suppose," I say quietly. "I saw how you watched me last night."

"I knew you were a sharp young lady, Lucy Westenra," he says, nodding with approval. "Yes, my eye was on you when Mr. Morris took out his silver cross and began to pray. But the sight of it affected you not, nor does the smell of garlic."

Nor the sun, I think. *Nor does human food taste repellent to me.* Perhaps the limitations do not take effect unless I am a full vampire. Then again, my own face has changed in the mirror. My hands tighten around the garlic flowers, and I hear a stem snap under the pressure of my fingers. "Then I have a question for you, Dr. Van Helsing," I say. "If these hellish creatures are kept at bay by such items as you mention, why, then, can *I* tolerate them?"

Jack looks shocked. "Lucy! You are not one of those creatures."

"Do not classify yourself thus," Dr. Van Helsing says, his face fierce and intent. "You may have been infected by one, that is possible. But you are not and can never be one."

"Why not?" I ask softly. They regard me in silence. "Why could I not transform into a creature such as you describe, after having been attacked twice?"

"Because you are inherently good," Jack says, and the older man nods in agreement. "Because you are a young lady who lives a clean, pious, and modest life. What Dr. Van Helsing speaks of is the stuff of penny dreadfuls, not fit to be read, in my opinion. But if there is any truth in it at all, none of it would apply to you, so pure and virtuous as you are."

I long to scream at their determination to think of me as some perfect angel. All I have ever asked, all I have ever wanted, is to be treated as a person. *But women are not people*, I think bitterly, knowing that if I said as much to Mina, she would have a thing or two to say back. "I am tired," I say, dropping the flowers on my bedside table. "Could I be alone for a while? To sleep?"

Dr. Van Helsing shakes his head. "I'm afraid one of us will have to sit with you."

"What for, Doctor?" I ask, exasperated. "Are you afraid that this creature will somehow fly through my windows and drink my blood again?"

"As it happens, yes," he says solemnly. "That is precisely what I fear."

I grit my teeth, longing for the peace and solitude of the mist. Of the churchyard in my dreams, cool and grey and silent. "I would prefer to sleep without being watched every minute, as though I might attack someone. For that is why you pulled Arthur away from me last night, did you not, Doctor? Because you thought I might bite him?"

"I do not yet know the details of your condition," he says calmly. "But I rule nothing out. It is my life's work to study rare infectious diseases, and I have seen many strange things in my time. I ask you to trust me and forgive me for anything you deem unnecessary or intrusive."

Jack purses his lips in sympathy. "We could leave her door open and go into a different room. At least then the poor girl would have some measure of privacy. It must be hard on her to always have people prowling about," he adds, and I give him a grateful look.

Dr. Van Helsing frowns. "I'm not certain that—"

"We will be right across the hall, where we can hear everything. Look around, Van Helsing." Jack points to the garlic bulbs and flowers covering almost every inch of my room. "You've created a veritable minefield for this beast, in whose intelligence I strongly doubt."

"Very well," the older physician says, his brow still furrowed. "But Lucy, I want you to call out if there is even the slightest disturbance or sound. Will you promise me this?"

"I promise," I say at once, and they leave.

Across the hall, my newly sharp ears hear Dr. Van Helsing whisper, "Whatever you do or do not believe, I advise you not to underestimate the intelligence of this creature, Jack. For anything that understands how to travel from Whitby to London, perhaps even by train, and how to follow and target that poor girl, is no simple wild beast but a being of preternatural cleverness and sophistication." He pauses. "A predator, obsessed with its prey."

CHAPTER TWENTY-SEVEN

I drift to the surface of sleep. A chilly wind ruffles my hair, and I try to pull my blankets up to my neck but cannot. Someone is sitting on the edge of my bed, pinning the covers in place. The room is full of thick grey mist creeping in from the wide-open windows.

"Wake up," Vlad says.

At the sound of his voice, I gasp and reel back against my headboard, shivering in the cold. Outside my bedroom, the house is silent. "How did you get in here?" I ask, looking around in a panic. "Where has all the garlic gone?"

He crosses one leg over the other. "It was none of my doing, I assure you. Well, not *directly*. I persuaded your simple-minded housekeeper to invite me in and get rid of the disgusting bulbs and flowers, and she was very obliging. Was that truly the best your doctor could do to keep me out? Such folly for a supposedly intelligent man."

"Where is he? What have you done to all of them?" I demand, my heart in my mouth.

Vlad raises a dark brow. "Calm yourself. I have not harmed anyone, especially not your mother. She seemed quite touched by my concern upon hearing how you had been attacked by the same creature for a *second* time. If only she knew you had asked for it."

I grit my teeth. "Where is she?"

"Drugged into slumber, like all the rest." With a movement of his fingers, the mist rises and bleeds even more thickly through my window and into the hall. "I think you'll find that none of them are a match for me. Or you, for that matter. We are creatures that hell spat out, as the doctor so aptly put. He actually believes himself to be a worthy opponent for me! I have to say, I admire his arrogance. I came in here to kill him, but I think I will keep him around a bit longer." He smiles at me. "You know how I love to be entertained."

"I asked you to help me cheat death," I say, struggling to remain calm. "I gave myself to you instead of to Arthur. Did you ever truly intend to grant me my request?"

Vlad's dark blue-green eyes are maddeningly serene. "No."

"That's all you have to say to me?" I ask, and he shrugs, enjoying my anger. "After biting me to trick me into thinking that you had accepted my bargain?"

"There was no bargain. I agreed to nothing, and I made you no promises. I asked if you wanted me to bite you, and you said yes, and I obliged. Quite generous of me, I must say."

"But you *knew* what I wanted!" I shout, and he turns away in distaste. Fear and anxiety rise in my throat like bile. I force myself to speak in a more even, measured tone. "Both of the times you bit me, you took enough blood from me to sicken me for days. How could you be certain that Dr. Van Helsing would know how to save my life?"

"I wasn't."

I stare at him. "I beg your pardon?"

"I wasn't certain he would know how to save your life." He places a hand over his chest, feigning apology. "Do not take this the wrong way. I am glad he *did* save you. You have been a most welcome diversion for me, but no, I have never seriously contemplated making you my companion. You have not the qualities I seek, as beautiful and charming as you are."

"You were just going to let me die," I say in disbelief. "After all I have been to you?"

Vlad looks around my room with casual detachment. "I told you, I talk nonsense when I am infatuated with a woman. But my infatuations always run their course, Lucy, as this one has."

"That is a lie," I say, my jaw clenched. "You *do* care for me. Why else spend so many evenings listening to my troubles? Why share so much with me about your life and what you are? Why release Jonathan Harker at my request?"

"To keep your trust in this game I am playing with you," he says patiently. "But just as I was unsure whether you would survive my bites, so, too, did I let Mr. Harker go without any hope of his survival. My mountain home is rather treacherous to humans, you see. I assumed he would die in a snowbank or a ravine or be eaten alive by wild animals. I planned to have a telegram sent to Miss Murray, telling her of his untimely death whilst traveling home. And I would be there to comfort her when she received it." He gives me a conspiratorial wink.

"You know nothing about love," I seethe. "It was because of love that Jonathan survived. Knowing that Mina was waiting for him helped him fight his way through those dangers."

"How touching," Vlad says, bored. "He is a minor problem, easily eliminated. I think I *will* wait, however, with regard to the doctor. He knows too much, but he interests me quite a bit. Yes, I'm curious to see what else he can do, this irritating little man from the Orient."

"His name is Dr. Van Helsing," I bite out.

"Yes, him."

I take him in, this man who is a stranger and yet not a stranger. Tonight, there is no affection or kindness in his manner. His eyes are the North Sea, cold and unyielding, and he will destroy anyone he considers to be "a minor problem" without mercy or a second thought. Jonathan Harker, who knows who and what he is and where he lives. Dr. Van Helsing, who is unearthing the truth about him bit by bit. And me. What of me? "You will not hurt them, Vlad. Any of them," I say. He ignores me, so I lean forward and touch his cold hand. He looks at me, his face impassive. "You are lying to yourself. You talk of people like pawns in your game, and perhaps they are, but *I* am not. What I have been to you and what you have been to me . . . on the cliffs, in the mist . . . all of it is much more than you will admit to yourself."

"You think you know my own mind better than I do?" His quiet tone is laced with an undercurrent of malice. "You think after five hundred years that I don't know myself?"

"I think that in five hundred years of loneliness, you have never met anyone like me. You became angry when I said we were equals. I struck a nerve because you are afraid of me and what I have come to mean to you." I tighten my fingers on his hand. "I don't believe for one moment that you left me to die. You knew I would have help, but you also knew that I am like you. A fighter. A survivor. Someone who surrenders easily to no opponent, least of all death."

Vlad turns to face me more fully, his eyes gleaming in the shadows. I have surprised him. Or impressed him. Or angered him. Likely all three.

"We are kindred souls, you and I, and it frightens you," I say quietly. "That is why you will not make me a vampire, though you took my blood and my virtue."

His voice is low and soft, coiled like an adder. "I took nothing from you. What you gave me, you gave of your own free will. Do not blame me. You alone are responsible, you who are so fond of making your own choices. I told you that my existence is a curse, yet you refused to listen. I bit you with violence that first time as a kindness—"

My laugh is full of derision and disbelief. "You call what you did to me a *kindness*?"

Vlad's face changes, like a mask slipping, and I press back against the headboard. It is like looking into an abyss, cold, dark, and utterly without pity. Sharp pinpricks of pain blossom at my temples. I gasp at the invasion of my thoughts and clutch my head, berating myself for not being on my guard. "You blame me for distressing your friends and sickening your mother with the prospect of your death. I can see it in here," he says, tapping an icy fingertip against my forehead. "But the fault is yours alone. Twice have you manipulated me into biting you, wanton and disgraceful as you are. You forced my hand and now you play the innocent victim?"

"I forced nothing!"

"You are no lady, Lucy Westenra. You disgust me. No upstanding, well-bred young woman of good society would even *think* of doing what you have done. You have overstepped, my dear. You have reached too high." He regards me, his expression cool and smug like that of a judge delivering a well-deserved punishment. "But perhaps Arthur will still have you. He seems noble enough to accept damaged goods. He may not reject a glass of champagne that bears the marks of another man's lips. I will leave you all to him now."

I hate myself for crying at his cruel words, but I cannot stop my quiet, hopeless sobs as Vlad gets up and walks over to the door. "Where are you going?" I demand. "You have made me yours. You cannot leave me like this. You have soiled and dirtied me!"

"Goodbye, Lucy," he says pleasantly. "Enjoy your married life. I am sorry I cannot attend the wedding. Perhaps we will see each other again . . . or perhaps not."

I get up and follow him with rising desperation, still weak and unsteady on my feet. He cannot be let loose in this house, not with Mamma and the others sleeping and helpless. And he cannot leave me, not when I have been thoroughly poisoned with his venom twice, brought to the brink of dying twice, felt my fingertips brush immortality twice. I have given up everything I have to evade death, driven my own mother to illness, betrayed my beloved Arthur, and lied to my friends. I have come this far, and I must not, *will* not let my chance slip away.

In the doorway, I seize Vlad's arm. "Do not leave me. You cannot show me a way out and then take it away from me. I will reveal everything you are."

He laughs. "And reveal yourself at the same time? The doctor has seen your reflection. He will put two and two together, and they will all know what you have done to yourself. What will Arthur or Mina think then?" He smiles at me. "I did enjoy you, my naïve little Lucy. Thank you. But our affair has run its course, and you have bled me of quite enough of my time."

You have bled me.

The words are a wind stirring the embers of my mind. That is the answer. *That* was the memory I had been trying to find in the depths of my illness. "I bite my victim multiple times," he had told me when we danced at the ball. "And when they are sufficiently infected with my venom, they must drink *my* blood and make their first kill before the next sunrise."

I must drink Vlad's blood.

I must complete what I have begun, but I must be cautious or I will lose my chance forever. I must tread into the lair of the great grey wolf one silent step at a time—prey hunting the predator with a rope behind my back, ready to slip over his neck when he least suspects it.

Mina once said that we have to live according to the rules of men, because men own this world. Well, then. If this is a game, then I will play by Vlad's rules. And I will win.

I tighten my grip on his arm, envisioning once more the shield of silver protecting my mind. I hold it there with sheer force of will and fix my eyes upon his face. "You are right," I say, humble and appealing. "I am to blame, and not you. You warned me, and I refused to listen."

Vlad's brows come together as he studies me.

"You were kind to me. You made me feel understood. I think perhaps you are the only person to have ever seen me." My voice quivers with genuine emotion and I am glad of it, for the most convincing lies are the ones threaded with truth. I put my arms around him and look up into his face. "You once called me your friend. And so I ask you, I *entreat* you, as a mark of that favor of which you once thought me worthy, to please release me. End my misery and suffering. I do not want to live on, unwanted by you and too stained for Arthur. Free me from the guilt of what I have done and let me die without further blemishing my soul. It is my final request, Vlad."

A thousand needles dig into my scalp, probing at the tender skin, coaxing it to yield my innermost thoughts. But I am too angry, too determined. Papa used to say that I am as stubborn as a storm—that once begun, I am all thunder and lightning, wind and rain, and the sun will not show its face until I am done. Vlad does not know he is standing in the arms of a hurricane.

"How are you doing that?" he demands, the line between his brows deepening. He takes my chin roughly in his hand as though he can rip my thoughts from me by brute force.

The pinpricks in my head strengthen, but so, too, do my efforts to keep him out. "You are right to doubt me," I say, my voice strained. I can feel my energy sapping, still low from my illness. "But I am ready to accept the consequences of my choice. I wish to die." The words burn my throat like acid, but I remind myself that this is only a game. A part I have to play.

Vlad's gaze sharpens. "Then you admit that you deserve to be punished?"

"Yes," I say without hesitation. "I tricked you into biting me. I forced you to take what rightfully belongs to Arthur. He thinks I am an angel. If you give me a merciful, dignified death, then perhaps I can leave him still thinking well of me." I let go of him and slowly back up until I reach my bed. "Bite me one last time. Drain me completely of this poison. Take it all. Take me."

His eyes never leave me as I lie back down and turn my head to the side, exposing the left side of my throat, my black hair fanning over my pillow. The ocean hue of his gaze darkens as he takes me in, my body soft and fragile and yielding in white silk.

"You gave me so much pleasure that night," I breathe as he approaches me like a predator stalking his next meal. "Let me remember, one last time, how it was with you."

And then so suddenly I do not see him move, he is on the bed with me, elbows and knees braced on either side of me, his face inches from mine. His eyes are now as black as ink or blood in the shadows. "You were hungry for me," he whispers against my lips. "You moved against me like waves on the shore. You moaned my name. You gave me everything."

Every inch of me is starving for him. I think of his fang catching on my lip, of the feel of him between my thighs. I want to lock my arms and legs around him. But he wants a woman who will run, who will deny him. A victim. So I ignore how my body aches for him as his eyes rake down the length of my throat to the soft swell of my breasts beneath my nightdress.

The mist coming in through the windows thins to a trickle.

"Everything you said is true," I whisper. "I cannot deny it. I deserve to be punished for giving you something that was not mine to give. Something that belongs to—"

His nose brushes mine. "If you say *Arthur* one more time," he says, low and vicious, "I will tear your head from your shoulders, Lucy. I swear I will."

"Then do it," I say through gritted teeth. "It would be a mercy. Kill me, Vlad."

I feel his cold breath as he angles his mouth toward the wounds on my neck. "Then you have come to your senses?" he asks quietly. "You will no longer make demands of me and call yourself my equal? You will die a pure, clean, and virtuous death?"

It takes everything in me not to pull him closer. My nerves roar with unbearable longing, but I lie still and pliant beneath him. "Give me a goodbye worthy of my memory," I whisper, and I shiver as his icy lips find my neck. But I do not feel his fangs, only his gentle kisses.

"Yes," he says, smiling against my skin, "I have enjoyed you more than I thought I ever would, Lucy. And I think I may miss you as much as you will clearly miss me." He looks down at where my traitorous hips have lifted of their own accord to press desperately against him. His hand curves around my waist, his stroking thumb further strumming my need for him. "Look at you. Your body cannot deny me, even when you are about to die."

I touch his cheek. "Give me what I need. Please. Give me mercy."

He looks at me with eyes as black as night. His lips part to reveal sharp white fangs. "Goodbye, Lucy," he murmurs. And then his teeth are sinking into my half-healed wounds with unerring, pitiless precision. I gasp at the bright, blinding pain mixed with the pleasure of his arctic lips and tongue on my skin. His huge, heavy body crushes mine, pressing me into the mattress, and I hold him tight as he drinks from me for the third time.

Stars explode in my vision. My heart beats weakly against his deadened chest. The life is quickly fading from me, and I cannot wait any longer to do what I must.

I slide my hand beneath his collar and yank it down to bare his shoulder. And then, with all the force left in my jaws, I clamp my teeth down, ripping open his cold flesh to taste the thick, metallic, sour-sweet gush of his blood. My body is on fire. I am a wanderer in the desert who has been given a draught of fresh cold water. I cling to him greedily, but my drink is short lived.

Vlad jerks upright, his knees still on either side of me. My blood drips from his mouth, as his does from mine. He touches the wound on his shoulder. "You little bitch. You *dare* to drink from me." There is a quiet and inexorable hatred in his voice, much more frightening than if he had shouted. But there is also wary recognition. In his face, I see the two halves of him: the man who had called to me on the cliffs, with his fleeting tenderness and manipulative charm, and also the dark menace, the beast of the shadows hiding beneath the guise of a benevolent friend.

"I am not sorry, Vlad," I say softly. "I let you drink from me, and I have drunk from you. I have made my choice, even if you hate me for it."

His laugh is low and almost gentle. "Do you know what you have done, you stupid girl? Do you understand the existence you have chosen?" He looks at me with those red-ringed onyx eyes, his bloody mouth still stretched in disbelief at my daring. I have impressed him against his will and regained his interest. So much for his infatuation running its course.

"Yes. I have chosen to belong to myself. Only myself."

And then, as he watches, I pull my nightdress up over my head and throw it on the floor, which is now fully visible through the thinning wisps of mist.

The ring of blood around his pupils glows an even deeper scarlet. His breathing becomes ragged as he takes me in. "Lucy," he whispers. "You would give up your soul for this?"

"A soul," I say, "is a very small price to pay."

And then we are kissing, angry and hateful and venomous. He kisses me as though he would like to kill me with his lips, taking no care with his fangs this time. They cut my fragile skin, adding more blood to the mess around our mouths, but I scarcely feel the pain through my uncontrollable desire. My hunger for him has only intensified after my first taste of him.

He tears down his breeches and yanks my hips upward to meet him. The violent force of our joining sends the headboard crashing against the wall. A pillow flies into the lamp on the bedside table, knocking it over with a shattering of glass. I arch my back, crying out for more, my appetite growing with every rough, slick, delicious glide. With every moan I utter, I strip away the remains of my old self. With every movement I make, I declare that my body is my own, my soul is my own, and the old Lucy Westenra has vanished entirely. I have given myself up not to Vlad, but to a new world in which I will have the power to choose whatever I wish.

I raise my hips higher, inviting him in even deeper, his iciness never melting in the scalding heat of my body. If I am to be infected, then let it be fully. Let it be complete. Let there be no ambiguity or regret. There is no going back now.

I pull Vlad's face down to mine and kiss him again, our mouths melding in a bloody brawl as our bodies collide in a rising frenzy. More glass shatters as a painting above the bed comes plummeting down. Vlad buries his fangs into my neck again and I lap up what blood is left on his shoulder, taking in every drop of him hungrily as my excitement retraces its steps up the now-familiar ascent. But my release does not come this time. Instead, I feel a sudden terrible, shocking cold, as though what little blood is left in my veins has been replaced with ice water. I cry out, not in pleasure, but because my body is racked with chills.

Vlad stays still on top of me, his face pressed into my neck as he finishes with a long, low groan. And then he gets up and turns his back on me, tugging up his breeches and tucking his shirt neatly in. The mist is now completely gone, and I can see him clearly silhouetted against the night sky outside my window.

The bed shakes with my shivering as an intense, devastating cold grips my body. I grab at my remaining pillows and any blankets that have not slipped to the floor, but I cannot get warm. The cold has reached into my very bones. "What's happening to me?" I gasp.

"You're dying," Vlad says shortly, broken glass crunching under his feet as he moves toward the window. "That is what you wanted, is it not?"

"No! I thought that . . ." I trail off, my teeth chattering as the realization strikes me. "I have to kill before sunrise. I have to take a life."

He keeps his back to me, hands braced on the windowsill. "If you stay in that bed, you will die as a human at sunrise. I have drained you completely, though you do not deserve that mercy, and the only thing keeping you alive now is the blood you stole from me." His voice is flat with loathing. "But if you drain and kill someone before the night ends, you will die and reawaken with the curse for which you have given up everything."

My head swims with pain and cold and anger. My vision blurs as panic rises within me at the thought of Mamma, of Arthur or Mina coming to find me dead. "I will lose my life, no matter what I choose? You never told me that! I thought—"

Vlad turns, his teeth gleaming red in the hollow of his smile. "Yes, either way, you will have to die. Vampires must first relinquish their human lives. Did I neglect to share that? How careless of me." His smile twists into a grotesque leer as he turns back to the window. "I doubt you have the courage, but I certainly don't care enough to stay and find out."

My muscles are so tense with cold that it is excruciating. "Vlad, don't leave me!" I beg.

"You have a house full of people to choose from. And if I'm not mistaken, two of them are watching you right now." And then, in the space of a breath, Vlad disappears. A monstrous bat the size of a small dog spreads its jagged wings wide to catch a current of night air. It sails out of my window and melts into the black sky as I turn my head slowly, painfully, to the door.

Dr. Van Helsing and Mamma stand there, gazing with horror upon my naked, ravaged body and the chaos and destruction around me. Vlad had allowed the mist to fade in his distraction, freeing my mother and the doctor from their induced slumber. Even as I feel myself drifting away weakly, not knowing whether it is into sleep or into death, I wonder how much of our encounter they saw.

And then Mamma collapses to her knees. Her eyes do not even close as her lifeless body sinks to the floor, rigid and still and lost to me forever.

CHAPTER TWENTY-EIGHT

I have no time to grieve for Mamma or reflect on what has passed between Vlad and myself. I do not even have time to get dressed. As the household awakens from its unnatural slumber and my room becomes a maelstrom of panic, with Jack Seward barking orders, Quincey Morris carrying my mother's lifeless body from the room, and the servants crying and scurrying about in the mess, Dr. Van Helsing strides over to my bed and picks me up, blankets and all, with more strength than I would have expected from his slender form. Without speaking or looking at me, he carries me into the next room, where maids scramble to fill a tub with steaming water.

"More water! The hotter, the better!" Dr. Van Helsing shouts, depositing me into the bath. "Harriet, ensure that Miss Lucy stays in the tub. It is imperative that she get warm."

Jack appears, looking pale and harried, and he and Dr. Van Helsing turn their backs to preserve my modesty. Even in my cold and pain and terror, I cannot help laughing, knowing that the doctor must have seen or at least guessed what had happened between Vlad and me. But my mirth dissolves into violent shivers. The hot water is doing nothing to warm me, even though Harriet and Agatha are frantically pouring bowls of it over my shoulders.

"What's wrong with her?" Jack asks. "I could kick myself for being dead asleep."

"Then you must kick me as well," Dr. Van Helsing says grimly, "though I think it was not our fault that we fell into such a heavy slumber. Did you see that strange mist?"

An infernal buzzing begins in my ears, growing into a steady roar like the rushing of the ocean. It is so distracting that I barely notice when

Harriet pours another bucket of steaming hot water into the tub. Through the din, I hear an odd cacophony of noise: a water glass clinking on a nightstand three houses away, the flapping of an owl's wings in the park, carriage wheels rattling in the next neighborhood, a man coughing and guzzling liquor at a streetlamp two miles away. I can smell the liquor, too, and the fetid sourness of his breath. My nose is assaulted by a thousand different scents, rank and heady and intoxicating, but always there is the underlying iron velvet fragrance of blood, thick and rich and pure. I hear it pulsing through Harriet's veins as she leans over me, worried, saying, "Do not fear, Miss Lucy. We will get you warm."

"Harriet, be careful," Dr. Van Helsing says sharply, striding over. "Do not get too close."

"Is it infectious, Doctor? Whatever poor Miss Lucy has?" she asks. The beating of her heart is like the fluttering of butterfly wings, frail and hypnotic, beneath her sensible apron.

"It may be." The doctor looks at me, ever honorable and dignified, his eyes fixed only on my face though the whole of my naked body is visible in the water.

I can hear *his* heart, too, and smell the contents of his veins. His blood is like himself: swift, determined, and clever, and I can guess at the surprising sweetness of its taste. Something in my face must alarm him, for he takes a full two steps away from the tub and pulls out a large bulb of garlic from his pocket. Watching my eyes, he holds it up in the air.

The scent of it fills my nostrils, cloying and powerful. It gently tickles the passages of my nose and throat. I close my eyes, and I can see the soil from which the bulb had sprung. I can smell rain running into the earth, tenderly encouraging the plant to grow. I think of Papa and the meals he had loved that his grandmother had made for him, dishes that he had asked our cook to practice, filling our house with the savory aroma of fried garlic. I think of his big, warm laugh as Mamma hurried about, opening windows and shaking her head at him even as she hid a smile.

They had loved each other so very much. And they had loved me, but will love me no more.

"Stop it, Van Helsing," Jack pleads. "Whatever you are doing to her, stop it!"

I realize that I am sobbing as though my heart will break. As Harriet and Agatha pour hot water over my thin shoulders, I bury my face in my hands and I weep and weep and weep.

"I do nothing, my friend, but what I have done before," Dr. Van Helsing says, watching me with calm despair. "Remember how I placed these bulbs all around her room for protection earlier. I gave her the flowers to hold and none of it hurt her. Notice how she reacts now."

Yes, the garlic has hurt me. But not in the way he imagines.

The doctor sighs. "The creature has done his work. He has done it well."

"He?" Jack repeats.

"He was with her on the bed. He flew out of the window when he saw me. His eyes . . ." The doctor does not finish his sentence. He puts the garlic back into his pocket and turns away, but not before I can see that he, too, has tears in his eyes.

"Lucy, are you all right?" Jack asks. His eyes find my breasts, pale and buoyant in the water, and he looks away hastily. "Get her out of the bath and dry her well. Take her to bed."

The maids obey, wrapping me in thick towels, but I am so cold that it does not make a difference. Something about the garlic has sedated me. I feel numb, drained.

"I am so sorry, Doctor," I say weakly as the maids help me stumble past him.

"All is well, my child," Dr. Van Helsing says with forced heartiness. "Do not fear. Go and get comfortable under your blankets, and Jack and I will come and stay with you."

The buzzing in my ears has subsided, and as the maids put my nightgown back on me and tuck me into bed, I can easily hear the doctors talking in the hall.

"To fail here is not merely life or death," Dr. Van Helsing is saying.

"Sir, I mean no disrespect," Jack says. "But are you certain your mind hasn't been addled by lack of sleep? You say he flew from the window as a *bat*?"

"I have no energy to persuade you, my boy," Dr. Van Helsing says tiredly. "I have told you the absolute truth, and you must use your knowledge and your trust in me to help you judge. Lucy Westenra has been thoroughly seduced and infected by that beast who can transform into man, wolf, or bat. And it was not the first time. I saw how they were together."

"He . . . he took her?" Jack whispers.

"I saw it, and so did her poor mother."

Sobs rack my body anew at his words. Grief has become a wall, and I run headlong into it. My mind is a reeling, dizzying carousel of shame at having been witnessed in the most vulnerable surrender of my soul; rage at Vlad's blame and rejection; and fear at the reality of what I have chosen. Naïve, Vlad had called me, and stupid, too. He was not wrong. I have been a fool to trust him. I have put my hope into an ocean, turbulent and cruel and fathomless, and now I will drown in its unplumbed depths. He tricked me with his warmth and friendship, his tender promises and lingering kisses. He swept me up in the romance of his existence when he needed to frighten and impress me, but all the time, he was holding back so many truths.

What else do I not know about this curse? How on earth will I ever be able to take a life? And what does any of it matter when I will die, regardless of what I choose?

Grief twists in my gut, knife-sharp. Grief for who I was and can never be again, and grief for my mother, who had loved me more than life itself and who had left this world watching me make my most terrible choice. And what of Arthur and Mina? How did I ever think I could live on beside them and hide the truth of what I have become?

Dr. Van Helsing and Jack hurry in at the sound of my sobs. I am so empty—of blood, of water, of virtue—that I am astonished I can still cry, but I do. I want my mother so badly that I cannot help screaming out at the agony of it. I will never see her eyes shining with pride or feel her arms around me ever again. She died without the comfort of knowing that she would never lose me to death, never have to face the pain of my loss.

Jack takes my hand, his face twisted with sympathy, as Dr. Van Helsing watches us, tense and alert. Even in his pity, he is ready to fight me if I attack them. But I am growing too weak to even contemplate it. My lungs gasp for air as I fall back, limp against my pillows. What little blood left in me is sluggish, dragging itself through my veins with the last vestiges of life.

"Send for Arthur at once," Dr. Van Helsing says quietly.

Jack nods, his face white. He squeezes my hand before hurrying away.

"Doctor, I'm dying," I say, my voice faint.

Dr. Van Helsing places a gentle hand on my forehead. "Yes, my child, I'm afraid you are," he says, a tear slipping down his face. "I am so sorry I could not protect you."

"It isn't your fault. Only mine," I say, my eyelids growing heavy.

"You must never blame yourself," he says severely. "This was done to you. You could not have asked for it." Even here, even now, he wants to think that I am perfectly innocent.

I fall into a light, dreamless sleep, and I awaken to everyone gathering in my room. Dr. Van Helsing and Jack stand by the door, their heads bowed. Quincey is at the foot of my bed, his face full of emotion as Arthur cradles me in his arms, weeping disconsolately.

"Arthur," I whisper, burying my face in his chest. I smell the night air on his coat, damp earth on his shoes, and brandy, which in my careful Arthur is proof indeed of his unbearable sadness. It is the week before his wedding, and he thinks he will lose both his father and his fiancée. "Wait for me. I will return. This is not goodbye."

"Arthur, that's enough," Dr. Van Helsing says, his voice tight. "Come away."

"Just hold on a minute, will you? Give them some time," Quincey says sharply.

I move my face to Arthur's neck, where an artery pulses against my lips with a hypnotic rhythm. The scent of brandy in his blood is stronger here, rich and dark and bitter. It blends with the familiar smell of him, pine and cigars, making me think of our first kiss, and to my horror, I feel a tingling in my gums above my front teeth followed by two sharp pinches as my long, new, lethal fangs sprout from behind my upper lip. *No,* I tell myself. *Not Arthur!*

I clamp my lips together, my face contorting with the effort of resisting my hunger. *I cannot hurt this gentle man I love. I will not poison him!* But a teasing, tantalizing thought persists: that if I bit Arthur, I could make him truly and irrevocably mine, more than any ceremony or prayer book or exchange of rings. *No! I will not give in!*

With all of the strength left in my failing body, I put my hands against Arthur's chest and push him away from me, hard. He stumbles against a chair, one of its legs catching on my mirror.

"Lucy?" he sputters. "What are you—"

"Arthur, move away!" Dr. Van Helsing's voice rises with panic. He and Jack dart forward and drag Arthur backward, away from me. They have seen, and so has Quincey. In summoning my strength to push Arthur away, I had gritted and bared my teeth—*all* of them.

The men recoil.

Dr. Van Helsing, who had tried so hard to keep me safe.

Quincey Morris, who had asked me to sail to the New World with him.

Jack Seward, who had once sent blood-red roses as a token of his desire for me.

And Arthur, my own dear Arthur, who had loved me since childhood, who had watched and longed for me, who had asked me to marry him beneath a moonlit sky.

None of them are looking at me with love or admiration. Not anymore. They press together against the opposite wall, the whites of their eyes bright with terror. Dr. Van Helsing is clutching the bulb of garlic, and Quincey holds up the silver cross of his necklace, his lips moving fervently in a prayer, and they are all staring at me as though I am monstrous.

A creature that hell spat out.

The white sheet covering my full-length mirror has been pulled aside by Arthur falling backward, and I see the truth of what I have become in its shining surface: a young woman bled of her beauty by the pallor of death, her black hair wild and two wicked slivers of bone shining between her dry, cracked lips. And all over her skin, the frenetic movement of those pulsing, swirling droplets of blood, clumping into large splotches against her throat and her collarbone and her arms. I cry out and touch my own face, feeling the bumps of the fangs under my lip.

"It's a curse." I hear Vlad's laughter, low and cruel and full of the hatred with which these men who had once loved me now look at me. "I told you, I told you, I told you . . ."

"What have I done?" I moan. "Oh, what have I done?"

"It is not your fault," Dr. Van Helsing says.

"Do not blame yourself," Jack adds, and his pity is even harder to bear than his disgust.

None of them sees me. *Me*, as I truly am. I am still here and always have been, but the mirror may as well not show my reflection at all.

"None of you will listen to me!" I scream. Suddenly, I am standing on the bed with my fists clenched, towering above them. "Is it so impossible that I made a choice of my own, and embarked on a path of my own, without any of you to guide me?"

Quincey holds up his cross with one hand, and with the other, finds the gun at his side.

"You made a choice? Lucy, what are you saying?" Arthur asks, his voice breaking.

I have been a fool, utterly and completely—so entranced with the gift I imagined, the prize Vlad's words had painted for me, that I did not see the grave yawning before my feet.

"I love you, Arthur," I say, sick with despair, collapsing onto the mattress in a swoon. "I wanted so much to be with you and make you happy." My arms are trembling so much that I cannot lift myself back onto my pillows. I gasp for air, my breathing rough and labored. My gums pinch as the fangs retract, hiding themselves once more in the tissues of my mouth.

Cautiously, Dr. Van Helsing approaches me. Keeping one hand on the garlic, he feels the weakening pulse in my wrist with the other. The heat seems to be rising in the room, and where I was freezing minutes ago, I am now baking in the light of the lamps.

"Window," I choke out. "Please. I need air."

The doctor shakes his head. "No, Lucy."

"Surely it can't hurt to open one," Arthur says, hurrying to the window.

"I said no!" Dr. Van Helsing roars. "I will not risk that monster coming in again! Not when this child deserves to die with dignity. Yes, my poor boy, she will die," he adds in a gentler voice as Arthur lets out a heartbreaking sob. "Her pulse is weak, she has very little blood left, and her heart and lungs are struggling. It will not be long now. Come and say goodbye to her, all of you. It is safe. But for heaven's sake, the windows must remain closed." And as if to prove his point, he moves to stand guard in front of my bedroom windows.

No one moves for a long moment. Arthur weeps into his hands, and Quincey, who has put his pistol away but still grips his cross, is praying again with his eyes squeezed shut. At last, Jack comes over to me. He glances at Dr. Van Helsing, who gives an imperceptible nod, before leaning down to press his lips against my forehead. "Goodbye, Lucy," he whispers.

Quincey wipes his face with a rough hand as he comes over to me. "I told you before that you've got grit, and you still do," he says gruffly. "Thank you, Lucy, for teaching me a thing or two about bravery. I will miss your spirit." He kisses the top of my head and moves away.

My eyes meet Arthur's through a haze of tears. There is no need to speak. Everything we want to say is in the way we look at each other, and in the way he falls to his knees beside my bed. I hold his hand over my heart and whisper, "This will always and forever be yours." I look pleadingly at the doctor. "May we have a moment alone?"

Dr. Van Helsing hesitates, but he must deem it safe, for he leads Jack and Quincey into the hall. "I am afraid I will have to leave your door open," he says. "It is the best I can do."

I nod as they retreat, and even that simple movement saps precious energy from me. I wonder how on earth I would be able to *kill* someone by sunrise if I can scarcely breathe. But when I turn back to Arthur, weeping beside my bed, I know that I have no choice. I have come too far. To die as a woman would be to lose him forever. To exist as a vampire would also mean losing him—that is something I know now that I did not understand before. But at least I would be able to see him again and hover at the fringes of his life.

I must finish this.

"You have a house full of people to choose from," Vlad had taunted me. I would expect no less from someone without the ability to love. Even in the most intense throes of my unbearable new hunger, I had been able to push Arthur away, to save him from me.

Arthur rests his head upon my chest, and I wrap my feeble arms around him. "I'm sorry," I whisper. I want to say more, but the words snag in my dry throat. I cough and gasp, my lungs straining. I am burning hot and every inch of me feels rubbed with sandpaper. My skin hurts all over and my eyes sting, and I am desperate for just one breath of fresh air.

I think longingly of the mist, soft and cool. Vlad controlled it with just a movement of his fingers, and in his distraction, it had melted away into nothingness. I yearn for its chill to come back, to caress my feverish face and aching lungs. And when I look over Arthur's head, I see fog curling outside my windows as though summoned there by my need.

"Arthur," I whisper. "Will you open the window, please? I want air so badly."

He gets up at once. "Of course." He glances at my door, fearful that Dr. Van Helsing will come storming back in, but no one appears and we can hear the others murmuring in low voices across the hall. Very quietly, Arthur pushes one of the windows open. He looks back at me, his face worried, and he does not see the mist slipping into the room.

"Come here to me." I stretch my arms out and make room for him on the bed, and he lies down beside me, his head on the same pillow, all thoughts of propriety gone. I hold him tight, feeling his solid, reassuring warmth envelop me, so different from Vlad's arctic embrace.

The mist thickens. It pours through the window and pools onto the floor. I think of it surrounding Arthur and me, hiding and protecting us, and it rises at once at my silent command. Arthur relaxes against me, and his arms slacken as his heartbeat slows.

"Sleep, Arthur," I breathe. "Sleep here beside me."

"I love you, Lucy," he says drowsily, and then he is gone, lost to slumber. His face is so young and innocent and trusting in sleep, his lashes dark against his cheeks.

I hold him, tears scalding my face as I lift my hand to push the mist out the door. The conversation across the hall continues, low and alert; all three of the men are listening for sounds of struggle from my room. But they will not hear anything for hours. I will make sure of it.

I hear Jack's head droop against the back of the sofa, Dr. Van Helsing's suit rumple as he goes limp in his chair, and the thud of a heavy body hitting the floor—Quincey, who must have been standing. I whisper an apology and reluctantly pull out of Arthur's arms as the mist slides throughout the house like a somnolent cloud, putting every living being to sleep.

My knees quiver as I stand, gripping the bedpost for support.

I am alone, a monster in a house full of sleepers.

CHAPTER TWENTY-NINE

Time is hurtling toward sunrise as I move to the open window, stumbling and weak. The mist on my face seems to give me a few precious fragments of energy. It smells of soothing earth and dew, and every step I take feels easier than the last. I gasp as it helps me, lifting my feet so that I am floating inches above the floor, my long white nightdress fluttering around my ankles. I do not feel afraid as the mist gently carries me out the window.

I fly along the side of the house, light as a feather, breathless when I realize how far the ground is below me. I want to see my mother, and through the windows of her room, I do. Despite the shock of her death, her lovely face is serene on her pillow. I press my hands longingly against the glass, watching the candlelight flicker over her closed lids, pale and veined with blue. I want to stay there all night. I want to hold vigil and to grieve, kneeling by her side.

But there is a powerful, gnawing void at my core, impossible to ignore. I am starving. My body is screaming out for the blood that will render my transformation complete. I have no time to linger, for the sunrise is inexorable and the sky is already lightening from the darkest hours of the night. I drift downward in the arms of the mist, my long black hair floating behind me.

I fear for these empty streets, and for whoever will encounter me first. My *prey*.

The word makes me physically ill, and for a moment, I am forced to lean against a lamppost, heaving at the thought of killing someone. Of taking an innocent life. But I remind myself that I did not hurt Arthur. Even in my ravenous need, I had summoned the presence of mind to push him from me, and I will not hurt anyone else. I take deep, calming breaths as my ears pick up sounds from every direction: owls hooting, rats scurrying, foxes slipping through bushes. I will drink from an animal, I decide, and allow its blood to finish what I have begun.

"You stupid girl," I hear Vlad say in my mind, mocking and hateful.

"Curse you," I whisper.

"You're a fool."

I plug my ears with my fingers, a childish gesture that does nothing to keep his voice from my thoughts. I run through the mist, my bare feet making soft sounds on the pavement, and through sheer force of habit, I find myself at the churchyard gates once more. But this time, I have not sleepwalked there. This time, I lift the mist with my hands until it churns like the sea, making phantasmagoric shapes in the light of the gas lamps. I smell blood everywhere, pulsing through small animals. It is not as tantalizing as human blood, but it is blood nonetheless.

And then I hear it.

A strong, young heart beating. The rushing of fresh, hot blood.

I pause, listening. My newly sharpened senses focus on a creature behind me. There is an odd note to its smell, something I cannot place. No matter. The mist swirls around me as I stroll along the gate as though I have not a care in the world. I hear myself singing a soft lullaby, my low sweet voice lilting through the heavy silence of the dead. Why am I walking like this? From whence comes this music? I sing with a joy I do not feel, but I am as compelled to do it as I am to take air into my lungs. It is bait, I realize. I am setting a trap without even knowing how.

The animal approaches. The intoxicating scent of its blood strokes my nose, rich and savory. Everything slips from my mind but the bone-deep need to taste it. To feed. I continue to walk and sing, soft and blithe, but my muscles are already tensing, preparing to lunge and seize the prey that comes to me so willingly. Somehow, I know I could descend upon it in the blink of an eye, and that I am faster and stronger than anything within a hundred-mile radius. I could tear this creature limb from limb before it even had time to draw its next breath.

I turn to look at my prey, and my breath stops within me.

It is not an animal. It is a little girl.

She is about six or seven years old. She wears a long, shapeless coat too big for her, and her mousy brown hair hangs limp around her thin face. *That* was the odd note I had detected. I had been smelling the innocence and the fresh, tender skin of a child. Her enormous dark eyes never stray from my face as she stands there looking at me.

No, I think, recoiling. *No! I cannot.*

"I'm scared," she says in a small voice. "Will you help me, miss?"

The smell of her blood is overpowering. I am like a lost sailor seeing land or a thirsty man discovering an oasis in the desert. My ferocious hunger roars as the little girl scurries forward. My prey is *hurrying* toward me.

The new and evil instinct inside of me has me kneel with a smile, bringing my eyes level with hers. "Hello, little one," I hear myself croon, warm and kind, the way I have heard other women speak to children. "How did you come to be here all by yourself?"

I am a predator now, a monster whose sustenance is blood. But even through the presence of the newly awakened murderous beast inside me, I can still feel the human part of me reeling back in disgust, my stomach roiling with nausea even through my hunger. Never in my life have I had the gift or the liking for children that comes so easily to other women. This tiny being with its wet mouth and dirty hands and seeping eyes may be full of the blood I crave, but I am still repulsed by it. I cannot kill it. I *will* not.

Hope blooms on the child's face. "I'm glad you found me, miss," she says rapturously.

Why is she so happy to see me?

And then, as I stare into the wide darkness of her large eyes, I see the answer. I see my own reflection, and it is *nothing* like what I saw in the mirror after my transformation. In death, my beauty has magnified a thousandfold. My skin glows pale gold, as soft and flawless as the petal of a rose, and my hair and lashes are blacker and more luxuriant than they have ever been. My cheeks are a warm pink, but my lips are a brilliant rose-red as though I have rubbed them with rouge. I am transfixed by my own appearance in the child's eyes, for something in the giving of my blood and the taking of Vlad's has caused me to look this way.

As a human, I had been lovely. But as a vampire, I am utterly irresistible.

The child is relieved to see me because instead of being found by a vagrant or a drunk or whoever wanders these streets at night, I have come to her instead: a soft-eyed young woman in a spotless nightgown with an angelic smile and hair like the evening sky.

I am in awe and terror of the cleverness of this curse. This venom Vlad has introduced into my blood understands the concept of self-preservation. It knows that if it makes its host attractive and alluring, then the prey cannot help but come running.

As I had to Vlad. And as this girl has to me.

I think of what other children have called me before: a "bloofer" lady. A *beautiful* lady, one whose face attracts both their attention and their trust.

The girl throws herself into my arms and tucks her head under my chin, seeking the comfort of a mother. Oh, God, what am I to do? I am torn between devastating hunger for her blood, horror at the deed I am contemplating, and sheer disgust at the feel of this tiny, dirty, doll-like creature attaching itself to me like a tumor. My gums ache as my fangs threaten to snap down again, and I press my lips so tightly together that it hurts.

I will not do this. I will *not* kill an innocent child.

Awkwardly, I put a hand on the little girl's back, my fingers catching on her lanky hair. I remember that there is an orphanage nearby, an estab-lishment patronized by some of the ladies of Mamma's circle. Indeed, my mother and I have given money every Christmas to help feed and clothe the orphans. This girl must have wandered from there.

"Come, darling," I say, patting her head as my mouth waters at the seductive smell of her clean, fresh blood a spare inch away. "Let me walk you back."

She snuggles tighter against me, reluctant to leave my arms, and I think of how this is everything society has asked of me: to be a woman holding a child protectively, just like this. To first be a daughter, and then a wife, and then *this*, a nurturer of small lives sprouted from my own body like damp mushrooms from a moist log. Weeds from the wetness of my womb. I hold her against my weakly beating heart, trying to contain my revulsion at the stench of her innocence, tortured and unsure of what to do as the mist gently swirls around us.

The mist.

I can put her to sleep. I can push her far away from me so that the stains on my soul do not deepen and the reflection in the mirror does not grow bloodier with the blood on my hands.

But before I can take action, I smell new blood approaching, fanning the flames of my steadily increasing and unsatisfied hunger. In the dim light, they appear shoulder to shoulder like sentries in the fog: eight or nine small figures, their bodies frail, their clothes hanging loosely, and their eyes too big for their faces. They home in on us like an army of puppets moving in perfect unison, with identical expressions of hope and relief at the sight of me.

"Oh, miss!"

"We are lost."

"Help us," they chant. "Please help us, miss."

Their grubby doll hands find my face and my hair, their smelly bodies swarming around me like pale grubs on a festering wound. I am faint with horror and my senses are assaulted by these children I have somehow drawn to me through the mist, with their small voices, searching hands, and longing eyes. My head aches with the rhythm of their heartbeats. I can taste my own blood in my mouth as my fangs snap down, piercing through my gums in preparation for a feast.

I stand up and back away as the children paw at me, their plaintive voices shrill and the smell of their blood, velvety and unctuous, clings to my nose with invisible hooks. I am losing my sanity and my control as the tiny sacks of blood surround me. This will become a massacre.

"I told you." I hear a smile of triumph in Vlad's whisper. "I told you, I told you."

I clench my fists and scream, "No!"

The children go still.

Quickly, with trembling hands, I sweep the mist upon them like a shroud. One by one, they fall to the ground, their heartbeats slowing as they sink into deep slumber. I touch my face and realize that I am crying, looking down at these fragile, helpless bodies who had sought a loving young mother through the mist and found a monster instead. Found *me*.

"I can't do this," I sob. "You were right, Vlad. I have not the courage."

There is no response. Desperately, my insides quaking with hunger, I lick my own blood from my fangs. And then I use the mist to lift the children into the air before me, moving them back to the orphanage. Even before I reach the building, I can hear the worried voices of adults seeking them. Gently, I lower the bodies beneath a large tree and cry, "Here! I've found them!"

And then I flee, because I know I would not be able to help myself if the adults came upon me, too. I half run, half float, weeping as I move through the empty streets. The sky is several shades lighter. Sunrise will come soon enough, and I will die as a human. There will be no returning from that, no seeing Arthur's smile or Mina's bright eyes ever again.

"What am I to do?" I utter. "Oh, God, what shall I do?"

"Hello, love. What's a pretty piece like you doing out here all alone?" A man is leaning on a wall nearby, grinning at me with an almost toothless mouth. He is perhaps in his fifties, with ruddy white skin, thinning ginger hair, and a few large scars on his face. I can tell from his speech and his ragged clothing that he is a vagrant, and I smell old liquor on his foul breath.

I do not know this man. I do not know if he is good or bad, if he has fallen on hard times, or if the shadows of lost dreams linger behind those bloodshot eyes. I do not know his name, where he comes from, or whether there is someone out there who loves him.

All I know is that he is full of blood and I am empty of it. So, *so* empty.

My fangs are in his neck before either of us are even aware of it. My body is on fire as my new teeth, long and bright as shards, tear into the tissues and muscles of his throat to find his veins. The man thrashes in my arms, his cries incoherent under the glugging sound of blood leaving his body and entering mine, filling me with delicious warmth and vitality. I do not waste a drop, locking my mouth against his skin as I drain him of absolutely everything.

I let him go and he crumples to the ground, white as chalk. His milky eyes are still open, and in them, I see my own reflection once more. My face is pink with health and my pointed fangs drip blood upon my lip. And I notice something strange: my eyes are the same, wide and dark and tilting—not voids ringed with crimson, like Vlad's. Why have my eyes alone remained human? My old self looks out at me through them, lost and sad and tortured, racked with self-hatred at this violent, merciless deed I have performed tonight.

I have taken a life. I have killed someone.

This man may have had a family. He may have had a daughter my age. I imagine a vampire happening upon Mamma or Papa and I fall to my knees, heaving, sick to my stomach, but I bring nothing up. I have stolen a life to pay for my new existence, like some dark goddess or blood-splattered demon, and I know the weight of this death will forever be a chain around my ankle. The first human life I will ever take—the first of how many more? Oh, God, forgive me. I bend my forehead to the ground, trembling with silent tears as I hold the man's hand to my heart.

Vlad had lied to me. He had made subsisting on animal blood sound so easy. But he had not told me how it would smell as thin and bland as water in comparison to the bright, coppery bouquet of human blood. He did not tell me my predatory instincts would make it impossible to resist. But he *did* tell me it was a curse, and perhaps that was the greatest truth he had ever shared.

An eternity of killing. An immortal life of endless death.

My scream of torment shakes the night like the toll of a church bell. In my terror of death, I have chosen an existence that has inexorably married me to it. My body is strong, my limbs are powerful, and my senses are heightened . . . but only ever through the blood and the life and the soul of another. The rushing tide of grief, fury, and remorse in me could drown all of London.

"I've done it, Vlad!" I shout. "You thought I could not, but I have!"

Movement in the shadows.

I hear flapping, rustling, scurrying. From every direction come rats, dark and sly, oily fat bodies slipping through the grass; maggots, slimy with the sheen of corpses, pushing up from the earth; snakes, coal-black and poisonous green, undulating over the cobblestones. The creatures of the night join me, their eyes watchful, but Vlad does not come. I do not know if he heard my cry, but I suppose it does not matter; he cares not what choice I make. As the creatures watch me, I scoop the dead man into my arms and stand. I am a small woman, but he weighs almost nothing as I lay him with newly prodigious strength in the shadow of the trees.

"I'm sorry," I whisper, gently closing his eyes with my fingers. "I am so sorry."

Exhaustion overtakes me, so powerful that I am afraid I will fall asleep where I kneel. I turn my back on the man, knowing that the theft of his life has made its permanent mark on me. I wipe the heels of my hands over my wet face and clean what remains of his blood, and then I raise the mists and float home through the darkened streets.

I soar through my bedroom window and onto the bed beside Arthur, his long lanky body still stretched out in peaceful slumber. I tuck myself under his arm and press my face to his chest, committing every note of the music of his heartbeat to memory as I hold him close.

The mist wavers slightly.

Arthur stirs and looks down at me. "I didn't mean to fall asleep," he says drowsily with a sheepish laugh. And then he blinks in shock. "Why, Lucy. You look . . . you look so well."

I can see myself in the shine of his eyes, more radiant and full of life than ever. But it is only a dangerous illusion, one that will make it harder for us to let go of each other the way I fear we must. I caress his stunned face, my fingers moving over his nose and lips to his neck, where a vein throbs with longing. But it is safe from me, and so is the blood that rushes through him.

"You're glowing," he says, cupping a hand around my face. "There are roses in your cheeks. Perhaps Van Helsing was wrong . . . but you are so cold." He pulls me more tightly against him and covers me with the blanket, rubbing my shoulders to warm me.

"Van Helsing was not wrong. I *am* dying, Arthur, but not in the way we know. Not in the way you think I am. Will you trust me? When I promise that I will come back to you?"

His face crumples. "But how? How can you come back to me if you die?"

I look into the soft hazel of his eyes. "I told you that I have made a choice, but there is a price I must pay first. This choice means that you would never lose me. I would never grow old. You would have me until the end of your life . . . if you still want me."

"Of course I want you," he says, his voice taut with distress and confusion. "But—"

"If you want me as I am now. As I am in the mirror." He goes still at the memory of my reflection. I touch my upper lip, under which my fangs had emerged. "As you saw me earlier. I am the same Lucy who loves you, but there are changes in me. They are part of the price I must pay to be with you. To love you all your life and spare you pain."

Arthur touches my lip, too. "Those long teeth . . . and your face in the glass," he says hesitantly. "They are because that creature bit you?"

"Yes," I whisper.

"And you . . . you wanted to be bitten? That is what you mean by making a choice?"

"Yes."

He is silent for a moment, his eyes locked on mine, trying so hard to understand. "But what bit you? How did it find you? Why—"

"I will explain everything in due time. I promise."

He leans his forehead against mine, his face drawn and pleading. The imminent loss of his father has dimmed the light in his eyes, and I tighten my arms around him, every fiber of my being yearning to bring that joy, that smile back. "And you . . . you *will* come back, Lucy?"

I take his face in my hands. "I swear it to you," I say fervently. "I will see you again, my love, and this is not goodbye."

We lie there looking at each other, and my mind races with images of the future, even after the despair I had felt earlier, the certainty that I had no right to exist beside Arthur and Mina any longer. Arthur still wants me. He has seen a bit of what I am and he still wants me, and I would move heaven and earth to fight my limitations, to take no more lives, and to curb my hunger if it meant we could be together for his lifetime. It may be a dream. A fool's dream, perhaps, but it gives me more strength than I have felt in a long time.

"Kiss me, Arthur, before we sleep. Please?"

His mouth meets mine, soft and lingering, and then I lift the mist again. His eyes close, and he goes limp in my arms. I burrow tightly against him, my tear-streaked face pressed against his strong and steady heart as sleep overcomes me.

It is not the wedding night either of us had hoped for.

But we are together, and for now, that is enough.

CHAPTER THIRTY

I awaken in utter darkness, surrounded by the crisp scent of cedar. Astonishingly, I smell nothing else, nor can I hear anything. I move my stiff, aching limbs and find that I am lying upon a soft silk cushion. My elbows connect with a rigid structure on both sides, and I frown and try to sit up. My head hits a surface just inches above my face with a resounding thump.

As my eyes adjust to the dark, I see the polished grain of the wood that encases me. The cushion beneath my body is engulfed by my voluminous cream satin skirt. I am wearing my wedding gown, with white gardenias in my hair and on my chest, already wilting.

I have just awoken in my own coffin.

I panic, hitting my fists against the tightly closed lid, wondering if they thought to bury a bell with me. It is a common practice, in case a person who is still alive must ring for help.

But I am not still alive, I think with a dark humor bordering on hysteria. And then the thought begins to calm me. I am not still alive. I do not need air. But the gnawing emptiness in my core tells me that I *do* need sustenance. How long has it been since I fed? How many hours or days has it been since I abandoned that poor man in the shadows of an empty street?

Remorse threatens to choke me, but I push it aside. Right now, I must get out of this coffin. I think of how easily I had lifted that man, though he was bigger and heavier than me. This new existence has come with incredible strength, much greater than that of a human.

And so I make a fist with my right hand, the one that bears my great-grandmother's jade ring. Slowly, experimentally, I punch the lid. There is an encouraging cracking noise, and I cough as wood splinters rain down on me. I repeat the motion over and over until a jagged line forms along the center of the lid. When the pieces are fragile enough, I push them apart and try to sit up again. Once more, my head hits a hard surface— this time, unyielding stone. I lie back down in disbelief, staring at the solid granite that encases my coffin. Something sharp pokes my shoulder and I turn to see an iron nail, one of many that stud the edges of my coffin. Not only have I been encased in stone, but my coffin has been *nailed* firmly shut with dozens of slivers of pure iron. Someone clearly feared that I would rise again.

I give a heavy sigh. "Van Helsing."

This overly cautious burial has the good doctor's stamp all over it. But he is only trying to protect the living, as he had attempted to do for me.

I study the heavy stone above me, thinking. They must have put me in the main room of my family's mausoleum, near Papa and my grandparents. Their tombs are made of finely carved granite, and though the lids were not meant to be removed, they are separate and unattached.

If I am strong enough to break wood with my fist, then perhaps I can shift the lid of my own tomb. Impatiently, I push away my bridal bouquet and press my hands flat against the stone, exerting all my strength to shift it sideways. Slowly, grunting and straining, I manage to move it enough to see pale light filtering in from somewhere. My newly sharpened eyes take in every minute detail of the Westenra mausoleum's ceiling: a dead fly trapped on a cobweb with one iridescent wing broken; a clutch of milky white spider eggs tucked into a crack in the ceiling; and an errant leaf, long dead and dry, caught between two of the stones.

At last, I am able to wrap my fingers around the lid and slide it aside. I sit up, looking around at the mausoleum of which I have spent so many years dreaming. Not so long ago, I had harbored such silly and romantic ideas of death, in which I would be with Papa again and see everyone I had loved and lost. Vlad was right. I have been stupid indeed.

I brace myself against the side of the tomb and climb out, nearly falling as my heavy full skirts catch on the jagged wooden lid. Impatiently, I tear at them until I reduce them to a thinner, shredded layer of cream satin. The seamstresses had spent months sewing tiny seed pearls into the hem, and I destroy their work in seconds. They had made me a dress to catch the eye of my wedding guests, but now I need a dress that will be light and easy. I run my hands approvingly down the simplified gown and feel a small lump against my leg. Someone has stitched a pocket into the satin, and inside it, I find the bullet that had failed to kill Quincey Morris.

He must have asked my maid to bury it with me. I look down at this talisman of protection that had meant so much to him, my heart aching, and replace it in my pocket. He had not intended it to be of much use to me dead, but I will take any good luck charm *undead*.

I remove my delicate veil of creamy Devon lace but leave the crown of white gardenias atop my head. Someone has taken the trouble of intricately weaving and pinning the flowers into my long, loose waves of hair, and I am too hungry to take the time to remove them.

A freshly carved name on Papa's tomb catches my eye. The inscription now reads: *Phillip Westenra, Jr., and his wife, Audrey.* He and Mamma have been reunited at last. I bend to kiss their names and drape my bridal veil over their tomb, fighting back tears. Knowing that they are here together gives me both peace and unimaginable pain. I turn to read the etched words on my own tomb. "Lucy Westenra lies here. Lucy Westenra is dead and gone," they seem to assert.

But none of it is true.

Lucy Westenra is not dead and gone, and her hunger is growing every second.

I approach the mausoleum doors. An infinitesimal crack between them lets in light too pale to be that of the morning. I press my eye to it and see a blue velvet night sky stretching above the churchyard. Judging from the wilting flowers in my bouquet, I have been buried at least two days, maybe longer. How many evenings have passed since Arthur and I had fallen asleep together on my bed before sunrise? I cannot tell for certain.

I push against the doors, but they are locked as always and do not budge. No doubt the thorough Dr. Van Helsing made certain to watch the caretaker turn the key, or perhaps he locked me in himself, not trusting anyone else to do the job.

I look down at my slim, pale hands, knowing that they are now strong enough to break down the doors. But I am reluctant to damage this sacred monument of my family's, especially when they are all resting behind me. I quell my rising desperation and think.

The mist. It had carried me out of my house, drawn potential victims to me, and helped me return the children to the orphanage. Perhaps it can somehow help me escape this tomb.

A thin stream slips into the mausoleum at once, wrapping itself around my waist like rope. I begin to float and then, impossibly, I am drifting *through* the crack between the doors as though my body has transformed into vapor. In seconds, I am standing before the bench where I willingly gave Vlad my innocence.

An involuntary smile of glee creeps onto my face. This existence may be a curse, but it has also given me indescribable and untold power. No granite tomb or locked door can keep me out now. The world is open to me, laid bare for the taking, and I will hold it cupped in the palm of my hand like a firefly, to nurture or destroy at my will.

But just as quickly, my glee fades. I am ravenous again, and there is only one answer to the question of my unholy hunger. *I will not harm anyone,* I think, clenching my jaw. Somehow, I will resist temptation tonight. I will make do with animal blood, as thin and unsatisfying as it may be. Blood is blood, and I refuse to commit another murder. Arthur still loves and wants me, and I will not do anything that is unworthy of him. It strikes me then that perhaps I do not need to take a life. Perhaps I can drink only a little, just enough to satiate me without snuffing out another existence. After all, Vlad had bitten *me* twice and had sickened, not killed me, and he had told me about biting Jonathan Harker multiple times. I press my clasped hands to my stomach, against the tiny kernel of hope nestling in the maw of the starving monster there.

"Lucy, come here."

I tense at the sound of Vlad's voice. But the churchyard is empty.

"I said, come here."

My legs begin to move of their own accord. My feet in their white slippers take steps I do not tell them to take. The mist slips from my waist and curls ahead of me like a finger beckoning, leading me out of the churchyard. Something is compelling me onward when I do not even know my destination. I grab hold of a lamppost on the dark and empty street, trying to stop my legs. But my body is no longer my own, and my hands loosen and let go as I continue to walk.

"You cannot fight me," Vlad says calmly. "My word is your command."

"Where are you taking me?" I ask, frustrated and afraid, as my body moves like a marionette controlled by his invisible hands. "Tell me and I will come of my own free will."

"Ah, but I know you too well," he says with a smile in his voice. "And I will not take any chances. Do hurry, won't you? We don't have all night."

The mist lifts me off the ground. My long shredded bridal skirt flutters as I fly through the fog, past closed businesses and silent houses full of sleeping people. In the shadows of the night, I pass half a dozen tiny figures, shoulder to shoulder in the fog, their arms outstretched to me. "Not again," I gasp. "Not more children. Vlad, get me away from them."

"We cannot help who we attract. I, beautiful young women, and you, motherless urchins," Vlad says, laughing, but the mist begins to pull me faster, dragging me out of sight.

I end up in front of an ornate black iron gate. The red brick home it surrounds is elegant and luxurious, with large windows and a pair of white marble lions on the doorstep. Through the open door, I hear the sounds of a party: people laughing and chattering, glasses clinking, and a piano playing a joyful melody. The mist pushes me inside. I follow the noise and the warm glow of light to an enormous ballroom filled with candles and walls covered in oil paintings.

There are people everywhere, all in various states of undress.

A fat man wearing only a linen shirt chases after three naked, dark-skinned women, his buttocks quivering with mirth and exertion. A brocade divan groans under the weight of revelers experimenting with an array of substances. One man sniffs a handful of sparkling grey powder into his nostril, while the woman at his feet drains a glass of poisonous green liquid before going limp, her long black curls fanning out over his lap. Across the room, a rowdy game of blind man's bluff is taking place: a blindfolded woman stumbles about, her breasts bouncing as she attempts to catch one of the giggling, caramel-skinned girls circling her. Everywhere are sofas, chairs, and even beds occupied by people drinking and carousing, mouths bobbing between legs, hands stroking unclothed limbs, skin and hair of ebony or mahogany or copper gleaming.

But I find none of it appealing. All the people have unfocused eyes, vacant smiles, and a looseness to the sway of their heads. I shiver, watching a girl with deep-olive skin being tugged between two grinning men, their arousal evident as she staggers back and forth, eyes half-closed.

In the center of the room is a long dining table packed with food and wine, the china and crystal glittering in the candlelight. The people seated there seem even more somnolent; several of them have fallen forward onto their plates, their eyes closed, and one man with thick jet-black hair is drooling onto his own shoulder, his lids flickering open every now and then.

At the head of this table is Vlad in crimson velvet, his skin so white that it almost glows in comparison to that of the two beautiful, full-figured girls enthroned upon his lap. His long pale hands are like spiders creeping over the earth of their umber skin, seeking a place to burrow and invade. One girl kisses his neck while the other nestles against him, pressing her head of long, tight black curls into his chest, but he pays them no mind. It is clear he has been watching me since the moment I stepped into the room.

"Hello, Lucy," he says, his low, rich voice cutting through the noise of the party. His eyes are black pools and his fangs glisten in the light. He has been feeding, and feeding well, for every neck at the dining table is wet with blood. "How kind of you to come."

"Did I have a choice?" I ask sourly.

"Well, no. But only because this party is for you and I wanted to make certain you would attend." Vlad gestures to an enormous, multitiered confection of a white cake, dripping with pale sugar icing like lace. "I knew you would be dressed for this special occasion."

I glance down at my high-necked, long-sleeved gown, pristine but for the shredded skirts, rows of seed pearls still hanging on for dear life. "What do you mean, this party is for me?"

"It's our wedding, of course. Yours and mine."

"I am *not* marrying you," I say flatly.

"You already have. You became my newest bride the moment you stole my blood, and now you must honor and obey me as your husband." Vlad bares his fangs in a garish smile. He shoves the girls onto the floor, where they lie still, and pats his vacant lap. "Come here, wife."

"I am *not* your—" I begin, but I feel my body jerk into motion again as though his deep, magnetic voice is a rope tied to each of my limbs. I grab on to anything I can—the back of a sofa, the edge of a table, even a dazed partygoer's arm—and almost fall in my effort to fight him. But it is like trying to stand in the ocean as the waves pull and the sand shifts beneath me.

Vlad sighs. His eyes are lightening to their customary blue-green. "Why do you have to make everything so difficult? You should know by now that it is easier not to struggle."

"And *you* should know by now that I always will." I gasp as my body flies toward him and lands sideways in his lap. My arms lock around his neck as he kisses my cheek and hugs me close, burying his face in my hair. "Let go of me, Vlad."

He ignores me, touching my crown of white gardenias. "You smell lovely for someone who just came out of a tomb. I like these. Pale flowers become you . . . and so does death. How was your first feeding? Have you had a chance to weep and wail over it yet?" He laughs.

I grit my teeth. Sitting this close to him reminds me of the night we played our harp duet, when I had been entranced by him, when I had foolishly thought he was everything I wanted. If my arms were not fastened around his neck against my will, I believe I would hit him. "You made it clear you had no interest in me any longer. Why have you called to me?"

"To teach you about your new existence, of course. You thought I would be cruel enough to forsake you? How hurtful." He tilts his head. "Though it *would* have been fun to watch you struggle, crying into your food and trying to wander about in the sun. That would have exposed me to discovery, however, and I have not yet sampled all that England has to offer. I ought to teach you how to better dispose of your meals. If you keep leaving drained bodies under trees, you might just set that little Chinese doctor on my trail."

"I thought you weren't afraid of him," I snap.

"I am not afraid of him, my dear, but of the inconvenience of being on the run. You will know it well. It is something you never anticipated, did you? In your stupidity and arrogance." He flicks my nose with a fingertip, and I jerk away from his touch. "Most humans do not like vampires. I'm sure you can imagine why. Too often have I had to flee mobs waving torches and howling for my death. Once one of them gets wind of what I am, the fear will spread quickly to more of them. It happens in every place, in every age, sooner or later."

"You have been a vampire for hundreds of years and still have not learned to hide yourself?" I ask contemptuously. "You have spent immortality well, I see."

His eyes blaze with cold blue fire, but his voice remains calm. "Watch how you speak to your master. You will soon learn how difficult it is to move invisibly among the prey you hunt. You think you can hide what you are and stay with your precious Arthur and Mina all their lives without attracting fear and curiosity?" His gaze bores into mine, and pinpricks of pain pierce my scalp. "Vampires cannot stay with anyone. They cannot get close to anyone. They cannot *love*."

I wince. "Stop it."

"You think you are better than I am. I can hear you."

"Get *out* of my mind," I snarl, and miraculously, the pain disappears at once. I feel his invasion of my thoughts fading, though I have not even tried to envision my silver shield.

Vlad growls. "You are my property, and so is your mind."

Once more, I feel the sharp pain of his invasion. And once more, I push it out of my head as easily as breathing. Clearly, my new strength is not just limited to my physical body.

But my pleasure and surprise are short-lived as he pinches my chin between his fingers, hard. "You belong to me. You are an extension of me, however much you want to judge me for enjoying my victims. Can you not see what fun they are having?" Roughly, he turns my head.

The olive-skinned girl is on a bed in her corset and nothing else, lying with the men who had been tugging her about. Behind a billowing curtain, the fat pale man wrestles with the three dark-skinned women he had been chasing. Meanwhile, at the piano, a blond woman is playing with her head thrown back in pleasure. Another woman, naked and copper-skinned, who had been kneeling between the pianist's legs, gets up and wipes her mouth before collapsing to the floor again. Her gaze finds me, and in it I see a desperate plea.

"None of them are here by consent," I say, sick with revulsion. I look around the dining table at everyone fainting and limp in their chairs. "You forced them to attend."

Vlad chuckles. "How charming that you think consent means anything anymore. I am not only *your* master, but theirs as well. I could make anyone do anything I wish. I could have Arthur here in a minute, kneeling between *my* legs, or Mina waiting for me on that bed. They are all just animals. Slaves for my food and my pleasure."

My stomach roils with nausea. "How did you call so many of them to you?" I ask, and then I see what I had not noticed before. Every window of this ballroom is open, and the mist is slipping in like a vine of smoke. "You used the mist. You can make humans sleep—"

"Or put them in a trance, as you did to those poor children." He smiles at my shock. "You will find, my dear, that we are irresistibly attractive to humans. So much so that we can call to them even without meaning to. They will come running through the mist, those lucky few who are caught between two worlds. The waking and the dreaming . . ."

"And the living and the dead," I whisper.

"Those who sleep lightly are drawn to us, as are those who walk in their dreams. But you already knew that." Vlad's smile widens. "You judge me prematurely. You do not know how fun it can be to make them lose their inhibitions. Let me show you." He nods at the copper-skinned woman sprawled on the floor, who gets up immediately and stumbles over to us, trembling.

Her knees are red from having knelt in front of the pianist, and her head lolls to one side as though too heavy to hold upright. My gut clenches at the pain in her eyes, even as my newly awakened hunger roars at the clean apple-blossom scent of her blood.

"Let her go, Vlad," I say furiously. "Let them all go."

"And have you skip a meal? Don't be silly." Vlad strokes my cheek with a cold finger. "Go on and feed, Lucy. This is my wedding gift to you. Drain her dry."

Against my will, my body flies toward the woman until we are standing inches apart. She is much taller than me and painfully thin, and the holes on her neck are ragged and careless. Up close, her blood smells even more fragrant, as soft and warm and floral as a spring morning. I feel the pinch of pain in my gums as my fangs snap down involuntarily.

"No," I say desperately. "No, Vlad, I won't do this again. I cannot take another life."

"You can and you will."

"Perhaps I can take only a little. Just enough to satisfy me . . ." But even as I say it, I know I will not be able to control my devastating hunger. I seized every drop from that vagrant on the street in the blink of an eye, and the intense emptiness roaring inside of me now would destroy any willpower I had. I turn to Vlad, trembling. "You drink from humans without killing them. You did it to me, and to everyone in this room. Teach me. Show me how. Please."

"I cannot," he says calmly. "For I never allow my hunger to grow as uncontrollable as yours. That is something you will learn to do with time. For now, do as I say. Kill her."

I look up into the woman's drowsy face. Her features are sharp and clear beneath long waves of dark hair. Her eyes are large, dark, and filled with tears of horror and sorrow and hopelessness. In them, I see my own terrible beauty, showy and obscene as a full-blown rose, a virginal woman with blossoms in her hair. And I wonder if this curse will lead to an addiction to seeing myself in the frightened eyes of humans.

"Lucy?" Vlad prompts me.

"No," I say again, but then I hear the young woman mumble something. "Please."

"What did you say?" I whisper.

"Please," she utters again as a tear rolls down her cheek. "Kill me."

"Are you making her say this?" I demand of Vlad, appalled.

But he only says, his voice cold and even, "Drain her, Lucy."

I look into the woman's eyes, so conscious and alert and full of sadness. She blinks at me, and the plea in her eyes convinces me. She wants to be free.

"Kill me," she murmurs again.

My arms are around her, and my fangs are buried in her throat before I even register that I have moved. She lets out a sharp gasp and freezes as her blood—as sweet and mellow as it smells—gushes into my mouth. I hear Vlad laughing as I drink and drink and drink, and the woman sinks to her knees once more. I bend to keep my lips fastened to her neck, the salty taste of her skin melding beautifully with the honey of her blood. I have never tasted anything so delicious in all my life, not even the meals Papa had favored, full of garlic and herbs, or the strawberry cakes I had once loved above all else. *Stop*, I try to tell myself. *You have fed enough. You can stop this now. Let her go, let her live.* But my predatory body refuses to obey. My fangs remain embedded in her skin and my hands clench on her shoulders, and I am lost, lost to the oblivion of satisfying my all-encompassing need to consume. She gives a muffled moan, her face pressed into me as I drink until there is nothing left but an empty shell that crumbles at my feet.

My face is wet with my own tears. I feel a curious mingling of grief and exaltation—a simultaneous clench of my heart for this second life I have stolen and the spreading stain upon my soul, but also the relief of my hunger subsiding and the joy of the fresh new blood pouring through my body. Perhaps it will always be this way—perhaps this momentary despair and this intoxicating euphoria will forever appear side by side, with every person I dare harm.

I fall to my knees before the slain woman, weak with remorse and self-hatred.

"Do you see the peace on her face?" Vlad asks. "You have given her a gift."

"Don't," I sob.

"Now, watch carefully. This is how we dispose of our food." He lifts his hand, and the mist rises, wrapping itself around the dead woman's body like puppet strings and pulling her to her feet. She does not fall, to my shock, but stands with her head drooping to one side and her arms limp. The ropes of fog grow thicker and thicker until they cover her completely, and I see her eyes open, empty and sightless. Her mouth hangs agape as she staggers through the mist like a lost, dead wanderer, and the sight of it reminds me of my dreams—of sometimes seeing other people stumbling in the silvery fog, some of them dead.

"What have you done to her?" I ask shakily.

"I have hidden her in the mist. It is a world few inhabit, and the perfect place to conceal one's indiscretions. Her shell will wander on and on, as will those of everyone we kill, and not a soul in the waking world will be any the wiser. I did the same with that vagrant you drank," he adds, looking at me expectantly as the dead woman staggers deeper into the mist and finally vanishes. "Well? Where is my thanks?"

I stare at him in numb silence.

"What's the matter, Lucy? Have you realized the consequences of your actions at last? Do you finally understand that the foolish story you told yourself—about choosing this existence because you didn't want your loved ones to grieve—was a fairy tale?" Vlad comes over and tilts my chin up to meet the dead mirrors of his eyes, which refuse to reflect me. "It was purely selfish on your part. You wanted to hold on to Arthur and Mina, but without responsibility. To please him but earn your freedom at the same time, and to keep her without having to act upon your lust. Oh yes, my dear, I know every corner of your wretched soul."

I try to pull away, but his fingers tighten on my chin. "You know nothing about love," I spit. "Don't speak of Arthur and Mina as though you know *anything* about them."

"I know they will hate you."

"They will love me even now. Arthur said he would still want me."

Vlad lifts me onto my feet. "It would have been better if you had died," he says with quiet malevolence, leaning in until our noses almost touch. "And Arthur and Mina would agree."

I haul back and slap him across the face, my body reacting before my mind has even registered the thought. His head barely moves, no doubt having anticipated my blow long before it fell, but his eyes narrow to jagged pinpricks. My handprint appears, pink upon his white cheek.

"I made you, Lucy," he says softly, wrapping his large, brutal hand around my throat. "And I can unmake you. With one movement, I could snap your head off like a dandelion and render your choice useless. Everything you sacrificed will have been for nothing."

"I cared for you," I choke out, clutching his wrist. "I would never have loved you, nor you me. But I would have tried to make you happy had you been the man on the cliffs."

"And who am I if not that man?"

"Someone both cruel and common. Someone disappointing," I say, coughing. If I am to die, strangled by his hand, then I will die speaking my truth. "That man on the cliffs treated me as no one ever has: as a person with hopes worthy of respect. He was kind and generous, though I was mortal and he was all-powerful." My tears splash onto his hand, and he flinches. "Kill me, then, Vlad, for I know I will never see that man again."

"He is here, you silly, vain, self-obsessed girl. He is here, and *you* have changed."

"We both have," I say, my voice soft and full of grief. "You wanted me to stay a pawn in your game, but I refused. That is why you hate me now."

He lets go of me and turns away, but not before I see the rare emotion in his eyes. "It is not your business what I feel. You are only to do whatever I say. I'm afraid, my dear, that in your unseemly quest to escape from society's rules, you failed to take into account that there would be *new* rules. And as your husband and master, I have you at my bidding."

I ball my hands into fists. "You do not. I have power of my own—"

Vlad whirls around, his face full of laughter. "Power! You think breaking a flimsy coffin or floating upon the air is *power*? My poor, ignorant girl, let me show you the truth." He takes a seat at the head of the table once more. "Come and stand before me."

At once, an immense pressure drags me toward him. I strain with all my might, my limbs quivering with the effort, but I quickly grow weak and tired. The pull is too much to bear, as is the smug smile on Vlad's thin lips, and my feet slide right across the floor toward him.

"Good," he says approvingly as though I had done it of my own will. "Now, kneel."

"I will not," I snap, but I am yanked onto my hands and knees before him at once by an invisible force. I glare at him, breathing hard, humiliated and furious enough to rip him apart with my bare hands . . . or die trying, which is surely what would happen.

"Now do you believe what I say?" he asks gently. "I hate that I must resort to such measures with you, Lucy. You reminded me just now of how much I enjoyed those nights with you in Whitby, but you constantly and unwisely push me to the limits of my anger." He touches my cheek. "I do not hate you. And I could still show you that kindness and generosity of which you spoke if you would only accept the consequences of your own actions."

I refuse to look at him. "You call it kindness and generosity to force me into submission and insult me? To show disgust and condescension?"

"I am only trying to teach you, little bride, to own your mistakes rather than foisting the blame onto others. You just told me that you cared for me, and so you must listen well."

"I will never care for you again," I whisper, turning away from him. "That is over and done. You may not hate me, but I will certainly hate you."

Vlad sighs. "What shall we do with you, my petulant child? You could stay in your tomb, but I believe the doctor will come back to finish you off." He thinks for a moment. "Best to ship you off to the Carpathians with the other brides. You would be out of the way and would not endanger my reputation here. Why, I have hardly had time to decorate my new house, Carfax!"

Fear crawls up my throat like bile. "No, please! Please don't send me away."

"Are you begging me?" he asks, smiling.

"I will not go," I say, my chest tight at the thought of leaving Arthur and Mina, perhaps forever. "I want to stay here. Please."

"But you told me so often of your wish to travel," Vlad says coaxingly as though humoring a fussy child. "You wanted, quite desperately, to see the world."

"This is not seeing the world. This is being locked up in some old castle far away from the people I love." My voice trembles with panic. I could not even fight him when he had forced me to kneel. If he ordered me to cross the sea, I would not be able to resist, and we both know it. I push aside the tatters of my pride. "Please, Vlad, do not send me away from here."

He raises an eyebrow. "A moment ago, you flew at me, hit me, and told me that you hated me. And now you humbly plead with me to let you stay?"

"Only for the length of Arthur and Mina's lifetimes. It would be a blink of an eye to you, Vlad. You, who have lived so many ages. Let me have this short time with them, and I will be cautious and not risk your reputation. I cannot give them up."

"But what if they wish to give *you* up?" he asks softly. "What if they cannot accept you as you are now and reject you despite what the noble Arthur said?"

I think of how Jack and Quincey and Dr. Van Helsing had pressed themselves against the wall like frightened animals upon seeing my fangs. Of how hard I'd had to fight against the temptation of Arthur's blood. But I push the memories away. The men's fear had come from the unexpected, and if I could just show myself to them and explain everything, perhaps they would understand. "They will still care," I whisper, clasping my hands to hide their trembling. "When I return, they will be glad and welcome me back."

The pity on Vlad's face is infinitely more difficult to bear than his cruelty and mockery. "Let us strike a bargain," he says. "If your friends accept you, knowing what you are, then I will accede to your request, provided that you dispose of your food appropriately. You will *never* expose me. You will *never* speak of me to anyone." His words are slow and deliberate, an incantation, and somehow, I can feel the command sinking into my skin and bones.

I swallow hard. "And if they do not accept me?"

"If your friends are disgusted by your new nature—as I believe they will be—then you will go to my castle in the mountains without further argument. Are we agreed?"

I shudder, but only from habit. My muscles still hold the memory of being human, and human Lucy would certainly have quaked at such an ultimatum.

"Well?" Vlad asks.

"I accept," I say.

It is the only answer I can give.

CHAPTER THIRTY-ONE

In the mausoleum, I cannot rest, though I know I ought to try. Instead, I pace all day, surrounded by dust and shadows as the world goes on outside the tomb. I burn to see Arthur again . . . but I am also gripped by terror and anxiety. I am haunted by Vlad's certainty that Arthur will reject me, and that he—that *all* of them, from Mina and Jack to Quincey and Dr. Van Helsing—will fear and hate what I have become.

I sink down beside my parents' coffin, overwhelmed with despair, clinging to what Arthur had said on that final night: "Of course I want you. You *will* come back, Lucy?"

The sunlight is interminable. I will the sky to darken, but it refuses to, and a beam of yellow light slips through the mausoleum doors, just to the left of me. Tentatively, I reach out a hand, remembering how Vlad had disappeared when the sun had emerged in Whitby, for fear of being burned. Indeed, he imprisoned himself in a box of earth every day to avoid the light. But when I touch the beam, I feel nothing on my fingers except a gentle warmth. I lean forward and let it fall upon my face, tense with anticipation. But there is still no pain.

"How is this possible?" I whisper.

I get up and peer through the doors of the tomb. The churchyard looks so different in the daylight, the sky bright blue above the gravestones. There is no one in sight, so I call up the mist and let it take me slowly, *slowly*, out into the sun. I shade my eyes, squinting, my heart delighting in the fresh air and the smell of leaves and the sound of carriages and people on the street. I hold up my hands and study them. I touch my face. But my skin is cool and smooth and unhurt.

Vlad lied to me again. Or did he?

Perhaps he had assumed, as I did, that his limitations would also become my own.

The sun endangers him, but here I stand in its glow. He has no reflection in a mirror, and I do, albeit changed. His eyes become ringed with red when he feeds, but mine remain the same. And when Dr. Van Helsing had held up garlic, it had not pained me in the way it should have.

This condition is different in me than it is in Vlad. Why? And can he truly not know?

Voices reach my ears. The caretaker approaches, talking to visitors, and I hastily retreat. It would not do to have them see a woman in an expensive wedding dress, standing in front of a tomb when she ought to be lying dead inside it. And I have much thinking to do before the sun sets, for if vampirism has such strange and inexplicable exceptions for me, then surely I can think of a way to break free of Vlad's control.

The day passes more quickly now, and at moonrise, I slip back into the dark and empty churchyard. Tonight, I will find my friends and tell them all—but not before I have fed first, to ensure their safety. Fear twists my gut, but I cling to the hope that Arthur will not turn me away. We will marry, and we will be happy, and we will remain together for the rest of his life—many years for him, and a short time for me. And when Mina returns from Budapest, I will continue to be the doting friend I have always been to her, only young and beautiful forevermore.

These pleasant fantasies occupy my mind as I perform the unsavory task of seeking out small creatures in the dark: rats, squirrels, and even an unlucky fox. Their blood is bland or sour, but it does abate my hunger. I bury the bodies and take care to clean my face, hands, and teeth, fretting at the inconvenience of wearing a white dress as a vampire. The thought amuses me, for it is proof that somewhere inside me still resides the human Lucy, who had once worried about subjects as insipid as gowns and flirting and parties.

I am about to summon the mist to bring me to Arthur when I hear a small voice ask, "Where is my mamma? Please, can you help me find my mamma?"

"Not again!" I growl. "I have not the time for this!"

The child goes still, frightened. She is perhaps nine, with pale skin, golden curls, and blue eyes, the type of girl that other women would covet and call a *pretty little thing*. But to me, her eyes are too big, her hands are too small, and her quavering voice sets my teeth on edge. She wears a costly, beribboned nightgown, ridiculous on a child. Somehow, she has left the safety of her home to find me in the mist, either because she sleeps lightly or walks in her slumber as I do.

I hear myself hum a lullaby, low and sweet, as I kneel with a reassuring smile. *No!* I want to shout at the hunger that rears its head. The girl's blood smells of pear drops and sherbet lemons, and my mouth fills with saliva, longing to taste her after eating such unsatisfying meals.

But never, *never* shall I harm a child.

"Hello, darling," I say gently as the tips of my fangs poke down from my gums. "I am going to send you home to your mamma. Where do you live?"

"Sheridan Lane," she says. "In the yellow house on the corner."

"That is not too far. Let me walk you back."

She fixes her large eyes upon my face. "Will you come inside and play dolls with me?" she asks, and hunger and nausea battle within me at this eager invitation from my prey. She slips her hand into mine, warm and sticky and confiding, and I flinch at her touch. "Please? Mamma and Papa never have time to play with me, and Lily and Edith are too grown-up now for dolls."

"I . . . I'm not sure I can," I say weakly.

"Please," she wheedles, wrapping her arms around my neck. The sugary smell of her blood intensifies a hundredfold, and I am forced to close my eyes, struggling to regain control. "I think you are a very nice and very pretty lady. And I want you to be my friend."

"Thank you. But I do not—"

The little girl gives me a sticky kiss on the cheek. Her throat is an inch from my mouth, fragile and perfect and full of blood. "No, I will not!" I cry, as my fangs snap down from my gums. Frantically, I call up the mist to put her to sleep as I had done with the orphan children.

But my exclamation has startled her. She pulls away and sees my teeth, and her shrill scream stabs the darkness. Now, I am the one clutching her, desperate to quiet her and keep her from running away to awaken everyone on the surrounding streets.

And then Dr. Van Helsing is there. He must have been hiding behind a large gravestone, for he is only twenty feet away, his face blanched with horror as he holds up an enormous bunch of garlic. Once more, the cloying scent fills me with memories of my parents: Papa reading to me in a room soft with lamplight; Mamma cuddling a smaller me upon her lap; the three of us at Christmas, laughing as Mamma tries one of Papa's dishes and makes a face at the strong smell.

Other shapes appear from the shadows of the churchyard.

Quincey Morris's long open coat flutters as he brandishes two silver pistols, both barrels pointed at me. Jack Seward holds up a wooden cross, grim and determined. Arthur's eyes are wild with horror, and Mina, still wrapped in her blue traveling cloak, covers her mouth either to suppress a scream or keep from being sick. She collapses, white as death, onto the stone bench where I had surrendered my virtue to Vlad.

They look at me in a way they never have before: as though I am a rotten and revolting corpse. And I realize that the suggestive tableau of me gripping a frightened, shrieking child, my fangs gleaming in the darkness, is exactly why Vlad knew they would reject me. To them, in this moment, I am the image of a demon from hell, evil and irredeemable, my arms imprisoning an innocent child in some twisted perversion of motherhood.

"No," I gasp. "No, please! This is not what it looks like!"

"Let the girl go," Dr. Van Helsing says evenly, advancing a step.

"I was going to put her to sleep. I was going to send her home!" I babble.

"Why do you think we would *ever* believe you?" Quincey Morris demands, and his cold voice chills me to the bone. It hurts me as much as if he had already shot me. "You soulless she-devil, trying to murder a little girl right before our eyes. We all saw you!"

"No! No, I would never!" I sob. "She lives on Sheridan Lane. I was going to walk her—"

Quincey turns off the safety on his guns with a deafening click. His hands tremble only slightly. "Let her go or so help me God, I will put ten bullets straight into your head." Days ago, he had given me a bullet for protection. Now, he will give me another . . . for the opposite reason.

I release the child, who runs to Mina. Mina wraps her cloak around her as Arthur, *my* Arthur, steps in front of them protectively, his gaze on me horror-struck. I try to move toward them, my heart aching, but Quincey speaks again.

"Stay where you are or I will blow your head clean off, as sure as I live," he says.

I choke back a sob and go still, frozen on my knees before them like a penitent.

"So you see, Jack," Dr. Van Helsing says calmly, as though continuing a conversation, "I was right. The creature in Lucy's room infected her with a dreadful malady that can only be sated by the drinking of blood. We have now seen her crimes firsthand and—"

"Respectfully, now isn't a good time for a lecture." Quincey advances with his guns drawn. I see a tremor in his jaw, but there is also an utterly detached coolness in his posture, that of the seasoned hunter. And for the first time, I know what it is to be his enemy . . . or his prey.

Silence follows his words. And then Quincey shoots.

"No!" Arthur and Mina scream as two bullets blast through the air, directed at my heart.

But I am too quick for him. I heard his heart pick up, smelled his blood accelerate, and felt the air move before his fingers even squeezed the triggers. In an instant, I am floating high above them in the mist, missing the bullets by mere fractions of a second.

Mina screams at the sight of me hanging aloft in the air, my wedding dress shredded and my black hair billowing, as Quincey shoots me again. One of the bullets catches my gown just inches to the right of my leg as I command the mist to carry me to safety.

"Quincey, stop!" Arthur shouts.

"Please," I beg, now floating behind them. They whirl in shock and terror. "Please, Quincey, for the love you once bore me, do not shoot anymore. Let me speak."

"Love!" Quincey bellows, veins bulging in his neck. "You dare to think that I ever loved *you*! That love was for an innocent young woman with a pure and spotless soul. You are *nothing* like her!" His words strike at the very core of my being, and my grief must show upon my face, for Jack lowers his wooden cross slightly, looking uncertain.

"Lower your guns, Mr. Morris," Dr. Van Helsing says. "You are wasting your bullets."

Arthur moves to stand between Quincey and me. His fists are clenched at his sides. "Stop shooting at her," he chokes out. "Let us hear what she has to say."

"Don't let her trick you, Arthur," the cowboy warns him. "That is not your Lucy, but a demon fooling you into trusting her with that voice. She would have killed that little girl if we hadn't been here. Oh, God, God, that face," he adds with a frightened gasp as I slowly lower myself to stand before them. "She is more beautiful than ever. The devilry."

"I am not trying to trick anyone," I plead, holding my hands before me.

Mina buries her face in the child's hair, weeping, and Arthur's body convulses with silent sobs at the sight of me. I smell his desire and longing, tinged with his familiar scent of pine, and it is almost my undoing. I want to be in his arms as much as he yearns to be in mine.

But I remain motionless because Quincey's pistols are still pointed at me and I do not wish to discover whether or not a bullet can destroy me. For a long moment, no one speaks, and so I say into the silence, "Please. What is today's date?"

Dr. Van Helsing and Jack exchange glances.

"What could a creature like you want to know of days and months?" Quincey asks, trying hard to keep the steel and the anger in his voice. But the guns quiver in his hands, and his dark brown eyes on me are wet. "What can they matter to you?"

"Don't speak to her like that!" Arthur snaps. He turns to look at me, his face pale in the dim light. "It is the twenty-seventh of September, the eve of your birthday. And . . . and our . . ."

I feel a pang in my cold, unbeating heart. "Our wedding day."

"You told me you would come back," he whispers, shaking his head. "But I didn't believe you. I thought you were just trying to comfort me, and I woke to find you not breathing. I watched them nail your coffin shut. How . . . how can you still be alive, Lucy?"

"I am not alive," I say, and Mina utters a muffled half gasp, half sob. "Not anymore. Dr. Van Helsing is right. I was infected, and my blood has been poisoned by a—" A sudden excruciating pain racks my entire body. I close my eyes, dizzy and weak, but I recover in an instant to see them all watching me apprehensively. I try again. "When I was in Whitby, I met—"

"What is happening to her?" Mina demands, her voice shrill as I am cut off by another terrible wave of burning pain that sears through my muscles. I lean against a gravestone, shaking. This is how I had imagined the sun would feel on my skin now, hot and fierce and sharp.

"You will *never* expose me. You will *never* speak of me to anyone," Vlad had said, like an incantation sinking into my bones. Like a spell.

Again, the sensation passes quickly, as though rewarding my silence. I swallow hard and look at Dr. Van Helsing. "You came to see me because of this," I say, choosing my words with the utmost care as I touch my throat, now perfect and unblemished beneath the high neck of my gown. "It happened to me multiple times."

"You were bitten," Dr. Van Helsing says. "Attacked. It happened first in Whitby."

I nod. "Not by a dog, but by . . ." I trail off, already frightened of the pain that will come should I attempt to tell the truth again. "After the third time, I began to die. And I would have truly died had I not arisen before sunrise to drink blood myself. I found a man nearby, and I was so hungry, I couldn't stop myself. I—" My voice breaks, and I am unable to continue.

"Oh, Lucy," Mina whispers, tears streaming down her face.

"You were attacked by a blood-drinking beast," Dr. Van Helsing says. "I saw him in the guise of a man, though not very clearly in the shadows. He flew away in the form of a bat."

Arthur whirls on Quincey. "Do you see? I hope you feel proud of yourself, shooting at a helpless, innocent woman! It wasn't her fault!"

A tear slips down the cowboy's face. "But she isn't helpless or innocent anymore," he says, his voice cracking with emotion and uncertainty. "We all saw it just now. That child in Mrs. Harker's lap almost became her next victim. Any of us might. Especially you!"

"Hush," Dr. Van Helsing says sharply. His eyes are on me, shrewd and penetrating. "How did the creature find you, Lucy? He came to you first at Whitby."

I hesitate, struggling to find the right words.

Jack and Quincey begin to fidget, tense and impatient, and Dr. Van Helsing holds up his hand. "Let her take the time she needs," he warns them. "There is some sort of restriction, some coercion, that forbids her from revealing her attacker. Did you not see how it pained her?"

I feel a rush of gratitude for him. "Mina knows how much I love the cliffs at Whitby. And how I have sleepwalked all my life. I did it often this summer, and many nights, I found myself sitting there above the sea." I am too afraid to go on, but I see the comprehension in both Dr. Van Helsing's and Mina's eyes. Mina lets out a low moan of grief. "It was not your fault, Mina, darling. You could not have prevented me. I *wanted* to go."

"She was lured," the doctor says softly to Jack. "She was seduced."

"It is not that simple," I say shakily. "We spoke about immortality at dinner once, Doctor. Do you remember? I have always longed for freedom. The ability to roam, to experience, and to *live* as men do. But I felt that there was nothing more in life for me but to belong to Arthur."

Arthur's voice is as frail as taut thread. "I thought that was what you wanted."

"I *do* want it," I cry. "I want to marry you and love you and be happy with you. But I also want freedom afterward. After living life with you."

"And this was what *he* promised you?" Dr. Van Helsing asks.

I do not answer. I do not even nod. I only meet Mina's eyes, which are even bluer through the sheen of tears. "Mina, I could not help it. You know how death has stalked me, haunted me."

"Oh, Lucy," she whispers, her face unbearably sad.

I press my hands over my heart, which aches as much as it ever did, though it is still and lifeless. "Know that I made this choice. I did not understand it completely. But know that I *chose* it, however great a mistake I have found it to be." I bow my head, ashamed by my foolishness. I did not think it through. *Any* of it. For in this form, I must always mourn others; I must hide and not be close to anyone; and I must live on with the hateful, vindictive Vlad, not the kind and tender one I had first met on the cliffs. "I chose this for myself. Please, please try to understand."

"What do you mean by *choosing*?" Dr. Van Helsing asks slowly. "One does not choose to be attacked. Unless . . ." He trails off. "Unless you were never attacked, and had *asked* . . ."

"Asked?" Jack whispers. The arm holding the cross drops to his side.

"Asked?" Arthur utters.

They look at me and I look back. I had not thought the churchyard could get any quieter, but it does. No crickets chirp, and not a blade of grass rustles. It is the all-encompassing silence of death, of the tomb, hanging over us like some unseen shroud.

And then Mina falls to the ground, *screaming* with grief. Quickly, Dr. Van Helsing takes the terrified child and hugs her close as Mina beats the grass with her fists, ignoring Arthur's and Jack's attempts to help her up. "How could you, Lucy?" she asks, her words barely intelligible. "How could you do this to yourself? How could you subject yourself to such an existence?"

Everything in me wants to run to her and hold her. But I am afraid that Quincey will shoot me, so I settle for crumpling to the grass as well, several agonizing feet away from her. "I love you, Mina," I say, but my words are drowned out by her shouts.

"You have robbed us of yourself! Do you understand the cruelty of what you have done?" she shrieks. "You have stained and destroyed yourself beyond redemption. Your soul, Lucy! You feed on the blood of the living! I . . . I cannot—" Her weeping trebles the ache in my heart.

"But I am still here," I say desperately. "Here in the flesh, with you and Arthur. And I can be with you for years and years! I will never leave you. Arthur and I will marry, and we will see you and Jonathan, and we can all be together. Your children—"

"Her children?" Quincey gasps. "Mrs. Harker's children would never be safe from you!"

Arthur goes white and sinks onto the bench Mina has vacated.

"Arthur, please," I say, stretching my hands out to him. "You said, that final night, that you would love me as I am. You said—"

"You almost killed a little girl, Lucy," he whispers, rocking himself. "Quincey is right. We all saw it. I laughed in Dr. Van Helsing's face when he told me what he suspected. What he and Jack planned to do tonight. I came with them to show them how wrong they were to slight your name, to even *suggest* what they did. But that child was so frightened, and you had her, and you—" He buckles over, putting his head between his knees as though about to be ill.

"How could you think I would ever hurt her?" I plead, cut to the quick. "Do you not know me? Any of you? I would *never* harm that little girl!"

"Not the old Lucy Westenra, but you, *you*—" Quincey cries.

"Let her speak—" Jack begins.

"Can you control your hunger?" Dr. Van Helsing asks. "Your fangs? Can you be sure?"

They are all talking at once, Quincey and Jack arguing, the doctor asking questions, Arthur crying on the bench. But even so, Mina's words come through the commotion clearly.

"The old Lucy never liked children."

Everyone falls silent again.

"What was that, Madam Mina?" the doctor asks politely as though they are having tea and he had simply misheard a conversation. "What did you say?"

"The old Lucy," Mina says, her quivering voice rising as she looks at me, "never liked children. You thought you could hide it, but I knew you too well. And now that you have forsaken us to be a monster . . ." She breaks down sobbing once more, prostrate with grief.

Arthur sinks down and wraps his arms around Mina, cradling her like a child as they weep. It is the way he might have held me, with tenderness, with protection.

He will never hold me like that again.

The sudden realization, and the certainty of it, is like a dagger ripping me open from chin to belly, spilling my heart into the night air.

Vlad was right. Arthur and Mina will not accept me. The two people I love most in all the world would rather give me up than open their eyes to my new existence. *Monster.* My own dear and beloved Mina, for whom I would give the last drop of my blood, now thinks I am a monster, and even Arthur—who had loved me with every fiber of his being—would choose Mina over what I am now. They have rejected me, body and soul.

Quincey lifts his guns higher, Dr. Van Helsing raises the bundle of garlic, and Jack pulls out his own gun and points it at me, his hand trembling.

They have seen the wrath upon my face. Perhaps blue veins skittered around my eyes or my fangs in my wet red mouth caught the moonlight. I will never know, for I cannot get close enough to see my reflection in their eyes without one of them destroying me. But then my rage subsides, and hurt takes its place. The pain of Arthur's and Mina's rejection washes over me like the ocean, drowning me in the undertow. I have never felt more alone. I give in to my own silent tears, knowing that if Quincey shoots me again, I will not move this time. I will let him kill me.

But he does not shoot.

It does not matter, for I know that this is goodbye.

"I have been lonely all my life," I say, my voice breaking. I avert my eyes from the fear and hatred I know must be in their faces. "Not even those who loved me could understand what I wanted: a full and rich life on my own terms. To be loved, but also to be free. And now I have that freedom, but I have lost you all forever."

The silence stretches on.

When I look up, I do not see loathing, not even in Quincey. I see an impossible sadness.

"Thank you for trying to protect me, Dr. Van Helsing," I say softly. "And thank you, Jack. And you, Quincey. You are the bravest men I know." A lump moves in Quincey's throat. I turn to Arthur and Mina. "I love you more than I can ever say. I will love you for all my existence. You will never have to see me again. I will make certain of that. I am going away for good."

"I don't think we can let you do that, Lucy," Dr. Van Helsing says quietly. "If we let you go and endanger more lives, we would be aiding and abetting the beast that infected you."

"Then what, Doctor?" I ask tiredly. "Will you kill me yourself? Or will Quincey do it?"

"No!" Arthur shouts. "Don't touch her, either of you! Let her be."

"Arthur, you heard the doctor," the cowboy says. His voice, so cold and full of hatred before, is as thin and fragile as thread now. "We have to destroy her, or she will kill again."

"Don't, Quincey!" Mina begs. "Don't!"

My heart lifts for a fleeting moment. Arthur and Mina still love me, no matter what they say. They cannot stand to see me killed. I look Mina straight in the eyes and then Arthur. "I love you," I say once more, with all the feeling left in my cold body. "Goodbye."

"Lucy, wait," Arthur says with sudden desperation. "Don't go yet. Lucy, wait!"

But I am gone. I sweep the mist around myself and slip back into the mausoleum, where I sink against my own tomb and cry and cry until I am empty of tears, empty of emotion.

There is a movement in the air.

I look up to see Vlad watching me from the shadows. His face wears no expression, though I know he has seen and heard everything.

"Well? Go on," I snap. "Insult me. Berate me. Mock me. Tell me that you were right and that you always knew better than me. Rejoice in their rejection of me."

But he says nothing.

I take a few deep, shuddering breaths. My voice is as dead as my heart as I say flatly, "I will honor the terms of the deal we made. I will leave for your castle in the mountains as you commanded, and I will never return."

"Lucy," he says, and my name is a sigh upon his lips.

"Do not send me by ship, the way you came here," I go on in that dull, lifeless voice. "It is too slow a route for me. I understand the precautions, but I want to be gone as quickly as I can. I vowed not to expose you, and be assured I shall keep that vow by carriage and by train."

I wait, but he says nothing.

"I hoped to have you once," I say with a short, humorless laugh. "To be what I was to you on the cliffs. I thought I would spend all eternity learning from you, seeing the world with you, being with you. But I know now that I have lost you, too, as surely as I have lost Arthur and Mina. Whatever part of you I treasured is gone. There is nothing left for me here."

And then, as Vlad watches in silence, I crawl back into my granite tomb and slide the lid over myself, obscuring what little light is left.

CHAPTER THIRTY-TWO

I t is tempting to lie in the darkness of my coffin, cut off from the world and the ones I thought would always love me. If I am not alive, I reason, then I can simply ignore my hunger and linger here in the shadows, neither in danger of exposing Vlad nor harming another person as Dr. Van Helsing feared I would. A good, obedient little corpse, doing as the men tell her to do.

But death does not suit me. Lying still does not suit me. And before night comes again, my boredom grows even more unbearable than my sadness or hunger, and I tell myself that leaving is only sensible. Dr. Van Helsing will likely return to destroy me for good. Quincey and Jack will be with him, ready to finish the job. And Arthur? Will he watch as they send me straight into the fires of hell? Will Mina cry when I am well and truly gone, or will she be glad?

I wipe my eyes, slide the lid off my tomb, and sit up. To my shock, the mausoleum is full of lit candles. The trail of lights sends shadows flickering over the walls as it leads down to the crypt where more of my family members are interred. I step out of my coffin and hear a noise when my hand meets the granite. I look down to see that Arthur's ring has been moved to my other hand, next to my great-grandmother's jade, and Vlad's garnet is now on my wedding finger. I regard it bitterly, but do not take it off. This shackle is what I deserve, after all.

I follow the trail of candles into the bowels of the Westenra mausoleum and discover an enormous pile of goods scattered across the stone floor.

From a wooden chest spills an obscene amount of money, from the currency of England to that of France, Germany, and Austria-Hungary. There are traveling papers, documents, and trunks packed with gowns and veils, most of them black, all of them finely made and expensive. There are chemises, nightgowns, stockings, hairbrushes, and other toiletry items—though I note the absence of any mirrors—and shoes for all occasions. Against the wall sits a long narrow box of plain and sturdy wood, filled with earth that smells of rich forests and frost-tipped mountains.

Vlad has not only taken the time to thoroughly prepare me for my journey, but has left me one of his precious resting places to protect me from the sun and human eyes. I know better than to be touched, however, being all too familiar with his alternating kindness and cruelty by now—and after all, he is sending me away as though I am a bothersome child. What strikes me most is this proof that he does *not* know how differently the sun affects us, and it is a secret I shall keep to myself, in hopes that it will prove useful someday.

I ignore the gowns and choose a simple dark shirt, pants, and a cap to tuck my hair under, glad that Vlad was perceptive enough to include men's clothing, which will likely make it safer to travel. I put my wedding gown and slippers into a trunk, and as I am putting on comfortable dark shoes, I see a letter of travel instructions he has left me. His bold, scrawling handwriting is as forceful as a demand, and the words are cool, emotionless, and to the point.

"A carriage will come in three days' time," he writes. "Your belongings and papers—as well as you yourself, safe in the box of earth—will wait at the churchyard entrance, to be taken to a private car on a train bound for Dover. From there, a ferry will take you to Calais, then Paris by train and a series of other conveyances beyond. You will arrive in the Mountains of Deep Winter no later than the end of October." The final words give me a strange sensation, as though they are dissolving into my bones. They are a direct command to which I will be beholden.

Despite my impending exile and separation from Arthur and Mina, I cannot help but feel a twinge of eagerness to see places I had only ever hoped to experience in my dreams. My excitement soon sours into restlessness and anxiety, however, and I find it too hard to remain here, surrounded by the family I must leave behind. And so, even before the first rays of sunlight touch the sky, I decide that I will say goodbye to London. I hesitate at the doors of the tomb, both hoping to see Arthur and Mina still outside, concerned and repentant, and also wishing to avoid them if they are and save myself the pain of loving people I can never have again.

As though it has heard the emotions warring in my breast, the mist comes floating gently in and takes me in its hold. I feel my hair and skin and bones become particles of air, though my mind and consciousness are still present, and I soar out of the mausoleum in the form of the mist itself. I have no eyes to see and no ears to hear as I rise high above the churchyard and float to the back entrance, where the mist lowers me and I materialize as a woman once more.

I find several large rats with which to suppress my hunger and go out onto the empty street, pulling my cap low upon my brow. The city is just beginning to awaken as I walk along the rows of houses, listening to neighbors greet each other and carriages clattering along. I smell late autumn flowers, burning leaves, the remnants of cooking upon a man's jacket, the soap in a woman's hair, and candle wax wafting toward me from a shop.

Though it is day, I feel that I am sleepwalking again. A dreamy surreality overtakes me and a set of lines from Keats echoes through my head:

Was it a vision, or a waking dream?
Fled is that music:—Do I wake or sleep?

I move through the lanes and alleys of the city, one undead among the living. My hunger waxes and wanes as I take in a bouquet of tens of thousands of different types of blood: sweet or savory, fragrant or sour, fresh or stale, thin with illness or rich with health. But I restrain myself as I continue on, my feet finding all the familiar places—the avenues of the park where Mamma and I had gone on long drives, talking and laughing; the shops Mina and I had frequented, holding new hats and gloves up against each other as an excuse to touch; the houses in which I had danced and flirted and fallen in love, my smile dazzling to hide the darkness within.

Men and women alike had stared avidly at me in that former life, just as taken by my overt difference as by my beauty. But with my costly hats and splendid gowns, neat gloves and well-made shoes, they had made the effort—at least to my face—to be polite, and to treat me as Papa had promised they would as long as I strove to be perfect and unobjectionable in every way.

But now, in the plain dark clothes of a working man, with no lace or jewels to make my tilting dark eyes, olive skin, and too-black hair more palatable to them, I attract open hostility and revulsion. Ladies pointedly cross the street to avoid me, and governesses herd their charges away to protect them from such an unsightly foreigner. "The docks are that way! Go home!" one man barks. I ignore him and move past, but not before I hear him say, "Damned bloody Chinamen. They're everywhere now! Can they not leave their silks and spices and be gone?" to which his companion reminds him, sniggering, "Don't forget their opium and their women."

Minutes become hours, day melts into night, and sun and moon take turns rising and falling as I wander on in a daze, confronted by memories, sparks of joy and waves of grief, nasty comments and even nastier looks. I stop only to feed on birds, foxes, and squirrels, whatever I can find to dull the edges of my hunger. I feel no exhaustion, no compulsion to sleep.

And then, on the third evening, as sunset bleeds from the sky, I smell garlic, acrid enough to break me out of my daze. I find myself in a poor part of London, where the faces are thinner and more tired. I follow the scent to a food stand where an elderly Chinese couple is cooking hot, savory pockets of beef and shrimp. My mouth waters not for their blood, but for the dumplings, and when the wife waves me over, I approach, though I have avoided being too close to humans for the past few days. She scoops two dumplings onto a little plate and pours a dark, thick sauce over them that smells of even more garlic. I take them and hand her some coins in return from the supply Vlad gave me. She gives a short nod and turns her attention back to her work.

I look warily at the plate. Vlad cannot withstand garlic or the taste of human food. Garlic clearly does not offend *me*, but will human food repel me as well?

I take a small, tentative bite of a dumpling, expecting it to crumble like dust in my mouth. But instead, it is delicious. I close my eyes, over-whelmed by the palette of flavors: the tang of onions, the rich smoki-ness of the meat, and the snap and warmth of a dozen spices, all melding against my tongue. I imagine Papa here with me, kind eyes crinkling and a hearty belly laugh as he watches me eat something he would have adored. "You are my daughter," I picture him telling me, "and whatever choices you make, you make with good reason. Learn to live as you are now, Lucy, and try to be happy as you deserve. As you will always deserve."

My face is wet as I swallow the rest of the dumpling and then the other.

Perhaps this existence will not be as I had hoped. Perhaps it will come with a whole host of considerations that I, in my human selfish-ness, had not understood. But there may be flashes of joy like this, small and simple. I may learn, in that castle far away, to live with intention, to only satisfy myself with human food and animal blood, and to avoid doing more harm. And I may still be a daughter worthy of my parents' love and pride.

But no sooner have these hopes entered my mind than I smell it.

The fragrance stokes my hunger a thousand times more than the garlic did.

My eyes fly open, and I see a man. He is short and round, nondescript, perhaps Southeast Asian as I myself am. He has a scar on his chin and weary eyes, but when he smiles at the elderly couple as he purchases three dumplings, his face is kind. And his blood, his *blood*, with notes of smoky garlic, sun-ripened fruit, and clean cinnamon—an odd but utterly enchanting blend. I hold my breath, trying not to breathe in any more of the scent, but doing so only intensifies it.

I have not fed on human blood in *days*, and standing this close to the most indescribably perfect blood I have ever scented, I find it difficult to resist. No, not difficult. *Impossible*.

Papa's laugh. Mamma's smile. My conviction to lead a life of which I can be proud.

All of it vanishes in an instant, dissolving under the furious hunger that shoots sparks of need through my body. *I will not kill*, I tell myself, cajoling and persuasive. *I will taste him and then leave him be. I will try harder to stop drinking this time.* I have successfully abstained from human blood for days, after all. Do I not deserve a reward?

The man's eyes widen as I approach, and I see my reflection clearly in the dark pools of his pupils. In these few days of wandering, I had appeared to humans only as a foreign young man, threadbare and bedraggled. But now, my growing hunger transforms my skin and eyes, making them glow, and enhances my beauty in sharp contrast to my simple attire. My demonic infection has recognized its next victim, and it is doing everything it can to lure him in.

He asks a question in a language I do not know, hushed and awed. But when I move into the shadow of a building, he follows without hesitation, leaving the light and noise of the food stand and the small crowd that has begun to gather to buy dumplings.

I will take just a little blood, I think as my appetite roars. *And then I will stop myself.*

Tongues of mist materialize and wrap themselves around us, and people pass by us without a second glance. The man's eyes are now half-closed and the plate teeters in his hand. His breathing does not change as I take the food from him and set it on a doorstep.

What happens next is a blur.

One moment, I am looking at this man whose blood smells like a heavenly elixir. And the next, his body is crumpled at my feet with two little red holes in his neck, utterly empty of breath, of blood, of life. His blank eyes stare up at me sightlessly. The dead weight of his arm slides off his chest, and on his limp hand I see a wedding band of cheap metal. I collapse onto the doorstep, shaking. How can this have happened so quickly? I told myself I would stop. I barely remember my fangs snapping down . . . and now I have killed again. I have murdered someone's husband. Someone's son, or friend, or brother, or even father. I have robbed another person of blood they never owed me, and I have deprived another family of their loved one.

"I meant to stop," I whisper. "I meant to—"

"Lucy." Vlad's voice is so clear that I startle and look around, expecting to see his menacing shape, but he is not there. He is only in my mind. "Remember what you promised me."

Something in my body takes over. I lift the mist and wrap it around the dead man, as Vlad had done to the woman I killed. As soon as the man is on his feet, with his blank and unseeing eyes still open, he begins to stumble mindlessly through the thickening fog, swept away into the world of the mist, never to be found again. I watch him stagger toward the docks of dirty, ramshackle boats, my gut clenched with self-loathing. And then I am moving away, flying.

In the mist, I hurry through the dark streets of London, unseen by anyone I pass. Only animals lift their heads, tense and sniffing. I drift along lanes and alleys until I am in the churchyard again. In the Westenra mausoleum, I stand staring at the tomb that bears my name. And I know, I *know* I deserve Arthur's and Mina's rejection and Quincey's hatred and Dr. Van Helsing's determination to kill me. If a looking glass were here, I would see my true self: a demon, a beast of the shadows, my skin swirling with the evidence of what I have stolen.

I gave up my soul to embrace this curse with hungry arms, and all that awaits me now is an eternity of damnation and disgust, overwhelming hunger and deep-rooted loneliness. Vlad does not care what becomes of me, Mina and Arthur believe that I am better off dead, and I have lost Mamma and Papa forever. There is no one to love or help me, not anymore.

I descend into the candlelit crypt and my eyes fall upon a wooden hairbrush among my new belongings. I contemplate breaking it and burying the sharp point into my heart, freeing the world of the mistake of me. But *true* death would not erase what I have done. The stain of my deeds is already spreading like poisonous ink. What have I committed to? What have I chosen?

If I go on this way, I will destroy everything I touch and harm everyone I love. There is nothing for me now but to hide myself away from the world, for I do not deserve anything or anyone in it. And one day, when I have retired long enough for penance, I will find the strength to stake my own heart. I will find the courage to die.

Fury and grief and self-hatred war within me. I smash boxes of jewels and shoes, shatter bottles of scent, kick holes into the chest of money, tear up gowns and hats and veils and fling them into the far corners of the crypt. None of it matters anymore. None of it means anything. It is all nothing, just like me. My heel connects with a trunk, and I kick it viciously, sending it flying into the pile of travel documents. An envelope slips out from between the papers, and I seize it in a blind rage, preparing to rip it into a million pieces. I cannot take another cold and commanding letter from the man who had fooled me into thinking he cared, who tricked me and withheld information from me, and who had the gall to shame me for trusting him.

But I freeze when I see the handwriting, small and neat and perfect, on the thick cream-colored envelope. A governess's elegant and practiced hand.

For Lucy, Mina has written. And on the back, in tiny letters beneath the unbroken seal, she has added, as though not for my eyes: *Will you please see that she gets it?*

Who was she addressing? Vlad? Only he could have placed it here for me.

I stare down at the envelope for a long and breathless moment as that feeling of surreality returns. Surely, I am sleepwalking. I am lost in the mist and wandering in my dreams again, for Mina would never write to me now, not when she fears and hates me.

Mystified, scarcely daring to hope, I sink to my knees and tear the envelope open to find a thick sheaf of paper, all the pages filled on both sides in Mina's impeccable hand.

My cherished Lucy,

I write this on the 30th of September, two days after Arthur, Mr. Morris, the doctors, and I saw you. My heart had shattered upon receiving news of your death, and never did I imagine that I would see you again. No matter how my soul rails against it, I cannot stifle the joy that came from hearing your voice once more. It soothes my fear and horror at the choice you have made.

I wish I had been the friend you deserved, for then you might have felt that you could talk to me before making this decision all alone. You looked so sad that night, Lucy. Mr. Morris may have seen you as evil and seductive—at first, at least—but I saw your loneliness and despair. I want you to know that you will always have my love and friendship. That would not have changed with your natural death, and it has not changed now, with your . . . I hardly know what word to use. Your new state of being, I suppose.

That night, we saw you retreat into the mausoleum, and Dr. Van Helsing was ready to follow. He told us that piercing you through the heart with a stake of wood and cutting off your head would save your soul and send you to Heaven, where you truly belong. At this, your poor Arthur, always so quiet and mild, actually tried to attack him and had to be held back by the other men. He loves you still, Lucy, so much that I weep to think of it. Dr. Van Helsing and the others relented and agreed to go home after they had taken the little girl back to her family.

When Arthur regained control of himself, he said to me, "Mrs. Harker, I know you love Lucy as much as I do. The doctor believes she will sleep during the day for fear of the sun, and I have a notion that he and Jack will return in the morning to kill her."

"They can't! They mustn't," I cried.

"Mr. Morris is all for it. Which means that you and I are the only ones who can protect her. Please, Mrs. Harker. I hate to ask you when your husband is ill and you ought to be home with him, but I wish that you would please come back and help me keep Lucy safe."

I have never seen a man cry before. Jonathan never has, not even on the worst days of his illness, when I knew he wanted to. But Arthur wept inconsolably as he spoke, and I could only touch his shoulder and say, "Have no fear, my friend. I shall stand watch with you until dawn."

Well, Lucy, it was a lucky notion of his. I patrolled the churchyard entrance with him until sunrise, when Dr. Van Helsing—who is every bit as much of a hunter as Mr. Morris—came back with the other men in tow. When I saw his face, I knew he would not rest until you were no more.

I truly thought he and Arthur would kill each other. Arthur refused to move out of his way, so Dr. Seward and Mr. Morris pinned him to the ground. Oh, the violence with which they treated their friend! "I am sorry, Mrs. Harker," Mr. Morris said to me. "I am sorry that you stayed."

"I will not move, either," I told Dr. Van Helsing, prostrating myself before him. "Will you hurt me, too, Mr. Morris? Or you, Dr. Seward? I beg you to let Lucy be. Do not take her life."

"It is not a life, Madam Mina," Dr. Van Helsing said quietly, "but an evil, soulless existence that she must now endure. In the name of the love you once bore her, let me pass."

"Evil? Soulless? Take those words back!" I had never shouted like that in all my life, and the men went still with shock. "If you want to kill Lucy, you will have to kill me first. Go on! My head and my heart are here for the taking, and I would rather you destroy me than her."

Lucy, I meant those words. Every one of them.

They protested that you had almost harmed a child, to which I replied, "I should not have said what I did. Lucy may not like children, but she would never hurt them. Not even now. I have loved her long and well and ought to beg her forgiveness for making such an assumption."

Mr. Morris shook his head. "It wasn't an assumption, ma'am."

"The doctors examined the child thoroughly," I said. "There was not a scratch on her. Lucy did not hurt her, though she had the opportunity. Please go away and let her be!"

Dr. Van Helsing's eyes held such sorrow as he looked at me. "Madam Mina, you do not know what you ask." But something about my plea touched him, and the men vowed not to return that day. I believed them, but Arthur did not and stayed with you all afternoon. I went home to care for Jonathan, and when I came back, Arthur was on the bench with his head in his hands.

"I cannot leave her," he said. "I cannot leave my love."

For two nights and a day, we watched over you. I had to leave now and then to see to Jonathan, but then I would return to sit with Arthur. Writing this helped distract me from my fear, for always I sensed a presence watching us. My intuition told me that this being did not wish to harm Arthur and me . . . at least, not right away. And I knew they had something to do with you.

I am sobbing as I read Mina's words. The page ends with a large ink blot, and then the letter continues with one last sheet, her neat handwriting becoming crooked and agitated.

Oh, Lucy! Such distressing news since I last wrote to you!

On the third day, I stayed at home, as Jonathan was growing worried by my long absences and lack of appetite. He took a nap after lunch—sleep has *been elusive for him ever since his journey—and a good thing, too, because Arthur came to see me, looking frantic.*

"She is gone, Mrs. Harker," he said. "Lucy is gone!"

That morning, the doctors and Mr. Morris had returned to the churchyard bearing wood and iron, and Arthur had been too weak from lack of food and rest to fight them. They bullied the caretaker into open-ing the Westenra mausoleum . . . but what should they discover but an empty tomb? There was no sign of you. Perhaps you had not been there for days.

Where are you, my darling? Can I be writing this letter to no one?

No sooner had Jonathan and I returned to England than we received news of Mr. Hawkins's death. He had loved my husband as a son and had left his business and his entire fortune to him. You can imagine how touched Jonathan felt. Ill as he was, he insisted on going to London at once now that he was a partner in the firm. I came, too, to take care of him.

I was already worn down with grief for Mr. Hawkins and worry for Jona-than, and so the news of your and your mother's deaths almost destroyed me. I wrote to Arthur, telling him that we were in town, and he came to me on the very eve of your wedding, half-frantic with terror. He told me of a strange notion that Dr. Van Helsing had regarding your demise. I lied to my husband that night, telling him that Arthur had invited me to a gathering of your loved ones to celebrate your life. It was the first time I have ever been untruthful to him.

Oh, Lucy, something dreadful indeed befell Jonathan in those moun-tains. He has never spoken of it, and I fear he never will. All he would say was that he had kept a journal there and wished to spare me the details, but he would give it to me if ever I desired to read it. What a joy it is to be so loved and trusted by one's husband . . . and yet I am so afraid to even touch it, Lucy, even as my intuition tells me that it may be important to us some-how. Not just to Jonathan and me, but also to you. I cannot explain why, even to myself.

Lucy, please don't go. Don't leave us. Arthur and I love you and we want to help you. Read this letter, find us, and show us how. We are not afraid. We know you would never hurt us.

Stay, dear heart, and save us the agony of your loss. I know you have done wrong and your new existence compels you to commit awful, unspeak-able deeds, but there must be something we can do. We will come up with a plan and talk it over, you and Arthur and I, and in time, we may change Dr. Van Helsing's mind and enlist his assistance as well.

What a fine, first-class brain that man has! I sigh as I write this, for it sounds foolishly hopeful even to me. He is dangerously single-minded, cool, and calculating. He is like a train that, once on the tracks, will not veer until it reaches its destination. But we shall cross that bridge when it appears, shall we not, my Lucy?

I must end this letter and seal it with a kiss. I love you, I love you, I love you.

Please find me. Please don't leave us.

Your Mina

I read the letter again and again. I run my hands over the words and weep until there is nothing left in me. Mina wrote this. She wrote this as she and Arthur protected me, watched over me, and guarded me ferociously from Dr. Van Helsing. They love me still. They love me even now, as I knew they would, and they always will. I should not have doubted or let Vlad shake my faith in them. In the heat and shock of the moment, Mina had used the word *monster*, but she had not meant it. One would not write such a letter of love and devotion to a monster.

I hold the letter against my heart, trembling with joy and gratitude. But what could Arthur and Mina possibly do to help me? They are even more powerless against this curse than I am. They have not seen for themselves the horrors I have wrought . . . the lives I have taken.

I want to believe that they would be safe with me, but how can I promise myself that after tonight? I have no self-control. I can trust myself no longer. And I would only serve as a constant reminder of loss and pain and horror if I stayed with them. They are better off without me. Mina has Jonathan, and Arthur has his friends, and perhaps one day, a good woman who will love him better than I can, as excruciating as it is for me to imagine that.

I must let go of them. I must learn to live with myself and what I have done.

I have this letter, this declaration of love and friendship, to give me strength and remind me that once, I was loved—that I am *still* loved—and that will have to be enough.

I kiss Mina's letter and fold it into my corset, right over my heart. And then I pick my way through the wreckage of the crypt. I gather my travel papers and what undamaged items I can find and pack them into the trunks, and then I put on a long black traveling gown and a heavy veil of crape to conceal my face. I transform myself and my belongings into a column of mist and drift out to the churchyard gates to wait.

Everything I have done will forever weigh on me like an invisible chain. Link by link, I feel it around my neck, my wrists, and my ankles.

But somehow, I can bear it more than I could an hour ago. And when the carriage appears on the empty street, just as a new dawn touches the sky, I put a hand over my heart where Mina's promises of love and affirmation warm my ice-cold skin. And I allow myself to hope, even if it can only ever be just a beautiful dream, that one day, I will see her and Arthur again.

ACKNOWLEDGMENTS

Now Comes the Mist is a book that has been many years in the making, and it would not exist in this form—or indeed, at all—without the help, guidance, and support of a great number of people for whom I am incredibly thankful!

In February 2025, Tamar Rydzinski will have been my agent for an entire decade. There have been countless ups and downs in those ten years. Through it all, as I wrote book after book, switched publishers, and tried out different genres and age categories, Tamar has been there for me, a staunch advocate, astute business partner, and unwavering friend. It is thanks to her that you now hold this book in your hands.

I am so grateful to have worked with Melissa Frain, editor extraordinaire, on this book. Her keen eye, attention to detail, and ability to ask hard-hitting questions not only helped me tighten my writing but also got me to think so deeply about the characters and the romance.

Mist and I are lucky to have found such an enthusiastic and savvy group of cheerleaders in the Podium Entertainment team. Thank you to Annie Stone, who saw potential in this book and snapped it up out of obscurity, and to Nicole Passage, Cass Dolan, Taylor Bryon, Stephanie Beard, and Mindy Fichter, for their hard work on this novel's journey. Thank you to the sales and marketing teams, especially Cole Antos and Griffin Spurr, who brainstormed such wonderful ideas to get readers excited. Big thanks to Gina White, Hannah Grenfell, and the rest of the audio team, as well as to Ainsleigh Barber, whose voice I knew would be perfect for Lucy. I'm grateful to the artists at Damonza and to Leah Zink for a gorgeous, eye-catching cover, and to the talented Erin Bowman, whose graphic design skills led to the breathtaking final concept.

ACKNOWLEDGMENTS

I'm very fortunate in my friendships and I want to give a special mention to the people who have been there for me during *Mist's* often tumultuous journey: Naima Dennis, Melody Marshall, Hannah Reynolds, Rebecca Caprara, and Dhonielle Clayton.

Thank you to the Context Literary Agency team, particularly social media goddess Monica Rodriguez, who is always a vital part of getting the word out about my books. Thank you to our coagents overseas for working hard on *Mist's* behalf.

I'm endlessly thankful for the readers, bloggers, influencers, librarians, and booksellers who help spread the word about my stories. I appreciate all of you!

I am moved by the kindness and generosity of the following authors, who took the time to read my work and provide such glowing blurbs: Kiersten White, Natalie Mae, Wendy Xu, Jessica Rubinkowski, Alexis Henderson, Beth Revis, and Sue Lynn Tan. Thank you to each and every one of you. I admire you all and I'm grateful to have had you read *Mist*.

Thank you to my intrepid film agent, Jon Cassir, for everything you do on behalf of my books and me. And thank you to the Juvee Productions team, especially the brilliant Andrew Wang, for believing so hard in the fierce and bloodthirsty women I write.

As always, thank you to my loved ones for riding this rollercoaster of a writing career and cheering me on, no matter what wild path I decide to explore next!

I would be remiss to leave out Bram Stoker, whose classic novel has inspired me for so many years. And I hope that fellow fans of *Dracula*—especially those who have always wanted more from the female characters—will feel that I did justice to the canon and to Lucy Westenra, whose yearning soul it was a pleasure to have in my keeping for the past several years.

ABOUT THE AUTHOR

Julie C. Dao is the critically acclaimed author of many books for teens and children. Her novels have earned starred reviews from *Booklist*, *School Library Journal*, and *Publishers Weekly*, and won recognition as Junior Library Guild Selections and Kids' Indie Next List picks. *Now Comes the Mist* is her adult debut. A proud Vietnamese American who was born in upstate New York, Dao now lives in New England.

DISCOVER
STORIES UNBOUND

PodiumAudio.com